Larena's Fascination
Twelve Dancing Princesses Book Ten

Christine Young

ISBN: 978-1-62420-450-0

Credits
Cover Artist: Designs by Ms G
Editor: Christie L. Kraemer

Chapter One

1821

Standing atop the base of the lamppost, Larena Graham strained to see over the heads of the milling people while trying to shimmy higher. People in the streets protesting repression by the English government notarized this day. The citizens, in Larena's mind, had every right to want more from their government. They weren't asking for something they didn't work for or deserve. The citizens were proud and honorable people.

Over the years since the Napoleonic wars, food prices soared and wages fell. Fewer jobs existed because of industrialization and heads of families found it difficult to feed their children. All this seemed to be ignored by parliament.

"What do you see up there?" Tyna, Larena's friend, asked, peering up at her, one hand shielding her eyes from the setting sun. "It's got to be very interesting to have you so focused. I don't think you've moved a single muscle since you've been up there."

"Soldiers are lining up with guns pointing at the protestors. Give me a boost higher," Larena said, wishing either she was taller or the lamppost was easier to climb. "I can't see very much."

For a moment she was pushed higher. Without warning, the friendly hands disappeared and she found herself hauled from the post and into hostile masculine arms. She struggled against the force taking her away from her vantage point.

"Put me down. You've no right to be so upper handed," Larena said, furiously trying to punch the horrible man, hitting only air.

"Little fool, what are you doing here? You're coming with me." Gavin Broon wrapped his arms tightly around her and pushed her through the rapidly growing crowds to a doorway. "You take chances with your life, and I won't have you doing that." His brows furrowed together, his eyes dark with emotion.

Bumped and battered from all sides by the throngs of bystanders, "No," she protested, struggling against him. She pushed at his arms yet they didn't budge from around her waist. "You... you can't leave me for weeks then show up one day telling me what I can and can't do."

Crowds swarmed past her. Somewhere shots were fired and screams filled the air. "Little fool," he bit out again with a hot whisper close to her ear, sending shivers into her body. "What the bloody hell were you thinking? You could be shot or hurt by the stampeding masses of people."

"These individuals have a right to be heard. Those laws keeping them earning a decent living should be repealed and you know it. Only the wealthy who want to make more and more money at everyone's expense are for that law. They don't care about the citizens and their wellbeing. What do you believe? What do you stand for? I've a right to know."

"Are you finished?" Gavin asked, sounding exasperated and frustrated. It seemed he was totally out of patience. "You know what I think. I've never kept secrets from you."

"Do you want to hear more?" Larena didn't care how impatient he was and no, she didn't know what he thought. She had the right to her own pursuits of knowledge. She wanted to make a difference in the world. This was her chance.

"I'm sure you could recite all the laws and acts that have been passed since the Napoleonic wars, but we have something more pressing to do right now." His hands tightened around her, sending strange evocative sensations through her.

"What could be more important than the pursuit of free speech?" She still meant to protest his Neanderthal behavior, but she was fresh out of new arguments, at least ones she thought he might listen to.

"The extenuation of your life," he whispered close to her ear, sending more curious shivers within. She remembered their first kiss, but this was far more provocative and mercuric, causing heat and chills to sweep through her all at the same time.

Up two steps to a small protective space, Gavin stopped, turning her. His lips descended on hers while he ran his fingers through her hair, pins clattering to the earth below. Then with his hands around her waist, he pulled her close, trailing his hands up her ribcage, stopping below her breasts.

Then his large hands framed her face as he kissed her, using his tongue and his teeth to punctuate his caresses with more passion than he'd ever kissed her with before. He stopped to look at her, the steel glint of his blue-gray eyes searing her. An inferno simmered deep inside, a sensation she fought to deny. As much as she loved the kiss, had even yearned for it, she didn't want to give into his mandates, and she was afraid that was exactly what she was doing here.

Her breaths came in short bouts, her blood pulsing heat edly. She brought her hand up to slap him. "How..."

He easily caught her wrist and brought it down, holding it tight against his chest where she felt the thundering of his heart. "How dare I?" he finished her sentence for her. "Where your safety is concerned, milady, I will dare anything. You have pushed past the limitations of my patience. The last thing I want for you is to see you on the gallows, a prison ship or in Newgate."

His huge body blocked her view to the boulevard. Yet she was sure chaos seemed to encompass the street. Shouts and cries of pain reverberated through the narrow thoroughfare. In this tiny alcove they were secure for the moment.

"My safety was not in jeopardy until you showed up," she objected, struggling slightly in protest yet understanding he held the upper hand in this matter with his brute strength. "What is happening out there? I need to see." She squirmed to look around him, but it seemed he drew her closer.

As if to deny her statement, his mouth descended upon her s again, his hand on her derrière pulled her flush with his body.

He pulled her shirt from the waistband of her skirt, his hand ris ing against her back until his fingers found bare skin. "You should not be here," he whispered, his warm breath caressing her cheek.

It seemed at the moment he had no control, but she had longed for this for months now and she didn't want him to stop. Still, she objected. "Where I am is not your con—"

Stopping her protest, his mouth met hers again, his tongue drawing a line across her lips. Once more she tried to speak. When she opened her mouth, he filled hers with his tongue. A tiny squeak emanated from her as she wilted into him, wishing she didn't make this so easy. Too many months had passed since she felt the heat of his kisses. She'd thought he forgot about her. She braced herself, her hands against his chest in a feeble attempt to push him away. Something she hoped she couldn't accomplish.

He kissed her again and again, her lips swelling from the intense actions. She clung to his shoulders, barely able to stand and still his lips remained on hers, enticing and seducing in every way.

"Master Broon, you and your lady friend shouldn't be here." The voice seemed to echo around her in a hazy void.

Gavin turned, keeping her behind him and pressing her against the door. "Constable. Sorry, I got carried away for a moment. She's a fetching piece, don't you think? We'll be going on our way as soon as you tell us it's safe. Too many people running around on the street at the moment."

"It's safe now, won't be in another few minutes. This gathering is getting out of hand. We have orders to arrest everyone involved. You and your lady friend need to leave before it's too late. Find a place that's a bit more private for what you're doing."

Gavin cleared his throat. "As you can see, we are not involved in the protests. My little sweetheart and I just want to find a way out of here so we can be alone. My office is a block from here. Could you see us there?"

"Fetching piece, little sweetheart," she repeated, hitting him on his back, furious with his audacity even though that was almost what she wanted to be. "I'm not your lady friend or anything else."

Over his shoulder he stared at her, once more his glare shook her to the core. "Pretend."

"I'd be happy to help you," the constable said. "Follow me." He set off for Gavin's office at a quick pace.

"I don't want to go." She held back, refusing to move her feet to help him with this pretense. She was not going to pretend to be his whore even if it meant her safety.

"You want to see the inside of Newgate prison? If you don't move your feet, I'll carry you." His calm voice resonated, gave her chills of foreboding.

"Of course not. I would never get arrested and if I did, Aunty would call in some favors," Still she fought him, denying his words as well as his threats.

"Best you hurry," the man said. "The soldiers are heading this way. It's not the time to dally. If the two of you are having a lover's spat, wait till you're safe and sound," he chuckled.

"Don't push this any farther, Larena. If you make me, I'll haul you over my shoulder."

As if to give credence to his relationship with her, he wrapped his arm around her shoulder, letting his fingers rest over one breast. She inhaled a swift deep breath. "Gavin." She recalled The Duchess' words. *Kisses are fine but anything else you need to tell him no.* This, she supposed, was something else.

"Behave yourself then."

For a minute or two she feigned compliance. When she saw a small escape route, she jerked out of his arms. Freedom was close; she ran two steps before she found herself caught and unceremoniously slung over his shoulder. "No," she pounded him on the back, trying to wiggle herself from his shoulder. "You can't do this to me. I don't want to go with you."

His hand came down possessively on her rear and stayed there, his fingers moving on her as if he claimed her. "I already have done this to you, and while I would normally indulge you in anything you want, I can't tolerate this defiance to the law."

"Hurry up," the constable encouraged. "You're almost there. You and your lady friend will be nice and safe at your office until it's all over. It won't be long before everyone is put in the wagons the soldiers have brought. You don't want to be rounded up with the hoards."

"What's going to happen to these folks?" Gavin asked pleasantly, waving his arm, indicating those who were racing through the street. "Will they be released?"

"The wagons are lined up and ready to take everyone who doesn't get away to jail. They'll be tried and sentenced." The constable seemed eager to get them away from the crowds.

"What then?" Gavin continued with his questioning, seeming to need to make a point that was directed at her.

Larena was sure Gavin knew the answer. He was asking for her benefit, but she wasn't about to listen. Hanging head down she closed her eyes and tried to close her ears as well.

"Off to a penal colony, either Australia or Tasmania," he told them as if that was an everyday occurrence.

She gulped air, telling herself the lack of oxygen was due to her lungs pressed against his shoulder. Were the two of them in cahoots? She knew he would do anything to convince her he was always right.

"Long time to spend in the bowls of a ship with little food or water and nowhere to relieve yourself. Are the women raped?" Gavin queried.

"Horrible trip, I've heard. The pretty ones don't fare very well. Here you go." Seemingly intrigued, he stared at her as she lifted her head high enough to see where they were.

"Thanks, you're help is much appreciated." Not setting her on her feet, Gavin stepped into the building and taking the stairs two at a time, made his way upstairs to his rooms above the office.

"Put me down," she bit out, furious with him and unwilling to let him dictate her life. "I can't breathe."

"You should have thought about that before you tried to run into more trouble." Ignoring her, he strode through the rooms upstairs. She saw what looked like a sitting room, but he didn't stop there. Instead, he strode into a separate room and before she could take another breath, she landed on a bed.

He came down beside her, his hand resting domineeringly on her stomach. "Did you hear what the man said?" The frigid glint of his eyes and voice chilled her. She'd never seen him like this.

She tried to scoot to a sitting position, but his body weight stopped her. "I didn't listen to him, so no." He had taken liberties she didn't know yet if she wanted to give him. His absence from her life had shaken her confidence, and now he suddenly reappeared. A stubborn streak settled in, and she knew she would not agree with him just on principle.

His eyes shimmered his mouth drawn thin. "I worry about you." He gently pushed tangled hair from her face. "You're too beautiful. I don't want anything to happen to you, and you do things you shouldn't. As formidable as she is, The Duchess might not have been able to pull in favors soon enough to get you out of that predicament you were so eager to get yourself into."

"What do you care? I haven't even seen you in weeks." She was determined not to let him touch her heart until he proved himself to her. A few kisses every now and then were not enough incentive for that.

When he looked at her, it seemed he gazed past her. She'd never seen him so severe and hard; unyielding would perhaps be descriptive. This time when his lips found hers, they were gentle yet still demanding a response she was unsure of. This was Gavin and she'd wanted his attention for so long. He was doing this to her, making her want him, ready to give up everything. She steeled herself against his blatant seduction.

And yet...

Gavin touched her in ways she couldn't fathom. His hands moved on her and a molten inferno of his making rushed through her. His lips and warm moist tongue touched upon her neck and the curve of her shoulder, the line of her collarbone. She shivered in response, creating tiny noises in the back of her throat that he seemed to take pleasure in hearing.

Eyes half-closed, she watched him doing things to her she'd wanted for such a long time. She had given up on him, assuming she didn't interest him. Six months ago, two months, she would have given all of herself to this man who stole her heart the first moment she looked upon him. Now she held herself back, wishing for things that could have been. She looked to her future now and was unsure he held a place in it.

Coming to her senses and trying desperately to escape the sweet seduction of his lips and tongue where they met her flesh, "No, Gavin, not now. This can't happen." She pushed on his shoulders, her eyes wide open now. "You have to stop."

"This, milady, is our present and our future. In time I will have nothing but your sweet compliance," he murmured softly, the whisper of his breath against her still seducing. Yet he obeyed her request.

He rose from her, his gaze locked with hers. She would battle him with all her heart and strength. Here in London while he'd been gone, she found a purpose to her life and he must have found something somewhere else. He'd been away for so long.

She sat up, to no avail trying to readjust her clothing and hair.

"Gavin?"

Shoulders rigid, he strode into the main sitting room. She heard voices and while she recognized the other man's voice as Drake Montgomerie, her cousin's husband, she could not make out anything they said. When she drew closer to the door, she could finally understand some of their words.

"I found her," Gavin said. "Little hellion that she is, she's very special to me and I wouldn't want to see her hurt, her life changed irrevocably. She can't continue to run free with no guidance."

Her heart felt as if he slashed it with a knife. *Little hellion*, that was all he thought of her. For a fleeting moment, she'd believed he cared enough about her to find her. That his concern for her safety was sincere, but obviously she was wrong. He would not find a way into her heart.

Quickly, she set about tucking in her blouse and finding a mirror, trying to put her hair in order. Nothing could be done about her kiss-swollen lips and the total disarray he'd created in her appearance. A lone tear slid from her eye. Furiously, she wiped it away with the back of her hand. Setting her hands on a table in front of the mirror, she drew in a long deep breath in an attempt to settle her nerves.

Drake would surmise what Gavin did to her and how would she explain her appearance to Ella, her cousin? Then she would have to explain to The Duchess what had happened. Clenching her fists, she strode into the room, back as stiff as she could make it, remembering The Duchess' advice. *Men think with their cock.* It seemed she was right about Gavin.

Slowly, Drake looked from Gavin to her then back, his gaze held no questions. He knew very well what Gavin had done. She swallowed hard, thinking to stride from his apartment and hail a cab, but she doubted if either man would allow that to happen.

"It's not what it looks like," Larena said, still trying to put her blouse into her skirt and unable to meet his gaze.

Gavin strode to her, blocking Drakes view. "You should have looked in the mirror before you presented yourself half naked in the sitting room." His hands fell upon her blouse, fastening buttons that he'd skillfully undone, sifting his fingers through her hair as if he could replace the pins he removed.

She gasped at his words, looking down and feeling blood rush to her face. "You did this to me."

His arrogant smile left her breathless. Then he whispered, "I'm certainly glad it was me and not some other scoundrel. You could have told me no and rest assured, I would have stopped."

"What will he think?" she whispered. She truly didn't understand herself. Of course Drake would believe the worst, and he would tell Ella who would tell The Duchess. No, Ella would say nothing, but she would undoubtedly have a nice long talk with her.

"I need to get you home. You do know you cannot have anymore contact with these people you're associating with now." He ran his finger down her cheek, a strange tender look in his eyes. "You need to stay away from them. They mean you harm and are taking advantage of your naiveté."

"Says you. I don't believe for a minute Tyna would ever take advantage of anyone, especially not me." She challenged him in every way she could think of. Obeying this man was not possible. He had no hold on her life nor did she want him to command her obedience, and she was not naive.

"You will regret it if you disobey. The Duchess, your guardian, would demand the same things." The silver steel of his eyes sliced through her heart.

It seemed Drake had watched their interchange. "Gavin is right, Larena. There are elements in play here that could be dangerous. We both understand this is not about obedience, it's about your safety. I'm sure Gavin would never command you do anything you wished unless he was serious about it."

"Probably not. Where I'm concerned, he sees danger in the sunbeam slanting across a window and the wind blowing a leaf from a tree. At least today he does, tomorrow I won't see him," she replied, wondering if she was just being foolish and defying these men because she was angry with Gavin for abandoning her for months.

"Take heed, Larena. This is not a game to be played." It seemed Gavin couldn't stop himself from playing the autocrat.

"Whatever you wish," she said, smiling sweetly. She'd been so bored and frustrated with her life. She'd tried to find something useful to do that would make her feel good about herself. Then she met Tyna, who gave her new purpose and direction.

"Yes," Drake said, stepping in to the conversation once more. "No one knows for sure what their future will bring, but you dabble in politics you know little about. I don't understand the argument between the two of you, but both parties should figure out what is really bothering you before it's too late."

"I'm not ignorant and I understand the politics. If I were a man, this conversation would not be happening." She fisted her hands, anger growing inside. Feelings of helplessness swept through her before she pushed them back, just as she tried to push her hair from her face.

"You don't have all the facts, either," Gavin said. "Here, let me help." Somehow he managed with the few pins left in her hair to arrange it so she didn't look as if she just rose from his bed. "I don't mean to make you angry, Larena. I care about you."

"The people of London are incensed and some of them are using you," Drake told her as he paced the room. "You've got to understand the laws and that you must not be seen meeting with these people. That, in itself, could be construed as a crime and condemn you."

"I don't believe you. Who is taking advantage of me?" She wanted answers. No one she knew played her. She made all her decisions from facts and what she understood to be right.

"Your friend Tyna, for one," Drake told her. "She is part of the resistance to the laws that have been voted on by parliament. She not only fights to see the laws repealed but the throne abolished as it was in France. Obviously, the government as well as the monarchy does not want that to happen and will use all its power to see it doesn't."

She stiffened, inhaling a quick deep breath at his words. "Tyna wouldn't do that. She has not expected me to do anything. In fact, she's counseled against some of my actions." Yet the girl found her one day when she was riding in the park and befriended her, telling her stories of her childhood and the suffering she'd seen around her. She had believed everything the young woman told her. Suddenly, Larena wasn't so sure about her new friend.

"All you know about this woman is what she's told you," Gavin pointed out, his expression changing to one Larena didn't understand. "You are innocent and believe in the good of all. She is not who you think she is and yes, she is using you to her own ends as well as her brother's."

"I'm not naïve," she said, realizing in this she most likely was too trusting. Thinking back, she desperately tried to recall everything Tyna said to her, but very little came to mind.

Gavin looked away for a moment, and truly she wanted to know what he was thinking. She could not read his thoughts. What did he know she didn't, and why wouldn't he tell her?

"How you think of yourself makes no difference at this point. Your life is at stake here. I need your promise you will stay away from her," Drake said, seeming to step in where Gavin left off.

Perhaps it was a good thing the request was made by Drake. At this point, if Gavin had asked her to promise this, she would have promptly and without thought said no. Instead she decided to somewhat agree, "I will take your advice under consideration."

"I'm glad," Drake said, his hands behind his back, a dark shuttered look on his face.

"I'm supposed to meet her tomorrow for tea. I don't have any way to contact her. She always sends messages to me." Her body quivered, wondering if Tyna befriended her so she could gain something from her.

"Where? I'll see that Addie Winthrop meets the two of you. You can tell Tyna that Addie's your friend. In a way, she is. You did attend her wedding," Drake said. His words seemed to give her some encouragement.

"I barely know the woman. What I do know is that she was one of your spies, Drake," Larena protested. "How will I convince Tyna she's a friend?" This had taken on a new dimension. "I'm not going to spy for you and she's there to spy on me, I'll..."

"What Larena? Dig yourself a hole so deep you can't climb out?" Gavin spoke up, clearly finding it difficult to control his anger, which he tried to explain away as concern.

Drake broke into the conversation with a heavy sigh, "No one wants you to do that, especially not me. Addie will be there to protect you just as she protected Tavia at her wedding. I'm sure I don't need to remind you how she used her pistol to shoot the man who meant to murder your cousin.

Addie is a good person and a better friend. You couldn't have a better person at your side."

"Do I have a choice?" She didn't believe for one second she needed protection from Tyna. The girl had been honest with her about everything. She'd always told her there was danger in what she did.

"No choice," Gavin said, "It's either Addie or myself."

"I'll take Addie any day over you," she said and was cheered for a moment by the slight flicker of insecurity in his eyes then it vanished, replaced by the hard visage she had become used to in the last few hours, realizing suddenly what she saw was not insecurity but annoyance.

He watched her for what seemed an eternity and with a shrug, he said, "Have it your way."

"You should get her home," Drake said with a tinge of laughter in his voice. "Do you need help, Gavin?"

"I can handle this one," Gavin said with a raised eyebrow, seeming to search her for some reason she might have to refuse. His eyes raked her with a careless disdain. A sizzle of mockery touched his eyes then vanished with something seeming a tiny bit softer.

"The Duchess will be waiting. She has important news. I will see both of you later. I hope you work out this problem before you have to speak with Charlotte. Use the time in the cab to hash things out. A united front is always the best course." Drake turned on a heel and strode from the small apartment.

"Well," Gavin said, gallantly holding out his arm and smiling as if they were off to a picnic and had not spent the better part of the day at odds with each other.

She marched past him, head held high, her back stiff. There was no way she would talk anything out with the infuriating man.

~ * ~

By the time they hailed a cab and reached The Duchess' townhouse, the sun had set and streetlights were beginning to light the darkness. Gavin helped her from the cab despite her reluctance. He wished he'd handled the last few hours differently, but Larena had a way of getting under his skin, making him say and do things he didn't mean.

"Do you know this important news Drake spoke of?" Larena asked before they entered the house, having refused to speak to him for the duration of the ride. She suddenly needed to understand what was about to happen. "I probably should know."

"Come, she's expecting us in the parlor." It seemed both The Duchess and her companion, Scarlett, waited for them. Larena was correct, however, he had ignored her for months but not because he didn't want to see her and court her properly. He understood the simple fact that he had to reassure her and instill in her a reason to believe in him.

"You're not going to answer me, are you?" she said, her words clipped.

"The Duchess will respond to all your questions." He opened the door for her. They walked into the parlor.

"Finally," The Duchess said, tapping her cane, a plate of lemon bars available on a table. "What held you up? I thought you would be here hours ago."

"An altercation that couldn't be avoided," Gavin chose to reply before Larena could weave a believable story out of falsehoods. Then there was absolute silence while he watched The Duchess rivet her gaze on Larena and back to him seeming to search for answers.

"What say you to that, Larena? The Duchess asked impatiently, narrowing her eyes at her wayward charge. "Can you tell me about this confrontation Mister Broon speaks of?"

Larena did not meet her aunt's gaze, seeming to like the looks of the floor and rug better. "I'd rather not talk about our altercation. In any case, the dispute between us was really nothing." Her gaze shifted from the floor to Gavin.

"You probably don't want my rendition," Gavin said pleasantly, "but if Larena doesn't want to tell her story, I'll be happy to explain our tardiness. May I take a seat?" He needed to tell all the truth, but he didn't want The Duchess to judge Larena too harshly or worse, keep him from seeing her. Now that his business was finished, he planned on spending every accessible moment with her, and in the process changing her mind about him.

"Of course, I'm waiting with baited-breath for the story." The Duchess waved her hand, "Would you like something to drink or a lemon bar?" she pointed to the plate.

"Both," Gavin said, laughing, "A brandy if I may." He always enjoyed his sessions with The Duchess. In so many ways the conversations were always refreshing as well as eye-opening.

"Scarlett, see to their needs. I'm sure my niece needs a brandy too. The girls seem to have a penchant for the stuff. I'd prefer a fresh pot of tea today. Then we'll hear what they have to say."

Gavin sat down on a sofa next to Larena, lazily letting his leg touch her skirts, watching her as she turned to stare at him but made no attempt to move away. What was she up to?

Insinuating himself as far and as deep into her life as he could was his immediate intention. He didn't mean to give her a chance to run away from him, simply because he was pretty sure this was an act of defiance and not what she truly wanted.

"Larena, do you care to tell me what made the two of you tardy by a couple of hours?" Once more she tapped her cane on the floor. "I'm not getting any younger."

Larena cleared her throat, "As I told you previously, I'd rather not. It was nothing to concern yourself about. Just something I was interested in. Nothing important. Nothing..."

"If it were nothing, you'd tell me." The Duchess turned to Gavin. "If you don't mind, I'd like to hear what happened."

"That's alright, Auntie," Larena hastily said. "I was watching a peaceful protest and Gavin, for no reason what so ever, kidnapped me and held me hostage until it suited him to bring me home." Clearly agitated, her breaths were shallow and deep.

Charlotte tipped her head to one side, her brows coming together in concentration, "You've never lied to me before. Why now? Perhaps I do need some brandy. This might be a long night."

Larena shrugged her tiny delicate shoulders, sipping the drink she'd been given. "Everything I told you is true."

The Duchess waved her hand in the air, "Pshaw...a lie of omission is a lie. You've left much from your fairytale." She turned, her attention now focused in another direction. "Gavin?"

"Duchess," he smiled politely.

"This is between the two of you. I understand that. I have to hear the truth, but for now, I'll be patient." Turning to Larena, "I'm leaving for a few months. You will move to the Montgomerie estate while I'm gone. Ella and Drake will be your chaperones."

Larena rose quickly, "No. I won't go. I need to stay here, close to the city and my..."

The Duchess looked sternly at her charge then to Gavin as if asking him for help. "You don't have a choice or a say in this, darling."

"If it's a chaperone you want for me, Ella will not be able to fulfill those duties very well." Larena strode to the sideboard and after pouring another brandy, she downed it swiftly. "I won't go there."

"You need to stay away from the elements that are influencing your hasty and at times very bad decisions. I know Ella is no chaperone, but if you are out of the city, I'll feel you are safe." She turned to glare at Gavin again as if asking him for answers or another choice.

He didn't care and thoroughly enjoyed this altercation, which seemed to play into his hands. If he could get her away from the city, he could continue with his plans, without worrying about Larena's life.

"If you send me away, I'll return here," Larena said defiantly. "You know I will. I will go where I please."

"Your father left you alone too much. I suppose you can do that, but then I'll be forced to ask Gavin to take charge of your life. If you defy my orders, I'll hand you over to your young beau. I've done worse for my charges. Your life and safety is more important to me than your reputation."

Shocked by The Duchess' words, he looked to Larena for a reaction. He wasn't surprised. Larena's body shook with anger, he supposed. Her fists were clenched as was her jaw. Fury emanated from her so hard she quivered.

"And what does that mean?" she asked defiantly. "Do I live with him in his tiny apartment or does he come here? You do understand he has only one bed."

The Duchess leaned back in her chair, her hands resting on the top of her cane, a smile curving her lips. "I don't care. You and Gavin will have to work that out. I'm sure Gavin will have the last say. He doesn't strike me as the same type of man as your father."

"I'm meeting Tyna tomorrow. I won't miss it." Her eyes sizzled with a ferocity he'd never seen before. "Drake has arranged for Addie to be there, so I assume you'll agree to that rendezvous at least."

His soon to be fiancée had a temper he hoped he could turn to passion. Gavin sat back, settling an arm around her, touching her and to his delight, she didn't flinch away from him. Instead, it seemed she inadvertently leaned into him as if asking him for his support.

"The last person you should be seeing is this Tyna woman. She is at the root of all your bad decisions." The Duchess turned to Gavin, again seeming to implore him to do something.

"I will see that Addie meets them. I'm sure the trained spy will be able to take charge of the rendezvous if it turns in an awkward direction." The mercuric shimmer in Larena's aqua eyes could melt glass. Yet he took advantage of the rare moment and trailed his finger down her arm then back up, enjoying the slight trembling and wondered if the response was her fury speaking or desire.

"Addie must have better things to do than babysit me," Larena pointed out indignantly. "It's supposed to be a private conversation. She's my friend and she doesn't mean any harm."

"Private conversations are against the law," The Duchess told her. "More trouble is brewing, and I don't want you in the middle of it or on the wrong side of the law."

"Ah, you forget that if you refuse to go to the Montgomerie's residence, I suddenly become your chaperone; an intriguing idea." The Duchess' judgment seemed to have deteriorated. She would know Larena would never remain a virgin if he was alone with her for very long. Maybe that's what she wanted.

"How on earth can a cad and a womanizer become my chaperone?" Larena turned to The Duchess, fists clenched at her sides. "You're going crazy in your old age. I thought you had more common sense that that." She suddenly stopped, her hand over her mouth.

Taken aback by her statement, Gavin cleared his throat. Despite what she thought about him, he was pleased with the new situation the two of them were just now thrown into. This way he could keep Larena from finding too much trouble. "While I'm hardly a suitable chaperone for a young lady such as yourself, I've never been a cad or a womanizer." He didn't like that his intended thought the worst of him.

"It is the wisest choice of all those presented to me as well as all the ones you refused," The Duchess said, the strange smile remaining. "Gavin will make a fine chaperone."

"Well, I don't like any of the choices. I'm perfectly capable of living here by myself. I've no need of a guardian," Larena declared heatedly. "Especially not Gavin Broon."

"I think you protest too much, sweet one." Gavin pulled her closer, wrapping both arms around her and for the moment declaring his possession of her. In his mind, she would always be his to protect and cherish. He did regret his too aggressive display of affection earlier today. She needed to be wooed gently, and he meant to do just that now that he was handed a golden opportunity.

"How well will this role work for you when all you want is to get me into your bed?" she shook his arms from around her and moved away.

"Hmm..." he paused then laughed softly, pleased with himself and the new opportunity. "In my bed would be a dream come true for me, but not until we're married. I planned to hold to tradition in this matter unless of course you manage to seduce me."

"Seduce you? Marry you? What makes you think I'd marry you or would want to seduce you? If you haven't figured it out yet, you haven't asked." She turned on him.

"Consider this a proposal," he said, watching her intensely, his heart beating furiously.

The Duchess clapped her hands together. "Perfect! I was hoping something like this would happen. Perhaps the two of you can wed this evening. I'll call in a favor."

"Stop right there," Larena said, pointing a shaking finger at her aunt. "I'm not getting married tonight or tomorrow. I don't care a fig about a grand wedding any longer, but Gavin has paid no attention to me for months now. He can't just saunter into my life and think to marry me."

"Saunter into your life?" he repeated with sarcasm. "I was tied up in litigation then I was in Scotland to attend to my mother's estate. I can assure you I thought of you every single day and night when I was sleeping alone in my bed." He was disappointed she didn't understand the messages he sent her or the urgent necessity. What he hadn't thought was that she would act out because she thought he ignored her and put her life in danger.

"See, there you go," The Duchess seemed pleased with herself. "We have a match made in heaven."

"My answer is still no." She stood swiftly, her skirts flying around her so he was graced with a peek at her tiny ankles. Larena turned back to the room. "I'm going to bed now."

"If you don't intend to wed Gavin tonight, I insist you stay here until the carriage is loaded and I'm on my way." The Duchess tapped her cane. "I'd like the two of you to see me off."

With a heavy sigh, Larena returned. "You are leaving tonight? Is that safe? It couldn't possibly be safe."

"I prefer to travel at night, and I've enlisted several men to guard the carriage. I have found that in my old age I sleep while traveling. I sleep like a baby, makes the journey go so much faster." The Duchess turned to Scarlett. "Are the bags and snacks ready to go?"

"I'll check with the butler and the cook," Scarlett said and left the room.

"Good, then the two of you need to find a way to cohabitate. I really have great expectations for the both of you as a couple. Gavin, you need to keep Larena safe from herself. I fear for her impetuous behavior. She doesn't ever think of the repercussion. Promise me that if you have to, you'll haul her off to Gretna Green and wed her before she does harm to herself."

"Duchess..."

"Promise me," she tapped her cane once.

"It won't come to that but I promise. One never knows exactly what the future will bring. However, Larena will have to agree to a marriage. In any case, I would make sure to get her out of town." The trap The Duchess seemed to be laying was deep and intricate. But the ruse was for Larena not him. This was exactly what he wanted, only he needed to figure out a way to stop Larena's irritation with him.

"I'm not going along with anything so absurd," Larena protested. "I don't know what has happened to The Duchess, but I'd like her back, please. Where is my aunty?" She clasped her hands beneath her chin her eyes wide, regarding her aunt Charlotte.

"The facts are simple, dear child. I'm a woman who learns from her mistakes. Every precaution I took with your sisters and cousins were to no avail. They and their beaus did exactly what they pleased despite my wishes and objections as well as all the care I took as a chaperone. I'm leaving the two of you with a clean slate. You can do whatever you want with it, paint any picture that suits the two of you. I'm exhausted and so I'm leaving for a bit of relaxation in the Highlands."

"The carriage is ready."

The Duchess rose, "Come, give me a hug, darling. I'm truly sorry for any inconvenience I've caused you. I do think this is for the best."

While Gavin leaned casually against the doorframe, Larena ran to her aunt and gave her a huge hug. "Don't forget to write, Aunty. I will miss you and I really don't think you're making a prudent decision here."

"I'll return each of your letters with one of my own," The Duchess told her. "Now, the two of you take care and don't do anything I wouldn't do."

"But...you and the Duke," Larena said, pointing at her with a shaking hand.

"Of course, dear, and if he's the one for you and you're the one for him, I expect no less. Just as it was with most of my darling charges, I did manage to get the ring on Ravyn's finger before Aric took her virginity, but she was the only one to my knowledge. No, I think Eveleen also had her virginity intact, but I can't be sure."

Gavin heard every word and smiled, his heart enjoying every second. The Duchess turned over Larena's future to him, and he'd have it no other way. Larena was his. She just didn't know it yet or accept the idea. He followed the ladies from the house and with Larena watched the carriage and her guards disappear.

He heard the muffled sob from Larena and moving closer offered comfort in his arms. "I won't be a demanding chaperone. I promise." This was something new. He didn't know what to do with a crying woman.

"I won't come to your bed willingly," she protested as he wiped a few tears away with his thumb.

"I haven't asked," he laughed.

"You had me on your bed this afternoon," she told him, a tinge of defiance in her tone.

"Of course I did. I can have you on your bed tonight if I wish and you won't say no, but I'm not going to." He tilted his head slightly, studying this fragile determined woman he was trying to understand.

"Oh," she picked up her skirts, whirling then stepped into the house. "Arrogant... Infuriating... Annoying..."

Rocking on his heels, he looked at the moon, which cast soft tendrils of light on the ground. He wished he'd finished the renovations to the home in Scotland before he felt an urgent need to return home. It was something The Duchess had written that prompted him. His office and established clients waited for his arrival. Convincing Larena she belonged with him might take a few months as well as a great deal of patience. At this moment, time was precious and he intended to make the most of minutes and hours he'd been allotted.

Slowly he turned, walking up the steps to find Larena sipping brandy in the parlor. He'd been sure she would have fled to the safety of her bedroom, yet she stayed.

When he strode into the room, she looked up and held up her glass. "Would you like another brandy?"

"Don't mind if I do." Before he poured a drink for himself, he topped off Larena's. "You like to drink?"

"Only when I'm so angry I can't think straight," she told him sweetly. "Lately, you have a tendency to make me that way."

"So, what makes you angry?" he baited her, unsure of his reasons yet he loved to see her passion, wanted to feel it first hand and he needed to know more about her.

"You." She held her glass so tightly her knuckles were turning white. "You make me so furious I can't think."

"Me?"

"You arrogant man. Don't play innocent with me." She swirled the amber liquid before sipping. "You do what you want, take what you want..."

"I've only tried to do everything The Duchess and you as well wanted. My sacrifices make you mad. Now, I'm going to have to sleep in a strange bed." For a moment he thought she might toss the brandy in his face, instead she downed the liquor then held her glass out for more.

Reluctantly, he poured more brandy into her glass, understanding if he refused she'd get it herself and be even angrier with him. To hell with it all, if she got herself drunk, he'd be there to help. "If you get tipsy, it will be easier for me to take advantage of you."

Regarding him over the rim of her glass, her eyes narrowing, "I don't think you would do that."

"Do what?"

"You know, what you said. Take advantage of me."

That seemed to be an about face to Gavin. "Would you even know what I'm talking about?" He set his glass on the table and striding toward her, he took her glass from her and placed it on another table. Pulling her into his arms, "I've wanted to do this all night." His lips found hers while he held her still, his hands on either side of her face.

To his surprise she responded to his advance. Her tongue swept his mouth and he let her inside, allowed her the offense. Her teeth c losed on his lips, biting gently then eliciting a groan.

She ran her small fingers through his hair, pulling him closer. He let her lead, enjoying her passion derived, he supposed, from her anger.

Pulling away, she said with an angelic smile, "I like the way you taste, brandy and something different...you."

His heart stopped momentarily. "It's the brandy you savor." If he let this go on much longer, she would be in his bed tonight. That was not part of his master plan.

"Maybe, but I believe it's more than that," she told him, her innocence staggering to him.

"Part imagination, I suppose." His laughter was quick and easy, enjoying her weakness for brandy. It seemed to serve him well. She was relaxed and so unlike the temperament she'd been in most of the day. This was the Larena he'd come to know months ago.

"No, I taste you, something beyond the brandy. It was the same this afternoon when you kissed me." Her hands were on his chest, tiny fingers grasping the cloth of his shirt.

"Perhaps we should table this discussion for another time," he murmured softly, his voice trailing away in a haunting sigh. His knuckles brushed over her cheek and his fingers whispered against the length of her throat. She gazed at him, unmoving, not protesting.

She stepped back, seeming to realize all she said and the implications. "I despise you."

He laughed, catching her wrist and pulling her toward him so their bodies met. "Despise? That's a very strong word when we barely know each other. But, my dear one, I promise you there will come a time when you don't loathe me. Just as I believe you're lying right now."

"Bastard!"

"Ummm... Perhaps I am in some ways, but I can assure you my mother would take issue with your claim." He agreed and the touch of his free hand traveled lower, teasing the mound of her breast. She stiffened in his arms while his fingers continued their exploration, touching her breast, grazing her nipple through the fabric of her gown. Then once again he laughed and his touch vanished.

He handed her the brandy he set on the table then picked up his glass. "You were right. We should talk," she said.

Sipping his drink, "Are you sure you haven't had too much to imbibe." His gaze ran her length then settled on her mouth. "You tasted of brandy but you smelled of the sweetest flowers."

"You may sleep in the room down the hall." She sat down, smoothing her skirts, keeping her gaze focused on her hands.

"No."

"There must be some sign of propriety." she looked at him, her face flushed and her eyes blazing once more but it seemed they burned with passion not fury.

He knew she wanted him. "Why?" He strode through the parlor, picking up items and regarding them before placing them into their proper positions, waiting for her reasoning.

"Because."

He shrugged his shoulders, anticipating an answer she didn't seem to be able to form into words. "Yes." One eyebrow rose in speculation.

She fidgeted. "You don't want to ruin my reputation. You said so yourself. Said you'd marry me before that happened."

"As long as I'm the man ruining you, I don't care a fig about your reputation. When the ton discovers I'm living in this house alone with you, well..." He wanted her to finish the sentence.

"They will assume so many things that aren't true."

"And if you continue to play games with these protestors, you will find your reputation also ruined. You will have to choose, but I intend to do everything in my power to keep you from falling."

"I don't understand."

"Your well being is my only concern right now."

"That's hard to believe after you've..."

"Kissed you, touched you and came very close to ravishing you? Is that what you mean? And I thought I acted the perfect gentleman."

"Gentleman?" she was on her feet, her body shaking with fierce emotion.

Once again he touched a spark. "True, you've had the opportunity to feel my kiss and my touch against your flesh, but there was so much more I could have done. I believe I've tremendous restraint." Bloody hell, but in his mind he was a saint.

She stood, "Restraint? You call that restraint. I'm going to bed."

"And I will be right behind you. I'm sure the room next to yours will be very acceptable."

~ * ~

"Do you think that was wise?" Scarlett asked. "Leaving the two of them alone with each other?"

"I don't know what to think any longer. You know as well as I do the young folks will do whatever they wish regardless of what people will think of them." Of course she had regrets about this, but the trip to the McLellan castle was necessary. "I need to see David. I've missed him and it seems to have been so long since Tavia's wedding and we were together."

"But to leave the two of them alone and in the same house?" Scarlett repeated her question, removing her gloves. "That just wasn't wise."

"I know they might explode. I saw the fire simmering between them. All it will take is the smallest trigger."

Scarlett leaned over and patted Charlotte's hand. "Remember, Larena was seen with an insurgent and as far as we can tell this Tyna is his girlfriend. The pair is dangerous and they will jeopardize Larena anyway they can just to get what they want."

"Gavin understands what is at stake here, and it's more than Larena's reputation. It could very well have repercussions on her life. He will do all that is necessary to stop anything that might happen. Drake was called in to help, but he can't possibly spend the needed time with her. Gavin can."

"Charlotte, we are getting too old for all this subterfuge. I say my heart goes out to the young ones. Life is so difficult now, not like it was when we were young." Scarlett wiped a tear from her cheek.

"I still worry about Tira and Aidan, Aidan especially. The two of them are totally alone. Ravyn and Amorica live miles away. If Blade finds Aidan, the fire between Gavin and Larena will be nothing compared to the explosion waiting to happen with Blade and Aiden."

"Those two girls were not with us long enough." Sniffles overtook Scarlett. "I miss all of them so very much. Why did they have to move away?"

"No, perhaps if they stayed, Larena would not have become involved with the social protestors. Until Larena got tangled with these people, I'd forgotten about the Peterloo Massacre. Half-a-dozen people were killed and so many more injured. I know Gavin returned sooner than he planned simply because I summoned him, needing his help."

"Gavin won't let anything happen to our sweet Larena."

Charlotte pulled a newspaper from a large bag sitting next to her, handing it to her companion. "Take a look at this."

Scarlett's gasp didn't surprise Charlotte. "This can't be. Say it didn't happen. No, no, no..."

"I wish I could. No, Gavin's going to have his hands full, already does. She's just as stubborn and impetuous as the rest of the girls." The Duchess wasn't sure what else could be done. She pulled open the basket of snacks cooked for them. "At least they will have good food while we are gone. Cook loves to have men to feed."

"Cook isn't eager to be the only one supervising those two as if she could, but she does love her job so she'll do her duty as best she can. I certainly hope the McLellan has an exceptional cook."

Charlotte gazed at the front page of the London Times for a bit before sighing and placing the horrible reminder that Larena needed a lot of looking after into her bag. "The butler didn't much like the job either, even though I told them they should just look the other way unless something occurred that might be life threatening." The Duchess tucked the bag into a corner, wishing she could tuck her fears away just as easily.

"I'm certainly relieved you wanted me to travel with you."

"You're my companion. I will always want you to be by my side. Oh look, Cook packed us a couple bottles of Logan's Chianti, my favorite. I'm sure the McLellan will have crates of both the Bordeaux as well as Chianti in his cellar, especially since Logan Maxwell is his son in law."

"A wonderful trip, relaxing, just what I need. I might just remain in my room every night with a bottle of each," Scarlett laughed, casting her blue eyes dramatically heavenward.

"I'm looking forward to spending time with David and reminiscing. I'm hoping he'll take me to this island the girls all rave about so I can see the danger as well as the draw." Charlotte continued to probe the basket, finding glasses for the wine and ham sandwiches for both of them. "I do hope you're hungry, Scarlett."

"Famished," she said as the carriage rolled to a halt.

Charlotte poked her head out the window. "What are we stopping for?"

Chapter Two

"She doesn't trust you, Tyna." Cale Johnson sat at the small table outside the eatery where Tyna agreed to meet Larena. "You have to do something to change that or our cause is lost. Larena is the all important key to our success."

"It's that arrogant man who tore her off the lamppost yesterday afternoon who doesn't trust me. Don't believe he trusts anyone, and more than anything it seems he means to protect her." Tyna cast her gaze skyward. "Don't much like him. Heard he's a lord and a member of parliament. He's probably working against us and everything we believe in."

"Lord Broon pulled the gel from a lamppost you say," Cale said, inadvertently rubbing his chin. "Then hauled her off to his apartment. Wonder what they did there if the kiss they shared in public was any indication of his feelings. We might be able to use his infatuation with the girl to our advantage."

"I'm not sure he's a lord," Tyna said, motioning a server to bring her tea, "but he thinks of Larena as his. She's enamored with him too but angry because he's ignored her for months."

"Tea?" one eyebrow rose mockingly. "Not your usual drink, Tyna."

"Just trying to fit in. Isn't tea the drink the aristocracy chooses?" She looked at the pot of tea that was just set on the table in front of her, squinting at the steaming beverage. Pouring them both a cup, she shoved the one for Cale toward him. "Drink up."

He obliged, cautiously sipping the hot liquid. "Bitter stuff, not good at all, needs some sugar."

Tyna tried it, seeming to think about what she'd say next. "Not much to my liking either. Think my mum must have drunk this stuff, but she put lots of milk and honey in it."

Cale stood before kissing Tyna on the forehead. "Our mum couldn't afford milk and honey, couldn't afford much of anything if you remember correctly after the good days vanished." He stood setting his cup on the saucer. "Suppose I shouldn't stay any longer. Convince her to have a meeting at her home. Once that feat is accomplished, we'll have her bound to us and if she chooses to defy us, we can hold that fact over her head."

"Shouldn't be too hard," Tyna laughed, swirling the liquid in the tiny cup. "She's got her head wrapped around the idea of noble causes. She doesn't really understand though. Just wants to do good deeds. Thinks she can change the world."

"She's a rich bitch with nothing better to do than play games she doesn't understand. If that man has her figured out, he needs to keep her barefoot and pregnant if he wants to keep her out of trouble, or it will be too late for us. Bloody hell, but we all understand we're either going to die or find ourselves shipped out. Parliament will never vote for the repeal of the corn taxes. We've put everything we are on the line, and we're willing to risk the consequences."

Tyna watched him leave, smoothing the tablecloth and lost in her imagination. "Larena Graham is my way out of this hell you've created for me, Cale. I'm going to use her but not how you want." She sipped the tea, grimacing at the foul taste.

"Tyna," Larena swept gracefully to the table, a smile on her face and impeccably dressed. "Tea not to your liking?" she asked laughing softly. "It can help keep a person awake."

"No, thought I try it though."

"It's an acquired taste. How are you doing? I see you got out of the riots yesterday unscathed." Larena pulled off her gloves, stuffing them in her reticule before sitting.

"As you did..." Tyna paused, casting her gaze upward. "Or did you? The gentleman who kissed you in that secluded doorway..."

"The kiss left me thinking of something I yearned for a very long time ago but no longer want. This place is charming by the way. How did you find it?"

"I thought you might like it. Discovered it one day while I was bored and restless. We've a lot to talk about today. I hope your young man's kisses didn't dissuade you from our mission."

Larena leaned forward, "This really isn't going to be..."

"Larena, what a coincidence meeting you here."

Newly married Addie Winthrop sat down next to Tyna, holding her hand out to her. "I'm Addie and who are you? Do the two of you mind if I join you? Of course you don't." Laughter spilled from her.

"Tyna," she said, extending her hand. "Nice to meet you but Larena and I really have some important things to talk about."

It seemed Addie ignored Tyna then went on to say, "Isn't this just a beautiful place and the weather, well one couldn't ask for anything better." Addie picked up the pot of tea, regarded it thoughtfully before setting it down. "Girls, we really must have something a bit stronger." She looked for a waiter, signaling for one then, "We'd like wine, please. Enough for a couple of glasses for each of us. We mustn't waste this beautiful day on something as mundane as tea."

Tyna looked from one lady to the other, seemingly awestruck. "How do the two of you know each other?"

"Just barely," Larena said, wondering what she'd said to Drake and Gavin to deserve a chaperone and furious that her independence was jeopardized this way. Gavin isn't here, she reminded herself but Addie was and she was spying on her at Gavin's request. It was just an underhanded way of keeping tabs on her. Next time she saw Gavin she'd make sure he understood her position, not that it would do any good.

"More than barely?" Addie shook her head before looking dramatically into the sky. She pointed a finger her way, "You were at my wedding, remember. The wedding was unforgettable. Oh, there is our wine." She laughed softly the sound whispering around her.

"I will never forget that wedding," Larena gazed at Addie thoughtfully, wishing the woman would disappear. She looked over her shoulder expecting to see Drake's men guarding her but she saw no one.

"Neither will I but it's over, both the enjoyment as well as the terror. Today I'm going to have so much fun, and I didn't even expect to see anyone I knew. London is so big and Hamilton, my dear husband, told me I could do whatever I wanted this afternoon. Wasn't that so nice of him?"

"It was, of course." Larena stared at the glass of wine Addie poured.

She wished Gavin would tell her she could spend the day doing whatever she liked. If he did, she'd probably faint. He didn't even have that right, yet he assumed he did.

"Your dear cousins Eveleen and Tavia were wed also but then you know that. Most of the wedding, ceremony and reception, was so much fun I nearly swooned. Cheers," she drank her wine then seemed to watch everything over the rim of her glass.

"The wedding was interesting, nothing I've been to before." Larena acknowledged Addie was good at her job. She had a way of diverting attention to something frivolous. If she didn't know better, she'd never guess she wasn't a woman with little to do but gossip and spend her husband's money. She'd never fathom Addie was a well-trained and experienced spy, a woman who was the best marksman Drake had ever known.

"No, it was hard to imagine three weddings in one," Addie waved her laced fan in the air smiling. "No one knew when they would say their vows. I tried to say mine twice before it was truly my turn."

"Addie," Larena leaned forward, placing her hand on one of Addie's, "We've, Tyna and I, have business to discuss, you know." She tried to no avail to send Addie on her way. It seemed nothing would budge her.

"Nothing that can't wait, I'm sure. Let's get some food. What would the two of you like? Oh, this is just so much fun."

Larena had to acknowledge Addie wasn't going anywhere. The woman was as much behind this ploy as Gavin Broon and Drake Montgomerie. "Whatever you would like."

"I favor meat and bread but of course I will eat anything," Tyna downed her glass of wine, setting it hard on the table.

"My, my, you must like the wine. More?" Addie filled her glass before Tyna had time to reply. "It is delicious. I might buy a bottle to take home and enjoy with Hamilton. I believe he would like this just as much as the Bordeaux and Chianti Logan gives us."

Larena wanted to laugh until she recalled all this was a ploy to keep her from getting into this too deep. She wanted to ask Addie where Gavin was but was sure he had eyes on her while he wasn't there in person.

Yesterday Gavin appeared seemingly out of nowhere. She hadn't seen him in months and now he seemed to be everywhere she was.

"I'll take more," Larena tilted her head to one side in an attempt to measure Addie's thoughts. She held out her glass.

"Yes, me too," Addie said, filling both glasses, a silly grin gracing her beautiful face.

Tyna looked to her for answers. "Why..."

"You know," Addie sat back after downing a liberal amount of wine, "I just feel as if the common people have been forgotten. The Corn Laws, the Peterloo Massacre and now the six acts that prevent people from meeting and talking are all wrong." She leaned forward sweeping her hands in a gesture to include the ladies. "Just like we're doing right now, meeting. What can the men writing laws be thinking to make something like this illegal?" Dramatically, she waved her hand in the air. Her voice fell to a whisper, "It's all wrong, all detestable. Don't you think?"

Bloody hell, Addie was good at what she did. No wonder Drake hated to lose her and Hamilton. At this point nothing this woman did would surprise her. Larena grinned inwardly, deciding here and now to become a spy for the cause. She could do so much more for the common people than she already was. After all, she had government contacts and Gavin as well who might be seduced to tell her things she could use.

Of course Gavin didn't need to know about any of this. Larena laughed, feeling lighthearted for the first time since Gavin yanked her off the lamppost. "This is such a beautiful day and look, our food is here, enough of this conversation. We need to put it to the side and enjoy."

"And I'm famished. How about the two of you?" Addie asked, sticking a fork in a strawberry before popping it in her mouth and chewing it slowly.

Larena studied Addie as the luncheon was served and the threesome placed food on their plates. Adelina Winthrop was so much more than a pretty face. She found a way to become a person of her own. That's what she wanted for herself. Once all she believed she needed to make her happy was a husband and children. Now, after meeting Tyna and Addie, that was no longer true.

"Why were the two of you meeting today?" Addie placed cheese and meat on a slice of bread. Holding the morsel in one hand she waited for an answer.

"Girl talk," Larena said, smiling purposely and lifting her shoulders. "I suppose we wanted to share stories about our beaus."

Tyna nodded her head, her mouth filled with food.

"That's divine. The closest person I've ever had to a girlfriend is your cousin Tavia. I really like her and it was so easy to talk to her when we were on board that ship." Addie sipped her wine, a slight nod of her head caught Larena's attention.

Larena cleared her throat, telling a tiny bit of Tavia's story. "Addie was on the ship with my cousin. Tavia pretended to be a cabin boy and well, the ship's captain, now her husband, knew who she was all along. They had a hard time coming to terms with all of the lies of omission."

Cale surprised them. "You need to come with me, Tyna," He placed proprietary hands on Tyna's shoulders. "We have business to take care of, and it can't wait until you finish this little party."

"We can meet another time. I'll send a message." Tyna stood, her hand in Cale's. The look on her face told Larena she didn't want to go.

Larena watched her leave. In her opinion, there didn't seem to be much of a connection between these two. When she looked back to the table, Addie had poured her another glass of wine.

"After you see the drawings and read the article, you're going to need this one." Addie placed a newspaper over her food.

Larena regarded Addie and noted the grim expression before she cast her gaze on the paper. She inhaled rapidly, her heart thundering in her chest. "No." For a moment she couldn't breathe and was sure her heart stopped. "It can't be, it just can't..."

"I'm afraid so," Addie tilted her head slightly pursing her lips. "All of London, at least those you know, have seen this and they will form conclusions. The gossip will circulate. There is nothing you can do about it now."

She whispered the headline in disbelief. "Wealthy lord ravishes young street woman dragging her from a lamppost." Larena looked up to stare at Addie with her mouth gaping open. "Who would have the nerve to write this? Has Gavin..." she paused still gawking at Addie.

"Yes, Gavin has seen this. You can imagine how he's feeling." Addie clearly pointed out for her benefit.

"What about my feelings? Does anyone care about them?" Larena folded the paper then handed it back to Addie.

"Well, the lord's features are clear in this drawing not yours. Even the second drawing..."

"Where he's kissing me?" She couldn't breathe, remembering that kiss and everything that transpired after it. For a few seconds yesterday she nearly begged him to make love to her.

"It's clearly Gavin, Lord Broon. Those who know you well and your relationship with Gavin will know it to be you."

Her heart in her throat, Larena searched the area outside the restaurant, feeling the hairs on the back of her neck stand on end. "Is Gavin out there? I know you've been sending signals to someone."

"Drake's man, no one else. You will have to answer some questions this evening when Gavin returns or earlier if he finishes his work. He knows where we are so who knows if he'll show up. This drawing and article will take a tremendous amount of damage control if the two of you are going to survive this unscathed."

"What does he do, really? He's always telling me he's in litigation. And it seems litigation is synonymous with *I don't have time for you*." Larena let all air from her lungs in a delicate huff.

"Men are busy. Who knows what they do?" Addie shrugged her shoulders before rolling her eyes as if she felt there was an excuse in his answer. "He was involved with an elderly couple who were trying to settle their estate before they died. There was family to take into consideration, and from a few of Hamilton's comments, no one could agree on anything."

"If we wed..."

"So you've thought about marriage. I'm glad of that. I'm sure that is what he eventually has in mind."

"If we wed, he would always be out of town. I don't think I'd like that. Besides why does he think he can't tell me what he's doing?" Larena pensively played with a tendril of hair that had escaped her chignon.

"Neither would I like it if Hamilton left me alone all of the time. Gavin probably just doesn't want to bother you with his boring life," Addie laughed softly.

"Lawyering is nothing like spying." Larena said in a huff. "I like boring because I don't want to worry. When Drake is gone, Ella is always pacing and weeping. Ashcroft, the baby, has helped but she still thinks about her husband all of the time."

"No, I suppose it's not."

"It seems Gavin never likes anything I do." Larena drummed her nails on the table. What did she care about his approval? He was nothing to her except a man who seemed to hover when he disapproved.

"I was lucky. Hamilton never stepped in my way. He recognized that what I did was dangerous, but he always understood." Addie stared at her over the rim of her glass. "More wine?"

"Might as well finish the bottle."

"Don't be so hard on him. You have to come to terms with your feelings, but Gavin does care. He would have to care if he was willing to risk his reputation by publicly declaring you his."

"The drawing said he ravaged me..." Sweat beaded on her forehead, knowing that if Drake had not shown up when he did, her ravishment could very well have happened.

"Did he?" Addie clasped Larena's hands in her. "Hamilton will take him to task if that's the truth."

She felt the empathy slide from one woman to the other. "No, I don't think so. He wasn't a perfect gentlemen either."

Addie chuckled softly, her gaze drifting away for a half-second. "No man, is at least not when they're infatuated with the woman they're alone with. If he ravished you without your permission, we wouldn't be having this conversation. I'd kill him."

Larena understood how capable Addie was when it came to using a pistol. Addie shot the man who abducted Tavia and James then tried to kill them at their wedding. A shiver swept down her spine, but it wasn't fear. Addie was a woman with too many skills to list.

"Do you think Gavin is infatuated with me? I didn't think he cared at all for me two days ago. In fact I truly believe he thinks it's time for him to marry and I'm available. I won't have that. I want a man who loves me with all his heart."

Addie made a little snort of frustration. "Men often don't believe in love. They want good sex and a woman who will admire them, a woman with passion to fill their evenings. Some want women who will obey, but I don't think Gavin is one of those."

"Is Hamilton?"

"No, he might be, with a different woman, but he knows me better than anyone else. I never thought I'd be able to say this about anyone especially a man, but he's my best friend. He knew I would do Drake's bidding and come today even though I knew he wanted to tell me no."

A best friend, that was an interesting thought. Actually, Larena could imagine Gavin as a best friend just not a husband. It wouldn't matter if a best friend only had time to visit once in a while. But a husband... She yearned for a man to love her and stand by her side to be at home every night.

"Were you best friends before you married him?"

Addie didn't have to think for even a second. "We were. There were times when we were assigned to the same mission. I believe Drake wanted me to have protection other than just my gun. In Spain I was so relieved when I saw him, I nearly swooned. Something in my gut told me the assignment would not turn out as planned."

"It's really none of my business but...well...I'm curious. You were pregnant at your wedding."

She smiled and a soft blush heated her cheeks. Moistening her lips before speaking, "We couldn't keep our hands to ourselves. In the last year whenever we saw each other if we could find privacy..."

"You love him very much."

"I do but I'm still waiting for him to say the words. Broaching the subject is not that simple or even saying the words myself is not easy. I want the words to be returned, and if I admit it to myself, I'm a coward."

"You should tell him."

"Easier said than done," Addie said, closing her eyes for a moment. "What about you?"

"Truly, I don't know if I love him. But I'm so very attracted to him." She put her hand on her heart. "When I'm with him, I want him to kiss me and after yesterday I know there's more than just kisses."

"What did he do to you?" Addie leaned forward, concern etched on her face. "He will have several men to answer to you if he did anything you didn't want him to do."

"Nothing really, it's just my body...I don't know what but..." She didn't know how to put her feelings into words. This was all so new to her. "He made me feel things I've never even thought of before."

"That's good to hear. I would have to kill him if he took advantage of your innocence."

"Please don't hurt Gavin. While he infuriates me in so many ways, there is something unique about him that keeps me wanting to see him. He steals my breath..."

"I do?" Gavin stood behind her, grinning.

She inhaled a swift breath of air, turning in her seat. "You do what?" she asked, not wanting to give credence to her words not meant for his ears.

"Ah, I believe I heard you say I steal your breath." He pulled out a chair, sitting down beside her and setting her hand in his. "I never thought I could do that, take someone's breath away."

"I think that's my cue to leave," Addie stood, turning for her wrap only to find... "Hamilton?"

"At your service." He grinned at her, bending over to kiss her on the cheek. "Are you ready to go? I've plans for this evening."

"Yes, we've talked and I've learned a bit about Larena." Turning to Gavin, "She is a really competent women. You should talk to her more. Let her understand your concerns and fears. And if you want her, you should tell her what you're doing and where you go."

Gavin turned to her, sitting back and crossing his arms. "I'm listening. What do you want to tell me?"

Larena wanted to laugh at him. He didn't understand anything Addie told him. She could probably talk for hours but unless he learned how to listen, there would be no improvement.

"Nothing." She smiled at him, clasping her hands in her lap. "Nothing at all. You could start by telling me what you've done today. You know I've been talking to Tyna and we're going to see each other again even though I know you don't want me to see her. She told me she'd send me a message." She watched his eyes darken and his brows draw together.

"Visited parliament today."

"Anything important happen? Any laws voted out of existence?" she asked knowing nothing would happen. The wealthy aristocrats out numbered the ordinary person. The farmers wanted the Corn Laws repealed and the taxes that created greater armies reduced.

"Not much but I do wish I could give you the news you crave and perhaps then I wouldn't have to worry about you so much."

"Thank you. Is there anything else?"

"Nothing that I want to talk about here."

Well, she had a lot she wanted to talk about with him. He was always silent when she needed to speak of something important. "You saw the newspaper." She challenged him.

His jaw clenched. "Would you like anything more to eat or drink?"

Gavin had this way of changing the subject when he didn't want to talk about something. "I've had my fill, besides I'm sure cook will have a meal prepared for us when we return. Unless you've decided you don't want to be my chaperone."

"I've a cab waiting but I want to stop at my apartment for a few changes of clothing. Last night came as a surprise to me, so I wasn't prepared." He leaned forward, shrugging his broad shoulders. "No nightshirt, you recall."

Blood rushed to her face, heating all of her. "By all means stop at your apartment." She waved her hand in front of her face in hopes of cooling herself. Had he slept naked last night?

"What are you thinking little sweetheart?" His knuckles softly whispered across her cheek. "What makes you flush so sweetly? Are you thinking about me lying in bed, naked?"

~ * ~

"I don't want to talk about it now." She turned her back to him and stood, her hand resting on the table.

He laughed, admiring her. "Pink cheeks become you. Does the thought of me naked in the room next to yours make your heart race? Does it, as you just said, steal your breath?"

She tripped on a chair in front of her, whirling her arms in the air to keep from falling. With one long stride he reached her and pulled her into his arms. "You should watch where you're going. While I love having you in my arms, if I didn't catch you...you might have hurt yourself."

"I did, it's just that..."

He turned her, needing to feel the length of her body against his. "Just what?" Her breath whispered close to his mouth. He needed to taste her sweetness, feel the softness of her lips.

"Let me go," she whispered and her breath once more caressed him.

"I would have you kiss me first." He pulled her closer, enjoying the closeness yet yearning for so much more.

She gasped, her eyes widening before assuming the color of a summer storm, violets, and dark blues. "That wouldn't be appropriate here in public."

"Appropriate," he laughed, smiling at her while he tried to put thoughts of her perched on the lamppost from his head. "Nothing about our situation is appropriate."

"That doesn't mean anything."

"Kiss me little sweetheart. I promise you won't regret it. After that, we'll take our leave."

She moistened her lips while she was still shaking her head no. "I don't know how."

"You'll figure it out."

"Please, can we just go?"

"After you kiss me," he persisted.

Her hands touched his shoulders and he felt the pressure as she tried to gain more height. He bent his head until their lips almost touched. "Gavin," she breathed.

"What are you waiting for?"

"We're in public." She was just a breath away.

He watched her moisten her lips while he waited. "We're not going anywhere."

She closed her eyes, her hands finding purchase in his hair, bringing his head down so their lips met briefly. "A kiss, now can we go?"

"That's not a kiss." He chuckled softly. "But this is closer."

Their lips met and he felt her body melt into his, heard the tiny sound emanating from the back of her throat. Quickly, he touched her mouth with his tongue, traced the seam and delighted when she opened for him. He pulled back, regarding her closely. Bloody hell, she had a strange, brain-numbing effect on him if we weren't careful.

"Gavin..."

"We can pursue this more thoroughly when we're alone." He slipped a tendril of hair behind her ear, reveling in the silken strand that seemed to set his flesh on fire with the brief touch. He wanted to know how it would feel wrapped around his naked body.

He let go of her, offering her his arm and she accepted. "Gavin, I like your kisses, but just because I like them I'm not going to obey you."

Sometimes she said the strangest things. "I've never asked. Ah, there's our cab now."

He sat across from her in the carriage as it rumbled along the street. She spent most of the time gazing out the window. He leaned back, studying the tiny female who was quickly stealing his heart.

She turned to look at him. "I don't want you to ravage me."

He needed patience. "No, I would never do such a thing." He paused trying to think of the right thing to say. She'd obviously read the newspaper and saw the drawings. She wanted to talk about it, but he still needed to wait for privacy and time to think about what he should say. He didn't want to offend or scare her but needed the right words. He just wasn't sure what they were yet. "No, I don't think you would like that, nor would I."

"What does it mean, ravaged?"

He cleared his throat before wrapping on the cab, a signal to stop. "We're here, almost anyway." Stymied for the right words again, he felt such tender yet mercuric emotions for her.

The vehicle slowly rolled to a halt. Gavin jumped out then helped Larena from the carriage. "You're avoiding my question."

"I am?" he asked pleasantly while he regarded her heartbreakingly lovely face. The lines were drawn tense, her lips moist and slightly parted. Tendrils of her hair moved softly, whipped by a tender breeze.

"Yes, and we're not here. I remember from yesterday."

"Almost," he pointed down the street. "Thought you might enjoy a bit more fresh air." He took her hand in his, relishing the feeling of her fingers interwoven with his. Truly, he didn't know how he was going to keep this relationship platonic if he slept in the bedroom adjoining hers and she kept telling him how much she enjoyed their kisses. His body wanted to know if she enjoyed more than just the kisses.

"Do you have the feeling we're being followed? I do." She looked behind her then across the street.

"Did being in Addie's company make you suspicious of everything?" He knew they were followed but what he didn't know was for how long or why and he didn't want to frighten her.

"No, not at all but I've had the feeling all day that someone was watching me. I thought it was you, but Addie assured me you were somewhere else and she didn't seem concerned. But then she'd know if one of Drake's men had been sent to watch me."

"The day is beautiful. It took awhile for the sun to find it's way from behind the clouds but now..." he gestured with his free hand. "We have sunshine. I love the feel of sun on my face. Do you?"

She hit him in the arm then blushed beautifully. "You do know that you have this way of changing the subject whenever there is something you don't want to talk about."

"Is it working?"

"No, I remember everything I've asked and you're going to have to answer me some time."

"We really are here now." He turned into the building but felt her holding back. "And I'll answer most of your questions when we have the needed privacy."

"I don't think I should go in with you. Not after yesterday and the drawings in the newspaper."

"You can't stay out here alone. The district is safe for a man but nowhere in London is it completely safe for a woman. If you don't come inside with me, well, I'll have to keep sleeping naked."

"Unless you're Addie Winthrop," she said, seeming to ignore his last statement.

"Now who's changing the subject? I'll let you get away with it though. Not even Addie is completely safe. True, she is more capable of defending herself than most but Hamilton would not want her so close to the docks alone."

"There could be more drawings. I really don't want this and if, well, I think anyone who might be following has seen my face by now."

"You can't stay on the street by yourself."

"I don't have a choice?"

She pushed him and every instinct he possessed told him he needed to find a way to let her make the right and safe decision. "Impulsive choices or ones that are made to make a point are bad choices. If you decide not to go inside, then I choose not to either."

"You can't do that."

"My little sweetheart, I don't need a nightshirt to sleep. Indeed, the clothing was not for my modesty but to reassure you. I always sleep naked. That sweet blush I'm growing quite fond of is painting your cheeks again." Inside, his heart seemed to melt.

"I believe we should walk upstairs to your apartment." She spoke slowly, pausing several times to clear her throat in order to form the words she didn't want to speak. "Do you always get your way?"

"Only when it's the right decision." He let her walk in front of him, leading the way. She had been in his arms yesterday and he'd set her on his bed, felt the rounded contour of her breast. With this little interchange he understood her better. Let her make the decision he needed her to make.

"Arrogant man," she said looking over her shoulder momentarily.

"I prefer confident over arrogant." He tossed his head back and laughed aloud. When he caught his breath, he saw her wounded expression. He wasn't at all sure why. It was another aspect of Larena he would have to uncover.

Once inside the apartment she sat down in the main office. He took his time, searching for items of clothing he knew he wanted. Although this trip had not been necessary, he would be in his office tomorrow and he had no plans to wear the dreaded nightshirt. As he told her, it was to reassure her. What she didn't know wouldn't bother her.

Along with his clothes, he picked up a few files he needed to review this evening. He didn't want to talk about the drawings in the newspaper, didn't want to confront the issues plaguing both of them, but he understood something needed to be said.

"How much are you packing?" He heard her behind him and before he could respond, she was in his bedchamber.

"Enough for a week," he told her, nonchalantly folding a shirt before stuffing it in his valise all the while his thoughts zoomed straight to the bed.

"Aren't you going to be here tomorrow?" She stepped closer, staring at the bed then moistening her lips, appearing confused.

"True," his body hardened at the thoughts leaping through his head. He was no saint but this tiny lady tempted him more than anyone he'd ever met. Just the way she gazed at the bed then back to him had him pushing all gentlemanly thoughts out of his head.

"Shouldn't we leave soon? The hair on the back of my neck is still standing on end. I really don't like that feeling. I'm sure no one is inside your apartment watching us, but shouldn't we be careful?"

"The truth is, I'm not eager to have you alone with me in The Duchess' townhouse. Her presence haunts the place. And I'm pretty sure I have need of her infamous cane. Where you're concerned, I'm not sure I can remain a gentleman."

She blinked several times, her visage unchanging. Usually her expression screamed her feelings. At this time he could not read her thoughts. Then pink rose to her cheeks. "I think we should go. This is making me very uncomfortable."

"You were looking at my bed."

"I was."

"Are you remembering yesterday? You shouldn't. It wasn't well done of me." He remembered the brief feel of her rounded breast and her hardened nipple on his knuckles.

Slowly, she backed from the room, shaking her head as she moved away from him. "No. No it wasn't, but it wasn't all your fault. I could have told you to stop."

With those words he knew she was remembering and wished she recalled the mercuric sensations he hoped he evoked in her with his touch. Yet the time wasn't right to recreate the impulsiveness of the day before.

She wasn't ready and if truth be told, neither was he.

"We can go now." He picked up his bag and offered his arm as he approached her.

Hesitantly, she accepted the proffered support. "Will you talk to me tonight? Maybe after dinner?"

He hesitated perhaps a second too long. "If that's what you'd like."

"Will you promise not to change the subject?"

"No." He would never promise something he probably couldn't do.

The sun had begun to set when they stepped outside and hailed a carriage. As last night it was getting dark when they arrived at the townhouse. A soft wind filtered through the greenery. Unlike last night, no one waited for them. The house was empty.

He dreaded the evening and the night to come. Sleep proved elusive to him the night before as he was sure it would tonight. Even though he knew he needed to discuss the newspaper and the articles repercussions with Larena, he didn't want to.

Inside, "I'll take this to my room," he said starting for the stairs, relieved he'd have a few moments of privacy before he spoke of the implications of the article with Larena.

She followed him. He heard the swish of her skirts behind him as they ascended. Once in the room, he turned to her. "Are you so eager for me to take your virginity that you follow me to my bedroom?"

He heard her gasp as she slowly backed away from him. "I wanted to make sure you had everything you needed. Do you?"

"With you here I do have everything I need." He set his hands on his hips, his feet braced apart, studying her.

"What does that mean?" She stepped farther inside his chamber. Curiosity seemed to draw her forward.

"Best leave that answer for another time," he said, tempted to pull her into his arms and show her the meaning. He respected her too much for that, needed to build a future for them.

"I want to know now," she told him, moving to his valise and opening it for him, beginning to unpack his things.

"No you don't." He swallowed hard, gripping his fists tightly. "You have no idea."

She pulled out a long white shirt. "Is this your nightshirt? Where do you want me to put it?"

"In the fire," he murmured.

She tilted her head slightly, her eyes wide. "What?"

"Never mind. In the armoire. So, you're bent on helping me unpack? I can do it myself. Why don't you see if Cook has dinner ready? I'm famished."

"You don't want me here. All right then, I'll get one of Logan's Bordeaux or would you prefer Chianti?"

"Either is fine," he ran his fingers through his hair.

"I like the way you look when your hair is all messed up."

He couldn't keep the groan from emanating from his chest. Her innocent statements made this harder than he'd ever thought it would be. "I'll see you in a few minutes in the dining room."

As she turned, her skirts swirled around her ankles and swayed provocatively as she walked from the room. If The Duchess knew what was good for her niece, she should return this instant.

He spent several minutes putting his clothing away then a few more pouring himself a drink from the whiskey bottle and glass the butler must have left on his nightstand.

Looking from his window he had a good view of the street. Nothing seemed abnormal, yet he noticed a movement down the road. Just an animal searching for something, he told himself. This time it was the hair on the back of *his* neck standing on end.

Focused on a shadow he waited for movement and was rewarded when he saw a man step from the darkness and make his way to a cab. He groaned, realizing there would be another article and drawing in the papers tomorrow. This time he was sure Larena would be identified.

The Duchess had not done right by her niece. This was an impossible situation. Even if he kept his hands to himself, Larena's reputation would be ruined. It already was. He would marry her today if she'd agree, but he didn't have high expectations. Larena wanted to make life more difficult for herself before she would accept advice from him, a man.

Inhaling a long deep breath, he swallowed the drink he poured for himself and strode down the stairs to the parlor where she waited for him.

In the time he spent thinking, she had changed her clothes. She wore a beautiful dark blue dress with a low neckline and tiny off the shoulder sleeves. The diamond and sapphire pendant she wore rested provocatively close to her cleavage. His mind traveled in a direction he'd been trying to avoid.

When he stepped through the parlor doors, she stood. "A pre-dinner drink?" she moved to the sideboard.

"What you're having." Hands behind his back, he studied her from the tips of her toes to the top of her head. Her waist was narrow and her breasts would fill his hands nicely. Her large expressive eyes enhanced her beautiful face, and full lips, and her dark hair compelled him to touch.

"Brandy." She poured two glasses then handed one to him. "Cheers and to the truth, all of it."

He cleared his throat, searching for the words he needed, "Cheers, and the truth is not always what we want to hear."

I do want to hear the truth, all of it, and you promised," she stayed her course.

"Is dinner ready?" He swallowed half his drink.

"You've done it again."

"What?" he asked, beginning to enjoy a conversation that could turn on him in a moment.

"Enjoy your dinner." Head held high, shoulders stiff, she lead the way to the dining room.

"Only if you do." Her safety from the ton and those who would ostracize her was his only concern. Confronting the reporters though would not help his cause.

"I should understand all the implications about our relationship. Don't you think?" she sat down next to him, picking up her napkin.

"I don't want to see you hurt." He knew the answer he gave would not satisfy her.

"I'll be hurt more if I'm surprised by things I don't understand. In this new world I refuse to be kept in the dark. I want to know what you don't want to tell me. My guesses could be worse than the truth."

"I want to protect you, nothing more," he told her, wishing this were easier.

"Knowledge will protect me not ignorance."

He poured the Chianti, breathing deeply, thinking about what she said. It seemed she had an answer for everything. "I disagree."

"Have you really thought about it? Women obviously can't be protected from everything. You can try but you'll fall short every time there is some type of diversity."

"The wine is really very good. I believe I'm going to like this connection we have with Logan. He's very generous. Don't you think?" He watched the play of emotions across her face.

"You've done it again. I'm not going to let it ruin my dinner though." She forked a piece of salmon into her mouth.

"Good, I'm glad you don't want your dinner ruined." He smiled, wondering what she would come up with next. The only reason he didn't answer her is because he couldn't figure out what to say.

"After dinner we are going to talk about the newspaper and what everything means."

"You're determined."

"I am. I very much believe knowledge is most important. How can I make rational plans and decisions if I don't understand the significance of the written word?" She frowned at him and he wanted to trace the lines with his finger.

He sighed heavily before downing his glass of wine and pouring them both another. Perhaps if she had too much to drink, she'd forget about the newspaper article.

"I promise that I'll do my very best to explain anything you ask this evening." He settled back in his chair, completely satisfied. Excitement coursed through him. She was absolutely correct in her desire to understand what had been written.

"Good." She stood and carrying her wine glass, she picked up the bottle. "If you're done eating, let's retire to the parlor."

"You think to get me drunk?" he queried with a bit of a chuckle.

"If that's what it takes to get you to talk to me, then of course I'll try anything." She flounced through the dining room doors.

He picked up his glass and followed at a slower pace, thinking about all he would say to her. It would be so much easier to show her.

~ * ~

Cale paced the tiny apartment where he and Tyna lived. Dust had settled on the tables and windowsills. There were no curtains or decorations in the tiny loft. He set the meat pies he bought from a vendor on the table near the kitchen.

"You really should learn how to cook," he told her, grabbing a spoon and digging into his meal.

"So should you."

"Nah, it's women's work. I earn the living and it would be nice if you could do something to help out."

"I've found Larena for you, a ripe gullible little fool whose only wish is to help people like us."

"And I thank you for that." He truly did and he supposed he should be nicer to his half sister. They were all each other had.

"Lady Graham thinks we're married."

"And you haven't disavowed her of the knowledge. Why?" He was curious about so many things. From the first moment Tyna told him about her new friend, he understood she could no longer be trusted.

"I'm not sure. She just made the assumption and I didn't tell her the truth. It seemed to be an easier explanation of our relationship."

"Ah, my little sister, what exactly are you up to?" He strode close to her, hoping he could read something in her eyes.

"Nothing," she murmured, sipping the ale her brother preferred. "Nothing at all. I want what you want."

"Your eyes give you away every time you lie. You're not thinking of betraying me or the cause?" He regarded her over the pint of ale. If that was the case, he'd have to set her straight.

"I don't care about the Corn Laws and I really don't want to end up in jail. That's not what I want for myself. I crave a better life, but Cale, I would never betray you. It's just that I'm not going to stay by your side forever. Your work is getting dangerous."

"You think the Lady Graham will see past your worn dirty clothing and hire you as a lady's maid. You're a bigger fool than she is, but if it's what you want for yourself, I applaud your aspirations. Just don't deceive my people and me. They trust me."

"Don't deny that you have aspirations too. I know you're working so hard to get these laws changed so you can make a decent living. You can't pretend in front of me. I know you better than anyone."

"I'd like to marry and start a family." His thoughts went to Celine, his golden girl. She was so beautiful.

"You can't do that if you're in Newgate or transported. These protests might all be for naught. Is that a chance you want to take? You could settle down and wed Celine. I bet Lord Broon would help you if I continue to make friends with Larena."

He downed the last of his food, thinking of all he had to lose. His sister pointed out a relevant fact. "Send the message tomorrow. We'll meet at The Duchess' residence after Lord Broon leaves. We need her help in this."

Chapter Three

Larena filled both glasses before she set the bottle on a nearby table. The window was open and a soft breeze whispered through, fluttering the lace curtains. Brilliant colors of the sunset had spread across the horizon earlier. Now moonlight brightened the land.

Wide eyed she watched the day end. She wondered what the remainder of the evening would bring. Touching her lips with a finger, she turned too quickly, stumbling into Gavin's arms, wine sloshing in her glass and threatening to spill. With ease she'd seldom seen, he took the glass from her hand, setting it on the sill.

"Ravish," he began, "is to become overcome with emotion as when I kiss you I hope I'm ravishing you."

Her heart thundered against her ribs and she momentarily lost her ability to think. "That's not what was implied by the article."

"No, it wasn't. Come, sit." He picked up her wine then held out his hand to her, a compelling smile on his face. "We can talk and perhaps I can show you a little something."

She trailed behind him to the settee. She'd follow him anywhere. "Exactly what aren't you telling me?" She frowned at him, trying desperately to slow her breathing, which was now racing out of control. Perhaps she shouldn't have been so adamant about this talk. "And what do you mean, show me?"

"I prefer the definition I gave you than the implied ones in the article. Don't you?" His knuckles whispered against her cheek, sending a sudden shiver down her spine.

"You haven't changed the subject, but you are talking around it. Why don't you want me to understand what's going on?" She was confused and growing irritated.

He shrugged exceedingly broad shoulders, still smiling at her as if nothing was wrong between them. "I suppose I like your innocence. It's endearing you know."

"Perhaps I don't want to remain innocent. I want to be worldly, Gavin." She picked up her wine, running a finger lazily around the rim before slowly closing her eyes and opening them.

"If you continue in this vein, you will lead me to believe you've lost that endearing quality, your innocence."

"What do you mean by that?" She quickly set her drink on the table as if the glass burned her fingers.

"You flirt impeccably for a virgin. Do you even realize what you're doing and what those looks can do to a man?" He leaned forward. "And I'm pretty damn sure you are a virgin still."

"I'm not flirting. I've no idea what you're insinuating," she stood, meaning to find the cooling air floating through the open window. His fingers circled her wrist, tugging until she collapsed on his lap.

"I like you close," he murmured as she felt the soft touch of his lips behind her ear as well as the stubble of a day's growth of beard. One hand held her face while the other settled on her waist.

"We shouldn't." She swallowed, her emotions simmering in anticipation of the coming kiss, but she lied. She wanted this more than anything, needed to find out what he inferred all the time and why The Duchess would use her cane on his back.

"But we are and there is no one available who will beat me with their cane when I take liberties I shouldn't." His hand traveled upward, coming to rest just below her breast.

"The Duchess always told us we could kiss as much as we want." Her gaze met his as she ran her tongue across her lips a couple of times. If she flirted, it was because he taught her.

"Kisses lead to other things." She felt his lips and teeth on her earlobe then his tongue.

She turned. "I'd like to know what those other things are. You should teach me before someone else does." She gently touched her mouth to his before moving away in order to see his reaction.

"No, you don't, not right now and no one else will teach you anything."

"Show me. You said you would." She challenged him, hoping she could entice him to do something more than kiss her.

"You will never know how much I want to do just that, but I promised myself I would wait until I married you," he murmured, his lips on hers.

Surprised, she tried to stand but he kept her firmly on his lap. Needing to get away from him, "More wine."

He laughed, letting her go, "If you keep giving me more wine, you're going to have to carry me up the stairs. That might be a little difficult for you."

While she was pouring the Chianti, "I will ravish you with wine, and you will tell me about the article. Perhaps you will show me a bit more about lovemaking. Can you do that without taking my virginity?" Yet she felt the affects of the alcohol and her mind was not as clear as usual. Momentarily, she felt the room tilt.

His head fell back and he roared with laughter, grinning at her. "More likely I will seduce you but...I don't know how to respond to your question. Yes, I can show you more about lovemaking without taking your virginity. I just don't know if I have the needed control."

She knew she'd had too much wine but still she meant to pursue the meaning of the drawing and the article in the newspaper. After all he promised to tell her. "What did they mean in the article, ravished? Please. Not the definition you gave me but the real meaning or at least what the author of the article meant."

He cleared his throat a couple of times, "I'm not sure what to say. What they meant really doesn't matter to me and shouldn't to you either."

"The truth always works the best. I want to understand what London is thinking about me...us," she told him, petulantly. "Your hesitancy has me thinking horrible things, writing my own story so to speak."

"Very well, I've been thinking about what to say all day. The article implied that I might have carried you off against your will since the first drawing depicted me prying you from the lamppost, which was what I did. You're stronger than I expected."

"You did that. You ravished me? Addie said she'd kill you if you did that. Why?" Whatever he did or people thought he did, the act didn't warrant his death. "I won't let her."

"This isn't getting any easier. She wanted to know if I raped you. Which of course I didn't." He paused. "There it's out."

The room swirled. She closed her eyes in an attempt to steady herself. She let her head fall against his chest. After a few seconds that seemed more like an eternity, she answered. "I told her that you didn't ravish me, but in some ways you did. The kisses and the way you touched me..." her body responded so intensely to his caresses.

"You ravish me every time we kiss," he murmured softly, his breathing growing heavier by the second. "I'm so overcome by emotions that I can barely stop with just a kiss."

She pulled away from him, looking at his dark simmering eyes. "You must understand. I need to know what else you would do besides kiss me. It's not fair that everyone in the world knows except me."

"Let's move on. What else do you want to know about the article? I feel another topic is a bit safer."

"The paper called me a street walker and a public ledger. I'm pretty sure they referred to me as a prostitute." She didn't really care about that unless they put a name to the face.

He shrugged broad shoulders, a grim expression on his face. "If I could change that I would and you're right. I have reason to believe there will be another article tomorrow. This time your face will be revealed, and no one in the ton will think you're a streetwalker but a fallen woman."

"The hair on the back of my neck?" she queried, knowing the answer before he could confirm her fears.

"Yes."

"I'll fall from grace." She realized she really didn't care if she fell. Just like her sister Fayth, her ruin didn't mean anything. Her cousin had been adamant she'd never marry, but she found Jarret and they fell in love despite a great deal of lies between them.

"I'll protect you."

"How? In truth my ruin or fall doesn't mean anything in the scope of this life. There are people dying who cannot get enough from their hard work to feed their families. What's in a name?"

"I'll marry you," he said simply as if a wedding proposal would make everything right.

"That's very noble of you." She found she didn't like that word, noble. Marrying for love was what she dreamed of.

"Is there anything else you'd like me to explain?" He emptied the bottle in her glass.

"No." Yawning, she rested her head on his chest finding peace in the sound of his heartbeat. "I've learned more than I bargained for tonight. Thank you, I think. I still want you to show me other things besides kisses."

"Perhaps you shouldn't be so very curious. For now kisses should be enough to keep that inquisitiveness at bay."

"Curious," she rolled the word around in her muzzled mind. "I've had too much wine. You?"

"No, this evening has left me wide awake. I feel...I need to do something...expend some energy. I'm afraid what I really want isn't viable."

She sat up suddenly not so sleepy. "What do you want? I can help you. I can make it feasible."

Shaking his head he groaned. "No, no this is something I have to fix myself. I'll find a way."

"Really, I could do something." She was eager to give him some type of aid. He'd gone beyond himself in telling her everything she wanted to know.

He set her aside, "Larena, you wanted truth?"

"Yes."

"If I let you help me with this issue I have, I would ruin you."

"How would you do that?"

He paused for a few seconds as if he thought; "I would take your virginity, break through your maidenhead, and ruin you for marriage to anyone but me. Yet that's exactly what my wine drenched mind is telling me I want, so don't tempt me anymore."

She smiled at him, "I don't know what all that means, but I'm willing to try."

"You need to go to bed."

She truly didn't know what she was thinking or even if she wanted what she was saying. "With you?"

He groaned. "No, by yourself."

She touched his chin then ran her finger along his jawline. "Do you always have hair on your face this time of night?"

"Can you walk up the steps by yourself?" he asked.

She looked at him, feeling chastised. "I've been able to walk up steps since I was two years old. Of course, I can."

"Show me." His voice sounded strained and a bit gravelly.

On wobbly legs she stood, her hand resting on his shoulder. She swallowed hard, looking at the parlor door as if it were a world away. It was moving. Quickly, she sat back down. "The room seems to be whirling." She closed her eyes. "Give me a minute."

"Don't think a minute is going to help."

"Of course it will," she told him, determined to walk up a set of steps she easily negotiated when she was two years old.

"I'll give you a minute then I'm going to carry you to your bedroom. Rest assured I will leave you in your bed then go to my room."

She wanted to be in his arms, but she needed to prove herself and do this by herself. "Okay. Are you counting to sixty or am I?"

"You are," he chuckled softly.

"All right then, one, two, three," she closed her eyes, thinking about his lips on hers. She began again, "One, two three, ten, eleven..."

"You can't count to sixty."

"Of course I can." She started over again.

He laughed and cradled her in his arms. She let him carry her up the stairs and to her bedroom. Gavin set her down, "Do you need help getting undressed? I shouldn't have said that."

She moistened her dry lips, needing water. "A glass of water, please?"

"I'll bring you some after you're ready for bed."

"There is some on the nightstand." She sat on the bed watching him, enamored of his broad shoulders and narrow hips while he poured her a glass and brought it to her. She wanted to see him without his shirt on.

She drank and blinked a few times, "Thank you."

"Anything else?"

Running her hands down the bodice of her dress, she tried to think.

"My corset, I need for you to unlace me."

"Good god, how did you lace it?"

She forced this morning into her mind and didn't come up with any recollections. "I don't know." She burped, closing her eyes and wishing she could sleep with Gavin, wishing he would hold her in his arms.

"Turn around."

His voiced warmed her, heated every part of her and gently seduced. Then his knuckles brushing against her skin sent a wave of mercuric emotions through her. Unknowingly, he was ravishing her, and she meant to savor every sweet second. "You do that very well." She turned to face him, holding the bodice of her dress to cover her.

"Experience," he mumbled.

"You've done this before?" A wave of jealousy swept through her and he probably ravished that lady too. "I don't like that thought at all. I don't like it that you did something to another lady you won't do to me."

"We're not talking about my past. It has no place where you and I are concerned. I've never implied or even said I've been celibate. I'm not a virgin, Larena." He backed from the room. "Anything else?"

She sat on the bed her head in her hands. "Could you get me my nightdress?"

"You can't do that yourself?" He studied her for a few seconds. "No, of course you can't. Where is it?"

"In my armoire," she pointed to it, slipping the dress from her body as well as the corset. "Need to wash."

"Here it is." He turned to her then stopped. "You're exquisite," he told her, dropping the fabric he held and backing from the room. "Goodnight."

He vanished. "Coward," she whispered softly. True, she'd had too much to drink but so had he. There had been many times where she and her sisters had spent the night drinking. She could hold her liquor better than most. And she wondered what she would have to do to find out first hand how it felt to be thoroughly ravished by Gavin Broon.

There was so much she wanted to understand and to feel. Gavin was the man she wanted to teach her, but she realized this wouldn't be easy. He had too many scruples. It would have been nice to fall in love with a man like Jarret who only had sex on his mind.

Yet she recalled Storm had to propose marriage to Hadden. She didn't want that, and Ravyn, her journey had been so fraught with horrible mishaps. No, she didn't want that either. This was her trip and she'd have to figure out how to bring Gavin to her. Right now she believed she'd taken the first step on that journey.

She stepped out of all her clothes and standing in front of her mirror naked, she wondered what Gavin would think of her. Pouring water into the small basin she washed then put on her nightdress.

One pin at a time she let her dark hair fall around her shoulders. Despite Gavin's reluctance she'd learned a lot tonight. But she wanted to put the knowledge into practice.

For some reason she didn't feel sleepy any longer, her body thrumming to life when she thought of his kisses. She pulled back the covers to her bed, sitting, hands on her lap.

She didn't know how much time had passed. Perhaps she closed her eyes but maybe she didn't. Her back was against the headboard as she listened to the muffled sounds that seemed to be part of her dreams.

Strange noises emanated from the adjoining room, grunts mostly and muffled yells. She straightened on her bed, pensive and so very curious. She tried to concentrate and hear the words. Tempted to check on Gavin, she stood but thought better of intruding on his privacy. Still intrigued as the noise continued and trying to ignore it, she found herself at the window looking out on the blackness of the night.

A loud crash caused her to jump. Unable to stay away, she strode to the door between their rooms and cautiously opened it. She inhaled a startled gasp. Gavin faced her, his chest bare and covered in a sheen of moisture that seemed to glow when the candlelight flickered across him.

"I didn't mean to wake you." He let his hands fall to his sides, his bared feet braced apart. Suddenly as if realizing he was practically naked, she searched the room in an attempt to keep from staring at his imposing frame.

"You didn't." Mesmerized by him, by his body in a trance she stepped to him, touched her hand upon his chest and heard the quick inhalation of air, felt the beating of his heart.

He set his hand upon hers. "Larena," he spoke her name slowly, his eyes gazing into hers.

She yearned to see into his mind, read his thoughts, "You're so different from me." With the slightest twist of her fingers she touched his nipple and delighted in the feel of him. She regarded him closely, smiling into his eyes.

He didn't laugh as she thought he would. His voice so sincere and strangely deep, he said, "I'm glad of that."

Unable to help herself, she brought her other hand and set it on his other nipple. "I like the way you feel. What were you doing that caused all that noise? What crashed to the floor?"

"Trying to get rid of pent up emotions, but I don't think it's going to help after this." He spoke slowly then, "The basin, as you can see it's shattered. I'll pick up the pieces in the morning."

"Pent up emotions?" She didn't understand what he tried to do, why he was grunting and yelling albeit quietly.

"My body wanted to do something my mind didn't." He ran his fingers through the length of her hair, bringing a strand to his face, touching his lips to it. "Silken fire, so soft I want to wrap it around me."

"You speak in riddles." She moved her hands lower, tracing the hair on his chest to just above the fastening of his pants then back, marveling in the play of his muscles where her fingers travelled. Intrigued by the obvious change in his breathing and fascinated she could do this to him.

"And, Larena, you really need to stop."

"Not unless you make me." She continued running her hands along his chest and upward to sweep them across his shoulders.

"It's best for you if I tell you no." He held her hands in his in front of him, placing light kisses on her knuckles. "You should go to your bed now before we both regret this night."

"I'm not sleepy. Indeed, my heart races and it seems I've grown hotter by the second. Don't want to spend the night alone. Want to be in your arms." She remembered when he barely touched her breast and the way her body quickly responded, and she marveled that perhaps she had the same effect on him.

"Come," he drew her to the door. "What you're innocently creating here is best left for the marriage bed. I'll walk you to your chamber."

"I want to stay with you." She realized she didn't care what others thought but rather she wanted to live in the moment. Only two of her sisters and cousins combined had waited for marriage to find out what happened to a woman in bed with a man. She didn't even know if she loved Gavin or wanted to marry him. She liked him though and who better to teach her?

"No. Not tonight," he told her, drawing her toward her room. Inside, he pulled her close and lightly pressed his lips to hers then let her go as if the touch burned him. "Your bed." He pointed in that direction then watched as she sat forlornly on the bed.

She watched the door close behind him then found herself at the window again. Shadows played across the street, and moonlight brightened the darkness. Below her a shadowed form strode quickly from the townhouse and a few minutes later she saw Gavin gallop down the street.

What had she done to cause this sudden departure? Men were such strange beings. She didn't understand anything about them. By leaving so suddenly, he left her unprotected.

~ * ~

Gavin had tried to release the tension in his body Larena created so easily. He thought he had his unruly thoughts and base desires freed from his body then she stepped through the door. Now after seeing her nearly naked, all the karate kicks and punches lost their effect on him.

The flimsy nightgown she wore revealed more than it hid. The candlelight around her silhouetted her form, and he could see the curve of her breasts as well as her waist and the dark triangle of her woman's mound. When she closed the distance between them and set her hand on his chest, her breasts with their hardened buds grazed his body. He fought the instinctive need to give her everything she asked for earlier.

He was not meant to be her chaperone, and this was only the second night. What new way would she find to torment him tomorrow? Even if she kept her hands and her thoughts to herself, he would have been hard pressed to ignore her. But she didn't. Her questions were always provocative and mercuric. When she innocently touched him, his emotions heated while his body hardened in anticipation of lovemaking.

Without further thought he dressed and strode from the house. Mounting his favorite stallion, he rode with a careless abandon through the London streets. Energy surged within him and, at first, he didn't know where he was headed. An hour later when he pulled up at the small lake on Drake's estate, he knew his subconscious had directed him here.

Disrobing, he strode into the lake until it was thigh high then dove into the semi-frigid water. With long sure strokes he swam to the middle of the lake before treading water, searching the area to make sure he was alone. He floated on his back trying to relax in the water. Living in the same house and sleeping in the room next to Larena's kept him in a constant state of arousal.

The chill and the exercise eased his condition. He turned and swam back to land and for a few seconds his mind and body were free of the woman who was slowly turning his world upside down.

"Needed a cold dip?"

Startled by the voice he hadn't anticipated in the middle of the night, he braced himself. "Drake?"

"Who did you expect?"

"No one." He found his buckskins and pulled them on before slipping his shirt over his head. Finding a large boulder, he sat down and pulled on his boots.

"What brings you here?"

He laughed harshly, not feeling the humor in his situation and in any case not wishing to relive the erotic minutes that had him swimming in the blackness of the night. "You wouldn't believe me if I told you."

"Try me. It's better than leaving me to write my own scenario."

"No, I think your version would probably be easier to comprehend than what is really happening to me." He ran his hands through his hair with a small grunt. "If I remember correctly, you stole Ella's innocence before the wedding."

"Try me. I've been known to listen to a man's troubles," Drake dismounted and handed Gavin a small container. "Drink?"

"No, I've had too much tonight." He paused, thinking. "Perhaps I gave her too much wine."

"From my experience wine can work in many different ways." Drake took a swig from his flask.

"Well, it had a deleterious affect tonight. She did things, acted in ways that would shock you, shocked me."

"You really must tell me a bit of what went on. Ella has her own way of surprising me," Drake said, smiling as if he seen inside his bedroom.

"So you can laugh at me?" One eyebrow rose in speculation then in an attempt to challenge Drake, "What has you riding to the lake in the middle of the night?"

"Not what you suspect. I've still paradise and passion in my bed. More than I can say for you. No, the baby was crying. Nothing I can do to help. Would rather take a ride than listen to the wails."

"Larena has changed me, changed my life and that has me forgetting the vows I made to myself."

"Well, you're not alone. Ella changed my life completely, and I never cease thanking her. I didn't know I could be so happy. Now, tell me, what happened?"

"She tried to seduce me." Lord but he should have let her have her way.

Drake roared with laughter, "Sorry, old man but I couldn't help myself. There is nothing sacred about waiting for marriage. A man needs to know what he's getting into so to speak. I hardly believe you've been celibate your entire life. Let her do what she wants then take the lead and teach her a woman's pleasure."

"Of course not, but I didn't think of marriage to any of the ladies who came before Larena." He'd never deprived himself of sex and now that Larena was becoming part of his life, he had become celibate, had been for almost a year now. Had been celibate since he made the vow to The Duchess that he'd never sleep with another woman as long as he was courting Larena.

"Make love to her if that's what she wants or just give her pleasure. Teach her how to pleasure you. You can always wait to take her virginity until the wedding night."

"You're providing me with excuses to ravish her." He grinned at his words. "Maybe I will have some of that," he said, holding his hand out.

"You've given me a lot to think over."

Drake obliged, handing over the flask. "Whiskey from your soon to be relatives, the Graham's. Between Logan and Larena's family, we'll never have to buy whiskey or wine."

"Thanks."

"So, what did she do?" Drake travelled back to his original question.

"Infuriates me, baffles me, women are such perplexing creatures." Gavin had never had an experience with a woman like the one he was having with Larena. "I've always been in control," he murmured.

"Control, I lost it the first time I kissed Ella. Even though I tried to dictate our lives, she had a way of speaking her mind and changing everything including the way I look at the world."

"Larena walked into my room, nearly naked tonight and when she saw me with my shirt off, the innocent that she is, she should have fled. Instead, she sauntered to me and put her hand on my chest and more." Somehow revealing the extent of her exploration to Drake felt wrong. This was private.

Drake didn't even try to choke back his laughter. "And she's still a virgin? My God, man, you have more restraint than any man alive. Guess that's why you're swimming in a cold lake."

"Frigid is closer to the truth." Gavin appreciated the older man's assessment of his predicament. He'd always thought he could control his emotions and his body, but where Larena was concerned, it was nearly impossible.

"Do you feel any better?"

He inhaled slowly then let his breath out in a long sigh. "No. Talking about what happened, thinking and remembering the way she looked and how her kisses taste, well, I need another swim." That was the solid truth, but he didn't have time for another swim. He needed to return before the sun rose.

Drake shrugged, "Won't get any better until you either wed her or give up that ridiculous promise you made to yourself and bed her."

"The way I understand what you're telling me is that I should ride home and after crawling into bed with her, I should make love to her."

"Ravish her. I read the article and saw the picture. That was Larena you pulled off the lamppost then, by the drawing, you tried to seduce her in that doorway. Am I right?"

"Pictures don't tell the entire story." Denial would only make him believe the opposite.

"No, they don't."

"Tried to keep her from hurting herself. If I didn't take her from that spot, she could have been arrested."

"I see."

"She believes she can solve all of England's problem by protesting the Corn Laws and unfair taxes. So far, from what I can tell she's only observed from a distance."

"You're afraid she's going to do more."

"She says as much. Wants to see the Corn Laws repealed and other things and she's seeing a lady who has ties to the men who seem to be leading the protests."

"I can loan you my hunting lodge for as much time as you need to persuade her that dissidence can be dangerous in these times."

"I would have to be there for several years..." He groaned, knowing he had to change her way of thinking sooner than later.

"Or until she is pregnant. Pregnancy has this crazy and wonderful way of curbing a woman's need to change the world. It seems the baby becomes the center of her existence and even her man has to work damn hard to claim her interest. Before Ashcroft, I wouldn't be out here looking for a diversion."

"Keep her pregnant and she won't want to dally in politics. A less than noble idea but worth thinking about. What I do know is that I don't want any bastards. So back to celibacy."

"I gave you another option," Drake pointed out with a chuckle. "For now, I need to get back. The sun is beginning to poke its head out signaling another day. Don't forget the lodge. Pleasure her and teach her how to give you pleasure. You can always invest in condoms, but they aren't always reliable for preventing pregnancies."

Gavin watched Drake disappear in the distance before mounting his horse. The ride back to town was more sedate, his mind filled with thoughts and plans. He wanted nothing more right now than to find his bed and sleep, but there were things to do. He still needed to read through the files he brought from the office and he had to send out missives to his retainers in Scotland. The work to his ancestral home was already in progress.

He'd never been quite so eager to see Larena imagining her walking down the steps to greet him. At the stable he quickly unsaddled his horse and brushed him down before striding to the townhouse to see Larena.

When he reached the front door, instantly he knew something was wrong. The butler stood at the side of the house motioning for him to come. He hesitated but the strained look on the man's face convinced Gavin this was some type of emergency.

He stepped quickly to meet Stewart. "What is it? You look as if there is a disaster waiting to happen."

"They took over the house, Sir. You have to get help." The lines on the elderly man's face were pronounced in his worry.

"Who are they?" Gavin had a horrible sensation he might have the answer to his question fury simmering deep in his gut.

"They, the man who is leading all these protests. Cale is his name, I think. I don't know what to do."

Gavin put his hand on the butler's shoulders. Bloody hell how had the morning come to this? "Larena? Where is she? Is she alright?" his heart pounded through his chest.

"She didn't want any part of this. She tried to get rid of them as did I, but no one would budge and they just kept coming."

"How did they get inside in the first place?" He ran his hands through his hair trying to figure out what to do. Summoning the constables was out of the question. This had to be handled in the private sphere.

"I think she let in a woman, Miss Tyna, she told me. She's going to hire her as a lady's maid but then all hell broke loose and nobody knew what to do. Pardon me for saying so, but you should have been here. It's why Miss Charlotte left you to chaperone."

"This can't be happening." He tried so hard to convince Larena she didn't understand everything that could happen. His heart pounded, energy he needed to control pumping through him. "Drake," he said wishing he knew what was going on here before he left the Montgomerie's summer estate. "I've got to get Drake. He has men he can send. How many are inside."

"Drake Montgomerie? The heir apparent? I could go get him." Stewart volunteered. The hesitation in his voice didn't go unnoticed.

"When was the last time you rode a horse, Stewart?"

Stewart hesitated, his face a bit pale, "Never did like horses."

"Who can we get?"

"The stable boy, he rides like the wind and he's loyal to The Duchess. He wouldn't want to see anything bad happen to her charge or you for that matter. But there's nothing you can do inside. Even with a pistol one man can't make them leave."

"I can give Larena some moral support, particularly if you say she tried to get rid of them."

"She did, she told me not to let them in but Cale was already inside and he stepped in front of me forcing me away from the door then letting the others through. There was nothing either of us could do to change the circumstances.

"I left Lady Larena in the kitchen. She was pacing and wringing her hands, tears slipping down her cheeks. Miss Tyna was trying to console her. Said the men wouldn't be there very long, but they had to make plans and this was the only safe place, but I think they have another motive."

Gavin left the butler and strode to the kitchen door. Stepping inside, Larena ran to him, throwing her arms around him. "How are you?" He put her down quickly. His only priority was saving her.

"Fine, where did you go? I..." she looked at him, fear clouding her beautiful blue eyes. He didn't know if she trembled to see him or if the shimmer in her eyes was meant as a plea. His heart leapt and careened to his stomach. They were in more danger than she knew.

He smiled icily then whispered furiously. "Doesn't matter." He strode through the kitchen into the hall, ignoring the men assembled in the parlor. Paper, pen and ink in hand he returned to the kitchen. The butler stepped inside.

Gavin quickly penned a message to Drake before handing it to Stewart. "See that the stable boy gets to the Montgomerie estate as soon as possible." He handed the note over. "Then I want you to take Larena and her maid to my apartment and office. Do you know where that is?"

"Yes." The butler turned to leave.

"Stay there. Don't go anywhere with the ladies and don't let them go anywhere. I'll join you as soon as possible."

"Ladies, go with him now." He cringed after he ordered Larena, something he planned to change but somehow it came out without his thinking. She didn't seem to mind or take the time to protest.

He watched as the home was vacated, his heart pounding. Yet knowing the ladies would be taken to safety, he could do what was necessary. His knife was secured on his belt, and he pulled a pistol from the kitchen drawer where he'd put it the first night he stayed at the house.

Walking into the parlor, grim thoughts and wishes this would be easy, he stopped at the door opening. The pistol in hand he stepped through and braced his feet, noting there were twelve men.

"None of you are welcome here. You all need to leave, now." His bravado went unheeded.

"We're doing no harm," Cale spoke up pleasantly, a smile on his face. "Why don't you join us? I've heard you've spoken in our favor in parliament. You can do a lot to change the current environment."

"This assembly is against the law and it matters not what I've done in the government. It is this moment I'm concerned with." Gavin stepped aside, leaving room for the men to file past. "You need to leave. You weren't invited and you're not welcome."

"I don't see how," Cale smiled. "Your vote is with us so do something to help the cause. Put your money where your mouth is."

"This is the private residence of The Duchess of Ravenswood. She would not take kindly to an assembly of men in her home. Men she doesn't know. It is time for all of you to leave." Reinforcements needed to arrive soon but it was a long ride to and from the Montgomerie estate.

"We were invited inside." Cale pretended innocence. "Not by you but by the lady of the house."

"She told me you forced your way inside so tell me, who invited you?" He knew what he would say.

"By your paramour of course. She has been consorting with us as you well know to repeal the unjust laws. Larena," he cleared his throat,

"Lady Larena Graham allowed us to meet in this home. Gave us her permission. Indeed she was eager to discover our plans. If you say otherwise, I'll dispute your word and I've men to back me up. Your word against mine," he smiled.

Anger threatened to overcome common sense. "The lady told me she had nothing to do with this, and the butler said you pushed your way inside. Did your sister help you with this?"

"Your butler is an old man. Didn't know we were invited; either that or he's making up stories to save the lady's reputation. Perhaps he forgot. Of course the entire world knows what she is, your whore. Tyna is on our side as you should be."

"None the less, you need to vacate the premises," Gavin said with a calm he didn't feel, his anger simmering deep inside threatening to burst. He had given Larena fair warning, had told her what would happen, could happen, but he never imagined the home overrun by these men.

"Not until I'm ready."

Unexpectedly, Drake with ten men behind him stepped through the front door. "My men and I think you will." Ungodly tensions knifed through the air.

Cale seemed to regard the burly farmers then the Duke's men. With a nod the men stood, fists clenched, ready to fight.

Gavin had no idea how Drake arrived here so fast. There is no way the stable boy could have reached the estate by now. Drake had a way, though, of discovering things. He must have had the house watched and knew hours ago the home had been invaded.

The intruders were no match for Drake's trained guards. Yet they did their best, determined to make sure their protest was heard. Cale met Gavin with a solid swing at his face. Gavin ducked and surefooted, he danced away. The other men engaged quickly. It was hardly a fair fight and was over soon after it started. Yet tables and figurines crashed to the floor as men landed upon them.

When the altercation was over Drake's men tossed the intruders from the home and left them sprawled down the street, choosing not to call the constables.

"Didn't expect you so soon," Gavin said. "Gotta tell you I was relieved when I saw you standing in the doorway."

"Was on my way into town. Ella wanted a certain hat and I needed to escape the house. Needed fresh air. Also had a man posted nearby."

"The crying child?" Gavin suddenly had second thoughts about children and wedded life.

"Not this time, just needed to escape."

"Same problem I had last night?" Gavin asked laughing. "Thought you might have had the house watched. Guess I was wrong."

"Not wrong but she's always so tired. Didn't expect that from my Ella." Drake shrugged, chuckling beneath his breath. "Last night she fell asleep while I was kissing her."

Gavin took note of Drake's comment while he surveyed the damage the ruckus created in the parlor. He scraped his hands through his hair, thoroughly frustrated. A few items were broken and one end table would have to be replaced. This was not how he'd anticipated his return to the townhouse and Larena from his late night frigid swim.

He picked up an ivory elephant that survived the fray. The consequences to Larena of this day's proceedings were unknown at the moment. For now it seemed Cale wanted to draw Larena farther into his web. He needed to make arrangements to leave town before this escalated to such heights he wouldn't be able to pick up the pieces.

"I'm going to bring Larena home. I told Stewart to take the ladies to my office where they would be safe." He couldn't think straight and perhaps he didn't want to use logic. His fear for her overrode any practical reasoning. Fury made Gavin's body shake.

"And I'm going to see about that hat," Drake gave him a friendly thump on his back. "Think on the advice we talked about last evening. It could take a load off your mind and make it easier to sleep at night. No more frigid dips in the lake and wild rides through the night."

Gavin watched Drake Montgomerie, the heir apparent to the Duke of Richmond, saunter away as if he was a man with no cares. Well, the man conquered his fear of marriage and was supposed to be a happy man. Yet here he was, trying to escape. No marriage is perfect.

Haunting sounds of Bach floated into the early morning air, catching Gavin's attention. He followed the perfectly played notes to the grand piano that sat in the music room mesmerized by the beautifully enchanting tones.

Larena's back was to him, and her fingers danced over the ivory keys. Leaning against the doorframe, arms crossed in front of him, he listened to the sweet sounds, feeling his troubles float away. After several minutes he pushed away from the frame and walking to her, sat down beside her.

"May I?" His hands hovered above the keys eager to play, waiting for her consent. Since childhood music had been his one escape from his three brothers and their constant teasing.

She smiled and nodded. "I believe I'd love that," He joined her, playing the lower notes while she continued with the higher ones. The music seemed to join her soul to his, and while they played, he felt one with her.

When they finished the song, "I didn't know you could play," she said as the music ended and the serenity of the moment vanished with the sound of the notes and the ensuing silence. "It seems you continually show me unique and different sides to your personality.

"Why are you here?" When he saw her sitting at the piano his heart caught in his throat but the music seemed to ease the fear. "You're supposed to be safely tucked away in my apartment. You don't obey very well."

She shrugged her slim shoulders beginning a lively Irish melody. "Never have and I didn't want to go. Don't much like it when people hide me away. At least it wasn't a closet you chose to put me in for my protection."

He'd been ready to throttle her when she told him she chose not to do as he wished. He froze when he heard the last of her statement. "Put you in a closet? Why would I do that?"

She continued to play and ignore his questions for a minute then she stopped, "That's what my sisters did for my protection. When I was a child I was always shuttled here and there, and I was always told it was for my protection."

His thoughts turned inward, suddenly despising her sisters and realizing she was the youngest and like him must have been the butt of many jokes. "They put you in an armoire."

"Afraid of dark, closed-in places. Always have been, I'm terrified of the dark."

He felt the shiver that seemed to sweep the coldness into him. "I'm afraid I don't really understand." He saw her fear, felt the horror sweeping into her at what he supposed were the memories.

She turned slightly and setting her hand on his forearm. "I thought you knew about my parents and all the miscarriages."

"No, tell me."

She blinked, her mouth turning downward and a single tear slipped down her cheek. "My father wasn't a nice person. I'm not sure why my mother married him. Perhaps he was different when they met and courted or he pretended to be someone he wasn't. He was horrible to her but my sisters tried to keep the terror from me only to create a new fear."

"All men are different when they are courting," he said, realizing the words were true.

"Even you?"

"Even me, but you haven't told me about the armoire." Knowing the memories caused her pain he wasn't sure he wanted her to talk about them. "It's alright if you don't."

"One time it was a trunk. That doesn't matter now but you should know. Bradford, my father, wanted an heir more than anything else."

"He had four daughters. I think you told me that a long time ago." He didn't care if he had boys or girls he realized, and he would never force her to have children.

"Yes, and in an attempt to get that heir he kept mother pregnant. After I was born all she had were still born babies."

"Selfish bastard." He bit out, clenching his fists and wishing he could take the pain away as well as the fear. "Are you afraid I might be like that?"

"Maybe, but not like my oldest sister. Ravyn was hurt the most. She had to bury all the tiny babies, and she believed all men were like our father. My sisters put me in our armoire every time father forced mother and every time another baby died. They didn't want me to hear mother crying and screaming. They believed they did what was best for me."

~ * ~

"How do you think your young charge and Gavin Broon are doing?" David McLellan spoke to Charlotte as he helped her through the tunnels of the McLellan castle. She finally convinced him she needed to see the place and now they headed to the island.

"Are you sure this is safe?" Charlotte avoided his question, feeling the guilt of leaving Larena to fend for herself against a man who was enamored of her. She swiped cobwebs from her face. "This is horrible. You didn't tell me there would be spiders."

"Yes, according to the girls the trip to the island is perfectly safe, but I did send a few men to the island to make sure we have no intruders. We're here."

"Where is that?"

He opened the heavy door leading to the steps. "I've had the stairway repaired and a hand railing installed. Take your time and be careful. I wouldn't want you to slip. They would walk down the steps then sail to the island."

Charlotte inhaled a swift deep breath her hand on his chest. "Oh my. The girls went down that without a handrail and they survived? No wonder Hunter banned them from the island."

"They did and that's why I took extreme measures and sent Christel to you as did the other fathers. The girls were all too careless with their lives. Then Eveleen..." he paused. "That was a father's worst nightmare. Thank god Logan was there or she might have died. I don't know if I could have survived that."

"Isn't there another way to the island?" The stairs began to spin and she grabbed the railing tightly. Blinking a few times and concentrating on the first step in front of her, the world seemed to calm.

"If you want to walk a couple of miles to get to that wee spot below where the sailboat is waiting for us," he chuckled.

She stepped tentatively then another, swallowing her fear and telling herself she could do this. Half way down she turned to David with a smile. "I was never a courageous girl, but I'm proud of myself now."

"I'm proud of you too. You're conquering your fear of the steps as well as the height."

"No, of falling to my death. I've never been afraid of a few measly steps." She laughed softly, enjoying the fact a handsome man cared for her. It had been such a long time.

In a few more minutes they reached the sailboat. David swept her from her feet and waded through the shallow water to place her in the vessel.

"Put me down. You'll hurt yourself." She pounded on his shoulder to make her point.

"There you go. Now just sit back and enjoy the beautiful day, the sun and the breeze. Don't worry about a thing. This boat will take us to the island where I can have my wicked way with you if you'll allow it."

"I forgot my parasol." She looked to the steps wondering if she dared sail with the McLellan or if she should run now. His wicked way with her, what on earth was he talking about? It couldn't possibly be...

He laughed and the sound filled her heart with joy. It had been so long since she heard a man's laughter intended to warm her heart. David pulled out a parasol from near the tiller. "My lady..." he gallantly handed her the sunshade. "No excuses now. I intend to show you a wonderful day and the tiny island that sent the girls to you."

Her heart fluttered and she was reminded of her first outing with the duke, her debonair husband who died much too soon. She watched as David pushed off the beach and the small boat floated on the water. He steered it expertly and in the secluded bay there were few waves.

She told herself these romantic and sensual feelings were foolish and had no place in her life. She wondered if the duke would understand if she found someone else. Foolish old woman, what could David possibly see in her? He'd been her sister's husband for much too short of a time. Gracie was elegant and sweet, so unlike her. At one time she could put on as many regal airs as any Duchess, now she used her position and power to get what she wanted. She was anything but sweet. Sometimes she wasn't even nice.

Before any more disturbing thoughts swept through her, the boat slid on the island's beach.

"We are here." David jumped from the boat, pulling it farther up the beach then cradling her in his arms, he set her on dry land, grinning at her as if he saw her naked.

At that thought, her breath caught in her throat. "Thank you." He held her a minute too long, gazing into her eyes. She moistened her lips, her heart racing while he touched her face gently with a calloused fingertip.

"I've been wanting to do this all day. May I?" Slowly, he kissed her, pressed his lips on hers. It was sweet and short but sent a wave of heat coursing through her. He smiled at her, "Come see what the girls did. It will give you some insight into why they acted the way they did and some of their preposterous ideas."

Clasping her hand in his, they walked up the trail to the small one room building the girls built. Amazed at the beauty of the small island, she suddenly understood why her willful young charges couldn't stay away from this enchanting place. If this had been something she discovered and built, she wouldn't have been able to stay away either.

Chapter Four

"I don't want you to feel sorry for me, just don't put me in a small dark space and I'll be just fine." She cringed at the thought but tried for a lighter note. For the most part she'd outgrown her childhood fears.

"The repercussions of today could haunt us. You understand a carefully placed word or an insinuation could implicate us in a very bad way. What happened here could be considered a public meeting and those are against the law. We could both be jailed, your aunt too."

"I know that's what you believe." She challenged him even while insecurities assailed her. "But how can ten people in The Duchess' parlor be considered a public meeting? Would every aristocratic ball be considered in the same light?"

"It's what they were talking about that makes it a public meeting instead of a ball," he reminded her.

"We should leave town before the authorities find out what happened here. You need to think about The Duchess and her reputation. Yet I'm thoroughly glad you are listening to my argument not just disagreeing."

"True, but where would we go? I don't want to ruin my reputation. I'm not like Fayth, my sister." She leaned against Gavin, absorbing his strength into her. "I've made a mess of everything."

"You're agreeing with me?" He laughed, gently touching her cheek with the back his knuckles. "You haven't made a mess of anything and together, we will fix this."

"Don't be so surprised. Tyna has said she wants to get away from her brother and the protesters. If she stays here, he'll always have a hold on her and a way inside this home." She wanted to give Tyna the means to get out of a life she dreaded.

"You're set on keeping her as your lady's maid?"

"Unless you want to help me dress and undress every day." She lowered her lashes before looking back to him. "Besides I like her a lot."

Gavin cleared his throat, running a finger between his cravat and neck. "Probably not the best idea."

"Then..."

"If you like Tyna then of course hire her, but you don't need my permission for that. Although I'll always appreciate that you ask my opinion."

"For some reason..." she paused in thought. "For some reason your approval seemed important to me. Gavin, you didn't tell me where we would go." Upheaval was not something she enjoyed and somehow she managed to create more than anyone needed.

"Drake offered me the hunting lodge. It's the only plausible place for us right now. We need to disappear until all that happened here is forgotten and another scandal has taken our place in the gossip."

"I won't go. I told you I don't want to fall from grace. Taking me to the lodge would set the ton gossiping, and I'd never be able to hold my head up in front of any of them. I'm not like Ella or Fayth. What people think of me is important to me."

"Perhaps my home in Scotland then," he said. "I have family there and chaperones in abundance."

"But we'd be alone in the carriage for days. Is there another choice?" Her heart raced at the thought of being alone with him, but she tried desperately to hold on to her values.

"A chaperone would help."

"Lady Larena." Tyna stood in the doorway her hands folded in front of her rocking on her heels a distressed look on her face.

"You're back. Were you able to leave before your brother arrived?" Secrecy for the time being was important although she understood it could not be kept from Cale forever. Perhaps it would be better for Tyna to leave too.

"He wasn't home. When he does get home though, he's going to know where I am. I hope this doesn't create more inconvenience for you and that he doesn't come looking for me." She curtsied as if she wasn't sure what to do next.

"I'll make sure the doors stay locked. Don't let him in." Gavin strode from the room.

"Come on, I'll show you where you're going to stay." Larena stood, extending her hand to her new lady's maid. "The room is in the attic and it does get a little warm in the summer, but there's a nice breeze that flows through the room when you open both windows. We might not be staying in Aunt Charlotte's home much longer though."

"Thank you, my bags are at the bottom of the stairway. Stewart told me he'd carry them to my room. He's really sweet."

"That he is. Stewart has been with Aunt Charlotte for almost twenty years." They met the butler at the bottom of the steps.

"Ladies." Stewart nodded his baldhead, his eyes twinkling as if he enjoyed every moment. "This is much more to my liking than riding a horse cross country."

The sunny day created more heat than Larena remembered. Once inside the two-room apartment, Larena opened the windows, humming the Irish tune she'd been playing earlier. "Tomorrow, we'll go shopping. Would you like that? New curtains and bedding is a must, and I'll send the housekeeper up first thing tomorrow morning to dust. Should have done it today but..." She really had so much on her mind she was having a devil of a time remembering anything.

"My brother had his own agenda," Tyna said. "And I'd like to go shopping, but I don't have money."

"Don't worry about that. I'll take care of everything." She leaned out the window to look at the garden below. "It's an excellent view, don't you think?"

"Of course, yes," Tyna said seeming a bit awkward.

Larena wiped the dust from a chair with one of the curtains she took down before sitting. Leaning forward, "Something I don't understand," she paused, tilting her head slightly to better observe the young woman she hired. "You seem well educated and well-spoken yet your circumstances don't," she paused. "I don't mean to pry it just seems..."

With the back of her hand, Tyna rubbed her forehead. "You noticed. Most people don't or can't be bothered."

"Your current status doesn't reflect on your upbringing. Tell me, what happened? If you want to." Larena asked as she looked around the room, taking note of the lack of various items.

Tyna shrugged, "The usual."

"And what would that be?"

"My mother inherited a small fortune when I was about ten and for awhile my parents were happy. Father, my stepfather, Cale's father, started a business. He was an excellent chef. With the money he was able to establish a restaurant. They both worked hard and their small fortune grew. I had a dowry at one time. Pretty dresses... a beau..."

"I've a feeling there's more to this story. How did you lose everything?" She waited for the answer to her questions.

Tyna plopped on the bed. "One night our father went out drinking and whoring with his friends. I can't begin to understand why he committed adultery. I always thought he loved mother. I've heard some men just can't settle for one woman, and he didn't see anything wrong with it if he had sex with a prostitute. He didn't think he was cheating or doing anything wrong."

"Adultery wouldn't cause your family to lose everything? One night and one bad mistake cost the business and your home? There's got to be more."

"No, but syphilis would. He went to a brothel and contracted the horrible disease. He felt so guilty for a while he didn't touch mother. For that I'm thankful."

"But they can cure syphilis, can't they?" Larena had heard talk of a cure but she didn't remember what it was.

"No, the cure killed father before the disease could. He took mercury pills and used the mercury ointment then an unorthodox gas treatment that took our last coin. It was expensive."

"So sorry." Larena's heart went out to her and her family. "That must have been awful."

"You don't need to feel sorry for any of us. I've come to terms with my life as it is and so has Cale. I just don't want the same things Cale wants. I want a husband and a family and he needs to tell people what he thinks. He takes chances with his life that he shouldn't because his actions involve me too."

"What happened to your mother?" Larena felt empathy and sorrow for Tyna. She understood the loss of a mother as well as a father since both of hers were gone too.

"I think she died of heartbreak. I heard her crying every night when I was in bed. Until that one horrific night they had a wonderful life, at least that's what Cale and I thought."

"How old were you when all of this happened?" She tried to remember her age when her mother died. She must have been only nine or ten. She'd never really known her mother. What she did know was that she'd never really been happy until she was older and could understand more of what happened.

"Cale was twenty-one and I was sixteen. His fiancée of more than a year left him and all my friends left me. He was devastated at the loss yet determined to make a life for himself."

"They weren't your friends then, were they? Friends don't leave you when things are hard." When Gavin heard her story, he would feel different about Tyna. He would lend her his support.

"No, I suppose not." Tyna's heavy sigh sent an arrow straight to her heart. "I still don't have any friends, except maybe you if you can forgive me from using you. It was Cale's idea and I didn't know how to tell him no."

"You have me as a friend." Larena told her sincerely feeling the emotion. "I am your friend and you can count on that friendship."

"Larena, you're my boss. You can't be my friend too. Things just aren't done that way."

"I wish I could do more for you and it doesn't matter to me our status. If you haven't noticed yet, I've a reputation for doing what I want. Aunty Charlotte is best of friends with Scarlett, her companion, and together they're visiting family out of town."

"What could you do for me? Let me think. Introduce me to an eligible young man who will love me as I am, a Lady's maid. I don't care how much money he has as long as the man is honest and faithful." She laughed as if it was a dream she once had. "And he doesn't beat me."

Larena leaned forward and set her hand on Tyna's. "I will do what I can and I'll ask Ella for help. Perhaps we can find someone who will make you happy and give you everything you dream about. The Montgomerie's have a lot of people working for them, good people."

"Does Gavin make you happy, really happy?" Tyna asked, showing a lopsided smile.

She pursed her lips in thought. "I don't know. He confuses me and frustrates me until I want to throw something at him. I'm happy when I'm with him, but I don't like it when he thinks he has the right to dictate my life." Until he started telling her what to do, she fancied herself in love with him.

Tyna laughed, the sound contagious. "You shouldn't have to think about such a thing. Do you like it when he kisses you?"

"Everyone saw that drawing in the paper, didn't they?" She put her hands to her heated cheeks. "To tell the truth I was shocked when he pulled me into that doorway." They shared kisses before but none like that one or the one on his bed.

"Also, the drawing today." Tyna tilted her head sideways her gaze riveted on Larena.

"Today's paper? It's been so hectic I've haven't seen a newspaper, although Gavin thought there would be another drawing and article. I truly don't understand why anyone would want to read anything about us. We're both such nobodies."

"You can't be that innocent. Don't you know who Gavin Broon really is?" Tyna took Larena's hands in hers. "He is anything but a nobody, and he shouldn't lie to you."

Larena frowned, searching Tyna's face for some clue. "He's the fourth son of a wealthy family and a well established lawyer here in town. His oldest brother inherited everything from his father. He told me today he has a home in Scotland, but that's all I know about him."

"All that is true, but his family has multiple holdings and even though he's the forth son, he has inherited from his mother's side all of her family's holdings. He's not the heir apparent but the Duke of Millsglen. He might not have openly lied to you, but isn't a lie of omission the same thing?"

Larena could barely breathe. "Gavin is a duke," she spoke slowly trying to absorb all she heard, closing her eyes as if she could clear her head of her previous misconceptions. "How can that be? I never fancied myself falling in love with someone like that."

"Obviously, he hasn't told you," Tyna said laughing.

"Why not?" She would have thought a man would be eager to tout himself. "Why wouldn't he tell me his true status? Another thing about that man that doesn't make any sense whatsoever."

Tyna smiled a bit and waited. "Perhaps he wants you to love him for who he is, not his titles or money. Men can be like that you know. Do you love Gavin?"

Once more, her hands on her cheeks, confused, and so baffled by this knowledge. "I don't know what love feels like, but I've never cared about titles or money. Never expected to have anything like that. I like him and the way he makes me feel. I love his smile and how it warms my heart and his eyes when he kisses me."

"Gavin must know or at least sense that about you or he wouldn't be here protecting you. So, do you like his kisses? The drawing today was another one that depicted the two of you kissing on the street near his office. He must like kissing you."

"Have you had kisses you liked?" Larena asked, trying to change the conversation from her to anything else that wouldn't make her blush.

"I don't know much more about kissing than you do, but I did have a few kisses before my family fell from grace. One I didn't care for, the boy was Cale's friend and he thought he could take advantage me. But there were ones that left me breathless and hot then there were ones that left my stomach churning."

"Gavin's kisses leave me breathless and hot. And his body, my goodness, I've touched him, his chest and..." She closed her eyes, the thoughts having the same affect. She could barely breathe thinking about last night and when he stood nearly naked in front of her.

"You touched his naked chest? That's scandalous. Tell me more. How did it make you feel?"

"It was nothing. He was making strange grunts and groans in the room next to mine so I walked in on him. He wore only his buckskins and his chest was shiny with sweat. He told me he was practicing some type of martial arts. I forgot exactly what he said."

"So, it's either lust or love," Tyna laughed, falling back on the bed, arms spread wide. "I so long for either one. Lust or love," she mused thoughtfully. "Love before lust would be nice, but I think it usually happens the other way."

"Lust or love... How does someone know the difference?" Larena wondered what Gavin felt for her.

"I don't have the answer to that, but I wish I did. Maybe you could ask your cousin Ella. She must know. All of London knows that Lord Montgomerie ruined her reputation and The Duchess agreed to it. Is that why your aunt left you here alone with Gavin? She wants your reputation ruined so you have to marry the Duke of Millsglen?"

Larena needed to ignore Tyna's last question. "With Ella it was lust from the very beginning. Drake needed to know if she was like his mother, a cold bitch was what he called her, or a warm willing woman. He took advantage of her innocence."

"But they're happy now."

"Yes, so much so it's something we would all want. But Gavin hardly ever touches me and when he does, he seems so restrained. It's like he's trying to stay as far away from me as possible. Last night after I walked in on him, I saw him riding away from the houses."

"I believe he must have been leaving for a different reason than boredom with you."

"What would that be?" Larena was more confused than ever.

"If my limited but more extensive knowledge of men tells me anything, it's that if he didn't leave, he might have tossed you on the bed and made love with you."

Larena stood, smoothing her dress, needing something to do with her hands and time to think about all that was said. "I'm going to need you later this evening to help me undress. I'll ring the bell. Until then you're free to do anything you like. Cook is amazing and will have dinner waiting for you in the warming oven whenever you're ready."

Tyna ran to hug her. "You can't know how thankful I am. You've helped me achieve a few of my dreams, and I'm sure Cale will understand when I tell him how I feel and everything I want."

"I hope so. Don't forget we're shopping tomorrow." Walking

slowly down the stairs, Larena mulled over everything Tyna had said. Still she had no idea how Gavin thought about her or what she felt for him. She wanted desperately to know how love would make her feel and she was sure Gavin could teach her.

She wandered through the house, through the music room, the parlor and the kitchen. Gavin had vanished.

Her footsteps took her outside and into the gardens. The sun still shone bright and strong. She'd left without a hat or a parasol. The small gazebo beckoned and enticed her with shade and a temperature a bit cooler.

She sat down, hugging one of the pillows close to her breasts then shut her eyes for a second, dreaming dreams of childhood, wishing for love and a life different from her past, one with a caring and hopefully loving husband. When she did marry, she didn't want to be pregnant for the rest of her life. Didn't want to be expected to give her husband heirs' just beautiful children.

She closed her eyes again, tears running down her cheeks for no apparent reason. She realized she didn't want to lose Gavin. Even if she didn't know if she loved him yet, she understood how much she needed him by her side. She trusted him more than she'd ever trusted anyone in her life. She could confide in him and even though he might get a dark shuddered look on his handsome features when he didn't like what she was saying, she was sure he listened to her.

He tested her in ways she'd never been tested. Yet he was so stoic and seldom showed his emotions. His uncanny ability to change any subject he didn't want to talk about had her smiling.

"What are you grinning about?" Gavin sat down beside her, wrapping one arm around her shoulder before pulling her close.

"Nothing." His chest was hard against her curves and she relaxed into him.

He leaned in close to her, his breath whispering erotically across her ear then his tongue touched the inside. "I don't believe you. Let's try this again. What were you grinning about?"

She turned and their lips were inches from each other. She gasped. "Why are you smiling, Gavin Broon?"

"Because I've got you to myself." Instead of kissing her, he drew a line gently across her lips with a fingertip. "You're turn. Tell me what you were thinking about that made you so happy."

She moved closer to him, needing to look into his eyes. She touched his chest with one hand, remembering the way his naked flesh felt against her hand. "I was thinking about your uncanny ability to change the subject thus evading my questions."

"I see and that makes you happy. I'll continue to make you happy. Do you want to kiss me?"

"Not right now," she teased, waiting for the dark shuttered look she expected to cross his face. "I want you to kiss me."

Obliging, he kissed her forehead, the tip of her nose then a quick peck to the lips. "Is that what you want?" he sat back looking smug and handsomely debonair. His confidence exuding from his posture.

She avoided his question, thinking it was time to ask something important. "How does a person know if they're in love?"

"Have we had this conversation before? I can't recall." The shuttered expression took over and his smile vanished.

"I don't remember." The lightness of the moment was gone. Dejected she studied her hands. "Did I say something wrong?"

He touched her chin, his thumb moving in small circles. "I'm sorry. I didn't mean to make you sad. What did you and Tyna talk about?"

With a heavy sigh, she leaned against him, taking comfort from him. "She's had a sad life. I feel so sorry for her and Cale."

"I'm sure Tyna has convinced you of that and I'm sure a lot of her story was laced with lies."

She pushed away from him. "I don't think so. She was so sincere. Unless it happened to you..."

"What happened?"

Larena told him everything, the money, the restaurant, the horrible disease, the cure that was worse than the disease and the losses. "Both her parents died. Brother and sister made the most of what they had left. Tyna just wants a better life for herself. She doesn't want to be caught up in her brother's politics. I'm glad I hired her. Except for Ella I've no friends here."

"I admire her if it's the truth. Come, let's talk about other things. Would you like to walk in the gardens?"

"Is it still so hot?" She felt lazy and wanted to stay right where she was, tucked beneath his arm her hand on his chest.

He stepped outside, his arms outstretched. "There's a cooling breeze and the sun is lower on the horizon so we can stay in the shadows. A walk will do us both a world of good." He held out his hand to her.

Reluctantly, she rose and let him hold her hand a bit disappointed the conversation about the kiss had ended. They walked the outskirts, staying in the shade. His fingers closed tightly around hers before relaxing. He stopped, bringing her hand to his lips, kissing each knuckle. "What haven't you told me, Larena?"

"What do you mean?" She trembled as she spoke, wondering what he was asking. "I can't think of anything."

"Something is bothering you," he persisted, holding her hand to his lips, his eyes shimmering.

"Nothing but," she paused trying to figure out how to broach the subject. Nervously she licked her lips.

"But?" one eyebrow rose in question.

"Did you see the newspaper today?"

"I don't want you to worry about it," he said, placing his hands on her waist and pulling her close. "No one is here right now so no one can draw us if we decide to kiss."

"I don't like what all of this implies about me." She shivered when he ran his hands up her back then down.

"It's just gossip and will blow over when something else comes to light." His fingers tightened around her waist.

The gesture sent a shimmering warmth through her, heating her and telling her all she cared about was Gavin. She caught her lip between her teeth. "Everyone knows it's me."

"And they all know that I'm living here with you and The Duchess has left town. One kiss won't cause more gossip." He lightly brushed his knuckles across her cheek.

"What are your intentions?" she asked, unable to keep herself from asking. "Do you need, like Drake for me to prove myself in some way?"

He frowned, "Prove yourself? My little darling, there is little for you to prove save your loyalty to me. I need to know if the woman I marry will always stand by me. Will you?"

She couldn't help herself and she didn't want to keep secrets. "Tyna told me something today."

"There was something you didn't tell me." His voice gentled. "You know you can tell me anything."

"I forgot about it until now." She wasn't so sure about letting him know she found out he was a duke."

"What is it?"

"She told me I shouldn't say anything to you, but I don't like secrets between us." Her heart raced with fear or anticipation she couldn't be sure. He could turn and never come back. She didn't want that. She drew in a deep breath and held it for too long.

He watched her closely, his hands still around her waist. "Secrets are never good."

"Are you really a duke," she blurted then looked down.

"Tyna told you that, did she? I didn't want you to know." He caught her chin with a finger and lifted so they looked into each other's eyes.

"Why? I've never cared about titles or money. It frightens me to think of you in that way. I want the fourth son of a lord, nothing more. A man who earns his living as a lawyer."

~ * ~

"That's nice to hear," he mused, wondering how he should feel about what she just said. She didn't want a duke but that's what he was. "At least I suppose so. You're not happy for me?"

"Of course I am, oh my, I didn't mean to imply... Bloody hell," she muttered, "you have me so tied in knots I don't know what I'm saying." She pushed away from him, turning and running.

In a few steps he caught up with her, swept her into his arms and whirled around in circles, laughing. "I like it when you swear. It's so refreshing and honest."

"Put me down." She pounded on his shoulders.

"Now why would I want to do that?" He thought about Drake's words to him. Pleasure her and teach her how to do the same to you and you won't be taking trips to my lake.

"Maybe because I asked you to." She hit him on the shoulder again.

"You're going to have to hit me harder than that to make your point." He pressed his lips against hers while he walked, his tongue drawing lines across her lips, waiting for her sweet response.

Inside the gazebo he sat down with her perched on his lap, one hand resting on her ankle, smoothing a path up to her knee, finding the ribbon tying her stocking on her leg. No, he couldn't do this now, not when anyone could find them but he could introduce her to a little more lovemaking and he could finish later this evening in his bedchamber.

"What are you doing to me? You've never..." She clung to him, her eyes huge and filled with passion.

"It's the beginning of your education, Larena. I think you're going to enjoy it. We're going to learn how to give each other pleasure."

"You already know."

"You'll love everything I do."

"I told you I don't want you to compromise me. I'm not that kind of girl and even if the entire world believes one thing, I'll still know the truth."

"Oh my Larena, I won't compromise or ruin you, technically you'll still be a virgin but an educated one. I mean to teach you so much pleasure you'll beg me for more." Good lord but he wanted her schooling to begin now and never end. They could be so much to each other.

Larena hit him again but not very hard. "Gavin, you can't do what you're talking about. We're not married. We're not even engaged and I'm not asking for a proposal."

He smiled drawing back his lips. "Tutor you? Are you a slow learner, Larena? When I wed you and I'm pretty sure you and I will be husband and wife someday, I don't want an untaught virgin in my bed. I want someone who can give and take pleasure."

"I don't understand anything you've just said." She blinked a few times, moistening her lips.

"You will and see, you're getting ready for my kiss right now. You brushed your tongue a couple of times across your lips. I do like your mouth wet." But he didn't kiss her, he wanted to feel the satin smoothness of her leg and touch her woman's core. He needed to know if she was ready for his loving.

"I'm not doing any such thing. You can't make me," she protested, her breasts moving up and down with each heavy breath she drew.

"Of course you are and I'm not going to make you do anything." His hand inched higher, his fingers coming perilously close to her soft wet core. In his arms she squirmed, moving her legs apart, unknowingly giving him better access to the soft folds he longed to touch. She did want him in the most elemental and primal ways and she didn't even know how instinctive her actions were.

"I am not." Her whispered protest brought another smile to his lips. "Besides you're not kissing me. You're doing something else, and I'm not sure you should be touching me there."

"Last night you saw me nearly naked. Did you like what you saw? It seems only fair I can gaze upon you, touch you like you did me. Would you like me to touch your rosy pink nipples that call for my caress?"

Her eyes widened, he supposed, with alarm but prayed it was desire instead. "I don't think The Duchess would approve. It's different, I imagine, when a woman touches a man. I'm pretty sure she would never use her cane on me, Gavin. After all I was just curious."

"No, you're right of course. The Duchess would still wrap me on the back with her cane, but it doesn't mean I'm not curious. I'm very curious and I want nothing more than to see you and touch you."

"Somehow that doesn't seem fair."

"Your sweet aunty gave her full consent to anything we wanted to do when she left us alone and without a chaperone. In truth she left me in charge of you. She bade me to keep you safe from yourself not from me." He looked up for a moment. "If she didn't approve, she'd be here, her cane landing squarely across my back."

"But..." She moistened her lips again, catching the bottom one beneath her top teeth.

He placed his hand beneath one breast. "See, your heart races in anticipation and longing for my caress. I can feel it. He touched the tiny sleeves of her dress. These are for decoration and to make it easier for a man to slip them down a woman's arms. Why do you suppose that is?"

"This isn't like before," she said, her voice wavering.

"How so?" He grinned.

"Before, I knew you just teased, now I'm not sure what you plan. Gavin, this can't be right but I don't want to tell you no. I like what you're doing to me and if I'm honest," she paused. "Do you want me to be honest?"

"Always."

"You mean that?"

"What we're doing is right when it's the right man," he murmured then he tugged on both sleeves, lowering them so he could see the valley between her breasts, pressing his lips there. "Are you ready for your teacher?"

"I don't know..." Her words were a tiny wail.

The dress slipped lower and her breasts were bared for him. "Look at your beauty. The shape is perfect and the color such a beautiful ivory, the tips a pale pink. I can barely contain myself."

She closed her eyes, shaking her head. "Gavin," his name was barely a whisper in the air.

"What, my darling? Do you want me to teach you a woman's pleasure? I can do that right now if that's what you want. Yet perhaps we should wait for more privacy or not. I don't hear anyone coming."

All he heard was a tiny sound in the back of her throat. "I'll take that for a yes. Remember how you let your hand rest on my chest and my nipple? Yes, I know you do. Well, you'll like the sensation as much as I did."

He rested his hand so the palm lay on top of her breast. He rolled the peak beneath his palm before he caught the rosy bud between his fingers. He delighted in her small gasp of pleasure and surprise.

"Do you like that? Let's see, what else did you do that night? You let your hand roam down then up my chest. Would you like me to do the same thing?" He turned her enough so he could unlace her corset. Before she could say yes or no or perhaps even think, she was nearly naked, her dress was on the floor and she wore only her chemise and stockings.

"Gavin..."

"You don't need to thank me yet. I'm not even close to being

86

finished. You're going to beg me for more but understand now you never have to beg. All you need do is ask."

"I can't breathe..."

"Nothing to worry over. You can catch your breath when we're done. Now raise your arms so I don't tear your chemise." When she didn't "Ah well, I'll buy you a new one." Despite his best efforts the garment, did not make it unscathed.

"What are you doing? I shouldn't..." She tried to cover herself with her arms and hands.

He held her wrists away. "So beautiful. My god..."

"Gavin, we can't. What if someone comes?"

"No one is home except the butler and cook. They never go in the gardens." So enchanted by her, he'd forgotten about that possibility. "That's an archaic notion. We can do anything we'd like. This is almost the way you were born. Except for the stockings."

He rolled one taut pink bud between his fingers and bent to take the other one in his mouth. Her fingers wove into his hair, holding tight to him while her hips arched in anticipation of his lovemaking, something that wasn't going to happen tonight. Not until they were wed.

"Can I touch you like I did that night." She nearly spun away from him when he bit gently on one swollen rosy bud.

"Not yet."

"Please..."

"How do you feel?"

It was a tiny wail. "I don't know. Hot and wet in places..."

"Good, that's how you're supposed to feel. When I finish, you'll like everything I'm doing and beg for me to do it again and again. And I'll want to do it again and again rest assured of that."

"Do what?"

"Pleasure you and I'm also going to teach you how to give me pleasure. Will you like that?"

His hand drifted downward, stopping just above the soft fleece of hair at her woman's mound. He paused several seconds in anticipation of watching her when she reached that sweetly painful pleasure.

"Don't stop," she whispered softly. "I couldn't bear it if you stopped."

"I won't stop unless you ask me to. Open your eyes, little darling." He needed to watch her eyes when the ecstasy claimed her.

"Why?"

"Because I asked you to and you'll like it. Trust me in this." His fingers drifted lower, finding her virgin's flower and the cream telling him she wanted him as much as he did her. He massaged the nub hidden deep inside and watched as she responded so sweetly to him, her hips arching. Then he slipped a finger inside her, pushing higher until he reached her maidenhead. He tapped it gently, knowing he would be the one to break through the fragile barrier.

He paused, lifting his head and listened, a tiny noise from the direction of the house had caught his attention. "I'm sorry." Quickly he reached for her dress. "Slip this over your head."

She did as he said, her eyes panic-struck, "What's wrong?"

"We're about to be invaded. We aren't alone." He worked on the fastenings of her dress, her corset still lying beside him.

"Lady Larena? Lady Larena are you out here?"

"Tyna," she whispered.

"You need to answer her," Gavin whispered close to her ear. "Tell her she needs to go back to the house. Tell her you don't need her for anything."

"I am. I'm fine. Just wanted to go for a walk. You need..."

"Is Gavin..." Tyna's words trailed off, her hands suddenly clasped beneath her chin as she gazed into the gazebo. She turned. "I didn't mean to invade your privacy. Guess you won't need a lady's maid tonight. I'll just go to my room. Sorry."

Gavin watched the young woman race away and wondered how much she actually saw. The mood he'd so artfully created evaporated into the evening air, and he didn't think he could recreate the gentle seduction he'd constructed. "We should go back."

"Like this? I've got to dress first. My chemise and my corset..." Her voice squeaked. "I don't have any clothes on."

He laughed, loving the sight of her but wishing they'd not been discovered. "You have your stockings on. I will tuck the corset and the remnant of your chemise under my waistcoat in the case we run into anyone else. No one will know or ask what we've been doing."

"I will know," she reached to put her hair in place, running her hands along the cushioned bench in search of the pins that had fallen out.

"Let me help."

"Really, haven't you've done enough." She found a few pins and frantically tried to put her chignon into place. A tear slipped from her eye and he wiped it away with a finger. "This really didn't just happen. What will Tyna think? I don't think I can look at her again."

"I've embarrassed you. I never meant to do that, but my intentions were in the right place. Tyna will believe we're in love and she will think nothing untoward of what she saw tonight."

"But we're not in love. Compromising me was your intention, why? This is hardly the right place or time."

"I'm a selfish bastard. I was looking for sexual relief for both of us. Although it's something you haven't realized yet, it will make you feel a whole lot better. I never meant for this to go so far tonight, but you enchant me and it seems when you're with me I can't think straight nor can I keep my hands to myself."

"I'm ready to go back, now." She rose, methodically smoothing her skirts and adjusting the bodice of her dress. "You have to take me back and I think it would be best if you slept in your office apartment tonight. If you sleep next door there, will just be more gossip."

He smiled. In all her dishevelment she was beautiful and regal. He wanted to pull her into his arms again and let her kiss him senseless.

He touched her elbow, guiding her toward the house. She pulled away. Little fool, she needed to learn where she was weak and how she was strong. She protested too much. Once more he set his hand upon her arm. "Stay close, you are still half dressed. Remember I tore the fabric. While I doubt if we will see anyone, we can never be sure. I don't want anyone but me seeing you naked or very nearly naked."

She stiffened but this time she stayed by his side, staring straight ahead as they walked. "Gavin, nothing is as it should be. I flirted with you, enjoyed your kisses but what you did to me, I don't understand. You made me feel things I don't think I'm supposed to feel."

"Someday you will understand the sensations and emotions you just felt are normal and a woman is supposed to feel them. I hope to be that man who teaches you, sees your eyes when you climax. You'll want me to never stop. I promise."

"If you say so," she tilted her chin higher. She looked as if she wanted to argue the point. "But we're not wed and those feelings are for married couples. That's why The Duchess keeps her cane handy."

"I do say that's the way it will be and don't forget The Duchess thought this was appropriate or she wouldn't have left," he laughed watching her as she tried to make sense of the physical sensations she just enjoyed. If she'd felt the sting of pleasure though, she'd know what he was trying to teach her.

"Do you need to go for another ride tonight?" she asked, leaning into him now, seemingly at least for this moment in time at peace with what just happened between them.

"No ride or swim if you're willing to continue the lessons when we reach your bedroom. It will be private there. Larena, I should have insisted on your room before I began. I knew the butler and cook wouldn't look for us, but I forgot about Tyna." Truly he had not thought this out very well. He hadn't been thinking with his head. Yet he'd run into her quite unexpectedly.

Her aqua eyes shimmered hotly and she was shaking her head in a feeble effort to tell him no. "That wouldn't be wise. If we continued, I might become pregnant and I don't want that. Do you?"

"I promise that wouldn't happen. I won't let that happen." He didn't want to believe the night for them was over, but he was willing to wait until a better time.

"I have to get up early. I'm taking Tyna shopping. I want to make her apartment more appealing, homey. She needs clothing too." It seemed she was looking for any excuse to keep him from her bed.

"How are you going to pay for all of that?" He smiled lazily at her, stopping and running his finger along her jawline, felt her shudder against him and knew if he wanted to be a cad, he could continue his seduction and her tutoring when they reached her room.

"I've enough money." She straightened her shoulders and lifted her chin.

"You do, how much Larena? Do you know what your allowance is or has your aunty Charlotte been paying for everything your heart desires? Do you even have an allowance?" He didn't mean to sound condescending, but she was too innocent by far.

"I've no idea," she admitted reluctantly, "Aunty let us spend whatever we wanted on whatever we needed. I do have a running account at the dressmakers and the fabric shop. I doubt if Aunt Charlotte would mind if I fixed up the attic and bought a few things for Tyna."

He wanted to give her money but knew her pride wouldn't allow the gesture. And while the evening had gone as planned until Tyna showed up, it had gone downhill since.

They entered the house through the kitchen door. He grabbed a chunk of bread from the counter and taking a bite before putting it back down, he escorted her up the stairs and to the door of her chambers. He turned her and with his finger lightly beneath her chin he slowly lifted it and pressed his lips on hers careful to make this kiss more of a soft caress than a demand for more. Spreading one hand over the nape at her neck, he urged her face up and deepened the kiss just a little bit. Tentatively, her arms went over his shoulders and he felt the tenor of the contact change. He could press his advantage but knew she'd regret what they did.

"Good night, have good dreams." He opened the door for her and watched as she blinked a few times, clearly confused by his actions. "Your corset." He pulled it from beneath his waistcoat.

She moistened her lips again, "Good night."

It seemed she hesitated before walking into the room. Quickly before he could change his mind, he closed the door. Leaning against it for a few minutes, his mind searched for the possibilities and how besides another wild ride to the Montgomerie estate including a swim in the lake could he ease the condition he found himself in.

He thought of the older woman he'd been seeing before Larena entered his life. She had probably moved on to someone else, besides he had no desire to see her. Now that he'd kissed Larena and seen the beauty she possessed, he could think of no other woman.

When Gavin finally strode the steps to his bedroom, the dark sky was beginning to lighten. The ride and the swim helped but as soon as he set foot in the townhouse, thoughts of Larena swept through his head. The calm he'd felt vanished.

He saw her, naked and in his arms. Remembered the feel of her breasts beneath his hands. He needed to feel her surround him and take him deep inside. During the morning ride he made some decisions. Now it was up to him to set them in place.

In the library he gathered paper and pen.

Charlotte,

It has become necessary to take Larena out of town. I originally intended to take her to my mother's estate in Scotland. Part of the castle is under renovation but it's not yet ready for occupation. Mother owned a home on the outskirts of town and that would be my destination. Drake Montgomerie has offered me the use of his hunting lodge if I would like to go there. I will decide my destination when all that is happening in town becomes clear.

Larena's ties with the protestors have grown. They are deeper and stronger than even she realizes. She has hired the sister of one of the leaders as a lady's maid. Tyna is a nice young woman and seems to want to better herself, however, Larena is too much the innocent and an easy mark. Anyone with nefarious plans will find it easy to persuade Larena to do their bidding. I must protect her from all enemies including herself.

A few days ago, Cale, the sister's brother allowed twelve men into the townhouse. I was lucky enough to contact Drake. His men helped me rid your home of these men but not before there was some damage. I have replaced a broken end table but the other pieces that were smashed, I will pay for when you return home and can pick something out to take their places.

Be assured I wish to marry Larena but have not had the chance to ask her. She has told me she doesn't know how she feels about wedding me or even how she feels about me. She has so many questions that need answering. Believe I can persuade her. She needs you now more than ever.

Drake has agreed to send an announcement to the newspaper of our upcoming nuptials. I'm sorry but there will be no fancy wedding. In the small village near the lodge is where we will wed, if she agrees or in the chapel of my family's castle and holdings. Since she doesn't want to be ruined, I'm sure she will accept my proposal. She does only have two choices. You're leaving her in my care has essentially ruined her without my doing anything to further the gossip.

I hope all is going well for you at the McLellan castle and the rest and relaxation you were looking for is there.

Sincerely,

Gavin Broon, Duke of Millsglen

Quickly he reread the letter to make sure he's said everything necessary before sealing it and setting it aside to give to a messenger. Earlier in the day he'd called in some of his men who were staying at the Broon summer estate and they would arrive tomorrow late in the morning.

Pulling a glass and a bottle of whiskey from the desk drawer where he sat, he poured two fingers. He leaned back, swirling the amber liquid before sipping. If all went as he planned, in a few days time he'd be a married man.

~ * ~

Cale paced the small room where he and Tyna lived. He'd known for a couple of years now that she yearned for more than he could give her. Perhaps this would all work out well for his sister. She'd always longed for a loving husband and children to hold, a family such as the one they'd once had.

Tomorrow a huge protest was planned in the center of London. Parliament would be in session and he hoped the men who wrote the law s of the land would receive the message they intended to send. He understood the risks but this was England and all had the right to speak their mind.

He thought of the beautiful Larena. She looked so much like his ex-fiancée. Remembering his lost love, a small sigh left his lips. Once he planned to continue the restaurant and had thought to have children. "Fool, that was a time long past and you'll never get it back," he murmured to no one.

"Hey there, you look a bit wistful." Jonathan Stone entered the room without knocking and immediately found the bottle of whiskey Cale set out. "You should be proud of what you've accomplished and be looking forward to the coming day."

"True but it's something not worth thinking about. There are so many things I'll never have. As you just said we need to focus on tomorrow. Do we have an escape path if things get out of hand? If we're shot at, will we shoot back?" he asked.

"We do and there will be no shooting unless your life is in jeopardy." Jonathan set down a map of the city with lines drawn indicating several streets. "We can't be sure but most of these alleys are too small for the police or soldiers to get through except in single file. We've planned to have horses for us at the end of these two alleys."

"So we can get away and fight again," Cale laughed, the danger hitting him in the gut. Since his fiancée left him, he'd felt he had little left to live for. Now he lived for the exhilaration danger gave him.

"Don't want to end up in Newgate or worse, Australia. Don't want to spend months in the bowels of a prison ship. You got feelings for the Lady Graham? Best you forget about her. She's not for the likes of you. Heard Gavin Broon has his sights set on her."

"From what Tyna has told me, you're right. Just she reminds me of someone I cared about a long time ago." For a wistful moment Cale wished for happier times and a different life. It seemed unfair that one bad decision made by another person could turn his well-orchestrated life into a disaster.

"Do you have your speech ready?" Jonathan laughed. "You do have a way with words."

"I've ideas in my head nothing more. I'm going to let the atmosphere of the day dictate what I say." Cale had a gut instinct deep inside this day was not going to turnout well. His gut usually served him well. He'd even thought, momentarily, about aborting the mission. "Whatever happens, Jonathan, take care of yourself first. I'm so lost, my life doesn't mean a hell of a lot. Don't try to save me if I'm taken."

"Can't do that. We live or die together, Cale. You know that." Jonathan tossed back the whiskey he poured for himself then set the glass hard on the tabletop.

"Tyna was here earlier today. She's moving on, doesn't want to be involved with us any longer. Does it matter to you?"

"You know I love her but she's never returned the love even before I was diagnosed, so I don't have that to blame on her. I'm smart enough to understand there is no future for us. She wants someone who can love her and give her a family. I can't do that, at least not the family part. She knows I don't want children. Can't have them either."

Cale drummed his fingers on the table, thinking and remembering the early stages of his father's disease. He downed the whiskey he poured earlier. Then, "You've the pox." He didn't have to hear the words. He saw the answer in Jonathan's eyes.

Slowly he nodded. "A whore house... I just wanted someone when I couldn't have Tyna. Children would be disfigured and born with the disease, and I wouldn't ever give it to someone else."

"Does Tyna know?"

Jonathan shook his head, sitting down, tears in his eyes. "Don't have the money for the cure."

"Mercury ointment and pills are no cure. It's pure poison and it's just as bad as the pox. The pox doesn't drain all your resources. If father had just let it take its natural course, the family would still have the restaurant and our home," Cale said bitterly.

"Here's to tomorrow and our fate then." He raised his glass in a mock salute to his future.

Chapter Five

The day dawned bright and unusually warm. By the time the girls set off on their spending spree the sun loomed high in the sky. Larena looked forward to this shopping day with high anticipation.

The trouble with men was that they were somehow necessary. Larena wasn't sure why but she distinctly remembered The Duchess saying those very words. How she longed to sit down with her aunt so she could ask for advice about men in general and Gavin specifically. When Aunt Charlotte left a few weeks ago, Larena had no idea she would miss her so much.

When she stepped into the kitchen, Cook had two plates set out, both heaped with bacon and eggs. Larena didn't feel the tiniest bit hungry. The night before after Gavin left, riding hell bent out of town, she returned to the kitchen for a midnight snack.

Between the half loaf of bread she ate and the hunks of cheese downed with nearly a bottle of wine, there just wasn't room in her stomach for more food. She'd hoped to see Gavin this morning and ask him once more about his midnight ride, but when she finally rose and made her way downstairs, he was nowhere to be found.

Sitting at the table and toying with her eggs, her mind drifted to the things Gavin had done and said. She loved every moment but felt as if she missed something. A woman's pleasure, that's what she didn't have and her body wanted more. Tossing and turning all night long, she'd not been able to sleep and she blamed Gavin for that. She yawned, wishing sleep had not eluded her.

Tyna helped her dress, lacing her corset for her as well as the tiny fastenings running down the back of her dress and told her she'd be down just as soon as possible but that had been hours ago. What was she doing that would take this long? Tyna had been fully dressed when Larena saw her.

"Sorry, am I late? I had an urgent errand to run and there was no time to waste." Tyna asked stepping into the house through the back door and sitting down quickly. "Would you like more tea, milady?" Tyna asked, teapot in hand or more eggs.

"No, I've had more than enough food and drink. Where were you?" Larena had questions and she didn't like the sudden and unexpected rush of doubt about her lady's maid. She asked even though she understood it was none of her business. Much to her chagrin, Gavin had planted the seed of doubt deep.

Tyna smoothed a napkin on her lap before facing her. "I had to see my brother, milady. I promised him yesterday that I would stop by and tell him what we were doing. He only wants the best for me."

"Why would you keep going to him? You no longer owe him your allegiance, and he has no right to know what I'm doing or you. I don't like this. It smells of danger." Larena felt a small shiver of fear sweep through her at Tyna's words, unable to understand why Cale would want to know where they were going.

"Truly I don't think he meant any harm. I certainly didn't. I want this job too much to put it in jeopardy. The protest will go on today at noon. We have to stay away from that part of town. He told me the place and time so we could do just that. Neither the dressmakers or the fabric store is anywhere near the site where the people will gather."

"That's a relief," Larena leaned forward, her hands together. "Thank you for the information. I don't want to be any part of your brother's plans or the protests. Gavin would be very upset if he had to rescue me again. And I'm not at all sure I agree with the way your brother is managing these events even though I do agree with the ideas he professes."

Tyna dug into the food in front of her and all Larena could do was watch. Her stomach churned with nausea and fear about today. She studied her maid and realized her features were shuttered and she didn't look at her. Perhaps she was just hungry.

"Is there something you're not telling me, Tyna? It might not be a good idea to continue with our plans. We could wait until tomorrow for our shopping spree." She had the distinct feeling things were being left unsaid and she didn't like it.

Tyna set her fork on her plate, her lips pressed together. "I'm sorry I interrupted you and Gavin last night. It wasn't well done of me. I wanted to apologize for last night, but I was afraid you'd fire me before I got a chance to start."

Larena stiffened her back, not wanting to recount the evening before, which was meant to be so private, with her maid. "What did you see? You can tell me. I won't hold it against you," but Larena really needed to know, her emotions unraveling one thin strand at a time.

"More than I ought to." She rose and set her plate on the counter by the sink before turning to look at her. "I really don't want to talk about what happened yesterday and my impropriety," she said before returning for Larena's plate. "No, not something we should talk about."

"I really need to know." Larena meant to press Tyna on this issue. She knew she could truly be embarrassed.

"Everything. I saw everything." She inhaled a long breath, closing her eyes for a second. "Yes, if you must know I saw you naked except for your stockings and in his arms, his hands where they shouldn't be. I didn't want to truly I didn't but... It's private and not for my eyes."

Larena realized then that Tyna had been in love before and maybe even naked with a man. "You've been in love and you've been with a man that way, haven't you?"

Tyna sat down again. "It was a long time ago and no, we never did anything like that, like you and Gavin. I loved him but he doesn't want anything to do with me now. He didn't even tell me why he left me. He's one of my brother's best friends and he was there this morning."

"Maybe your brother warned him off. I would wager older brothers might be like that." Once more Tyna had all her sympathy. She'd loved a man and he rejected her. She wasn't sure about love, but she knew she didn't want Gavin to reject her and set her aside.

"No, Cale never knew Jonathan and I loved each other or even that we cared about the other as lovers might. Well, I cared about him. Jonathan only wanted to get me into his bed and when he couldn't, he left." Tyna's words were bitter. "You did the right thing, milady, and I'm so sorry I interrupted the two of you."

"You should ask him." And from only a few minor encounters with Gavin, Larena knew her words were easier said than done. She could never confront Gavin about anything like that, and she realized she'd be devastated if Gavin left her without an explanation.

"I tried to talk to him and tell him how I felt in hopes of persuading him back to me."

"What happened?"

"He told me that I was better off not knowing why he refused to have anything to do with me save friendship, and with that said he turned and left without another word. I cried for days, cried until I made myself sick. Cale finally made me so angry, I left the flat and walked along the Thames, thinking about throwing myself into the water."

"I'm glad you didn't, Tyna. That man didn't deserve your tears or the love you felt for him. And for that matter your brother should not still be a friend of his. He should stand up for you." Larena's heart went out to her.

A lone tear slipped from an eye sliding down her cheek, a sob followed before more tears flowed. "Cale told me this morning why Jonathan left me. He told me I deserved to understand what happened and that Jonathan still loves me. I guess my brother did know we were sweet on each other. I'd been so sure we kept the secret from him."

"The reason better be good." Impatiently, Larena drummed her fingers on the table in her mind creating different scenarios. "A man can't tread on a girl's heart and expect to come away unscathed."

"The reason is horrible, and the harm done to him more than anyone deserves. Just like my father he didn't care enough about our fledgling relationship to stay true to me but he paid," she drew in a deep breath, "is paying for his one indiscretion. One night he wanted a woman and when I refused to ruin myself, he had one. I'm just glad we were unable to see each other very often."

"What are you trying to say?"

"Jonathan contracted syphilis, the pox. I guess I'm a lucky woman. When he found out, he left me. He never slept with me because of it." She let her head fall into her hands and sobbed.

"The pox touches too many people." Larena never understood anything about this horrible incurable disease until now. There had to be a way to prevent something so dreadful.

"In my life, yes, all of the men I've ever loved except one, my brother, have contracted the illness. Now that I know why, I think I can start fresh, let someone worthy have my heart. But you know, I'm not going to give myself or my heart to just anyone. He's going to have to put me first in his life."

"That's good and right. I should do the same, but I'm afraid the only man I really know and the only one I ever think about is Gavin." She really had no experience with men and isn't that just what they wanted; an ignorant woman, one they could mold and shape to think exactly the way they wanted them to think. She wasn't going to be that woman.

"Mr. Broon, the Duke, men like that are different. They have mistresses and they don't go to whores to see to their manly needs. They're not going to get the maladies ordinary folks get."

"I certainly hope not, but I know I don't like the idea of Gavin keeping a mistress or going to a whore house for his pleasure, whatever that is." If she'd been confused last night, she had questions today and she meant to ask Gavin about all these things she just talked to Tyna about. Perhaps his midnight rides had been to see his paramour. Her gut churned.

"Will Cook clean the kitchen?" Tyna began to clear the table. "I don't want to leave a mess."

"Yes, go tell Stewart we're ready to leave and he'll have the stable boy bring the carriage around. We've got a lot to accomplish in one afternoon of shopping." Larena tried to put a lighter air on today.

Larena watched her maid leave, mulling over all that had been said. The Duchess would have known nothing of the pox, or would she? The disease that had no cure had never touched her life. She never spoke of her husband's death. No, Larena shook that thought from her head. She thought someday to ask Charlotte how William died.

She waited on the front porch. Tyna joined her. "Our ride will be here in a minute. I've put a damper on your day, haven't I? I really didn't mean to do that you know."

"On our day," she corrected. "You've put thoughts into my head.

Gavin says I'm innocent. I don't want to be and the more I know of the world and the ways of men and women, the more knowledgeable I'll be." She had few people she could talk to about relationships. Ella was wed and had a child, so perhaps her cousin was her best source. Gavin would approve of a visit to Ella. Addie was a friend too and she was wiser in the ways of the world than her cousin. No one would consider Addie an innocent. Addie had experienced so much more than anyone else she knew in her short lifetime. No, there was nothing innocent about Addie Winthrop.

"You shouldn't tell the duke we talked about things like that, about the pox, or about the man who left me. Men want to be the ones who decide what the woman in their life knows."

Larena stiffened, realizing she wanted to decide what she should learn and not be dictated to by a man. "Gavin can try to be my lord and master, but he will have a fight on his hands." Larena skipped down the steps to the carriage, Tyna following at a more sedate pace.

Letting the coachman help them into the carriage they settled in for the short ride into town and the markets. As they approached the city, sounds of vendors and other carriages filtered through the window. The noise had a soothing effect on Larena's rattled nerves.

They stopped in front of the fabric store first. Inside the bolts of cloth filled the room. The store was stocked from floor to ceiling with bright as well as somber colors, everything anyone could imagine.

"What colors do you like?" Larena held a bolt of deep lavender for Tyna's inspection.

"Yellow is my favorite and the sunnier the better. I want something bright and cheery at the windows." She reached for a bolt of daffodil yellow and presented it to Larena. "Is this okay?"

"Anything you enjoy is perfect." Larena knew it had been a few years since Tyna had the opportunity to shop and pick out anything she liked.

They shopped for everything that would make the dreary attic room appealing and comfortable for Tyna: curtains, bed sheets and coverlets. Tyna would need a nice rug too.

"Can you sew?" Larena asked, realizing she missed creating dresses and the peace of mind sewing gave her. In London life seemed so hectic.

At home she could leave the house anytime for a ride or go swimming at their favorite lake. The confinement of the city made her feel smothered.

"I love to sew and I've even created a few designs of my own. When father owned the restaurant, mother and I fashioned most of our clothing." Tyna grinned at her.

They bought fabric for dresses, lace for embellishment and numerous other things including intricate fasteners. Larena was correct in assuming her aunt's credit was extended to her purchases. With arms piled high, they dumped the acquisitions into the carriage and walked to the dress shop.

"Larena, you don't mean to buy more things for me. You've done more than necessary. I can use the fabrics we bought to make all the dresses I need. The bright yellow curtains will make my new room feel like home."

"You need things now, don't you? A single dress cannot be worn everyday. Just a few purchases to tide you over until you can finish the dresses we bought fabric for." This was almost as much fun as shopping with her cousins and Aunt Charlotte. Those first few days before Tavia and Tira left had been so much fun, filled with laughter and even gossip. The Duchess treated all of them to new clothes; everything from the inside out, as well as top to toe.

Suddenly a man throttled her, grabbing her around the waist, a hand over her mouth. She stumbled, her arms whirling until the man pulled her against him. "Don't scream, Larena. It's me, Cale. I mean you no harm, but you need to come with me."

Tyna had disappeared into the dress shop without seeing her brother or noticing she wasn't behind her. Shaking her head in an attempt to say no, Larena reached out as if she could pull her maid back. Cale drug her with him, her feet barely touching the ground. So many people filled the streets they didn't seem to be aware of her reluctance to go with this man. Either that or they ignored her plight, believing it wasn't their problem.

In his arms she struggled but she couldn't dislodge herself. "We're almost there. I'm not going to hurt you, but you and I have become the face of the protesters. You're going to stand with me when I give my speech." He went on, seeming to pick his words meticulously. "I know your duke will not like this, but I really don't care how he feels. The cause needs you here today. When we're done and all is safe, I'll let you go back to him."

She watched Tyna emerge from the dress shop and look around. Larena reached out to her. Tyna saw her and started forward, but a tall handsome man restrained her. This was not what she wanted. At one time, yes, she wanted to be part of all this, the cause, but now, now Gavin had convinced her this was a game she was playing and it was a dangerous game that could cost her all she wanted in life.

Suddenly, she stood beside Cale on a platform, above the crowds, his hand around her waist. "Don't try anything. There is a pistol pointed at your head. You are a beautiful woman, Larena. I could enjoy having you." He laughed when she squirmed and he pulled her closer. "Ah, I know the duke would kill me if I tried and I do so wish to live."

"Gentleman and ladies, if there are any in the crowd," he began in a loud booming voice, one Larena knew was made for speeches. He knew how to play the people and win them over to his side. "We are gathered here in protest of our government's desire to keep us from our freedom to assemble. We have rights and parliament wants to deny us those rights. Our fathers have fought for years so we can speak our minds without fear of repercussions, yet these men who say they represent us do not."

"Here, here," the cry went up through the crowds, cheering so loud it kept him from speaking but he raised one fist in victory. "We can make them hear our words."

"No more corn laws. No more corn laws." The new chant rode on a wave through the crowd.

"Cale, Cale," another cry reverberated around the small public square where they stood. Cale held one hand in the air, grinning at the immense crowds who gathered here and spoke their minds.

Then, "Larena, Larena!" The chant continued. She cringed, trying to place herself behind Cale. She didn't want to be seen or recognized and prayed this all be over before Gavin knew where she was.

"No," she whispered. "Let me go. I don't want to be here. You've got what you want. Leave me out of your plans."

"When the afternoon is done, sweet Larena, then I will personally escort you to your home." His fingers tightened around her waist. "Right now you are serving my purpose well. Smile at the people who revere you."

A shot was fired into the air then a few more. British soldiers appeared from all sides, guns pointed toward the crowd of civilians. It seemed there were more soldiers than citizens. They emerged from the tiny alleyways and the larger streets.

"This can't be happening," she whispered, searching the streets for some way to escape. "Let me go, please. This is done here. You're finished. I have to get away."

"Stay with me. I'll find a way to get you out of this," Cale spoke softly. "Jonathan will lead the way."

Jonathan reached his arms for her and helped her from the platform. Cale jumped down beside her.

"Keep your head down." She stumbled, following the men who said they would keep her safe. They raced through the throngs of protestors, bumping into people. Hands reached out, touching her, grabbing at her. One sleeve was torn then she heard another part of her dress rip. Gasping for breath, Cale kept her hand in his.

Winded, she inhaled deep labored breaths filled with little air. Yet some feeling deep inside, told her these men were her best chance of escaping this unscathed. Then someone wrenched her away from Cale's hold. The bodice of her dress ripped. Cale turned and for a second their gazes met. He shook his head and mouthed, "I'm sorry."

She pounded on the soldier's chest, but his hold upon her was iron tight. "You won't get away. You're going to a place where you'll have no freedom." Kicking at his shins did nothing to loosen the man's hold. "I got you, little whore, and I'm not letting you go."

The soldier gripped her around the waist, her feet barely touching the earth. They were close to the prison wagons. Her heart lodged in her throat. She searched the sea of people for a friendly face. Then she was thrown into the wagon. She landed hard on other prisoners who pushed her against the iron bars. The door swung closed and the soldier hit it twice.

The wagon lumbered slowly through the street. Both men and women had been thrown inside. Larena leaned her face against the bars of the wagon, her hands clasping tight, tears rolling down her cheeks.

She had not meant to be here this day. Tyna had said the protestors would not be close to the fabric store or the dress shop. It had not even been curiosity that drove her to be in the city but shopping had motivated her.

Cale lied to his sister. He'd told her where they shopped was safe and far away from the center of the protest, or Tyna lied to her. She didn't want to believe her new employee would tell her falsehoods and, in the process, sell her out. She needed to hold on to that thought and trust Tyna to help her.

Gavin told her she would go to other side of the world or to Newgate if caught. At least if she went to the prison, maybe Gavin could get her out. He could use some of his power. Nothing or no one could help her if she was bound for a ship to Australia.

Cale and Jonathan must have gotten away and Tyna was most likely safe too. She smelled the sea, heard the cry of seagulls and her heart sank even farther. More tears slid down her cheeks.

The people inside the wagon grabbed at her, clawing and tearing at her clothing. Even while she knew what they did, her mind floated in a fog of fear now. The world was in a haze, one where she felt no fear or pain. She seemed to float away from her body.

Until the door swung open and her fingers were pried from the bars, she didn't know the wagon had come to a stop or that a man was negotiating with the guard.

Then she heard his voice. "Gavin."

~ * ~

Gavin sent the letter he wrote to The Duchess by messenger in the morning then he set about preparing for his and Larena's journey northeast. Lightness in his step was an indication of his relief and happiness the decisions he made were about to be set in motion. Larena would be safe from herself and her crazy beliefs. She would be his and as soon as their lives settled down, he intended to ask for her hand in marriage.

His carriage with his crest sat in front of his riverfront office apartment ready for him to retrieve Larena. As soon as a basket of food and a valise for himself were packed and inside the vehicle, he would set off for the townhouse. He inhaled fresh air, enjoying the crisp scent and the sound of the seagulls.

Inside his office, he stood on the small Juliet balcony and watched the town. The protestors were assembled and a small platform in the middle had been built for speeches. Larena had mentioned shopping for fabric and maybe a few purchases at her favorite dressmakers with Tyna this afternoon.

A lump formed in his throat. That platform was a short distance from the dress shop. "Bloody hell... This can't be happening." Deep in his heart he knew Larena was in trouble. "Alistair!"

"Sir? Everything's in order. The carriage is here and waiting. We can leave anytime you give the order."

"Get downstairs and wait for me. Don't go anywhere unless I give the order." His mind raced, yet the most prominent thought was for Larena and her safety, for her bloody life.

"Yes, sir."

Gavin looked out the window one more time. He wasn't sure why but he felt his name on the breeze. What he saw churned inside his gut. Larena stood on the platform with Cale, his arm wrapped around her. The distance wasn't so great that he couldn't see the distress clearly etched in her face. She was not a willing participant but there under duress.

"Larena..." he raced down the steps, taking them two and three at a time before jumping the last five to land solidly on the ground. On the street he grabbed Alistair's horse, praying the mount wouldn't shy when faced with these circumstances and the horde of people. Expertly, he weaved around protestors and soldiers.

His pace slowed as he approached the platform. Fear closed in on him as he searched the area, seeing no sign of Larena.

The horse clearly distraught, his head moving up and down, continued despite his anxiety. Gavin reached forward, his hand on the stallion's face. "Easy boy. Just hold it together a bit longer. You're a fine boy. You can do this." The horse whinnied and kept the slow pace inching forward as men raced in the opposite direction.

In slow motion he watched as Larena was grabbed and tossed into a prison wagon. "No," his cry reached no one. "Bloody hell, there will be consequences paid for this injustice." The wagon headed for the river. He eased around more people, slowly and steadily he closed the distance.

"Hold." The prison guard stopped the wagon at his command and approached Gavin.

"What can I do for you, Sir?" He wiped the sweat from his forehead, his eyes wide with question. "Don't stop for just anyone, Duke."

"The lady there," he pointed to Larena. "She's important to me. I believe she was in the wrong place when running a few shopping errands. I'd like to retrieve her before she's put on that ship." He nodded toward the prison ship swaying on the river. "She's to become my wife in a few days."

"Can't do that. She was in the middle of the rioters, even stood on the speech platform. We've strict orders to round up as many of the protestors as possible and get them out of London where they can't cause any more trouble."

Gavin pulled out a small bag of coin, he planned to use on the upcoming journey and handed it to the guard. "This can just be between you and me. I'm sure you can put it to good use."

The man looked inside the wagon then to Gavin and back to the wagon. "Suppose we could've got an innocent bystander by mistake. Thanks for bringin' this to my attention. Wouldn't want someone important to you hauled off to another part of the world."

He unlocked the bars and Gavin stepped forward, sweeping Larena into his arms. Even while her eyes were glazed over with terror, her body trembled and tears streaked her smudged face. "Thank you," he told the guard. "I'll double that coin as soon as I can. You've my gratitude forever. If you ever need anything, contact me."

She was nearly limp, her body in shock. He'd seen this in soldiers when death was imminent. "Larena, can you sit this horse? If not, I'll carry you to my office. Everything will be fine. Trust me."

She stared at him, her eyes unfocused, the trauma of the last minutes taking their toll on her. She didn't answer yet she touched his face with a delicate fingertip.

"I'm going to set you on my horse. You need to stay there. Don't fall off." He didn't dare put her behind him, unsure if she could hold on even for the short ride to the carriage. "Do you understand what I want you to do?"

She tilted her head slightly, moistening her lips as if she wanted to speak but still didn't say anything. Once she sat the horse, he mounted behind her and adjusted her onto his lap. "That's good. Now hang on the best you can, little darlin'." By then the crowds had dispersed slightly and the ride to his office was easier. In his arms she'd never felt so tiny and fragile as she did now. He'd failed to keep his promise to her aunt. He'd failed to protect her.

"Alistair, help Lady Graham down." She was so light it took little strength for him to hand her to Alistair. He'd never really noticed how very small she was. Her thoughts and actions had always seemed bigger than life.

"Yes, Sir. Your driver is here. He's in your office."

Gavin set her in the man's arms then quickly dismounted. "Listen carefully."

Taking Larena, Gavin carefully set her in the carriage, "I'll join you soon. Just relax now. We can talk later."

Alistair nodded. "Whatever you need, Sir."

"Go to The Duchess' townhouse and see if Tyna, Lady Graham's maid, is there. It's her choice. She can stay at the townhouse or she can go with you. If she wants to follow her employer, bring her to the inn we spoke of near the Montgomerie hunting lodge. By the time you get to the townhouse and speak with her, it will be too late to start on the journey. I've another carriage the two of you can use. You know where it is."

"I do and I'll go right away. Is there anything else?" He waited, his shoulders straight.

"Have Miss Tyna pack a bag for Larena. If she decides to go with you, it will be safer to stay in my office apartment tonight. It's too dangerous for you to start the trip in the evening."

"Sir," Alistair strode into his office and emerged with the driver then he mounted his horse and left.

Stepping into the carriage, he gave the signal for the driver to start before sitting back to regard the woman he cared deeply for.

He sat next to Larena, afraid to touch her or talk to her. She gazed out the window but didn't move. He set his hand on her back in an attempt to ease her fears, realizing only time could do that.

"Everything is going to be alright. You're safe with me now. I know you didn't intend to be there. Cale forced you." He massaged her tight shoulder muscles, wishing he could have somehow prevented this travesty from happening.

She turned, gracing him with a weak smile. Before she spoke she closed her eyes for an instant. "I'm not sure I believe you. Nothing feels right or safe. I don't think I even know who I am."

"Trust me."

She blinked a few times and delicately touched his face with the palm of her hand. "I wasn't there by choice. Cale grabbed me outside the dressmaker's and put me on the platform," she murmured, letting him take her hand in his. "I told him no but he just didn't care."

"I know you didn't choose to go with him." At first sight he hadn't been sure, but he remembered the look of distress on her face. "Did Cale force you by his side?"

With a sob, "He told me there was a gun pointed at me and that I'd become the face of the protestors so I had to stand by his side. I don't want that, don't want to be the face of anything."

"No, I don't want that for you either." He tried every way possible to console her and to ease the uncontrollable trembling of her body.

He pulled her close, needing to hold her and reassure her. For some time they traveled the rest of the way in silence, the sun slowly descending. A beautiful sunset stretched across the horizon the hues changing as the sun began to disappear. Twilight followed. Still the carriage continued.

Luck had been with him this afternoon when he saw her in the middle of the protestors. If he hadn't looked out the window, he would have never found her in the prison cart. She would have vanished. Yet he knew people and he could have enlisted help, pulled in a few favors. His fists tightened at the thought of losing her. Cale had no right to bring her into his cause, compelling her to his bidding.

If the situation had forced him to extreme measures and it had been necessary, he would have followed her to Australia or Tasmania. Bloody hell, how had he let this happen? He had been sure he convinced her to stay away so he'd let down his guard. She had stayed away, he reminded himself. She was at the dressmakers.

"Gavin," she pushed away from him, her eyes swollen from the tears. She looked as if she wanted nothing more than to hide away where no one could hurt her. "Where are we going?"

"You don't need to worry about that. Somewhere you'll be safe. A place I won't have to constantly look over my shoulder to make sure you're alive." Gavin tightened his fists, not liking the constriction of the muscles in his gut.

"We're a long way from the city. All I see is countryside. The townhouse isn't our destination and neither is your office." She shuddered against him, his hold tightening. "Don't you think I deserve to know where you're taking me? This is my life."

"Not tonight but in a day or two we're going to stay at Drake family's hunting lodge near the border. Thankfully, the summer retreat is located in Scotland. For now I want to get as far away from the city as possible."

She seemed to mull over his words. When she moistened her lips, he knew she was about to object. "Is there no other choice?"

"Not that I can think of. You've gotten yourself into a great deal of trouble. Only extreme measures will guard your life. Law enforcement could still come after you." He smiled trying to reassure her but understanding a smile wouldn't really help.

"There is no chaperone."

The true statement sent a knife into his heart even though he planned to marry her before they spent time at the lodge. "Not a single volunteer for the duty. Your aunt is too far away and Tyna wouldn't be considered suitable if she and Alistair decide to join us, and you couldn't stay in the city."

"Alistair?"

The mention of his man seemed to bring her back to the present. "Alistair works for me. His mission is to find Tyna and see what she wants to do. If she intends to continue to work for you then she needs to go with him. He will make sure they arrive safely at our planned destination."

"You've been planning this for a while." She wiped the tears from her cheeks and found them smudged with dirt. "When were you going to tell me?"

"Here," he handed her an embroidered handkerchief. "This might help wipe away the pain and the memories of this afternoon as well as the dirt."

She suddenly realized the state she was in. "I'm... "

"A bit in disarray," he told her smiling, not wishing to alarm her over the state of her clothing, more appropriately her lack of clothing. "But never more beautiful."

"I don't have anything to wear. This," she smoothed her torn skirts and bodice, "is all I have and it's very nearly shredded."

"When we stop you can wear one of my shirts and in the morning, I'll find a shop where I can purchase something for you."

"It's not that easy. I haven't told you I'd go with you to the lodge or anywhere else for that matter."

"You can't go back to London or recapture your innocent appearance to the ton. We can only go forward and make the best of whatever is thrown in our path. I intend to do a better job of protecting you, Larena."

"My life is in such a shambles. I don't know where forward is," she murmured, leaning against his chest, her hand touching his.

The time wasn't right for telling her he hoped she would become his wife. Didn't know how to tell her the announcement had already been placed in the newspaper and that he'd already informed her aunt Charlotte. He'd truly jumped ahead of the game but knew how necessary his actions had been.

"Are you feeling better?" he asked.

"If you mean am I no longer in a deep haze afraid of the people I'm imprisoned with and mulling over all the horrible scenarios you planted in my head, then yes, I'm feeling better. But exhaustion has consumed my body and mind. I feel as if I need to sleep for a week."

"Feeling better or exhausted?"

"Both."

"Do you have enough energy to begin discussing what is going to happen?" He knew he said that wrong, and he also knew she wouldn't agree with him if he made it seem as if she had no choice or a voice in her life. But she didn't, at least not a viable one. She couldn't go back to London alone and unprotected, so she had to accept his plans.

His words didn't go unnoticed. "Are you telling me I don't have a choice?" She ran her hands through her hair. "I'm tired," she said. "I don't think I've ever been this tired." She closed her eyes for a second, pressing into him as if she wanted his warmth or perhaps the closeness another human offered. "I didn't sleep at all last night, not after what you did, we did..."

He smiled at her confession. Sleep had been elusive for him as well. "We have plenty of time to discuss our future. Take this time to rest and sleep if that's possible under the circumstances." He hoped she would sleep. He needed time to figure out what he was going to say to her and how he could convince her to his way of thinking.

"What if I say no. Where will I go? Are you going to send me back to London unprotected? If anything, this incident has made me well aware that I can't do this entirely on my own. I suppose I can always go home. I'm sure my sisters will be happy to see me."

"Do you really want to force this conversation right now? I don't. I want you to rest and find some rational thoughts not just defiance. Really, Larena, I'm trying devilishly hard to be patient, and I'm not a patient man." Only a few minutes prior he wanted to talk this over with her, but in that time he realized she was in no condition to make cognizant decisions about her life.

"I don't know," she said quietly, her gaze cast downward. "I think I've a right to know what's going to happen to me even if I don't have a say. I do understand you want to wait but I really don't."

"Both are true. You've a right to know and I believe you've lost the opportunity to have a say in this other than agreement with my plans. I've only your best interest at heart, but I will listen to any suggestions and we can talk them over." So much happened to her today he didn't think she could handle anything else.

"You don't know how strong I am, Gavin Broon. I'm not a fragile delicate female who needs guidance or protection. I can take care of myself." She sat up straight. "I've decided you're going to tell me everything I want to know and you're going to do it now."

"Only what I want you to know." He did mean to hold his ground in this conversation. Whether she liked the idea or not, she needed him to safeguard her life. She didn't have to agree with him.

"That's not fair and you know it." She wound her hair into a knot to keep it from her face.

"I didn't realize your hair was that long. It's beautiful. You know that don't you?" He'd run his fingers through the silken strands and felt the fire. He wanted to wrap its length around his body. Soon, when they were wed and she was officially his.

"It's an ugly color," she murmured.

Bloody hell if her raven hued hair was ugly. He couldn't believe she thought so little of her beauty. "Not to me it isn't."

"Gavin," she sighed softly, his name whispering in the darkening night. "Where are we going?"

"Oh, look, we're here." The carriage rolled down a long path toward a three-story building.

"Where?" she asked.

"Guess."

The carriage stopped in front of the porch stairs leading upward. His family's servants assembled in a line on the porch, some waving some with their hands clasped in front of them waiting for orders.

"This doesn't look like an inn."

To Gavin she seemed frozen to the seat. She didn't move for a few seconds and he wondered if she did guess where they were. "It's my family's summer home. No one except the servants are here right now. My brothers are either on vacation somewhere or in town. It's ours for the night."

"Sir, Lord Gavin," the butler stepped forward. "Welcome home. It's been a long time."

"Thank you. It's good to be home. I understand none of my siblings are in residence."

"No one."

"Good, take my valise to the master chamber. The Lady Graham will reside in the room next to mine. Circumstances kept her from packing a valise so I would appreciate it if you found something for her to wear this evening. Perhaps my sibling's wives have left a few articles of clothing behind. I'd like baths for both of us and dinner in my room with a bottle of wine and perhaps some tea. I'm not sure what Lady Graham would like this evening. "

He heard her gasp at his instructions and understood she might protest, but these retainers of his family's were loyal and would do his bidding no matter what she said to them. Again rumors already abounded about the two of them. Nothing they did here would change that fact. They had no reason to assume airs for the sake of propriety.

She'd held back for a few minutes, but eventually the driver helped her from the vehicle before he drove away.

"Come, I'll show you to your room." He held out his arm hoping etiquette would keep her from making a scene.

"Do I have a choice?" he heard her mumble beneath her breath while she remained firmly in one place.

"Always, what would you like? The adjoining room or sharing with me?" His gaze remained straight ahead.

"A room of my own."

"That's what you have," he smiled and brought her hand to his lips. "I always think of everything."

"It's next to yours."

"For your protection. We are not far from town and I'm not going to take any chances with your life. I promise you I will not come into your room in the middle of the night and take your virginity. That is something a woman chooses to give to a man."

"So you say now," she told him. "You don't have any problem ruining my reputation."

Despite everything he told himself about their situation the words stung. "It's ruining mine too."

She stopped midstride. "Men's reputations can't be ruined. They can do anything they wish any time." She stalked away from him, her back rigid.

He let her go, watching while he grinned. When she reached the steps and turned, left he said, "Do you know where you're going?"

Hands on her hips one foot tapping in agitation. "No."

"Then let me guide you." The moment he said the words he wanted to take them back.

"Arrogant," she said but she waited for him.

He held out his arm, determined not to budge until she accepted what he offered. Seconds ticked by while she stared at him seemingly just as determined then with a huge sigh she accepted.

Gavin felt her fury pulse into him and become one with his heartbeat. Unity, however small and in the face of anger was better than distance and disenchantment. He didn't mean for her to bend to his will, just accept what was best for both of them.

"Milady," he spoke elegantly. "Your room is this way. I hope you're pleased with the accommodations."

"I wish we didn't have to pretend." They walked slowly, her exhaustion evident in every move.

"There is no pretense on my part, Lady Graham." Even though she tried to hide it from him, the limp became more pronounced with each step taken. He was convinced she'd admit to no injuries.

"Liar, you're pretending I mean something to you but look you're taking me to a bedroom adjoining yours." Her words lacked conviction.

Gavin stopped in front of the door to her room before opening it for her. "Make yourself at home, Larena. Your bath should be prepared for you in a few minutes, and we'll have dinner in my room. Knock on my door when you're ready." He stepped back and regarded her as she took hesitant steps into the elegant and pretentious room she would sleep in for one night. His oldest brother's wife had lavish and expensive taste in décor.

She turned then, dark shadows beneath her beautiful aqua eyes, exhaustion and trauma taking its toll. He'd thought she'd recovered quickly, but he now had serious doubts.

Purposely he strode the short distance to his room and stepping inside was pleased to see the bath filled and ready for him. Quickly, he disrobed and slipped into the hot water. He didn't intend to spend much time, just enough to wash and dress in clean clothes. Out of the tub, he donned new clothes. The butler had time to lay out buckskins and a white shirt he must have found in his room on the other side of the house.

The message he sent just this morning telling the staff they were coming must have arrived in a timely manner. He wanted Larena close to him just in case the prison guard he paid off gave him away.

The knock on the door stopped his musings. "Come in."

"Sir, your dinner is ready."

"Put it on the table. I'll take care of everything else." He hummed as he set out the dinner plates and silverware. The meal sat on a tray beneath a dome to keep it warm, and the tea and wine were set on a separate tray. He poured wine for both and put the teapot and cups on a separate table.

The hesitant knock from the adjoining door put a smile in his heart. Setting everything aside for a moment, he strode to the door. Opening it, he grinned at Larena who had a shawl wrapped around her shoulders even though it was warm in both rooms.

"I see they found you something to wear." He held out his hand. "I can't say it's the best fit but you look stunning."

She accepted and he escorted her to a place in front of the fire.

"It's a little big," she pulled on the sleeves, trying to bring them higher on the shoulders. "I feel nearly naked with this on, but it was the only choice I was given."

"Sit by the fire and you can dry your hair. Are you hungry?"

"Not really, although I've not had a bite since last night after you left for your midnight ride." She fanned her hair, trying to dry it, but in the process the shawl fell from her shoulders.

He closed his eyes at the site before him, and when he opened them, he couldn't help but focus on tender flesh revealed by her sagging bodice. Clearing his throat, "I can comb your hair if you like?" Bloody hell but he needed a diversion.

She looked down and quickly pulled the gown upward. "I'm sorry. It's a little too much fabric for me. Yes, I think I'd like for you to comb my hair. If I tried, the dress would be at my waist."

He laughed for the first time today and sat down with comb in hand. Slowly, he drew the length of her hair through the comb and his fingers, "Silken fire," he murmured.

She sat so very still. After a few minutes, "I'm sorry you had to change all your plans just to rescue me."

What she didn't know is that the only thing he changed was their immediate destinations. All of this had been set in motion before she found herself in a prison cart on her way to a ship bound for Australia.

"Your life is worth any change. Besides, what you should probably understand is that all of this was planned. I still had to ask you but I had every intention of doing that when you finished your shopping spree." He watched the change of expressions wash over her face.

"I'm confused. You had this planned?" She turned then taking his hand, hers eyes wide. Quickly, she pulled her hair together and tied it into a knot to keep it from her eyes.

Reluctantly, he nodded while his heart pounded. "I wanted you to see my home in Scotland. It's where I hope to put down roots."

"We...we're going on a trip together, without a chaperone? Perhaps we should eat." She stood but misjudging her step, she swayed.

"Larena," he steadied her before she fell.

"I'm fine," she smiled at him. "Just tired. That's all. Nothing a night of sleep won't cure."

"I need to feed you and put you to bed." He laughed at the frown on her face. "In your bed. I'm not going to take advantage of you. That will come some other time," he paused thoughtfully and for her benefit said, "after we are husband and wife."

"You're a cad." She accepted the chair he held out for her. "I won't let you do that, take advantage of me." It seemed she chose to ignore the tiny bit about marriage.

"When we make love, I promise you'll be a willing participant, no one taking advantage of the other."

Fresh salmon, spring peas and more were the fare of the day. He watched her pick at her food, but eventually she ate most of the portion he set on her plate. She sipped the wine but didn't finish the small glass he poured for her.

When she finished, he stood and walking to her chair, he knelt and reaching into his pocket, he pulled out a ring. It was an heirloom passed down from his great grandmother to all of the women on his mother's side. There were no women left, so the sapphire engagement ring was bestowed on him.

"Larena, will you marry me?"

~ * ~

Tyna raced into the townhouse breathless, eyes swollen from the tears flowing down her cheeks. Cale betrayed her and betrayed the nicest lady on this earth as well. She could never repay Larena, would never see her again. Hidden in the doorway of the dressmaker's store, she watched Larena fight to get away from her brother and Jonathan as they raced through alleyways they were familiar with and Larena was not.

"I'm sorry, milady. I'm so sorry." Her sobs filled the tiny attic room. "I couldn't reach you in time and he lied to me just so he could get at you. I detest him and will never forgive that horrible act."

"Excuse me."

A deep male voice shook her from her self-pity. She stood, addressing the strange man, her arms wrapped around her waist, her voice trembling. She backed away, finding herself trapped against a wall, "Who are you and what are you doing here?"

"The name's Alistair, lass. I was sent here by Lord Gavin Broon Duke of Millsglen. I work for him."

"Lord Broon sent you?" Her breath nearly stopped, sure he would see her punished for what happened to his lady.

"Aye, lass, you're to pack a bag for Lady Graham then you can decide if you want to go to her or if you want to stay here. Of course if you choose to stay in London, you need vacate this home immediately. You will no longer be employed by Lady Graham."

Shocked, she bent over, her hand on a night table struggling to breathe. "She's alive and not in prison? How? I saw her put in a prison cart." For the first time since this afternoon she felt a moment of hope.

"Milord rescued her from the prison cart, and even now as we speak, they are escaping the city in a carriage. If you want to meet her at the final destination, there is a carriage at the duke's riverfront office apartment waiting for you. I will see you get to your destination safely."

Before this moment, she'd not really noticed the man. With his legs braced apart, she followed the line of his form from the ground up, past narrow hips, broad shoulders to a chiseled jaw hidden beneath a reddish brown neatly trimmed beard.

"I want to go with milady." Her prayers had been answered in a miracle she never expected.

"Then you need to pack a bag for the lady and one for yourself. I can help or wait for you downstairs. Can you ride?"

"A, sure... yes," she said. She was positive she could ride a horse. It seemed so simple when she watched others, and at this moment in front of this devastatingly handsome man she didn't want to admit to a weakness, and she didn't want to be left behind because she'd never ridden a horse.

He frowned at her, his eyebrows drawing together in disbelieve, but when he smiled, she was sure she'd convinced him. Now all she had to do was convince herself and learn to ride before he would know her for the liar she was.

"Good, do you need help with the packing?"

"No," she spoke to quickly. "No, I can do this, no problem." She knew what she would pack for both of them. "Where are we going?"

"Just know the first destination and I must keep it secret." He watched her, seeming to regard her closely.

"Secret?"

"For the Lady Graham's safety. I'll wait in her room on the second floor. You might need help with the bags bringing them down the stairs." He smiled at her again, and it seemed her heart melted.

Not many minutes later, Tyna appeared in Larena's room. Packing her valise had been a simple matter. She had few possessions. Rummaging in Larena's armoire she found garments to clad her from her toes to her head and inside out. She guessed Larena would need something of everything.

When she finished, setting the two valises on the floor, Alistair grinned and took possession of both suitcases. "Shall we?" he asked gallantly. "After you."

She led the way to the stables and looked apprehensively at the horses. He tossed the bags into a small cart and tied two horses to the back of the vehicle. Then he offered her a hand to help her onto the seat.

Poking her head through the window, "Why did you ask me if I could ride if we're taking a wagon?" Having lied, she now felt a bit indignant.

"Needed to know if I should bring one or two horses with us." He nodded his head at her, a brilliant smile on his face. "Now just relax and enjoy the short ride through town. We'll spend the night at the duke's apartment then we'll be off first thing in the morning."

He didn't wait for her shocked reply. They would spend the night in the duke's apartment? Well, what had she expected when she decided to run off this way with a man she didn't know?

He climbed into the driver's seat and they were on their way. Good lord, but he was the most breathtaking and heart-stoppingly gorgeous man she'd ever set eyes upon and when he grinned, his features softened making her think of him as a gentle puppy dog. "Now, Tyna," she spoke to herself sternly, "you've got to get yourself under control or I won't be responsible for what you do. He's only your escort, nothing more so no more thinking that way."

"Ninny, he hasn't shown an iota of interest in you and why should he?" She let out a long deep breath closing her eyes only to imagine the feel of his well-muscled arms around her.

"You can't, no you won't give yourself to this man tonight. He would think you're just a whore, a woman he can take advantage of. Besides you don't even know what to do. You'd make a fool of yourself." She recalled the expression on Larena's face when she saw her in the gazebo and wondered if his lovemaking would create that expression.

If he offered, she truly didn't think she had the will to resist any overtures he might make toward her. She touched her lips, the feel of Jonathan's tentative kisses vanishing when she imagined Alistair and his mouth upon hers and his tongue gliding inside.

One minute the horizon was blended with colors and the next the sky darkened. The cart rolled to a stop, and before she could get down, Alistair was there, his hand out to her.

"May I help you?" he smiled at her.

Her heart pulsing frantically, she accepted his hand and watched as three young men scurried around the vehicle, one taking the horses to what she assumed was a nearby stable another driving the wagon and the third hefted the two bags from the vehicle and strode in front of them through the doors to the Duke's office and apartment.

She followed, soaking in the ambiance yet terrified of the night to come and the possible decisions she'd have to make. When she held her hands in front of her, they shook and she didn't know if the trembling was because of anticipation or fear.

Once inside and they were left alone, he spoke calmly, "You need not be afraid of me, lass," Alistair said, his deep voice enticing her with unknown promises. "I don't mean you any harm, although I've got to admit you're a wee bonny lass; one I'd certainly enjoy making my own."

She sucked in a huge lungful of air, her legs barely able to keep herself standing. "I..."

"Ah, I see you're at a loss for words. If the way you're staring at me is any indication, you like the looks of me as much as I appreciate your beauty. Perhaps the night won't be boring."

"Arrogant man," she swatted his hand away. "I'm more afraid of myself and my feelings than you."

He let out a roar of laughter that lightened the mood. "Would you like to take a look around the apartment? Lord Broon said there would be food for us in the kitchen and a bottle of wine if you care to indulge." He strode through a door looking over his shoulder at her as if he waited on something.

She watched him go, the swagger of his strides, the confidence emanating from him, and knew she'd hopelessly lost her heart to this handsome man. Walking through the sitting room, she peaked in various doors. For obvious reasons there was only one bedroom and one bed. A tiny shiver of apprehension and excitement shimmied down her spine.

He wasn't going to talk his way into her heart and her bed so quickly, not on the first night. Although if truth be told, she knew if he wanted her in his bed, she wouldn't object and if he gave her enough motivation, she'd never be able to tell him no.

Stepping into the kitchen and watching him hum a lively tune while he set out plates and utensils, "There's only one bed."

He shrugged broad shoulders as if he didn't have a single care in the whole wide world, "I'll take the couch," he said, handing her a glass of wine. "Do you like meat pies, lass?"

"That won't be comfortable for a man of your size, and, yes, meat pies are one of my favorites." She really felt as if she was babbling. "Thank you for the wine."

"I've slept worse places in my life, and the wine is compliments of Lord Broon." He shrugged, a glint of something indefinable in his eyes and looking as if he truly didn't care if he slept on a tiny little sofa.

"You're so big," she murmured, letting her gaze roam from the tips of his shoes to the smile on his lips.

"I'm a man," he said as if *what else would I be besides large.* "And you, my petite, are tiny and delicate, a fragile flower who needs tender loving care in order to blossom."

She felt heat rise to her cheeks and covered them with her hands. She was tall for a woman and she didn't think she'd ever been considered a delicate flower. Part of that thought warmed her heart, and the other feeling was to put him in his place. Then she stiffened, and on the defense said, "There are men no larger than me."

He laughed and she liked the sound of his laughter, one more attribute binding her to him. "True, but you're dealing with me and I'm charged to protect you with my life not ravish you, although if you were willing, I wouldn't object."

Her heart staggered, changing direction. She pulled herself inside the shell she'd built around herself for several years, wishing she wasn't a job to him but something more.

"I've survived on my own for quite some time. I'm sure I don't need a man's protection." The truth was she craved to have someone want to stand by her and help her through difficult times. For years after her parent's death, she had felt alone and unloved.

"Ah, lass, I didn't mean to hurt your feelings. No one, even a man, should have to do it alone. Let's eat and when your belly is full and you're able to relax, perhaps you'll see things my way."

"Just what is your way of thinking?" she asked, staring at him over the rim of her glass. "I'm not a whore." She regretted the words as soon as they left her mouth.

"Never thought you were. Miss Graham wouldn't hire a lady of the evening, a dirty puzzle."

"Oh," she said, unable to think of anything else.

"Don't want to give you all my secrets now, lass," he laughed, pulling out a chair for her before sitting down himself. "What is your way of thinking?" he challenged her.

She swallowed a bit too much wine and started to cough, "I'm overwhelmed by the situation we're in, and you might need several weeks to figure that out since I'm not going to tell you and make figuring me out an easy task."

"That long?"

For the next few minutes they ate in silence. She mulled over how she felt about this Alistair and all the things he'd said to her, and still she found herself no closer to the truth of her feelings for him.

"I'll take the sofa," she stood too quickly and had to sit back down.

"Not on my watch you won't."

"I'd fight you for it but I know the outcome. Truly, we are adults. I've shared a bed with my brother and there's no reason we can't both sleep there." Her heart raced while sweat beaded on her forehead, knowing her feelings for Alistair were a far cry from a brother.

"Ah, lass you wound me. I've no intention of ever being as a brother to you. We could share but I'm not sure I want to be responsible for what comes during the night."

She didn't want him for a second brother either, although she was ready to disown her current one. "Your legs would hang over the couch if you tried to sleep there."

"Or my head. No, I'd pick the floor instead of something that threatened to divide me into two pieces. A soft pillow and a cover is all I need. No, a willing woman would be nice..." he gazed at her, one eyebrow cocked suggestively.

The intensity of his eyes sent a wave of heat to her cheeks. "I can sleep on the floor." Suddenly, she couldn't breathe and she swallowed hard, attempting to clear her throat.

"If both of us are going to sleep on the floor, it only makes sense that we should share the bed." He laughed again.

"So, what is it we are doing? Talking in circles?" She poured herself a second glass of wine before standing once more and walking to the bedroom, hoping he would follow.

He was suddenly behind her, his arms around her, pulling her against the hardness of his chest. His hands spanned her waist, and she felt the heat emanating from him into her. His moist lips pressed against her neck and the softness of his beard left a unique sensation.

She closed her eyes, knowing he could do anything he wanted but hoping he would respect her enough not to press the issue this first night. "The bed is huge, just waiting for the two of us to share it."

"We could place pillows down the middle."

"Ah, lass, if you wanted me enough that would not keep me from your side of the bed."

She did want him, but not that much and not tonight. "I need to get to know you and who you are. Right now all I know about you is that you work for Lord Broon. I'm attracted to you in the most elemental ways and you're a large man. I know nothing about your character."

"It's enough for me to know you're attracted to me. In the most elemental ways, whatever does that mean?" He chuckled softly, seeming to enjoy himself and their conversation.

"I'm not at liberty to say. It might go straight to your head." She told him, tilting her head a bit to one side.

"So, lass, we share the bed with a barrier of pillows. That could prove interesting come morning, but I can't give you my word I won't compromise you."

Chapter Six

At his question of marriage Larena sucked in a lungful of air and her world tilted crazily. "Marry you? Why? You don't love me."

He shrugged lazily, gazing at her, "Does love matter? We care for each other and get along quite well. I do enjoy your company, specifically our conversations as well as the way you seem to melt in my arms."

Melt in his arms was so true. She collected her thoughts, trying to think of something to tell him that would sound reasonable. "Everything you say is true, but marriage is for a lifetime. You're talking about a few months of companionship."

"We've known each other over a year. I suppose you can sleep on the question, but a marriage will simply stop all the gossip you so abhor." Gavin managed to put their situation in a simplistic manner although compelling.

"I would marry for other reasons than stopping the rumors from flying through the ton. The gossip will end soon enough." Her heart shut down for a moment, and she felt the pain of this ridiculous proposal. She'd always fantasized about a love that would transcend all time. Not a marriage between two people who enjoyed conversation.

"As I said, I care for you more than anyone I've ever met. I suppose it could be love, not sure the meaning of the word though. What about you? Can you swear undying love to me or anyone else?" He challenged her.

She choked back the answer trying to jump from her lips and remained silent, moisture forming a barrier in her throat.

"No, I see you can't. Do you enjoy my company?" he queried, leaning toward her as if to better hear her answer.

Speechless she could only nod at him.

"Ah, that would be a yes then." He smiled, clasping his hands behind his back and rocking on his heels, seeming to empathize with her moments of confusion and indecision.

"I should retire for the night. Would you have a shirt I could borrow. It seems your siblings' wives left nothing of that sort." She tugged on the bodice of her gown that constantly slipped downward. If she wasn't careful, there could very well be a repeat of the other night.

"That would be too intimate if we're not an engaged couple, don't you think?" he asked trailing a finger across her exposed collarbone. "Wait, let me think. I've seen you with almost nothing on. What would the esteemed members of the aristocracy think about that, I wonder?"

"My nakedness in the bedroom adjoining yours would be even more intimate. I'm already ruined. What more can be done to my reputation? Borrowing one of your shirts would not cause further gossip since no one but the two of us would know." His attempt at psychological blackmail was working.

She had come to London in search of a husband and in time a family. The first second she set eyes on Gavin Broon, she wanted him and had been half in love. But now she didn't know what love was. At every turn and with The Duchess' help he found a way to compromise her. In her mind, that could not be love, only lust for his purposes.

Now she had two choices, go to the hunting lodge as his paramour or go as his wife. For a few moments she weighed the pros and cons. "All right then, I'll marry you."

"You won't regret your decision." He slipped the ring on her finger. Pulling her into his arms, he pressed a tender kiss to her lips. The touch was sweet and gentle and asked for nothing in return. It was something she never expected from him and was nothing like the other night, yet the caress still sent heat waves pumping through her body.

"I pray that I don't. Now about that shirt, I really don't want to sleep with nothing on." She watched the strange male reaction emerge on his face and immediately regretted putting something in that vein in his head.

"No, Larena, not tonight but you'll soon be quite comfortable sleeping with nothing on your beautiful body. Night clothes are for taking off as they only get in the way of more delightful pastimes." His sultry voice seemed to purr with sexual innuendos.

She closed her eyes, remembering the time in the gazebo. He

awakened so many sensations that evening, ones that if she were honest with herself she wanted to pursue.

She looked up, her eyes wide open in so many ways. He'd introduced her to new pleasures, and she yearned for so much more than he presented her with that evening, "Gavin Broon, what I do know is that I don't want anyone but you seeing me with nothing on or touching me intimately."

A purely masculine and surprisingly possessive smile graced his lips. "I'm glad to hear that. We are in agreement in this, so I'm sure there are more things we'll deal with nicely. I would kill anyone who saw you with nothing on but your delicate embroidered stockings."

She yawned, trying to ignore his statements and feeling utterly defenseless in this verbal battle. It was a fake yawn but she really needed to escape to another room or she'd be in bed with him, her virginity gone before the wedding night. She realized quite clearly that unlike a few of her cousins, she wanted her wedding night to be the first time she slept with him.

"I'm going to bed. Can you find that shirt for me?"

"Sure you don't want to stay a bit longer? Have some more wine?" his voice deepened to a throaty rumble, clearly meant to seduce. Yet she guessed he was teasing.

"Don't be a tease. You've kept me out of your bed this long. You're not going to entice me there tonight when you have something else in mind, something called a wedding night and my virginity. Just get the shirt for me and I'll leave to my bedroom." She was rushing to depart, knowing the downfall of staying too much longer.

"You do have a point. Even if you stayed for another glass of wine, your dress could slip to your feet if you moved the wrong way. I'm truly going to have to find something else for you to wear tomorrow."

She was sorely tempted to have another glass of wine. "Perhaps you wouldn't mind pouring me some and I can take it to my room. This conversation has not been good for sleep. I'm totally alert. Wide awake, my eyes wide open. Wine has a way of helping me to sleep."

"And I'm completely aroused and ready for whatever might happen." He poured her a full glass then rummaged in his valise until he pulled out a clean shirt. "This will cover all of you, at least to your knees. I've seen your knees and they're quite beautiful."

"Gavin," she paused, "that's no way to send me alone to my room. You promised and I'm going to hold you to your word."

"Very well then," he leaned against his bedpost, arms crossed in front of him and watched her depart the bedchamber.

After closing the door behind her, she let the oversize garment slip to the floor. Too late she realized she'd never be able to unlace the corset by herself. She really had few qualms about Gavin seeing her in her corset and petticoats tonight after their last conversation. He'd already seen her almost as naked as the day she was born, she reminded herself, and he hadn't ravished her yet.

Hoping he was still awake and not in bed, she slipped through the adjoining door without knocking. "Gavin?"

He turned, his chest bare and she recalled the last time she'd seen his naked chest and touched him, explored the muscled expanse of his chest. She paused, sucking air as she tried to breathe and calm her racing heart. He was just as magnificent as she remembered.

His slow smile was calculated as well as enchanting. "I see you wanted more of me. Another provocative kiss maybe? One that would test your strength of will and mine." One eyebrow rose a fraction. "Ah, you need me to undress you again. It's a pity women need so much help dressing and undressing. Will you need me tomorrow morning?"

"Please," she sighed petulantly. "Just undo the bloody thing and I'll disappear until morning."

He let his head fall back and roared with laughter. "I do enjoy life better when you swear. Women should really learn to let their emotions out more often. Doing so releases so much tension. Let's see, are you angry or frustrated? Maybe confused and tempted. Do I arouse you, Larena? I'd like that."

More than he could ever guess. "Gavin? Please unlace my corset so I can breathe again and so I can go to sleep. And if you really need an answer to your ridiculous question, yes, you tempt me beyond endurance. I want to know about a woman's pleasure and this climax stuff you teased me with. If I weren't so terrified, I'd ask you to teach me right now."

"As soon as we are wed, I'll teach you everything you want to know, my little darlin'. Ask and you will receive." He bent close to her ear and whispered, "I don't want you to be terrified of me ever."

She shivered, feeling his warm breath against her and tried to calm herself. "There is that. You were more than willing to educate me the other night before we were interrupted." She put her hands on her hips, turning so he'd have better access to the laces. "And now you want to wait. How is that? Men make no sense whatsoever."

"We could try tonight, but in my condition and state of mind, I might not stop at a woman's pleasure."

"In your state of mind?"

"There is such a thing as a man's pleasure too, and if I pursued that course you would lose your virginity before the wedding night. No, it's really best if you sleep, as planned, in the adjoining room, alone."

He unlaced the corset, pressing kisses across her back as he did so. She trembled in response to the sweet feel of his teeth gently scuffing her skin. Closing her eyes, she didn't move, didn't even breathe. His hands settled on her waist. She clung to the front of her corset with both hands and waited for what she wasn't sure.

"You need to go to your bed. Now," he whispered close to her ear, tongue whirling inside for a half-second. The gesture sent another wave of heat pulsing through her. "Before I take this any farther."

"Yes, that's what I need to do," she mindlessly agreed, unable to think clearly. If he told her she needed go to his bed, she would have followed him. She didn't have a coherent thought in her muddled head.

He guided her through the door and to the bed. Placing a chaste kiss on her forehead, he swept her into his arms and set her down.

"Get under the covers," he told her. "You need to stay warm and cozy so you don't come seeking me out."

She did and regarded him closely as he pulled the sheet and blankets over her. She didn't want him to leave. Yet she said nothing as she watched his back disappear with the closing of the door. A deep yearning for him settled in parts of her she'd never even thought about before meeting Gavin Broon.

Unable to relax, Larena sat up, leaning against the backboard, trying

to make sense of this evening. She picked up the glass of wine she'd set on an end table, swirling the contents before sipping. She wondered if he'd take another midnight ride to somewhere. She'd never had the chance to ask him why he left in the night or where he went. Sometime she'd like to go with him.

Pushing the covers down and walking to the window, she watched for a while but saw nothing. As it had happened before, she heard grunts and groans emanating from his room. She came to the conclusion that somehow he was working off his need to find pleasure.

She could not sleep either. Frustration ate at her but she had no idea how to ease it and find sleep. She wandered the room then sat back on the bed, sipping the wine, hoping it would make her sleepy. Whatever it was he was doing in there didn't stop.

She finished the glass of wine, wishing she had the rest of the bottle. A quick search of the furniture in the room, she found half a bottle of brandy. Smiling, she poured some into her glass. The drink burned a path down her throat and where she'd not felt the wine, the brandy sent heat pummeling through her body and an even stranger feeling of disconnect.

Still the noise continued until it did not. She woke from a dream. The prison cart unloaded its cargo to a ship and the people were herded below to the bowels of the vessel and were tied to posts.

She cried out for Gavin, but no one came, no one rescued her. Nausea welled in her stomach from the stench surrounding her. A guard pulled her to him and once more she cried out, praying for rescue when his beefy hands explored her.

She bolted upright, a slick sheen of sweat covering all of her. His shirt was damp from the perspiration. In the darkness of the night the terror had never before been so real. Even though she pulled the blankets around, her she couldn't stop the shaking.

"Larena," the voice startled her yet gave comfort at the same time. "What's wrong? I heard you scream my name."

"Gavin."

"Hush, everything is alright. It's just a bad dream. No one is going to hurt you. Talk to me."

"I need you," she told him, her body shaking from the chill

encompassing her. "I need you to keep me warm. I'm so cold. Hold me, please."

It seemed he hesitated for a moment, "Bloody eyes," he murmured before joining her and pulling her against him. "Can you tell me about the dream?"

She shook her head at him, knowing she didn't want to relive the nightmare. "Just keep your arms around me, keep me safe from the darkness and the terrors of the night. I need you so much."

"Damnation," he swore softly. "This should never have happened. Damn Cale."

Larena leaned into him, felt the warmth and the strength that was Gavin, and she knew she wanted to have these feelings for the rest of her life. She didn't know how long she slept or what time it was when he woke her with tender kisses across the back of her neck.

"Rise and shine. It's time to get up, little darlin'. We've a long day ahead of us and the sooner we get started, well then..." he paused to draw her hair away and kiss her earlobe.

"The sooner we will get there. What are you doing in my bed?" she turned in his arms, confused for the moment.

"You don't recall? I'm offended." It seemed he tried to stop the masculine grin from spreading across his face.

She searched her mind for the answers, "I had a nightmare and you kept the darkness away."

He smiled, kissing her lips then, "You need to close your eyes so I can leave the room. While I don't care if you see me naked, I suppose since we've waited this long for the wedding night, we shouldn't spoil anything."

"Seeing you naked would spoil the wedding night?" she questioned. "Is your body that spectacular?"

He roared with laughter again. "You never cease to surprise me. I don't believe so. You see, I'm extremely aroused and I don't want to frighten you."

"A virgin."

"Well, yes," he hesitated, raising one eyebrow in silent question. "Would my fully aroused body scare you?"

"I don't know." She smiled, thinking how much she did want to see him fully aroused.

"Then best we don't leave this to chance. I'm not about to have our wedding night ruined."

"Gavin," she crossed her arms. "What am I going to wear? I certainly can't wear that horrible gown all day."

"I thought of that too. While it's not the best solution, I remembered a few things. Mother never liked to throw away anything, so I prowled the attic after you left for bed last night and found some of my old clothes I wore when I was a boy. Something might fit better than the gown."

"Britches and a shirt?" she clapped her hands together, a smile on her face, eager to try the new type of clothing. "Before Tavia left we bought her some and she said they were so comfortable, much more so than the dresses and corsets we wear."

"I'll dress then bring them to you. Now close your eyes."

"Alright, if you insist," she said, her hand over her eyes and watched as he sauntered from the room. All she could see was his back but she silently applauded everything about him.

A few minutes later he returned with the garments. "You peeked."

She was shaking her head, trying to deny the accusation but unable to keep the grin from her lips. "How did you know?"

"Your cheeks and neck are a brilliant crimson. Here, as soon as you're ready we can eat and be on our way."

Still sitting on the bed, she looked over each piece of clothing, settling on a dark brown pair of pants and a white shirt. Slipping out of Gavin's shirt she folded it and set it aside to bring back to him.

The pants were a little tight around the hips but otherwise fit. The others were all smaller. The shirt was large but thankfully was made of material thick enough she hoped to hide her breasts.

"Gavin," she poked her head around the opening of the door. "I'm ready," She stepped into the room. "What do you think?"

His eyes widened and his mouth dropped. "Perhaps the oversize gown would be better."

Her heart fell. She'd thought this was perfect for the carriage ride. "What's wrong with these?" Her hands followed the curve of her body from beneath her arms to her thighs. She had no idea how the simple move would affect him, but the way his eyes suddenly shimmered and heated with fire, told her she provoked him in some mercurial way.

"Nothing if you want me to ravish you right here," he said, his voice a deep throaty whisper.

"You don't like them?" she turned sideways then all the way around, enjoying the fact she was in control for the moment.

He pulled her into his arms, "I like them too much. Little darlin', I can see all of you, the sweet curve of your breasts and the enticing outline of your nipples. And your derrière is begging for me to feel its feminine curves. If you don't take care, we won't leave this room anytime soon."

She put her hands on her hips and moving away from him straightened her spine, "These will have to do. If you must know, nothing else even came close to fitting."

"I don't want anyone but me seeing you." His voice a low growl sent another shiver of heat down her spine.

"We'll be in the carriage, so no one else will see me." She saw the eggs and bacon on the table, her stomach suddenly rumbling. She was famished she realized.

"Not when we stop to rest or eat."

"Famished." She picked up a piece of bacon, breaking off a piece and stuffing it in her mouth. Chewing slowly, "Gavin, I'm sure you'll think of something in those instances. Perhaps a jacket, one of yours would do nicely. This is what I'm going to wear. It's all I have." Before she sat down to eat, she raced back to her room to retrieve his shirt. "Here you go."

He put it in his bag. "You should have some of your own things by the time we reach the next town, well the afternoon after. If everything goes as planned, Alistair and hopefully Tyna should be there shortly after us."

"Is our next stop the hunting lodge?"

"No, we'll stay overnight in the small village below the lodge. It's there we'll marry, hopefully in the morning, and I plan on our wedding night in the lodge."

She mulled that over for a while. "I never wanted anything simple, always dreamed of a large wedding with all my family and friends, but a quick I do in a town where there is no one I love..."

"It's for the best we wed as soon as possible. As my wife I've more means available to protect you."

"I've been so foolish," she sighed setting her fork on the table, suddenly unable to eat another bite. She thought back on all the impetuous things she did. Why she was just as impulsive as Tavia and Tira, and she condemned them for their rash decisions.

"Rest assured, what happened the other day is not your fault." It seemed he spoke with conviction.

"Of course it is," she disagreed. "I set everything in motion, and now it's coming back to haunt me and you as well. What happened yesterday was directly related to my previous actions. If I'd never met Cole or acted so recklessly, none of this would have happened."

"You relied on Tyna who in turn trusted the word of her brother. There was nothing more either of you could have done."

"I barely know Tyna. Why did I believe her? She could have been a part of what happened."

"If you like, once our lives are more settled, you can have another wedding. I'm sure The Duchess would love to plan one, just as she did for Eveleen and Tavia. Ella was not pleased when she discovered what I intended. Tavia and Addie would surely love to be included."

"She would but...they all would, but it seems after the fact is a bit strange. Eveleen and Logan had a second wedding, though as did Tavia and James." And that wedding was fraught with danger just as first one had been controversial, in haste and against Eveleen's will.

"And it was fine until—"

"Yes, until someone tried to murder Tavia. We'll see. I want to get through with this wedding before I think of another one." She realized after the words were said, get through with it was probably not what he wanted to hear. "I'm sorry. I guess I should take that back. This is all so sudden and in many ways terrifying."

Without replying he drummed his fingers on the tabletop staring, at her as if he could read her mind. "If you're finished eating, we should leave. The trip is a long one and if you recall, we're running from the law."

"My shoes. I need to get them."

He waited at the door. She didn't miss his chuckle. At least the heels on her boots were small. She looked ridiculous, but there was little she could do about it. She was covered somewhat.

Before they left he wrapped his waistcoat around her, covering her. She slipped her arms into the sleeves and pulled the sides closed. "Now there is nothing to be seen."

Days later darkness had fallen when they finally stopped in front of an inn. The village stretched along the base of a valley. Even in the blackness, mountains rose above in a picturesque display silhouetted by a slivery moon.

"Larena, time to wake up. Rise and shine, pretty one." He whispered, his voice close to her ear, tickling and enticing as well.

She opened her eyes, stretching and yawning. Every muscle in her body ached from the sideways position she slept. Inside the rustic inn gaslights lit the foyer, brightening its natural darkness. The high beams and the long stairways were beautiful. "Where did you find this place?"

"My family owns it," he murmured as if he didn't want her to hear. "Many of the employees came here when mother died. They are all loyal to the Broons.

"I believe there is much about you I don't know."

When she walked down the flower-strewn aisle on Alistair's arm, her beauty stunned Gavin. With the help of Ella, he'd bought a wedding dress as well as other items before they left London. The cut of the white satin gown was simple but molded against Larena's curves like a second skin. He inhaled a deep breath, realizing marrying Larena was the best decision he'd ever made.

Tyna waited as a witness at the end of the long walkway. She wore a dress purchased in the village just this morning.

They stopped and Alistair gave her hand to Gavin then took his place as a witness beside him. He smiled at her, seeing her anxiety through the veil. Ella had handpicked everything from the dress to the shoes and the veil. She wore blue garters on her stockings, he was told, and the pearl earrings she wore were borrowed from her aunt Charlotte. Alistair carried the ring he was going to place on her finger.

The minister nodded and the few people assembled in the room sat down. He cleared his throat and began a short sermon on love and loyalty. After that a hymn played and more words were exchanged between them.

Gavin held her shaking hands in his, smiling at her in an attempt to reassure her. He'd wanted this wedding to mean something even though her family wasn't in attendance to stand witness and lend support. He'd mentioned a few of his mentors from his childhood who now lived here.

The somber vows were spoken with quiet sincerity then the ring was given to her. He felt the impact to the depth of his soul when he slipped the ring on her finger. She was his now for better or for worse and in sickness and in health for all eternity. He believed in his vows with all his heart. And forsaking all others.

Then, "With the powers invested in me, I pronounce you husband and wife. You may kiss the bride."

Smiling broadly, he lifted the veil and was pleased to see the soft smile on her lips. He bent and kissed her, knowing what he meant to share with her later this evening would not be so chaste.

Holding her hand, he stared down the aisle. When he returned his gaze to his new wife, she looked at him, her expression unreadable yet he was sure he saw a quiet peace within her expression. He hoped she was pleased. The attending people rose to acknowledge their first appearance as the Lord and Lady Broon Duke and Duchess of Millsglen.

He never cared about the title but was thankful now that it was his, and he didn't have to rely on anyone for help protecting Larena from the authorities. Anyone would have second thoughts where a duke was involved. The people working at the inn and most in the town were loyal to his family and would guard her with everything they possessed.

He bent close to her. "Are you happy?"

"Now that it's over, yes." She squeezed his hand.

"Me too, I couldn't wait for this to end and we can celebrate its culmination," he said.

She laughed and it pleased him, "You just want to teach me those things you talked about earlier."

"You know me so well. Come on, there's no reason to dally. Our pleasure will come soon enough. Now is the time to celebrate our nuptials"

Once outside they made their way via carriage to the inn where they'd stayed the night. It was too late to ride to the hunting lodge this evening. The morning wedding he'd hoped for turned into a later one. He'd arranged for a small celebration at the inn and reserved a room upstairs.

The table was strewn with a variety of dishes all tempting to the pallet. The chef at the inn's restaurant had been the chef at the castle in Scotland when Gavin was growing up. He'd stolen many a meat pie from his kitchen when the man wasn't looking as well as other delightful sweets.

When his mother passed on, most of the castle's staff left the failing castle to find employment here. They were all eager to wish Gavin well and congratulate the lucky couple.

"Are you hungry?" Gavin asked, leading her to the food and picking up a plate and utensils then handing a set to her. "What would you like to eat?" He held a strawberry between his fingers and touched her mouth with it, tempting her to touch his fingers with her lips.

She rose to his challenge and let him feed her the berry, "We're really married, aren't we?" she whispered, softly accepting her plate then and with each moment her cheeks grew hotter. "Look at all these people who barely know us."

"They want the free food," he laughed, casually tossing a grape and catching it in his mouth. "Many were my childhood friends. When my brothers teased me, I'd often find refuge where they were working. Over there," he pointed to a corner in the room, "Mary used to clean my parent's solar and all the chambers upstairs. She would listen to all my tales of woe. And Aaron worked in our stables. He used to let me ride any horse I wanted, and he'd take me on the different trails around the estate. I was pleased when they remembered me and wanted to wish us happiness in our marriage. So I promptly invited each and everyone to the reception."

"That was really nice of you," she told him, lowering her sooty lashes until they rested against her pale flesh.

"And self-serving, I didn't want to celebrate our union alone."

"I'm nervous about tonight," she told him bluntly. "I don't know why but this all seems so new to me. I almost wish you'd compromised me before the wedding then I wouldn't be worried about something I'm ignorant about."

"Don't be nervous or afraid. You've had a taste of what's to come and you enjoyed my kisses, the feel of my hands on your body. This is the way it's supposed to be."

"You had affairs."

"That's different. Men aren't supposed to be virgins when they wed. They are supposed to understand how to pleasure their wives."

"Shhh, someone might here you." The continuing obviousness of her innocence and the beautiful blushes gave him reason to believe in his future with her, and he was overcome with his good fortune.

"I love it when you blush so delightfully." He held up a glass of wine, "Here's to my beautiful wife and our night of pleasure."

"And may you have lots of children," someone called from the behind them as if they overheard the conversation between them.

"Here, here, kiss the bride," and the chant grew, taking over the room and reverberating into the rafters.

"I believe I'm going to have to kiss you or they'll never stop," pausing a moment, "not that I need a reason," He moistened his lips, bending to meet hers. Knowing what the well wishers wanted, he swept his tongue across her lips, opening them while he pulled her closer, his hand splayed upon her back. For a moment she responded in kind, accepting him into her. The applause and cheering was deafening.

Slowly he pulled away, smiling and gently tracing a line across her jaw then down her neck. "I can barely breathe," she said so softly he had to bend forward to understand what she was saying. "You never fail to steal my breath and make my heart race."

"You are beautiful. I'd like to whisk you away right now and forget all the well-wishers. I want you all to myself."

"We should cut the cake," she said. "Perhaps then we can leave without anyone taking offense."

"You are as eager as I am to find our bed." He turned her so they faced their new-found friends and reacquainted older ones then lifting their glasses in salute to them.

"I wouldn't say that, but I'm exhausted from all the traveling as well as the trauma of the days before."

"It's the wine talking," he told her, bending to kiss her cheek and enjoying the slow rise of heat.

"I haven't had any yet," she told him, "and you know that."

"Then I best do something to remedy the situation." He left her side for a few seconds and retrieved two glasses. "Here, this will relax you and hopefully not put you to sleep before we can consummate our marital status. The last thing I want is for my bride to fall asleep before I can school her."

The lively sound of bagpipes filled the air and the dancing began. She sipped, seeming to watch the gaiety and the laughter. They were having so much fun. Tyna and Alistair whirled around the room with the others. He wondered about the two people who seemed to have become a couple over night.

"Would you like to join them?" he asked, taking her glass of wine to set it on the table.

"It looks like so much fun," She held out her arms to him. They merged with the dancing group, the music changing to a different tune, some slow and haunting others gay and lively. It seemed as if hours passed before they stopped.

She leaned into him, breathing deeply. "I need to rest."

"As do I."

She drank the wine and danced then it seemed everything was repeated. He lost count of the dances as well as the wine. The gaiety enticed him, a man who'd never liked the frivolity of balls.

She leaned into him, pressing her body into his, her eyes slightly glazed over. "We still haven't cut the cake."

At that moment, Alistair and Tyna stood beside them. "People are thinking of going home. Shouldn't you cut the cake?" Alistair asked. "Not wishing to intrude on your fun but the hour grows late."

Alistair held up a crystal glass and with a knife sent a ringing tone throughout the room. The musicians stopped playing. The guest stopped dancing and everyone turned their attention to Alistair.

"The Duke and Duchess of Millsglen will cut the cake now. I hope all you stay and enjoy a piece. There is still plenty of food and wine so stay longer and enjoy."

Gavin took her hand in his. The cake was cut and a piece to share set on a plate. She broke off a small piece and fed it to him. He was so tempted to spread at least a small amount of the confection on her face so he could lick it off. It could be the beginning of this night's seduction of Larena.

"Gavin, don't."

He grinned, knowing he'd have more fun licking the icing from her lips than being polite. He tried to be delicate but she grabbed at his hand to keep it away. The cake and icing smeared on her mouth and cheek. "You're beautiful with a bit more decoration."

Slowly, he touched her lips with his thumb smearing a bit of the icing then licking it with tip of his tongue. He continued, much to the appreciation of the guests. "You taste wonderful, you and the cake and I'm sure all of you. I plan on tasting every inch of your silken flesh in not too very long."

"You shouldn't have done that," she said, her eyes narrowing.

"Why ever not? You can't mean to tell me you're not enjoying this as much as I am." Yet he wondered how she would retaliate.

The tiny sound from the back of her throat gave him reason to smile. "Ah, you can't talk and you like my attentions. Admit it, little darlin'. You want more of the same."

"Gavin Broon, you are a wicked, wicked man. Do you have no scruples? Will you stop at nothing to get your way with me?" she sighed into his mouth, her breath whisper-soft against his flesh.

"Time to go to our room," he told her, and grabbing a bottle of wine, he lifted it high for the people to see and with his arm around her waist turned toward the stairs. He tilted the bottle to his lips and drank.

Then he handed it to Larena. She slanted him a puzzled look then, shrugging her delicate shoulders, drank. Swaying into him and laughing, "Have I had too much wine?" She smiled sweetly at him, licking her lips with a tiny pink tongue sending him a signal she didn't understand.

"I wouldn't know. How much have you had?" he asked her but thinking he felt a bit muzzled, she was so much smaller. Inwardly he groaned, realizing the wedding night might be put on hold. It seemed he had a way of jinxing the consummation of their relationship.

Pulling her closer, he ran his hand along her tiny ribcage stopping when he reached the underside of her breast. She drank from the bottle again and handed it to him.

"I've never felt like this before. The walls seem to be spinning," she murmured through a hushed whisper. "Are you seducing me? We aren't even in our room yet." She tipped the bottle of wine, drinking a bit more.

He'd needed her relaxed but not drunk. Gavin wanted her to remember this night vividly. In her state she wouldn't recall anything. Stopping on the landing where their room was located, he kissed her again, his hands bracketing her face. She tasted of wine and her skin smelled of the sugary icing he painted on her. She gave everything to him, making tiny little sounds that sent heat pulsing through his body straight to his shaft.

When he let her go, she drank again then handed the bottle to him. It was nearly empty. They reached the door and he swept her into his arms, kissing her as they crossed the threshold.

The room was spacious. Servants had set a fire blazing and on the hearth, they placed bread and cheese along with another bottle of wine. He laughed softly, realizing the irony of the situation. He set her on her feet but kept his hands around her waist to steady her.

"Look, more wine," she sat down on the fur rug in front of the fireplace. "I don't think I should have any more."

"No, you probably shouldn't but tonight is not about what you should do, it's about what you want. Larena, would you like one more glass of wine before we go to bed? Before you see me naked and fully aroused?"

She moved her head a bit and he took that for a yes, "I'd like food more too." She mumbled getting her words crossed. "Know you," she paused for several seconds, "I forgot... Oh, all that, that remember...food and I don't remember, did I eat...if I ate anything. Did I eat?"

"Some," he broke out laughing then followed with breaking off a chunk of the bread and handed it to her. She reached for a slice of cheese.

"All I recall is the strawberry." Delicately, she placed one on her hand then holding it with her fingers, murmuring, "berry, like would you?"

"If you're feeding it to me" She placed the fruit on his mouth. He took the strawberry then held her hand, sucking on each fingertip before kissing her palm, letting his tongue draw circles there.

"I'm not sure what just happened exactly. What did I..." She finished the wine in the bottle they took from the reception before sipping at the new glass of wine and staring at him with half closed eyes.

"You're postponing your instruction," he laughed at her antics even though the wedding night would come tomorrow at the hunting lodge as he originally planned. She was in no condition to make decisions or understand the new sensations he meant to introduce her to his evening.

She smiled sweetly at him, pensively chewing on the bread he gave her. "I guess I am, but know you, I'm relaxed—very. I think I would quite enjoy anything you did to me."

"Tomorrow when I ask you if you enjoyed our lovemaking, you won't remember anything." Yet he didn't want this night to end. "Would you like to get more comfortable?"

"I would. Is this the beginning?"

"The beginning of what?" He wanted to hear what she had to say.

"My lessons?"

"If you wish to think it is, then yes. It can be whatever you like." He sat down behind her, his legs spread and adjusted her so he could reach the tiny pearl buttons that ran the length of her wedding gown. His large fingers fumbled with each one, and he was tempted to wrench the fabric apart but he wanted her to decide what happened to the gown. He knew some brides kept the dress in hopes their daughter, if they had one, would wear it at their wedding.

"What's taking you so long?" she sighed. "I want you to kiss me again. Maybe you could kiss my neck. I think you did that once a long time ago. I like it wherever you kiss me."

"A long time ago?" One dark eyebrow rose in speculation. "Kissing and all that, will all come later," he said, thoroughly relishing this moment even though he understood there would be no lovemaking between them this night. She fascinated him, completely and fully, "The buttons are tiny and my fingers are large and there must be at least one hundred of them."

"There are a lot," she acknowledged. "Tyna had trouble with them but they are beautiful. How did you come by this dress?"

"Ella had it made at your dressmakers. She thought you would like something simple but elegant. She told me the pearl buttons and Belgium lace made it exactly what you would like. Ella wanted to be here and in some ways was here even though she couldn't be in person." Now he was beginning to sound a bit drunk, slurring some of his words.

She leaned against him, her hand coming up to rest on his face. "Did you know she's pregnant again? They are going to have a second child soon. She must really enjoy sex with her husband."

Gavin couldn't help himself, he laughed once again at her remark. "And if we ever have the right environment, you will really enjoy sex with me too." He kissed the nape of her neck, his tongue drawing tiny circles before he gently closed his teeth. "Sit up and I'll finish with the buttons."

She obliged, reaching for the wine. He was so tempted to bid her stop. Not only would they not consummate the marriage tonight, but she'd wake with a blinding headache in the morning. He accepted the fact they would get a late start tomorrow.

Surprising him, she set the glass down. "I'm hot," she waved her hand in front of her face. "Is it you or the wine?"

"A little of both, and I'm finished with the buttons." He slipped the fragile material down her slender arms. "Stand up and you can step out of the dress. I'll help you."

Using his shoulders to brace herself, she rose. Her dress pooled around her feet. Slowly, he loosened the ties of her corset then turned his attention to her stockings.

"You should get comfortable. Are you hot too? Let me help you." She fumbled with his cravat, unable to make headway. She sighed then pulled the shirt from the waistband of his trousers, her fingers resting on the fastenings.

Gavin sucked air when her soft fingers found his flesh and explored. He wasn't sure he could withstand her ministrations, but he wanted to give her everything she asked for tonight. "You can do whatever you want."

She turned and he wasn't at all sure where to direct his gaze. Under normal circumstances it wouldn't matter. He could look and touch wherever he wanted. At the moment his gaze was drawn to her cleavage and what was beneath her undergarments. Ella had also purchased as a wedding gift lingerie she told him that would leave him breathless. He'd planned on giving it to her tonight but it could wait for tomorrow and their real wedding night.

"I believe...wrong order. First waistcoat," she sighed softly almost wistfully, "I just can't seem to say what I want." She helped him from his waistcoat then with his help, she undid his cravat and started on the buttons. When she finally finished, she sat back and smiled at him. The flat of her hands rested on his chest then she slipped his shirt from his shoulders.

"Is that better?"

"Almost," while he didn't dare take his pants off, he had to loosen the fastening. His fingers hovered there.

"Let me do that."

"Just the fastenings," he warned.

When finished, she leaned against him. Her breathing slowed and within a few minutes she slept soundly. He lifted her. Walking to the bed he set her there and regarded his wife for a few seconds.

"Sweet dreams, my sweet little darlin'. You don't know it yet but you are everything to me," he whispered then kissed her forehead.

He had not wanted to take any chances and hoped to consummate the marriage this evening. He failed to pay attention to what she drank. This was all new to him. A wife, one who loved her wine, he laughed.

Moving into the living room he wanted a nightcap, no more wine. He found the whiskey he'd asked for and poured two fingers. Nursing it he recounted his plans for the morning. They would have to be adjusted to accommodate the lateness and the probable hangover.

Perhaps it was better they get a late start. He could send Alistair and Tyna ahead to get everything ready and make sure all necessities had arrived. He sat back, closing his eyes before retrieving a pen and paper from an end table. The Duchess needed to be informed of his new plans.

Dear Charlotte,

We are wed, finally. I'm pleased with my new bride but what I haven't told you is that I had to rescue her from a prison cart. I was able to bribe the guard with a sac of coin but I'm sure it was not as much as he would have liked or expected to maintain his silence. I realize you're engaged in what is to be a relaxing vacation but I implore you to call in any favors you can. I fear for Larena's life. Now that she is my wife, it will be difficult for the authorities to press charges. Still we don't know if that is their intention.

We head for the Montgomerie hunting lodge tomorrow midday. My new wife had a bit too much wine and I was loath to stop her. I don't enjoy telling her what she can and cannot do even though she believes differently. But tomorrow she is bound to wake with a bad headache and hopefully she will learn from her actions.

Again, hoping your time in Scotland is relaxing.

Yours truly,

Gavin Broon the duke of Millsglen

He sealed the message and set it aside before walking to the bed to gaze at his new wife. She was curled in a tight ball, her breathing slow and even. He sat next to her and finished unlacing the corset. It slipped easily from her without waking her. Next he pulled all the pins from her hair, letting it spill over his hands. Left with just her chemise covering her body, she would sleep more comfortably.

Thundering hooves reverberated from the street below. He walked quickly to the window, his heart in his throat. Five British soldiers rode through town stopping at the inn's hitching post. Horrible scenarios rushed through his head, his breath catching in his throat.

Striding through the room his mind set on Larena's safety, he grabbed his shirt, slipping it on as he raced down the stairs. He was surprised to hear Alistair's footsteps behind him.

"You heard the horses," Gavin said, never breaking stride.

"Saw the redcoats." Alistair fell in beside him.

In the lobby the two men found a seat, carrying on a conversation while they watched the soldiers approach the desk. Gavin's gut tightened. The conversation seemed to last forever but the people assigned to the desk were his people. Apprised of the situation, they would never give anything away.

"If this is nothing, just British soldiers looking for a place to sleep you and Tyna can ride to the lodge first thing in the morning. Larena and I will follow later in the day."

Without turning to look at him, Alistair tilted his head confirming the order. "How is your evening going, other than this interruption?"

"Fine and you," they looked at each other for a spit second and laughed.

"Too much to drink." They said in unison.

"No wonder you were on my heels when these men arrived in the middle of the night," Gavin said, still observing.

"Until the reception I didn't know the two of you had any interest in each other," Gavin said, studying his friend.

"Seemed to be an instant attraction, one I was hard pressed to ignore but I have to say she surprised me. I think I might have enjoyed more tonight than you."

The men were handed keys and it seemed they were given rooms on the first floor. It was too soon to know their true purpose and their presence in a small village in Scotland was questionable.

"Go to bed, I'll come get you in a few hours. You can keep watch until they're gone. Don't leave for the lodge until we know where the soldiers are going," Gavin ordered.

"If they leave, I can get a few hours of sleep after I get you up."

"Sir, don't give yourself away." Alistair picked up a newspaper and after handing it to him, walked up the steps.

A few minutes later one of the soldiers appeared from the room and strode outside and was joined by two more of the men. The scent of cigar smoke filtered into the lobby.

Gavin could hear the conversation but couldn't understand what the men were saying.

Trying to be inconspicuous, he moved closer to the door and sat down. He kept his head buried in the paper, listening.

He heard a few words.

Ships and Australia then laughter and there was talk of the announcement of his marriage in the London Times. He'd not said where he would wed. Most of the conversation revolved around gossip, and he and Larena had been the most talked about couple in London.

The men returned still laughing and chatting before disappearing into their rooms. He prayed this was just a coincidence, but he didn't believe in chance and the facts their conversation revolved around caused him concern.

He blended into the shadows, waiting. The dawn heralded itself in brilliant colors, casting light in every nook and cranny. Gavin rose, striding purposefully to Alistair's room. He knocked twice.

"Sir?"

"They haven't risen yet."

"Tyna is getting ready for the trip to the lodge. I'll let you know when the soldiers leave. I'll check out their destination then Tyna and I will be on our way. I'll see you at the lodge."

~ * ~

Laughing and kissing after the reception, Alistair carried Tyna to his room. "You've had a wee too much to drink." His lips settled on hers as he opened the door then kicked it closed behind him.

"And so have you, my gallant Scotsman. You're not to be judging me," she poked a slender finger on his chest. "Now set me down before I get seasick way up here."

The last thing he ever wanted to do was judge her. He just wanted to love her. "If I set you down, it will be on the bed with me atop you. Are you ready for that?" he asked, twirling her around in circles. Her delighted laughter was magical and enchanting.

"Now that's a sobering thought. Let me see," she tilted her head as if thinking and placed a slender finger on her lips. "You won't think of me in a bad way if I succumb to your advances tonight. Promise me?"

"Never." She was more to him in this short time than any woman had ever been, and he couldn't figure out why. He didn't want to wait a moment longer to taste her sweetness.

"You're just trying to get under my skirts. I've heard my brother in just this type of situation. He didn't care for the girl, just wanted sex. Is that you? Did you get me drunk so you could have your wicked way with me? Now kiss me. I won't say yes unless you convince me it's in my best interest."

Cautious now, he settled on a large chair with Tyna in his lap, his hand resting below one breast. He didn't need convincing. His lips moved on hers, his tongue drawing a line across her mouth, urging her to let him inside. "Open for me. I want to taste the essence of your soul."

"Now you're talking nonsense, Alistair MacLeish. What does any of that mean or am I too muddled to understand? The essence of my soul, what the bloody hell is that?" She hit him hard on the chest.

"I thought you wanted me to kiss you."

His lips molded over hers again and with a tiny mew of pleasure, she did his bidding and opened for him. She didn't seem to know what to do which surprised him. Then she touched him while he pulled her tongue into his mouth. Her fingers dug into his shoulders while she thrust her hips against him.

He brushed kisses along her jawline to her tiny ear where he bit gently then swirled his tongue inside the lobe. She moaned softly and he delighted in giving her pleasure, loving the tiny sounds in the back of her throat that told him she enjoyed his attentions.

"You like what I'm doing? Tell me where you want me to touch you."

"I—I don't know." She breathed softly. "Never done this before."

He paused, wondering why she didn't want to tell him and why she would want him to believe she'd never made love before. His kisses lingered on the line of her collarbone then dipped lower to taste the soft swell of her breasts above her bodice of her gown. His teeth claimed the tiny sleeves that were barely there seeming to be mere decorations and tugged lowering her bodice for a better view of her delicate charms.

Her eyes wide she gazed at him then touched his face, ran her hands on his beard then returned his kisses. "It's so soft. I didn't expect your beard to be that way."

"Ye like my beard, lass?"

"I do," she whispered, kissing either side of his lips.

He was beside himself with need to taste every part of her; to see and touch and explore. "Lass, I want you so much I can barely contain myself, but I've a burning need to make this right for you."

"I don't believe you could do anything wrong." Her whispered words entranced him.

A final tug brought her bodice low enough to reveal her breasts. His breath caught in his throat. The small white globes with tender rosy buds inviting him were more than he could resist. With lips, teeth, and tongue, he paid homage to each, relishing the tiny sounds she made and the arch of her body drawing him closer.

"Tyna," he whispered as he rose and headed for the bed. He let her slide down his length while he impatiently turned her to unfasten the buttons and rid her of the corset. Her garments fell to the floor. She ran her hands beneath his shirt, touching him as he struggled to remove his clothing.

Finally naked, he fell on the bed with her on top of him then rolled, bringing her beneath him. He needed her now, wanted her in so many different ways. His hand settled on her belly then lower to touch the soft fleece of hair covering her most private parts.

He found the tiny lady bit inside, the soft wet feminine flowers protecting it. When he touched her there, she arched for him, crying out into his mouth that now covered her lips. "Alistair."

Her body weeping from his attentions, she was ready to accept all of him. He stroked her then slipped a finger deep inside her, testing. She was tight and small and so very hot. He gritted his teeth, trying for control, but when she moaned again and her hips arched needing him inside her, he could wait no longer.

"Do you want me lass?" he asked and when she closed her eyes and tilted her head slightly, he drove inside.

The cry of pain shook him to the core and he stopped. He just broke through her maidenhead and he'd taken no care to ease the way. "I'm so sorry. I didn't know you were a virgin."

Tears slid down her cheeks, but he wasn't going to let her hide from her feelings or him. He didn't move but waited for her to feel the pleasure once more as he knew she would. With time the pain would ease. He kissed her eyes, the tip of her nose and accepted the fact he had explaining to do but he meant to give her pleasure first.

Slowly, he felt her hips move beneath him, the sweet mercuric feelings running between them once more.

"I'm going to make this right," he told her, withdrawing a little before moving slowly inside.

"I didn't know it would hurt."

"Only once then nothing but pleasure." He stroked the tiny bud again and waited for her response. She spun away from him then, her hips arching, taking him deeper inside. He smiled as the ripple of her spasm spread down his shaft. Then he drove deeper until he could draw out the ecstasy no longer. One final fierce thrust and he felt himself exploding. Almost sobbing, dragging air into his parched throat, he withdrew from Tyna and let the essence of his sex spill onto her instead of inside her.

Chapter Seven

Gavin opened the door to an exhausted Alistair. Alistair regretted waking him, but his time was too important and consequences to dire. "You say the soldiers are still in their rooms?"

"They haven't left yet but I don't expect them to stay in bed much longer. I've got to check on Larena and get some sleep myself. Give me two hours before you wake me. If the soldiers leave, follow until you know where they're headed. If they're looking for me and don't realize I'm here, they'll probably head for the castle in Scotland."

"Get some sleep. I'll take care of everything."

Alistair watched Gavin step to his rooms then strode downstairs, stopping at the registration desk to ask a few questions.

"I'm Gavin's personal assistant. What do you know about the soldiers who registered last night?"

"They were looking for the Duke and his wife the Duchess. We didn't tell them anything they wanted to hear. Told him no one of his name stayed here but would let them know if that changed."

"Did you hide the carriage with his emblem on it?" He tried to think of everything recalling the ornate carriage Gavin left London with.

"Just a plain carriage. Nothing that would single him out," the man told him. "We made sure the vehicle wouldn't create any new questions."

"Thank you," Alistair handed the man several coins.

The man pushed them back. "The Broons are family. Don't need money to protect any of them."

"I'm sure your family could use a little extra coin, if not, buy something pretty for the missus." Alistair turned back to the lobby and finding the newspaper from last night he made himself comfortable.

Eventually, and still half asleep, the soldiers appeared and quietly made their way through the lobby. Alistair stood and after they left the inn, he followed, observing the northerly direction. As Gavin had said they traveled toward his property in Scotland.

In the stables he mounted one of the horses he had tied to the carriage several days ago when he and Tyna left London. Keeping the men at a distance and sometimes hanging back so they couldn't see him, he finally found a path running parallel to the road.

Sometime later and needing to get back to the inn, he decided to join the men and allow the distance to close between them. It didn't seem the soldiers were in a hurry to get to their destination.

"Hello," he said, "where are you heading?" He tried to make the question sound casual and unintimidating. He wanted answers without alerting them.

"Who are you?"

"Alistair MacLeish, I'm headed to the next village. Got a bonny lass waiting for me there. Haven't seen her for a couple of weeks, and I'm sorely missing her sweet charms."

The soldiers laughed. "The Broon castle in Scotland," one of the soldiers volunteered without hesitating, "there's an arrest warrant on a woman we think he's traveling with. There's a cell with her name on it waiting for her in Newgate prison."

"I see," he rubbed his chin and resting a forearm on the saddle horn. "None of my business but what's the gal wanted for? Five soldiers to bring a lady to Newgate tells me she's done something murderous."

"Not sure, don't pay much attention to those things. Just following orders. Don't believe she murdered anyone though."

"Heard she was part of a protest against the Corn Laws. Have to sympathize with her. My family lost their farm because of those laws. If they could be repealed it would be better for everyone."

"Don't forget our duty to the crown. We're bound to bring her home for trial and sentencing."

Alistair grimaced at what the men said, knowing how Gavin would feel. They'd reached a fork in the road. "I'm headed this way. You folks have a good journey. I'll be thinkin' about you when I've got my warm woman in my arms."

The laughter following his exit chilled Alistair to the bone. The men were following orders and had no idea why they were wrecking a man and woman's life. The outcome had nothing to do with them.

After what he guessed was enough time for the soldiers to be far enough down the road they wouldn't see him, he left the road. At the junction, he listened for the soldiers then, not hearing anything, he eased his way from the trees. The road in both directions was empty.

His ride back to the village so fast paced, leaving his horse heaving for air. He dismounted before the horse barely had time to stop.

While striding quickly to the inn, looking over his shoulder, "Saddle two horses and have them ready to go."

His pace increased as he entered the inn. He two-stepped his way up the stairs then he knocked on Gavin's door. Dark circles under his eyes, Gavin opened the door then walked outside.

"The soldiers are on the way to the Broon castle as you guessed. The soldiers had no concern about reporting this. As you suspected all along, they are after your wife. One sympathizes with her predicament. The others don't care, they're just following orders. They could easily be convinced to ignore the orders if my information is correct."

"I wouldn't want, well, I wouldn't want to jeopardize their lives. I'm hoping The Duchess will be able to call in another favor, but it's good to understand how these men feel. Thank you. Larena is still asleep. I trust you and Tyna will be on your way in the next hour."

"We will see you when we do, but if you're not at the hunting lodge by late afternoon, I'll come looking for you."

"You're a good man, Alistair, and faithful. I'm going to wake her in two hours. After I make sure she eats, we'll leave. I'm hoping by noon."

"See you then." Alistair's emotions were in a whirlwind. There would be no time to discuss the evening before with Tyna and he regretted that.

He entered, hoping Tyna would be ready and waiting for him. He was pleased to see she sat on a chair, her hands folded on her lap, her eyes closed with her bags at her feet.

"You're back," she smiled at him and stood. The sight struck his heart. "It took longer than I expected it would."

"It was necessary." He picked up the bags and nodded toward the door. "I had to follow the soldiers."

They were now standing in the stables, well, he was in the stables, Tyna stood at the door, seeming to hesitate, a frown on her pretty face. He tossed the bags in a small cart that would follow later.

He took the mare's reins, leading the horse to her. "Her name is Maisie. She'll treat you well, at least that's what the stable boy says."

He watched her eyes widen, her voice hesitant and trembling. "I thought we'd ride in a carriage. Is the cart going to the lodge?"

"What's wrong, lass? Are you afraid of the horse? You told me you could ride." He stood back, hands on his hips, feeling an urgency as well as fear.

She grimaced then made a strange face and shrugging her slim shoulders. "I lied."

"Why?" He didn't want to waste time with this conversation. "Why would you lie about something so insignificant? It wouldn't have changed the outcome of today, but I would have been prepared."

He watched her swallow before attempting to take a breath, "I didn't want you to leave me behind in London. I thought if I told you I'd never been on a horse in my life you wouldn't take me with you."

"We were riding in a carriage," he said, suddenly exasperated by the conversation.

"I didn't know that until after I lied," she sounded defensive.

"Doesn't matter now and even if you told me the truth, you would still have to ride to the lodge. The trail is narrow and rough. No carriage can make it up the steep path."

She eyed the cart. "There is that."

"It will be filled with supplies. Ah lass, I suppose the time has come for your first riding lesson. Perhaps it's your second." He laughed at the perplexed look on her face. "It's all part of the discussion and explanation you are owed. I would do it now but I've a duty to Gavin and you to the Lady Larena.

"I'll give you a leg up," he told her and continued to explain what she should do. Several attempts later she sat astride the horse.

"I didn't think this was how women ride a horse," she told him pensively, "but what do I know? Apparently not very much."

"No, you're right about women. They mostly ride sidesaddle. I took the liberties of getting you a regular saddle. The terrain is rough and you'll do much better riding this way. And, if you've never sat a horse before, this is the way you should learn. Are you ready?"

She looked from him to the horse then back to him, "I don't have a choice so let's get this over with."

"No, lass, there are no other choices and I love your feisty attitude. But you're sitting on your horse now. Don't show Maisie you're afraid," he said quickly as he watched the little mare sidestep and raise her head as if confused or distracted.

He was surprised to see her lean forward, her hand on the horses face. "There, you are pretty girl. I've never been on a horse and I don't want to be afraid. Will you help me?"

Maisie moved her head up and down as if in agreement. Then she whispered, "Thank you, and I'll do my best to take care of you too. If you don't mind, I'll have to ask Alistair for help."

Maisie nickered as if approving her statement. Alistair watched amazed at what he was seeing and hearing. Something else to add to the discussion they needed to have.

Wrenching the strange scene from his head he mounted. "Shall we?" he gestured toward the mountain.

~ * ~

Gavin woke Larena with a gentle nudge to her shoulder. She sat up, her hands to her head, her eyes still closed. "I've coffee and a few pastries for you. We have to go. I've let you sleep until noon."

She fell back, the pain pounding in her head until she felt as if her eyes were crossing, but she understood the source of her agony and knew she'd indulged on purpose. The excessive drink had been a delay tactic that only created more problems. She wished now...well what did she really wish for that she could do last night over? She was foolish to fear Gavin or his lovemaking. She knew first hand his gentleness. He'd never treated her anyway but with the greatest respect, even though he'd teased her mercilessly.

Determined, Larena sat up and accepted the cup of coffee, looking at the pastries skeptically." There is a hot bath waiting for you in the other room. I thought it would make you feel a little better."

"Did Tyna pack you a riding habit? No, I suppose you wouldn't know." He poked around her valise until he found a split skirt and a blouse. "Alistair must have mentioned something to Tyna."

Gingerly sipping the coffee and watching Gavin, she said, "Nothing but time, I suppose, is going to make me feel better, but I'm glad I've something appropriate to wear." She regarded him with eyes that seemed to question everything, the throbbing still the focal point of her feelings.

"I'll be in the stables when you're dressed."

She watched him leave, unnerved by the events of the past few days and dreading the ride to the hunting lodge. He'd told her it would take them at least three hours or more with stops to reach their destination. She'd never been on a horse more than an hour at any one time and remembered quite vividly how her body felt when she finally dismounted and attempted to walk.

Hot water and orange scented soap cleared her muddled head just a bit. Coffee, hot and bitter, had helped also, but what she needed now was a glass of cold water.

Out of the bath and into her clothes, she snatched a bite from one of the pastries Gavin ordered then quickly pinned her hair into a tight chignon. Chomping on the sweet, she checked the room to make sure everything had been packed then hurried down the stairway to the stables, trying desperately to ignore the pounding in her head.

Her favorite mare, Diva, was saddled and ready. She smiled at her new husband, wondering what he could possibly be thinking by the way his gaze roamed along her body. "Was that fast enough?"

"I barely had time to get the horses ready." He offered his arm and walked her to her mount before helping her up then he mounted and they rode from the stables.

A light wind blew down from the mountains, and the sun was high in the sky. The temperature was neither too hot nor cold. The day was perfect for a ride.

"Why were you gone from our room half the night?" She had been concerned about him then worried he had left her. When she finally fell asleep for a second time or perhaps third, she decided not to fret. The next day would be what it was, and he would tell her if it was important to her.

"There were soldiers in the inn." He turned to look at her.

She sucked in a breath of air her body tensing. "They were looking for me, weren't they? Is it safe?"

"News you don't want to hear, but yes to both questions. I don't want you to worry. Alistair followed them for a way, even had a quick chat with them. They are headed for the Broon estate in Scotland where they'll undoubtedly find a cool reception."

"Does it make a difference that we haven't," she licked suddenly very dry lips, "that we haven't consummated the marriage yet?"

"Yes again," but with a smile she was beginning to appreciate, "but not much longer. Besides, if anyone checked I took precautions."

"Precautions?" she felt confused, "I promise I won't drink too much again. I do regret it." She looked down for a moment, suddenly feeling shy in front of his questing gaze.

"At least not before we make love, otherwise you can have as much wine as you'd like. You do not need to fear me, Larena. I would never hurt you. But the consummation of our marriage is too important for me to have the patience you might like. If I do not make you mine, the authorities will not consider us wed," he finished, gazing at her. "News of your pregnancy should circulate in about four months."

"How on earth would they know?" She felt so strange that he would know more about these things than she did.

"The blood on our sheets." He held out his arm. "Precautions."

"I don't really understand what you're talking about." But she saw the small cut. "You put blood on the sheets?"

"A child, sooner than later, would be even better. Do you want children, Larena? I don't recall talking about children."

"You changed the subject again." Her mother had not been there for her, and her sisters had not hung around long enough to explain to their sibling anything about sex or wedding nights. Perhaps when they left home, they didn't know anything either.

"With good reason. Now is neither the time nor the place to discuss such things. It will be easier to explain after we've made love."

"Men," she muttered with a long drawn out and dramatic sigh. "You don't think my mind can understand something so confusing as blood on sheets. So you bade me wait for the right time."

"True."

"If I had to guess, I'd believe there is never going to be the right time. If it concerns me, I deserve to know." She wasn't going to let him get away with this nonsense.

"That would be wrong. I'm a true believer in telling the truth and giving explanations where they are appropriate. I won't keep secrets from you, Larena. But later is the right time."

"Well, I've yet to hear you tell me anything I've asked of you." She mulled her words over, trying to recall even one time.

His broad shoulders shook with merriment. "Larena, my bad habits must be wearing off on you. I asked you if you wanted children. If you don't, I can do my best to withdraw from you before I spill my seed, but then people will question whether we are truly wed."

Her body swayed and for a moment she thought she might fall off her horse so shocked by his words. "You can say outrageous things like that and you can't tell me what I asked?"

"True."

"Gavin, you..." she had no words so she started over, "Gavin, I've no idea what you're talking about."

"You have four sisters. Some of what I said shouldn't come as too great of a surprise. Women talk about things before they are wed. Mothers tell their daughters."

She grimaced, remembering the birth of Fayth's twins. That was all she knew about sex. These things he talked about baffled her. "Perhaps you're right, but not in my case. Ravyn is the oldest. She's eight years older than me. When she left for London she was, I think, twenty."

"So, you were twelve."

"Our mother died when I was six, and our father didn't want anything to do with us because we were girls. That's not quite true. He wanted to wed us to very wealthy men so he could reap the benefits. Money in his pocket is all we meant to him."

"And Ravyn left."

"A year or two later. Storm found a man from the village. She propositioned him when our father tried to barter her away to a very evil man. She proposed. I have to say it was a bit rocky at first. I spent most of the next few years at the McLellan castle with Aidan."

"And if I recall correctly a few things about past encounters, Aidan had no mother either."

"She's the youngest cousin. Fayth left and when she returned home, she had no husband but was very pregnant. I helped deliver her twins and that's pretty much all I know."

"If you saw the birth of a child, did that..."

"Make me not want to have children? No, the experience was breathtaking. It was like watching magic happen in front of my eyes."

"So, you want to have children."

"More than anything."

"Good, then no explanation is needed."

She cast him what she hoped was a disapproving look, but he let his head fall back and roared with laughter again. They rode in silence for a while. Larena felt her legs beginning to cramp but didn't want to tell him she needed to get off her horse for a few minutes. And yet...

"Gavin, I need to stop. Don't know how long we've been riding, but my legs are growing numb. I can't feel my toes." The growing ache in her legs transcended the headache or perhaps it was gone.

"I was so entranced by our conversation, I forgot you might need to take a short break. There's a shady place over there and grass to sit."

He dismounted then helped Larena down. Her legs nearly gave out when her feet touched the earth. She leaned into him, craving the physical and emotional support.

Gavin carried her to a cool grassy knoll and set her down before going back to the horses. He gave them water and smoothed their coats. Pulling two items from his saddlebag, he returned to her.

"I've some liniment and if you let me, I'll ease your muscles. Without it you won't make it to the cabin tonight. May I?"

She groaned softly her leg beginning to cramp. "Do whatever you can."

"Does either hurt more than the other."

"My right leg," she nearly cried when the leg spasmed.

Watching her, he pushed the split skirt as high as it would go before pouring some of the oil into his hand. Gently he began to knead the tired and strained muscle. "Is that better?"

"Hmm..." she leaned against a boulder, eyes closed. "I don't want to get back on that horse. I'll never make it unless I crawl."

"You mean Diva?"

"Yes," both legs shook with the exertion and her under-used muscles tightened.

He turned his attention to her other leg then alternated between legs, massaging and rubbing the healing liniment into her limbs. "You're beginning to relax, and the muscles are no longer knotted. I'm afraid though. I don't think you're going to make it to the lodge on the horse."

"Could we walk?" she asked hopefully. "For a little while?"

Gavin looked up the path, raking his hair with his fingers. "It's a long way to walk."

"At least we'll be moving. Walking shouldn't take too much longer than riding." Yet she knew the shoes she wore would mangle her feet sooner than later. The blisters might be just as bad as the cramps.

"We'll walk for a mile or maybe two, but if your feet start to hurt you've got to promise to tell me. Broken blisters can be just as unbearable and dangerous as cramped muscles."

She was shaking her head, acknowledging the truth of his words. "How did Tyna make it? I don't think she's ever ridden a horse." She felt sure they would find the couple alongside the road.

"Larena, think about her life. I doubt if she's spent much leisure time in her young days. Her muscles are stronger even if she's never ridden before. She's more equipped to go the distance. All your riding has been for fun and entertainment, nothing serious."

For some reason she bristled at his unthinking words. Storm owned horse stables. She bred horses for racing. As a young girl she spent her extra time riding and so did I. "I'm ready now."

"You're not." He handed her a bag of cool water. "Drink this. It will ease the ache in your head."

She stiffened once more at his words, sure he referred to something other than her alcohol-induced pain. "You must think me truly useless."

"Ah, the aristocracy tends to breed women who play the piano and dance, not hardy women who can plow fields and—"

"Ride horses."

"I'm not trying to undermine you. I've heard you play and I've held you in my arms to dance. I don't want a wife who can plow a field. I want you, so you're going to have to live with that, and I pray you want me."

She wasn't sure how to interpret what he said. But some of his words soothed her ego. She wanted him too, no other man would do for a husband.

"I know we need to get there as soon as possible, or I'll wager someone will send out a search party and I don't want to be embarrassed. I can walk now and it will stretch my muscles in ways riding will only tighten them again." She was determined not to let him down or show any more signs of weakness.

"We'll walk for fifteen minutes then ride for the same amount of time. I planned to stop twice so in an hour we'll rest again and I can tend to your legs and check for blisters."

Pleased with his proposal, she nodded her approval. He helped her to her feet and an hour later they stopped and he repeated the massage with the liniment. This time they rode. And so it went.

"How much father?" She looked up the hill, hoping to see a structure of some sort towering above the hilltops.

"About one walk and one ride and I believe we'll be there."

She stared up the path imagining her feet moving one step at a time then feeling Diva's sway one step at a time. She drank from the bag of water then extended her hand to Gavin for help standing.

"I can do this," she whispered determinedly one more time, regarding the path in front of her. "I can."

"Hold my hand, little darlin'."

She didn't understand but the tiny gesture made her feel better just as she didn't comprehend why her muscles had given out on her. "Thank you," she smiled at him.

He pulled her close, his fingers around her waist supporting her. The comfort gave strength where there was none and encouragement when she believed she could not take another step.

"You're doing fantastic," he kissed her forehead. "It's time to ride now." He brought her Diva and helped her up. "Be strong. This is the last leg of our trip then you can relax as much as you want."

"I will." Yet her body shuddered with fatigue and ached with the tiniest cramping of her thighs, as she clung to her horse. Tears slipped down her cheeks. *I can do this.*

She noticed the sun closing on the horizon and the tops of the evergreen trees swaying in the wind. A bird chirped in a tree somewhere, and as the day was beginning to end, the animals took that as a sign to rejoice, chattering with each other.

The world seemed to be locked in a haze. She closed her eyes, her body slumping and slowly she began to slide from her mount. She jerked to attention but at the same time cried out in agony.

"Larena, we're here."

Darkness closed around her, but she felt his arms catch her and pull her against his chest. Without thinking, her hand rose to touch his face even before she gave herself to the exhaustion encompassing her.

Gavin...

"All is fine. You can sleep as soon as I see to your legs. I do want you to be able to walk on the morrow." He kissed her forehead then the tip of her nose. She felt herself smile.

"I'm not that tired, really," she whispered softly. "You can put me down and let me walk."

"No." He carried her and she was too weary to see the inside of the lodge or to protest.

"Truly, I need to walk."

"Not on your life or mine." They reached the master chamber where a hot bath waited.

After disrobing her, he set her in a tub of steaming water. The heat jerked her awake but soon it soothed her muscles and she let her head lean on the back of the tub, soaking in the warmth.

"Gavin, are you there?"

"I'm bringing more hot water." He drew a bucket of water from the tub then poured in more of the steaming hot liquid.

"You should have a bath too. You must be tired."

"I'm going to wash in the lake," he told her. "Don't worry about me. I can take care of myself."

"You should have hot water too."

"Cold will do me much better," he told her, his voice taking on a husky tone she recognized as the sound of his voice when he kissed her and touched her.

"More hot water?" a servant waiting at the door asked.

"Last one."

Gavin repeated drawing and pouring a bucket. She sighed softly, enjoying the heat as well as the relaxing of her muscles.

"Gavin, will you help me out? I'm thinking I'm done here, and if I stay a moment longer, I will turn into a prune."

He stood in front of the tub, a huge bath sheet held out for her to step into. Helping her, he wrapped it around her before leading her to the bed. "Lie down and I will massage the oil into your muscles."

She did, lying on her stomach and resting her head on a pillow, her arms crossed so one cheek was against her hand. The oil was poured on her legs. His nimble fingers began with each foot and slowly moved up her leg before turning his attention to her other leg. Then he removed her towel to her waist and kneaded the muscles in her back and shoulders with liniment.

Inhaling deeply and totally relaxed, she almost turned over but he stopped her. "Do you think you can dress for dinner by yourself or should I call Tyna? I'm going to the lake."

"I can dress."

"No corset?"

"No."

"Good then, put some clothes on, and if you want you can explore the lodge. I've ordered dinner to be served in our room. Are you hungry?"

"I think I am."

"You should be starving after our ordeal today." He kissed her. "If you need anything you can call Tyna. Just ring the bell. I've asked her to stay downstairs until I'm back and dinner is served."

She observed him thoughtfully as he backed from the room, grinning. She wondered what he had in mind and why his smile looked so devilishly handsome. Finding a pair of pants and a shirt in the armoire, she decided she wanted to try comfort instead of fashion.

Ella must have left these for the times when she and Drake visited. She was a tiny bit taller than Ella but just as slender. Slipping the garments on, she studied herself in the mirror.

"Bloody eyes," she murmured. "If she wore this, he would be able to see her breasts, her nipples."

Quickly, she rang the bell summoning Tyna.

A few minutes later, "Larena, I'm so glad you made it. How was your trip? Mine was exhausting."

"Not without issues but that doesn't matter now." She waved her hands in the air. "It seems I drank too much and we didn't have a wedding night. More than anything I want to give him one tonight. What do you think?" She spun in a circle.

"What on earth are you thinking? You don't want to come to him dressed in men's clothing. Let's recreate last night. Where is your wedding dress?"

Larena shrugged. "He must have packed it because I checked the room before we left and I found nothing."

Tyna stomped to her valise and pulled out clothing until she found what she looked for. She held it up, examining the gown. "Looks good, no stains or wrinkles despite the way it was packed." She turned back to the valise and found the corset, stocking, garters and everything else that went with it. "You're going to look just as stunning the second time as you were the first night. Let's get you dressed so the rest of the evening can begin."

"Do you really think he'll like it?" She held the dress up to study the garment. "He did have trouble with the buttons. Maybe you should only fasten half of them." Larena wasn't sure about recreating a night that didn't turn out the way it should. She didn't want to jinx the marriage. Yet she did have something to prove to Gavin as well as herself.

"This is perfect. He will appreciate all the effort and thought that went into thinking about him. Your night will be just the way both of you wanted last night to go."

Dressed, Larena studied herself in the mirror, grimacing at her flyaway hair. "Can you redo my hair?"

"I'm not as good at hair, but for you I'll do my best." Humming to herself, Tyna began to work, doing much better than expected.

A little while later with a tiny amount of make-up applied to her eyes, lips and cheeks, she thought she was ready. "He told me to let him know when he should come up, but Tyna, I didn't ask you about your night. Did you have fun at the wedding?"

Tyna smiled and nodded then her cheeks flushed a brilliant crimson. "Yes. It was more than I expected it could be."

"Well, I hope Alistair's going to treat you right. You deserve the best. Is he a nice man?"

"Alistair was gentle and sweet although he wasn't a gentleman at all and I'm glad of it. He made my heart race and, well, it was a bit like that day when I saw you in the gazebo with Gavin."

"He made love to you?" Larena asked, wanting to know everything but was afraid to ask. "Tyna—"

She was cut short by the knock on the door and the trays of food being delivered. Gavin followed with a bottle of wine. His jaw dropped when his gaze fell upon her.

~*~

"Bloody eyes," he whispered, amazed at the vision she made.

"Is that good or bad?"

"I can barely breathe," he told her, "You're my dreams come true."

"One glass to help you relax," he told her, holding out the crystal, "Maybe a second one afterwards. You're beautiful again tonight. What made you think of wearing your wedding dress?"

"It was Tyna's idea," she looked to her maid then back to Gavin. "I was going to wear the pants and shirt I found in the armoire, but she thought you would appreciate this more."

"I do believe it's time for me to go. There are one too many people in this room." She turned quickly then gave Larena a reassuring smile before she slowly closed the door.

Gavin held out his hand to Larena and on wobbling legs she walked toward him, taking her hand in his. "I wanted to make this night special for you, something I was unable to do on our real wedding. I was terrified then and I really don't understand why."

"And I want to give you a night you'll never forget. One you'll look back on with fondness rather than regret." He pulled her into his arms, feeling her length against his body and wanting to make love to her now, even before they ate. He simply was no longer hungry.

"I think we should eat first," she told him, once again sounding shy. "Never mind, that's probably a bad idea. It seems I keep delaying the inevitable when it would be nice just to get it over with."

He didn't intend to just get the lovemaking over with as she would soon discover. "Of course, we'll do whatever you want." He led her to the fur rug in front of the hearth, motioning for her to sit.

"What would you like?" Without waiting for an answer, he placed something of everything on her plate.

She toyed with her food, nothing going into her mouth, and he knew her nerves were playing a huge part and once more they seemed to be winning. As the seconds ticked by, he saw the tension in her body escalating. He didn't intend to let this evening deteriorate.

He poured her a small glass of wine. "Drink some, it will help ease your mind." he encouraged while he held one foot in his hand and slipped the delicate shoe from her foot. He massaged her foot, placing it on his hand. "You're so small your foot in no bigger than my hand." The fact amazed him, terrifying him at the same time.

She gazed at him, her eyes wide, he hoped with desire. "You're a man. You're supposed to have large hands." Her breath whispered in the sultry air.

Laughing, relieved she could make light of the situation. "I'm happy. Let's suffice it to say, you're enchanting and this night should be as magical for you as I know it will be for me."

He did the same for her other foot, massaging and easing the tight muscles. "How are you feeling tonight? Are you better? Did the bath help? No more hangover?"

"Hmmm..." she sighed, whispering so softly he could barely hear.

"Whatever you're doing to me I don't want you to ever stop. I do believe most assuredly the massage is what eased my muscles the most. Without it, I don't think I could move." She closed her eyes, leaning against the hearth, seeming to soak up the warmth of the fire.

"You're wedding slippers are beautiful but nothing like the stockings on your legs. Somehow they shimmer with the firelight and beg me to touch." His hands explored the length of her leg, the dress moving higher on her limbs until he saw the delicate stockings with embroidered blue flowers and light blue garters holding them up. He sucked in a deep breath of air, inhaling the scent of her, his heart nearly standing still for a second. She could do this to him, unman him, without even trying.

Still within his embrace he turned her, "Ahh...I see your maid had my not so nimble fingers in mind when she helped you dress. This will not be as difficult as before."

"I told her you had trouble with the buttons last night. I didn't realize at the time you would be unfastening the same dress so soon. I should have just worn my corset and underthings."

"No, never, the sight of you once more in your wedding gown will be forever etched in my head. I believe I'll remember until the day I stick my spoon in the wall. Now, I've had practice and I've found that if I slant them a bit, they slip through the holes much easier." Each time he unfastened a button he kissed her, unlacing the corset as he slowly moved down her back. With every caress he felt her shiver, felt the pulsing of her blood beneath his lips. The tension in all her muscles seemed to vanish, replaced by a fine trembling.

"You're very good at undressing me," her sultry whisper sent a bolt of heat through him. "What else are you good at?"

He didn't want to tell her he had practice. Instead he pulled her against him, her back to his chest, his hands resting on her stomach. His lips and teeth caressed her neck. "You smell of oranges," he told her.

In his arms, she turned, "You need to take your shirt off. I want to feel you again, May I?"

"Anything you want, little darlin'." His body tightened hardening with the sexual need he'd grown accustomed to when he was with her. Now with the sweet promise of fulfillment, he fought the sensations he knew were only a few minutes away.

Her fingers tugged on his shirt, pulling the fabric from his waistband, her knuckles scraping against his stomach. His heart suddenly surged and once more he felt its fierce pounding in his chest. She stopped when she touched his nipples, running her fingers across them.

"Help me, raise your arms." He did so and while she leaned closer to pull his shirt over his head, her breasts pushed against his chest.

He needed her naked now. With an urgency he'd never felt except with Larena, he swiftly rid her of the corset and remaining garments save the silk stockings. "You're so beautiful, just like that sweet afternoon in the gazebo." Looking at her he broke out in a fine sheen of sweat.

Sweeping her into his arms he strode with her to the bed. He set her against the headboard then leaned over her. His hands rested on the slim length of her legs. Gently he caught her knees, parted them and eased his weight between them. Her hands fell upon his shoulder. The fingers of his right hand lightly brushed her cheek, his knuckles stroked down her throat, then over the bared mound of her breast across the tight bud.

Her breath came in ragged gulps. "Gavin, you're unraveling me one tiny strand at a time."

"Don't be afraid."

"I don't think I'm afraid, just hesitant and ever so curious. I want to savor everything with you, every precious moment. I know you will make all this perfect." Her eyes, alight with a shimmering glitter of pure aqua desire melded into his.

"We will do it right this time and we'll finish what we start. No one will interrupt us this evening," he whispered close to her ear, feathering kisses there. "And every time after our lovemaking will be amazing," he promised, then moving lower, to place light nipping kisses along her collarbone.

"Can you promise something like that?" she sighed into his mouth, their tongues meeting.

"I certainly hope so." He told her, his voice ragged with desire.

She cried out, making tiny sounds in the back of her throat as he continued to seduce every inch, her body trembling beneath his touch, responding in an age-old dance of love. His hand swept lower, over her belly, onto her mound. Between her thighs, touching, stroking, probing...a violent shiver seized her as his touch became more and more intimate. She created a smoldering fire within him and her body seemed to crave his touch, as he knew it would.

"Is this what I should feel, so hot and wanting something I don't understand or know what it is?" she gasped arching her hips closer to his heavy arousal. He brought his face very close to hers, her eyes all but scorching his. Her whisper was almost a caress against his lips.

"A hot wanting? He inquired. "Did you not feel this before when I touched you in the gazebo?"

"No, not like this...not as intense...we were interrupted. Gavin please I need something. Please."

"This evening there might be pain. It cannot be helped." He dreaded telling her this, needed her to know only pleasure.

"Is this something I should have been told by my mother?" she questioned while her hips rose inviting his penetration.

"Yes, but I will do my best to ease whatever discomfort you might have. The pain will be over quickly and afterwards you will know only the sweetest pleasure, a hot intense pleasure."

He rose above her and discarded his remaining clothing.

She reached out to touch him, seemingly amazed by what she saw. "You're so different."

"Relax now." He slowly lowered himself and thrust into her cautiously until he touched her maidenhead then he closed his eyes, the muscles of his jaw tightening, dreading the next moment. Quickly he pushed through.

She cried out, shuddering against him, beating on his shoulders, seeming to try to free herself from the invasion. Tears slipped down her cheeks. It didn't seem to occur to her that after he drove through her he had gone dead still. Her hands lay upon his shoulders as her nails curled sharply into his flesh.

His fingers wove into the hair at her nape. When she regarded him, her eyes blazed into his. "Sweet bloody hell!" he exclaimed softly. "My greatest joy should never bring you such pain. It will never happen again."

"Gavin, please," she gasped, barely keeping the words from being a sob. "I can't... You have to..."

"It will cease to hurt, soon. I vow. After this you will know only pleasure, no more pain." Yet he didn't really know how long it would take for pleasure to replace the agony.

She opened her lips to speak and his caught them gently. His kiss consumed and devoured, possessing her in every way he could. His tongue swept, hard and passionately, deep into her mouth, her throat. Molten steel rushed throughout his limbs, radiating to his throbbing sex. He could hear and feel the pulse of her heart, or his, and it was as if drums pounded mercilessly in his head. He prayed the sensations she was feeling were as mesmerizing and engulfing as the ones he was enjoying. He was moving again before she seemed to realize what he was doing. He simply couldn't help himself. His lips parted from hers, touched them again. His hand stroked her cheek, her breast then lower to her most intimate places.

"Your lips are so very soft," he murmured, his teeth closing over them, biting gently then moving on to other parts of her body.

This was more than he'd ever expected from their lovemaking. A whisper of tantalizing flame licked over him, inside him, a hint of something mercurial and as excruciatingly sweet he had never felt before. She didn't fight him but instead she clung to him, riding out the wildness of the storm he meant to create within her and feel the strange whispers of promised pleasure soon to overcome the ache he created and regretted.

He became increasingly aware of her, the soft curve of her body, straining, the fluid movement of her hips arching against him, soft, graceful, reckless relentless sweet as he plunged into her again and again until she cried out his name in wild abandon.

She gripped his shoulders as if she held on for dear life and burrowed her face into his neck. The whole of his body gave a massive shudder. He held himself taut and still above her, then moved once again, a groan tearing from his lips as a tidal wave of liquid fire washed from his body into hers.

He felt a trembling deep inside her and watched the beauty of her climax as spasms seemed to overtake her. He wanted to do this over and over again for the rest of their lives.

She touched his chest with one delicate fingertip, tracing a path from one side to the other. "Is this a woman's pleasure?"

"It is. How do you feel?"

"I want to touch you everywhere, to feel your kisses again and again. I don't want you to ever stop making love to me," she whispered, softly kissing his chest then his nipples. "You take me to heaven then into a magical enchantment I don't know how to define."

Hearing her words, he had gone still, but he had not withdrawn, enjoying the sensation of being one with her. Her lashes covered her eyes, silent for the time being.

His laughter echoed in the room as he realized he found something so very special with her this night. He withdrew from her, wishing he could remain in her tight sheathe. "I take it you enjoyed the first act of our wedding night. Be assured before this night is over, we will recreate the magic and the enchantment at least one more time." He swept her hair from her eyes allowing its silken fire to flow through his fingers. "Before we try act two, we need to eat. Does food seem a bit more palatable now?" He handed her the wine glass and picked up his.

She sat up, making a funny face at him and pulling something to cover her. "I'd like something to wear."

"I've seen and touched nearly all of you." He wanted to enjoy gazing at her beauty.

Heat rose to her cheeks. "I don't think I'm ready for this, to sit naked in front of you. I want to—"

"You're wedding night gift. You can put it on and while I'll tell you straight out it covers all of you it won't conceal you from my gaze. We will both get what we desire." He rose, standing above her then walked to his bag. "Here it is."

Pulling out a light blue negligee and robe he brought it to her. "Raise your arms and I'll help you into it."

She did and he slipped the sheer fabric over her body. "Thank you." She smoothed the garment across her legs.

He could see just as much of her as before yet it seemed to be more erotic through the flimsy barrier. "Is that better?" he handed her the sheer robe, unable to remove his gaze.

"Yes, Gavin, I don't know what I'm supposed to do or how I'm supposed to act." She clasped and unclasped her hands. "I feel so different now as if my life has changed in so many ways I can no longer count them."

"Natural, just do what you feel. Perhaps you're with child, Larena. I spilled my seed inside you. Would you like that?" He poked the fire and embers crackled, flying up the chimney while he waited for an answer.

"Is that what you meant, inside or outside. Outside if I didn't want children. I'm still not positive what you're talking about, but I've a better idea now. As to children, I told you before I'd like at least one, but I don't want you to keep me with child until I give you an heir."

He mulled her words over for a few seconds remembering her mother's story and the horrific way her father treated every one of his children, but he wasn't ready to address this issue yet. "You're a quick learner. I think I like that. Would you like me to put something on?"

"Well," she stared at him over the rim of her glass. "I...you're beautiful and interesting and intimidating all at the same time. It would be easier to relax if you put something on."

"You're not relaxed? Do you want to make love again?" He prayed her answer would be yes, that the passion he evoked tonight could be rekindled.

She looked at him a confused dazed look on her face. "Yes and no."

He placed his finger under her chin lifting so she couldn't look away from him, her eyes sparkling. "If you want you can make love to me. I'll let you do whatever pleases you."

"I wouldn't have any idea what to do."

"Pretty much anything will work. Just looking at you in your negligee arouses me. Touch me in the same way I caress you. Thrust your tongue inside my mouth, touch my shaft, caress any part of me that appeals to you. I will love everything you do, I can promise you that."

"What that means exactly eludes me but I like the sound of it," she murmured then sipping her wine, watched him.

He wanted to ask her some private questions but stopped. He would know soon enough if she carried his child without embarrassing her further. "Would you like to go downstairs? You haven't had a chance to explore the lodge."

"Dressed like this?" she held the fabric up, squinting as she suddenly realized how sheer it was.

"We're the only ones in the cabin. No one will be in the lodge except us. I will be the only one who sees you."

"Alistair and Tyna?"

"Have settled into one of the outbuildings. They've made it their own. I believe they are..." he stopped unsure of what she knew about her maid and his right-hand man.

"All right then, we can explore the lodge if that's what you want."

"It is what I want," he told her before dressing in a pair of buckskins.

Hand in hand they walked down the steps to the room below. "Tyna told me they made love last night. Do you think..."

"They spent last night together in the same room. I'm guessing they had a better night than we did." He thought to laugh but held it back.

"How do you know all this?"

"Alistair told me and since Tyna emerged this morning from the same room as Alistair," Gavin said.

"I certainly hope he treats her right."

"Now why wouldn't he?" Gavin paused in thought and wondering what Tyna said to her.

"Men aren't all like you." She graced him with a smile. "You know I'm not at all tired. Can we go look at the lake?"

"While I know no one will be here, I can't guarantee no one will be there, and I'm not a man who shares his woman with the world to see."

"It's dark and I want to touch the water, maybe even swim. I've missed swimming in the lake nearby. Would you like to swim with me?"

That was a twist he hadn't seen coming. Thoughts of a fine sliver of water between their bodies sent a heat and desire surging through him. Still holding her hand, he led the way to the dock. "We would have to swim naked."

"That doesn't bother me because you wouldn't be able to see me," she laughed then skipped to the door.

He had no reply, just the knowledge he would hold her and make love to her in the water. This would be act two.

She sat down, her feet in the lake, splashing the water and laughing.

"Are you serious about swimming?" He unfastened his buckskins and slipped them off. "You can come if you like?" Not waiting for an answer, he backtracked on the dock then waded into the lake until the water reached his waist. "Come on, when you take the negligee off, I won't look." With that said, he dove into the water, surfacing a few seconds after. The coldness penetrating his muscles, yet it was somehow invigorating.

She walked slowly, as if hesitating or thinking over what he invited her to do. He regarded her as she slipped the robe off before pulling the nightgown over her head.

"You said you wouldn't look," She whispered, stepping into the water. "It's so cold."

"All I can see is dark outline of your body. Can you swim?"

She answered by mimicking him. She dove and when she surfaced, she was in front of him. "As children we swam in the lakes around our homes." She turned and floated on her back.

He splashed water on her, enchanted by the enticing picture she made. She laughed and returned the water. He pulled himself underwater until he reached her legs, tugging her under while he wrapped his arms around her and kissed her. Together they surfaced laughing. Once again his lips touched upon hers, demanding and hard. He pulled her hips against his so she could feel the power of his arousal.

"Lay on your back and put your hands on my shoulders," he told her and when she did, he began swimming. Her breast pressed against his chest provocatively sending fire throughout.

Laughter from the beach caught his attention. "Wrap your legs around me," he told her and he treaded water, keeping her afloat.

"What was that?" she laughed then stopped suddenly. "You did tell me there might be others here. Do you think someone is here?"

He turned her so she could see two people laughing and running across the beach. "I believe we interrupted something. Now that I think about it the rowboat was gone."

"Alistair and Tyna?" she asked, her nails raking across his shoulders, the very essence of her pushing against his arousal.

"Most likely," he laughed," lie back again."

"Really, I can swim by myself. This is something that isn't new to

174

me," she told him, sounding indignant in her statement.

"I know, but I'm enjoying this so much I don't want to stop," he said and continued with slow lazy strokes toward the beach. When he could touch the bottom, he stood and brought her legs around him again. Then he was inside her. "Act two." His mouth settled once more on hers as he lifted her so her core touched his shaft.

She cast her head back and his kisses consumed her until his mouth moved to close over her breast. The cold water swirled around them. He made love to her, spilled his seed once again inside her.

It seemed the earth moved beneath his feet, never knew a touch so acutely, never imagined a man could know a woman so completely in such a short time.

When she set her head on his shoulder, he had never known such a gentle peace seize him. He held her still as thunder from the heavens rolled across the sky. Then a flash of lighting sizzled from one cloud to another, arcing against the darkness of the night.

An urgency possessed him. "We have to get out now."

Sweeping her into his arms he strode from the lake, pausing long enough to retrieve their clothing before racing to the porch while huge drops of rain pounded to earth. Hastily they dressed.

"Can we stay on the porch and watch the storm?" she wrapped her arms around herself.

"You're shivering."

"I'd really like to watch. Since I was little lightning storms have fascinated and terrified me. The coldness will vanish if you hold me."

"If that's what you want." He kissed her quickly before leaving, "I'll bring the blanket by the door."

He was back, wrapping the warmth around them before sitting on the porch swing.

The lightning created dazzling currents in the sky, and Gavin narrowed his eyes watching them. He spun a daydream as he held her, idly stroking her arm. The Duchess would come to his castle in Scotland. Charlotte would have used her considerable power to win Larena a pardon. This sweet sensual pleasure and madness could go on and on, forever. She could feel his strength and delight in his laugher and the fierce demand of his passion and desire... He would no longer need worry about soldiers beating down his door and carrying her off to prison.

"What are you thinking?" she asked him, running a fingertip along his chest, arousing him once again.

"That we are still wanted by the crown," he said huskily, "and that your aunt has to find a way to have the charges dropped. I don't know if that's possible. Yet some people believe she has extraordinary abilities when it comes to influencing the sweet evil people who make up the ton."

She stiffened, visibly shaken by his statements, "I'd rather not remember what happened to me right now. This evening has been perfect and those memories bring darkness instead of light."

"Sooner than later we will have to face the facts and figure out a way to make sure you stay safe. Hiding here can only last so long. Someone will give our location away whether purposely or inadvertently and we have to be ready for that day."

He pulled her closer, angry that he had no way of disappearing into the highlands with her. She tilted her chin, gazing at him with huge aqua eyes. Truly he didn't want to frighten her, but this was a fact they needed to discuss.

"We don't have to figure anything out tonight," she whispered softly. "I would rather forget everything even though I realize I can't. If we can, it would be nice to postpone reality until tomorrow."

He laughed and nuzzled her earlobe with a fascinating tenderness. "I don't like to put anything this important on hold, but I'm sure you're right. Tonight we can think of more pleasant things." This was to be their wedding night, and he didn't want anything to get in the way of her happiness.

He met her gaze, brilliant with desire and hunger, touched by her charming innocence. Her arms wrapped around him, letting him know in a way only she could that she wanted him. I have fallen in love with her, he thought with the deepest concern and dismay for his judgment. He never meant this to happen because he'd always thought love was for fools.

Suddenly the thundering of a horse's hooves interrupted the storm's vengeance, creating a fear of its own. One of his men jumped from his mount before it had even come to a halt, striding swiftly to the porch.

Gavin stood. "What is it?

"Two people are coming our way." His voice breathless reached deep into Gavin's soul while dark thoughts invaded him. "Don't know if they are friend or foe, but we all thought it best you should know so you could take necessary precautions."

"Alert Alistair immediately. He's in the outbuilding on the other side of the main house. He might be otherwise engaged with a lady so make sure you knock. Meet me here as soon as you give him the same message." His daydream would not come true this evening or anytime soon. The people approaching had to be soldiers. Who else would ride up the narrow path this time of night and in a raging storm?

Turning to Larena, he adjusted the blanket around her, concerned for her safety as well as her happiness. "We are going to our room and you're going to stay there until I come for you. Promise me. This could be dangerous and I don't want you caught out here unprotected. If there is gunfire..." He didn't want her caught in the middle and he would fight if necessary.

Desire in her eyes changed to fear while she tilted her head to say yes. "Have they come for me again? I won't go willingly. I did nothing wrong. We can disappear into the woods until they give up and go away."

"We will have to see. My man said people not soldiers. There's a possibility they could be friends, although I have no ideas who it might be." He took her hand in his and guided her quickly to their rooms, shutting the door behind them. Swiftly, he put on a shirt and boots before kissing her hard and fast. "Stay here." On his way out the door, he picked up his sword and pistol that he'd placed near the bed.

He met Alistair and the messenger on the porch then waited, jaw taunt, and hands clasped tightly behind his back. These could not be the same soldiers who left the inn just this morning on the way to the castle in Scotland. They could not have gotten there and back in this short a time.

Chapter Eight

Tyna slipped quietly through the bedroom door in the main house. "What is happening out there and what has Alistair in such a rush? He left in such a blinding hurry, I didn't even have time to say goodbye."

"Two people, Gavin fears they might be soldiers, coming for me," Larena said, the words stopping in her throat. "I'm tired of living in fear and it's only been a few days since the protest."

"There is nowhere to run." Tyna stood beside her peering out the window into the darkness, giving some support as she watched in terror. "It's just dark woods out there, nothing more."

"We can't see or hear anything from here. I need to know what's going on. We should go downstairs where we can listen to what is being said." She had to get closer. Did not want to be left in the bedroom waiting for some dreaded announcement. It was just like a man to put a woman out of harms way when he stepped right into the middle of the fray with no regard for his life.

"Alistair told me to wait with you, in the bedroom," Tyna said pointedly. "He told me not to go anywhere, especially not downstairs."

Sucking in a deep breath of air, she said, "As did Gavin, but I have to know what is happening. You can wait here if you wish, but I'm changing into the pants and shirt Ella left in the armoire, and I'm going downstairs where I can hear what is being said." Determined, Larena meant to have a say in her destiny. She wasn't about to let men decide her fate. Her future was too important to leave to chance.

"Perhaps it is good news and there won't be any danger." It seemed Tyna was trying to convince herself.

"The only way it will be good is if The Duchess managed to call in a few favors. She has dirt on all the dukes, admirals and even field generals in all of the British Isles. My auntie Charlotte could ruin so many people if

178

she's provoked. I have faith in her."

"Your aunt really has that much power?" Tyna asked, seemingly in awe. "I've never known anyone, especially a woman who could sway an admiral or a duke to do her bidding."

"She does, and it's amazing." It was too much all of this, the ton, the madness brought on by her careless behavior. Suddenly, she longed for home, with Fayth and Storm, tranquility and peace in Scotland. She wanted to ride free on the land surrounding their home; land they owned and she wanted to swim naked in their lake with Gavin. But they would hunt her down there too. She could flee to the United States and live with Ravyn, but she didn't think Gavin would want to leave Scotland.

Quickly, she left the robe and negligee behind and slipped into the men's clothing Ella left. "Are you coming?" she turned to her maid impatiently waiting for an answer. "If not, you're perfectly welcome to stay in this room and remain in Alistair's good graces."

Tyna was shaking her head no and wringing her hands, but when Larena started down the stairs to the living room, Tyna was behind her. Larena smiled to herself, knowing it took some bravery on her maid's part. She wasn't used to defying any man, least of all the one she cared for.

"I can't believe I'm doing this." Larena heard her mutter to herself. "Alistair won't ever trust my word again. I promised him."

Larena stopped midway down the steps and turned to her maid, "He will only be angry if we get in the way of whatever is going on. We are just going to listen and we won't get hurt. We'll stay in the background. I promise you. I deserve to know my fate." She didn't merit this and she knew even if Aunt Charlotte had not found a way to gain a pardon, Gavin would protect her. She could, after all, be carrying his child. He didn't love her but at least she knew he craved her body and she enjoyed his as well.

Downstairs she could see the three men who were still waiting for the people coming up the trail. It had to be too soon for The Duchess to call in favors. Several times she had the strange feeling Gavin was in communication with her aunt but she could never be sure. The Duchess could have sent a messenger to London. Perhaps the people coming here were friends not foes.

"What do you think they're saying? All Alistair does is nod his head," Tyna whispered, standing a bit too close to her.

"I'm sure they're talking about me and what is about to happen. I'd like to be outside with no one but Gavin watching the storm. Instead, I'm inside wondering about what exactly my future holds." She didn't want to admit to anyone the fear sweeping through her and the cold chills that seemed to settle deep in her soul.

Tyna stumbled over a chair. She caught it before the piece of furniture toppled to the ground but not before all three men turned to see what the noise was. "I'm sorry," Tyna murmured.

The mesmerizing sizzle of Gavin's eyes bored into her, yet she did her best to ignore the implied intent. She was sure she understood his thoughts, not that they were that hard to figure out. "I'm not going anywhere," she spoke softly and she was sure he couldn't hear but was also sure he understood. After nodding he turned his back to her. And she felt the impact of his thoughts. *You'll explain yourself later.*

Why are men so autocratic and obtuse?

Tyna tugged on her arm. "We really should go upstairs, you know. This could all turn out so badly, and Alistair is angry that I defied him. I can tell by the way he looked at me."

"Don't be a ninny. You don't have anything to be afraid of. He's just a man and all men believe, with all sincerity I might add, that they know everything."

"Really, I know what Cale would do. He'd lock me in my room for a week," Tyna said.

"Alistair is not your brother," Larena insisted, "and if Alistair locks you in the room, I'm sure he'll be locked in there with you because he won't want you out of his sight."

"Still, we should go back," Tyna persisted.

"We are not returning to my room. Not until I find out my destiny." Larena stubbornly stood her ground even though she understood the truth of Tyna's words. She'd never seen Gavin this angry. It seemed when she got herself into trouble before, there was always a glint of a smile on his face. This time his brows were drawn together and his eyes were dark, shuttered, his lips thinned.

"Men don't like to be defied. My brother...well he wasn't nice when

I argued with him or disagreed and even worse when I chose to go against his wishes," Tyna whispered, tugging on Larena's shirtsleeve.

"What do you think Alistair will do to you? He wouldn't beat you, would he?" Suddenly concern for herself faded.

Tyna backed toward the steps, fear in her eyes. "I don't know and I don't want to find out. I don't know him well enough to comprehend what he might do, but he has no hold over me. It's not as if we are married."

"I'm terribly afraid it's too late for that. He already knows you came downstairs against his orders. I'll bet he's just like Gavin. He says one thing but when I do what I want, then he ignores the facts that are staring at him right in front of his nose."

"I don't know, I really care about Alistair, and I don't want to ruin this relationship before it even gets started. I think I fell in love with him at first sight."

"Wait," Larena put a hand on Tyna's arm, stopping her from her crazed and silly flight up the steps. "Think about the precedence you're setting. What is it that you want? You need to stand up for yourself."

"I can't. I just want to be happy and have a family with someone I love." She shook off Larena's hand but stopped, tears sliding down her eyes.

"You love him then?"

"I believe so," Tyna whispered, looking wistfully up the steps.

"Someone's here. Look, it's not soldiers." Suddenly Larena's heart skipped a beat. She walked closer, bent over at the waist trying to see better but all that appeared to her were dark silhouettes, one obviously a female. "Who do you think it is?"

"How would I know?" Tyna said, following in Larena's footsteps. It seemed she was just as curious as Larena.

"Addie! It's Addie and Hamilton," Larena shot out the door, sliding to a stop in front of her friend then wrapping her arms around her in a giant hug before finally letting go.

"Hello to you too," Addie said stepping back in order to catch a breath of air. "It's nice to be welcomed here. We weren't positive it was the thing to do, barge in on your honeymoon. The two of you are married, right?"

Gavin answered in a gruff voice, "We are."

"I'm not positive but I'm not too sure Gavin is quite as happy that we rode all this way to visit as you. It's good to see you, Larena," Hamilton, always the gentleman, said with a wicked grin on a smug face. "It seems we've interrupted several somethings with our untimely arrival."

"Why are you here?" Larena asked so very curious as to the cause for this sudden and unexpected visit. "It's pretty unexpected."

"My questions also." Gavin spoke slowly. He still had his hand on his pistol and the other two men had not relaxed, remaining poised and appearing ready for any surprise.

"Had a visit from Montgomerie," Hamilton rocked on his heels, still grinning as if he knew something everyone else was waiting for. "The heir apparent graced us with some information we couldn't ignore."

"And..." Gavin appeared skeptical.

"Now Hamilton, quit bating them and tell them we were bored to tears and you went to Montgomerie for something, an assignment, that wouldn't be too dangerous. Be honest you wanted to feel useful again. You like spying on people."

"There is that. Boredom makes me want to do something and spying is in my blood, our blood," he amended, shooting a look at his Addie that could melt stones.

"Good idea, old man, tell us why you're here and quit stalling. Does it have anything to do with Larena and the warrant?" Gavin asked, his hand still resting on the hilt of his sword.

"Everything," Addie said. "The Duchess has been working night and day to overturn the arrest warrant which was groundless to begin with. She has put out feelers, well, threats to several people in hopes someone with power and authority will cave and produce the needed paperwork to overturn the authorization of your arrest."

"It seems she has evidence which was acquired by her late husband, William, that proves one of the field marshals involved with this was embezzling money from the crown, has been for eighteen years at least." Addie smirked at her husband who was now frowning. "And that's the only one we really know about, but some of those married men have had numerous affairs which The Duchess has kept secret."

"You've taken all the fun away," Hamilton said. "I hoped we could string them along for a few more minutes."

"I'm not sure why you think tormenting these two newlyweds is fun," Addie said indignantly, one hand on her hip, berating her husband with her words as well as the fire shooting from her gaze. "The peril to Larena is very real."

"My apologies. I give in to my wife's honesty and sensibilities. She has always been the rational and sensible one in our relationship." Hamilton bowed low, still grinning.

"Does The Duchess have a pardon yet?" Gavin persisted, his voice harsh, his fists closing tightly.

"Still in the works," Hamilton admitted reluctantly, "but The Duchess believes it will be official within the week. We truly hoped we would have the best news possible when we set out on this journey."

"That's good to know," Larena moved to stand by Gavin. He put his arm around her shoulders and pulled her close. For a moment she believed he forgave her, but now when she looked into his grim face, she paused, "Are you still angry with me for coming downstairs so I would know what I had to look forward to?"

"We'll discuss it later. Now is not the place." His curt voice sent a wave of chills down her spine.

"You're still angry." She inhaled a long breath of air, knowing a lecture would be forthcoming then it would be forgotten. She hoped by the time they could talk privately his temper would be cooled.

"We've a couple of spare bedrooms upstairs," Gavin suggested, nodding toward the second floor.

"Oh, no, we plan to camp. It's our way of recreating some of the moments when we fell in love, and we're..."

"Bored," Hamilton finished for her. "Stimulus and adventure are just the thing to counter boredom."

"He does that all the time," Addie said, taking off her rain gear before shaking the water off away from everyone else. "He has this need to complete my sentences before I can. Men."

"Does he order you around too?" Larena asked, obviously curious about these two unique people. She slanted her husband a frown in an attempt to imply he did just that and she didn't appreciate it.

Addie motioned for Larena then as they walked to the end of the porch, she whispered. "Hamilton does order me to do this and that or not, but since I've known him, I've made it my habit to ignore anything I don't like. I'm sure you'll figure out how to do the same thing. When they want you in their bed, they always find a way to entice you and you can always hold the argument over their head to get your way. In the end everything is forgiven."

"Already do this somewhat, I was just hoping there was a practical means to stop him."

"Convince him you have a mind and your capable of intelligent decisions?" Addie laughed. "Keep the thought in your head that you can't change a man. They are all set in their ways, but you can always reduce the sting of their disapproval when you seduce them."

"Something like that. Auntie always says men think with their cock and I'm beginning to realize the truth of that."

"Your aunt Charlotte is a wise woman. She knows, just as we do that it's just the way men are created. They like to think they're in control and it's truly possible to let them believe it most of the time. Don't assert your will unless it's important."

"I'll take your advice to heart and pass it on to Tyna. Putting that aside, in this storm you can't camp outside. You'll get soaked through to the skin. Really, you should consider Gavin's hospitality."

"Tonight," Hamilton cleared his throat, "since half of it is gone, we'd like to put up our tent on your porch if you don't mind. We don't want to be a bother to you or your new wife. In the morning we'll hike down to the river and stay there for a few days."

"Drake told you about all the scenic spots? You can take his fly rod and try your hand at fishing. I understand the hike can be treacherous though."

"Perfect," Addie said, "We'll find it cozy and romantic. Hamilton most certainly can fish, clean and cook it. I'm not going to touch the smelly things."

"Be glad to. I'm a great cook, particularly over an open fire," Hamilton said laughing.

"But can you catch a fish?" Addie asked. "You have to catch one before you can cook it and eat it."

"Ah, my sweet wife, I'm an excellent fisherman and you should remember all the excellent meals I caught and cooked on our route overland from Spain."

"Arrogant too."

"Confident," he amended, "Has an entirely different connotation and one I much prefer."

"Whatever you want to say," Addie said, batting her lashes. "We should let these two newlyweds go do what newlyweds do."

"Perhaps we could teach them something," Hamilton laughed.

"I doubt if Gavin needs any help."

"You're welcome to pitch your tent on the porch or take a room in the lodge," Gavin said. "And thank you for the news."

Hamilton pulled Addie into his arms for a long kiss then, "See you in the morning."

"The cook should have breakfast early." Gavin held Larena's hand in his, pointedly directing her inside.

She held back slightly, disconcerted by the upcoming conversation she was sure would come as soon as they were alone. The storm had eased, both the lightning and the rain but not the look in Gavin's eyes. He was still angry with her and she was about to learn what he would do when provoked beyond forgiveness. Trying her hand at seduction became an intriguing option.

"Larena." His voice sounded stern and intimidating. "You can't put this off no matter how much you'd like to."

For a moment she was resigned but thought better of an easy compliance, she stopped inside, "You've no right to order me around."

"I'm your husband. I've every right."

Knowing it was the law and believing that fact were two different things. She understood she'd never convince him he was wrong. Taking Addie's advice seemed to be the most prudent course of action, but she couldn't bring herself to give in this easily.

"You do have that right if you don't think I've enough intelligence to make up my mind by myself," she protested, not heeding the advice she just gave herself.

"If you're not going to walk up these steps, I'll carry you." He turned to her, his eyes blazing but it seemed to Larena the light shimmering in them was closer to passion than anger.

Without thinking she moistened her lips then realized what she did. "I'll walk when I'm ready. So no, you needn't carry me."

He didn't pause for a second. He swept her into his arms then sighing, "You have this way of saying no so positively thus making me want to do whatever you said no to more than anything. In short, you provoke me to do things I had no intention of doing in the first place."

"You do everything just as you please. Then you berate me when I assert my will," she said wishing she had not goaded him but trying for the seduction angle, she touched his lips.

"I'm a man," he bent to kiss her then grinned at her open and honest response to the quick intimacy. "Of course I do everything just as I please, and it pleases me to make sure you stay safe from any harm."

"Even from two friends who appear unexpectedly," she still challenged him, couldn't seem to stop herself.

"When you walked down those stairs against my orders, you didn't know the approaching visitors were Addie and Hamilton. For all either of us knew, they were soldiers coming to take you away."

"True, but..."

He kicked open the door and strode into the room. He set her on a chair and poured her a glass of wine.

"But...?"

"Whatever was going to be said or done was about me." She tried to make her case.

"My point exactly. Drink, you're going to need sustenance."

"Why?"

"When we're done with this conversation, we'll proceed to act three."

"No." After this she certainly wasn't going to be in the mood for seduction even though two seconds ago she tried for just that.

He grinned and after sitting down, he ran his knuckles gently down her cheek then slowly down her neck before coming to rest on her breast.

She couldn't help herself, she shivered at the caress as heat once more swept through her body even while she fought to deny the sensations.

"We do need to talk, Larena. You need to understand how I felt when I saw you in the living room. The fear that shot through my body, very real terror, that was for you. I can't live that way, fearing for your life."

"No," she said again trying to close out the sound of his voice and the truth of his words.

He picked up her hand, tracing gentle circles on the back then bringing it to his lips and kissing the palm then he set it back in her lap. "Let me tell you a story."

She sipped the Bordeaux before setting it on the table and watched Gavin pace. "I don't want to hear a story.

He stopped for a moment to focus his attention on her then began pacing again. "Too bad, you've given me no other choice. I want you to understand my position. Your cousin Ella, you remember her, right?" He paused midstride, turning to watch her.

"Yes, of course. What does Ella have to do with anything?"

"I suppose you were still on the other side of the island with your sisters. You only arrived in London for her wedding and so you can't possibly understand all that transpired before and the very real danger Drake and Ella encountered."

She tapped her foot, impatient for him to finish the story that seemed to be going nowhere. "Get to the point."

"You know there were bad men who wanted to hurt Montgomerie."

"It was his brother. I know that. He wanted to become the heir apparent so he became desperate when Drake decided to wed."

"True, but he hired others to attack them. They were spending a peaceful day at the lake by his summer home and suddenly men were shooting at them."

Her heart nearly stopped, and her hand flew to her chest. "I didn't know that part."

"Neither Ella or Drake talked about the episode. I believe The Duchess and Eveleen were the only ones who knew the extent of what happened that afternoon. They raced for the small cabin nearby, his men following because after Fayth was attacked near the dress shop, he suspected something like that might transpire."

"What happened to them?" Shivers ripped down her spine and she was now sure she could guess the point of the story. "But Ella was fine."

"Ella was lucky. She could have been killed, simply because she disobeyed a direct order. She has a scar that will last a lifetime to remember the paybacks of not obeying a husband. I don't want to take any chances with your life."

"You're sure of that."

"Ella and Drake raced inside, after he protected her the entire ride to the small home. When he told her to stay down—"

"She didn't." Larena's heart lodged in her throat. "That was more than she wanted to learn.

"Just like you she was curious about what was happening. After all it was about her so she deserved to see...to know why people were shooting at them."

"Well, she did what she thought needed to be done. We are all used to taking care of ourselves. Neither of our father's cared a wit about us." She found all the liquid in her glass vanished.

"And she was shot. Drake, believing she was fine because she wouldn't tell him she'd been hit, directed all of his energy to chasing the men who attacked them from the premises." He finished; so emotional his voice shook with the intensity of the moment. "She could have died."

"This was nothing like that." She still meant to argue the point, persisting in her rights as an individual. "No one was shooting at us and if the soldiers came, they would not have shot."

"No, it might have been far more dangerous. Addie and Hamilton could have been soldiers bent on bringing you to London to stand trial." He stopped in front of her chair, kneeling. Once more he brushed her cheek with his knuckles. "And understand this, if soldiers insisted on taking you, I would have shot. Bloody hell but I would have never let them take you from me."

"It wasn't though and nothing like that happened." She understood his position but it seemed she couldn't stop herself.

"If it had been, you would have been vulnerable, and," he reminded her once again, "what you might not realize or understand was that I and my men had every intention of fighting."

"You would have killed the soldiers?"

"If necessary, but I hoped all along a little smooth talking would send them away without a fight."

"What would you have done?"

"My men had an escape route planned. But it would have been more difficult than the journey here. Disappearing into the countryside is not an easy feat, but I have friends in the highlands."

Tears slipped from her eyes followed by a sob. "I'm so sorry but you can't expect me to understand when you don't explain. You have to..." sobs slipped from her as did the tears. "I can't read your mind."

"There was no time," he persisted. "The minutes were precious and they had to be utilized to protect not to inform. You have to learn to trust me."

"We had hours while we rode here yesterday."

"I would see to your safety no matter what, but if you do something so stupid as to present yourself to those who want to harm you..."

"I'm sorry, as I told you a second ago, I didn't understand. I was impetuous and careless just like my father always told me. I don't know that you can change me."

"Impetuous, Larena that's one of the reasons why you intrigue me, why your laughter and curiosity touch my soul but you must obey."

"I didn't see a reason and I thought you were just being...just being obnoxious and controlling, extremely autocratic, and the list could go on and on."

He stood in front of her and pulled her into his arms. "I'm not ever going to order you to do something unless I feel it's most important, unless it will keep you from harm."

"Promise?" she wiped the tears away with the backs of her hands.

"Act three," he told her as he touched her lips with his.

~ * ~

He couldn't recount another time he'd felt so terrified and helpless.

Nothing Larena had put him through to date could compare to the gut-wrenching sensation that hit him when he saw her through the window. Visions of her death had swept through his mind.

Addie's and Hamilton's arrival put his anger in the back of his head for a short time but now that he'd spoken his mind, he wanted to show her how much he loved her.

The night slipped by and when the morning sun began to find its way through the clouds, he kissed her on the forehead. "Go to sleep little darlin', I'll be back for you later."

"What about you? Don't you need to sleep?"

"Not with you naked in my arms I couldn't possibly sleep." He'd felt such an elemental need to bind her to him, to find a way to make her life as beautiful and fearless as possible. She was a bricky lass and it could get her killed if she persisted in this crazy behavior.

"We're going to have to learn for both our sakes," she murmured, a sweet blush rising to her cheeks.

"I need to see to some things before Hamilton and Addie leave for their camping trip. I'm sure there is more to their arrival here than we discussed last night." He paused trying to put her wants first, "I need to discover those truths."

Downstairs Hamilton was in the kitchen devouring eggs and bacon. "Where's Addie?"

"Sleeping, I hope. From what I've heard, the path down to the river can be treacherous. I want her to be rested and definitely sure of foot before we start on another adventure."

"You going to carry all that on your back; tent, food and clothing? That's a heck of a lot." Gavin knew there was more to this than Hamilton was willing to admit at the moment.

"I brought a mule with me. Drake seemed to think the pack animal would be able to negotiate the steep trail without a hitch. What do you think?" Hamilton's smile was disarming.

"Haven't been down but I'm sure Drake knows what he's talking about." Gavin pulled out a chair and helped himself to a plate of food then poured a cup of coffee. He hoped Hamilton would give him more information. He needed to know what the ex-spy was up to and at

Montgomerie's request.

"Beautiful country, reminds a bit of the mountains in Spain. That was quite the trip. We were always looking over one shoulder. Addie and I never knew if we were followed. Didn't really believe the brother cared about Addie once she vanished without a trace. Left some evidence pointing to an accident."

"Tell me the truth about Larena and the warrant." Gavin needed to know if his escape plans should be implemented anytime soon. Nervously, he drummed his fingers on the table.

Hamilton set his fork down. "She's not pardoned yet. The Duchess has been making her rounds and threatening everyone she has dirt on. All her bluster doesn't seem to be getting her anywhere. I imagine she is going to have to do more than threaten. She's used the same cards so many times I do trust she's going to have to show them she's not bluffing."

"Soldiers could be coming up here then." Gavin's gut tightened with that thought. He'd have to find a way down the mountain that involved animal trails and sometimes no trail at all.

"I don't think anyone knows where you are except Drake and me and Addie. I doubt if he told Ella your whereabouts. Montgomerie believes safety lies in numbers. The fewer people who know the safer everyone will be."

"Well, you're wrong there. Someone knows and right now they hold all the cards in their hand, and it seems they're playing games with us," Gavin said, setting his fork on the table, unable to eat a thing.

"It's the drawing that's doing her in. Someone drew her on that platform with Cale and Jonathan. I think you need to find out who has a grudge against you and take action."

That was something he'd never thought about. He'd put men in prison, sent them away to hard labor. He ran through the latest of his wins in court. "You might have something. I'll make a list. Alistair and I can go over it this afternoon." What if what he did had put Larena in jeopardy. Her little adventures might have nothing to do with any of this. Perhaps he was the object of the revenge.

"If you come up with anything, send up a smoke signal and Addie and I will cut short our little holiday and bring the information to The

Duchess. A person setting you up might cut more weight than her dirt, and I'm sure she doesn't want anyone to call her bluff."

Gavin chuckled, leaning back in his chair arms crossed in front of him. It would take more than a smoke signal to reach them. He'd have to take the hike down the trail himself.

Addie appeared, all smiles, "Glad you two didn't eat everything before I got here. I'm famished."

"And I thought you'd never get up." Hamilton laughed when she swatted him. "Thought I kept you up all night and you wouldn't be out of our tent until after twelve."

"You did keep me up all night." She sat down beside him. "Where's Larena? I'd like to talk to her before we leave."

"Asleep."

"Oh, I get it. After the lecture you convince her to make love to you more than once." She ate a strawberry, seeming to study him.

"I didn't lecture her." He smiled pleasantly at Addie.

"Then how did you express to her that she was to obey your every command? I know it's not my business, but if you want to ease my curiosity..." She left it hanging.

He shrugged, enjoying this conversation for the time being. *Wasn't about to tell her anything important and I certainly would never lecture my wife.* "Told her a story instead."

"Overheard you telling Hamilton one of the people you've sent to prison might have a grudge or someone who cares about them. My thoughts, he'd have to have access to money. It wouldn't be easy to railroad Larena and make everyone believe she was guilty."

"Could be a she," Hamilton reminded her with an arrogant shrug. "Just trying to give women folk equal opportunity here. As you've told me many times, women have minds and sometimes the means to be independent of their man."

"Of course darling, this person could most definitely be a she because we are indeed equal. In fact, this is the type of thing a woman would be more likely to do. Don't rule out Cale, Tyna's brother or Jonathan, her first lover."

"Cale or Jonathan." New thoughts swept through his head. "Would they put Larena and now his sister in danger?"

"Cale was obsessed with Larena in the few encounters they had and Jonathan with Tyna, only he couldn't have her because he has the pox." She continued to chew.

He felt the blood drain from his face and he was sure it was too late to tell Alistair of this new development. Bloody hell, how could she do that to a man?

"What's wrong?" Hamilton asked.

"I hope that's not true about Jonathan. If I'm right about Alistair and Tyna, it's too late." Then he thought over all Addie told him. "Jonathan and Tyna never had sex."

"From all we've uncovered that's the truth," Addie said. "But we obviously don't know everything."

"How long have you been working this case? All this information could be easily discovered." Gavin couldn't understand how he missed the intrigue.

"We actually started working on this before Larena met Cale," Hamilton said with a nonchalant shrug.

Addie massaged her shoulders and regarding her husband thoughtfully, "We were bored. We both agreed we wouldn't go on assignment out of the country but simple things like the situation you were in are exactly what we want to do. There was increasing protest and the crown wanted to know who the instigators were."

"Didn't you have a child?" Gavin asked, suddenly remembering the talk and gossip concerning them over a year ago.

Hamilton looked at Addie and she returned his gaze, a shocked expression on her face. "Hamilton, we forgot the baby. What should we do now?"

"Go home?" Hamilton asked, acting as if he was shocked by the revelation.

He let his head fall back roaring with laughter and Gavin had to assume it was because of his expression. "You didn't."

"No, we left the toddler with Ella and Drake. She was more than happy to have someone to play with her little boy. And little girls are so much easier to watch than little boys. Don't you agree?" Addie turned to her husband.

"Whatever you say, dear" Hamilton condescendingly patted Addie's hand. "Are you through eating? I had one of Gavin's men pack the mule for us. I want to see this river and catch us a fish."

"Do grab some of this amazing bacon for lunch. We can put it between bread and along with some cheese, it should be very tasty." She turned to Gavin, "Will it take very long to shimmy down the path to the river?"

"I've no idea," he told them, his thoughts racing and he had a fervent need to talk with his wife, but was loathe to wake her.

He watched the unique couple leave then strode to the porch. Leaning on the rail, he inhaled the crisp clean air. A storm always had a way of settling the dust. Lost in thought he didn't hear Larena but felt her presence next to him.

He turned to her, "I see you're up."

"I've done a lot of thinking."

"Am I going to like where this is going?"

"I don't know. I'm not used to this, someone telling me what to do. I think we've talked about this before. My father didn't notice any of us and particularly me. I was the youngest and when I was growing up my sisters were constantly running around just as they pleased. They certainly didn't care what I was doing. I promise you I'm going to try to do what you say, but you have to guarantee you will explain the reasoning behind the command."

"You can't expect to continue in that vein, and how will you raise our children? Will you let them run roughshod over our lives?" He spoke quietly, angered and frustrated by her need to set her own parameters and to hell with what he wished.

She seemed to bristle, clearly disliking his tone, but at this point he didn't care. By putting herself in danger, she put his entire staff in jeopardy. Alistair had been willing to lay down his life for her if necessary as he had, and she treated the situation with disdain and as much as told him she could defend herself.

"I will be a good mother." Her face flushed, she gripped the railing with white knuckles. "How dare you insinuate I might be otherwise?"

"Are you sure?" He had too many questions that needed answering. While her impetuous nature drew him to her initially, now that they were wed everything became real. The fun in her misadventures evaporated with the wedding vows and his newfound feelings for her. She thought in ways he couldn't ever understand or even tolerate.

"I'm willing to make compromises. To meet you part way. It doesn't even have to be half." Her voice rose as she closed her eyes. "Are you? Can you learn to listen to me?"

"No."

"I can't talk to you when you're like this." She left him, striding down the stairs and toward the lake, her back stiff.

"What does that mean?" He started after her but abruptly changed his mind and stopped, watching her intensely. Where her safety was concerned, he wasn't about to compromise even the tiniest bit. She couldn't possibly expect that from him. Confusion and frustration ate at him.

She took off her shoes and sitting on the dock, she kicked water into the air. This was not what he expected when she approached him with the comment that she'd done a lot of thinking. He could hear her out. Listening to her was an option, but compromising was not and never would be.

He wasn't going to negotiate this with her either. He wasn't. But he walked to the dock and sat down beside her and after taking his shoes off, he stuck his feet in the water, hoping she would shed some light about what she was feeling and thinking. Gazing at the water brought memories of the night before to the forefront of his mind. When he closed his eyes, he felt her naked body next to his.

Silence stretched across the water, filled in by the soft sound of the wind humming through the trees. A few birds sang in the trees, and he heard the sound of a fish jumping in the lake. He realized he wasn't in control of this. She was and somehow she was manipulating the situation to her advantage. He would not let his love for her influence his decisions.

After a few minutes, and without looking at him or speaking, she put on her shoes and walked away, her back stiff and started into the woods. "Larena," he called after her.

She didn't stop or turn to look at him. Stunned, his heart stopped then slowly began to beat once more. Curious, impetuous and now he could add another attribute, stubborn, to her list of characteristics. "You don't know where you're going. You don't know what could happen to you alone in the forest." He called after her in hopes she would hear some sense in his words and stop.

For a quick second she turned to look at him, her face streaked with tears, fists clenched tightly at her sides. A moment of hesitation followed as if she thought on what he yelled out then she marched down a trail that led somewhere. Neither one of them knew where it would lead. Well, they were about to find out.

He caught up with her before she'd gone very far and walked beside her, acutely aware of her distress and unable to think of anything to say. She cried silent tears, wiping them away with the backs of her hands only to find they kept coming. There was no bloody way he'd apologize.

"You should stop now. We've gone far enough and I see you're limping. The blisters on your feet?" He placed his hand on her shoulder but she brushed if off. "Talk to me, please."

She swirled, her mouth pinched tight and her eyes blazing with anger and something else he wasn't certain, unhappiness. Then she started down the trail again.

He followed her, wary and uncertain of how to handle this situation and what he could possibly say that would make this right. He couldn't give her the promises she wanted unless he lied. That falsehood would become apparent as soon as she tested him.

This was uncharted land for him. As they walked, the path narrowed and finally ended at a cliff. His heart stopped when he looked over the steep embankment that didn't seem to end. She wavered for a moment before regaining her balance and stepping backwards.

Moments later she sat down on a boulder, her head in her hands, long heart wrenching sobs tearing from her throat. He understood his words caused this pain, but he couldn't and wouldn't take anything back. He meant everything he said to her. "Larena, you have to be rational."

He sat down next to her and pulled her onto his lap. "Hush, it will all be right soon." He stroked her back then ran his fingers through her hair, pins flying everywhere. Silken fire that was her hair lingered on his hands. She was too precious to him to ever let her have her way in this argument.

"Let me go, Gavin."

"So you can walk over a cliff?"

"I didn't."

To no avail, she pushed away from him. He held her tight. "Larena, I do want to talk with you but not about obedience. Hamilton and Addie believe someone might be targeting you to get to me. One of the people I helped put away or even Cale and Jonathan. What do you think?"

"Nothing."

"You must have some thoughts on this," he persisted, wishing she would let go of her demands and pay attention. "You don't have to be so stubborn." She was carrying this too far and making the little disagreement into a huge one.

In his arms he felt the stiffening of every part of her then she tried to push away from him again. "I don't have an opinion worth listening to as you've so pointedly told me."

"Only in certain situations where it concerns your wellbeing." The moment he said the words he knew they would only make matters worse.

"So this is one I might be intelligent enough to comment on?" She tried to push away again.

He held her fast, deciding on the truth as the best course. "Yes, this is something you understand. You were with Cale a short time and Jonathan from what Addie says, loved Tyna. I know your maid has told you some stories about her past, her lost love as well as her brother."

"Cale was always intent on one thing, changing the laws. He saw me as a convenient tool to use in gaining what he wanted. He planned the speech right where he knew I'd be." And once again, she repeated herself, "I didn't want to be there with him."

"I never thought you did." He went on, "Addie says from her intelligence gathering, Cale was obsessed with you. He told numerous people he would have you one day." Unconsciously his hands tightened on her waist. "He won't. I'm not going to allow that to happen."

"That's laughable. You don't even like me and I'm your wife." Once again she wiped moisture away from her cheeks.

"You shouldn't read things into my words, and you shouldn't say untruths in a fit of anger, Larena. You've no idea how I feel about you."

"You could tell me."

"I don't know how you feel about me. Do you love me, Larena? Are you willing to build a life with me?" He supposed after the wedding was the wrong time to have this discussion, but he meant to see this as far as possible.

"What I'm feeling right now is so much more than anger, Gavin, and it's certainly not love." This time she did manage to push herself away from him. She turned and with hands on her hips, she said. "I feel used as if I'm just a pretty bauble for your arm. I'm more than that, Gavin Broon, Duke of Millsglen. I'm a woman and my wishes need to be respected. You married me. Why?"

Not waiting for an answer and walking once more, at least this time toward the lodge as she said she would do. He decided he'd follow her at a more leisurely pace. The crash in the woods caught his attention. He reached for the pistol he always kept in his waistband when he was in the woods but it wasn't there. "Bloody hell what kind of fool are you, Gavin Broon? One who's mind has been befuddled by a beautiful woman who can't see reason."

She stopped, waiting and looking around her. A mama deer and her fawn ran across the trail in front of her. He let out a long sigh of relief. The animals could have been a bear and a cub. Her foolishness and the very real danger they were in seemed to be permeating his rational mind.

In just those few seconds the forest seemed to come alive with noisy chatter. It seemed to be giving a warning of some thing bad coming their way. Then the surrounding foliage fell silent. He'd never been a superstitious man, but this sent a cold sweat throughout his body. Swiftly, he closed the distance between them.

"We can discuss our differences later. Now we need to get out of the forest. There is something wrong. I can feel it to the tips of my toes. Can you walk faster?" In his chest his heart thundered with fear for her.

She closed her eyes then tilting her head slightly she nodded. By the expression in her eyes she felt uncanny sensations too. He placed his hand around her waist and guided her, pushing her to walk faster, despite her poor blistered feet. By the time they reached the lodge she was winded, heaving long deep breaths of air.

"What was that all about?" She stayed close to him her fear seeming to overpower her anger.

"Something spooked me, the entire forest was strange," he'd realized. "There was something out there that caused the deer to run and protect her baby. You felt it too. I know you did. It had to be human. There is no other plausible explanation."

"I'm going upstairs. You can figure this out on your own." She left him watching her walk away, understanding they were on a shifting, crumbling plateau he didn't know how to rebuild. He cringed when he heard the door to the master slam shut then only a few minutes later she walked to another room. She would sleep with him tonight, he vowed. He would find a way to help her understand why.

Alistair knocked on the door, poking his head around the corner, holding up a piece of paper. "You alone right now? I found this in the kitchen and thought you needed to see it."

"Unfortunately, yes, what is that?" Gavin laughed not wishing to tell Alistair his troubles but at the same time longing for someone to confide in. They had shared many an adventure since childhood as well as a bonny lass from time to time. He grew up with Alistair.

"A drawing and as soon as I saw what it was..."

Gavin stared at the paper, his heart in his throat. He glanced at his long-time friend then back to the sketch. Wadding it into a tiny ball, he clenched it tighter. The picture burned in his mind. Someone had watched them in the most private and intimate activity devised by nature. The picture was a beautiful rendition of last night when he made love to her in the lake.

"Where did you find the drawing?"

"On the kitchen table."

"Whoever drew that was in this house?" His gut turned over, terror for Larena even more urgent than a minute ago when all he had were suspicions.

"I will put guards on both doors. Did you sense something strange in the forest just now?" Alistair asked still, standing at the door.

He didn't want to think of the drawing and what it meant. He needed to move on, realizing the person who drew this probably caused the uprising in the woods. "When it's just the two of us, you certainly don't have to abide by the rules of etiquette. Sit down. Help yourself to anything you might want. And yes, something or someone spooked the forest animals."

"I couldn't be sure, but I thought there were more people in the vicinity than we could account for. The drawing confirms this. It's the only thing that makes sense. I talked to your men and told them to stay alert."

"Someone is watching us and even with our men standing guard, we've no idea who this person could be. They've taken unconscionable liberties."

Gavin rose, striding to the sideboard, realizing those were his thoughts too. "Whiskey?"

Alistair looked outside before responding. "Yes, sometimes this seems too much like the old days when we ran around the forest near the castle with no supervision."

"We were boys and we had nothing to fear then."

"But we do now."

"Perhaps." Gavin handed him the glass, both standing at the window gazing outside. Unlike last night, the sky was clear, no clouds in sight but it was still eerily silent. "We would have grabbed our guns to find out the source and now we stay inside like old ladies guarding the house."

"What's in the house is too precious to leave alone," Alistair said then changing the subject. "I think I'm going to ask Tyna to marry me. I've never met anyone like her."

"Did you know she had a lover before?" Gavin watched for a reaction from Alistair.

He remained undaunted, "I figured that and I didn't treat her very well the first time we made love. If I'd known she was innocent, I might have waited."

"She's a virgin?"

"Was, I made assumptions and I hurt her that night. She forgave me though. Several times over," he grinned.

Gavin thought back on his and Larena's first night. He'd hurt her too but... "What could you have done differently?"

He downed his drink, setting it hard on the table. "Bloody eyes, I thought... I don't know what I thought but it wasn't that she was a virgin. I treated her as if she were a whore."

"You couldn't have known."

"Asking might have been the right thing or maybe treating her with tender concern like she deserved. I'm having trouble forgiving myself because I lost control."

"I suppose there is no real excuse. Make up for it every night for the rest of your life and in time you won't feel so bad."

"Many times over and I didn't deserve her. She is sweet and honest. Tyna was innocent and I carelessly took her virginity. She willingly gave something to me that was so very precious."

"You believe that now. Is she innocent in what her brother might be doing? Could she tell you something, perhaps something she doesn't even know?"

"What are you talking about?"

"Addie told me Cale was obsessed with Larena and his friend Jonathan fell in love with Tyna a long time ago. What happened between them to end their relationship? That fact could be important."

"You're trying to tell me that both of the girls are in danger from some crazy men?"

"Did she tell you Jonathan has the pox and that's why she's not with him? From what you've told me, Jonathan told her before anything happened between them. I doubt if he'll do anything to hurt Tyna. He's had her best interest at heart for a long time."

"The pox." He didn't want to believe it.

Gavin poured them both another glass of whiskey. "It's a lot to take in, I understand but we've got to be more vigilant here. I've relied on the men we posted along the trail but we both know someone was able to sneak past them."

"Do you know if there were warrants out for our arrests?"

~ * ~

The Duchess composed herself, smiling at the woman sitting in the chair across from her. Portia Melbourne had been a friend or more accurately an acquaintance for most of her adult life.

"Portia, would you like more tea and another lemon bar? Cook has truly baked the best ever, and I know how much you love them."

Portia smiled then hesitated, her hand outstretched, "I really shouldn't but they're so good," she said reaching for another one, powdered sugar coating her lips, her eyes wide with pleasure. She licked her sugar-coated mouth.

"Help yourself. There is more than enough. Now that all the girls are gone, I've been lonely and cook doesn't seem to realize it's just David and me. She continues on as if we were feeding a houseful of boys. All the leftovers we throw out. I really should do something about that, perhaps take them to the orphanages. Do you think they'd like them?"

"David? Who is David and why on earth would you feed those little devils who become pickpockets and whores?"

"The children have few options. They arrive there for various reasons, none of them good. Some are even bastards of wealthy gentlemen." The Duchess suddenly thought Portia deserved her unfaithful embezzling husband.

Portia waved her hand in the air, "Well, I've more important things to concern myself with." She leaned forward, snatching another lemon bar from the plate. "Who did you say David was?"

"The McLellan, my late sister's husband. We've both been alone for so long. I find comfort in his companionship and I hope he feels the same about me. He was willing to come with me for a stay in London. Wasn't that nice of him? He's been so sweet through all of this trouble with Larena. We didn't even get to attend her wedding to the Duke."

Portia sighed miserably, looking at The Duchess with tears in her eyes, "I wish I could find even the tiniest bit of comfort with my husband. He's been so distant for such a long time. After I gave birth to an heir... I think he married me for money and a position in the aristocracy." She paused, taking another bite of the confection, "And an heir."

"He's a field marshal, dear. Why would he want more than that? He's got you and anything money can buy." Charlotte's heart suddenly and inexplicably went out to this woman. She was right of course; the marriage was not made out of love.

"Ambition and a title. I couldn't give him a title." She bit into the lemon bar. "Could I borrow your cook for a day or two? These are simply divine. I'm going to have to tighten my corset."

"No, but I'll send some of these home with you, as many as you'd like." It seemed she didn't dwell for long on her husband's aloofness. Food was more important to her now and probably the latest gossip. Portia was just the type of woman who would revel in repeating stories about other people. What she didn't know was that if her husband didn't fold and give her what she wanted, there would be so many truthful and very hurtful rumors swirling around her she wouldn't be able to leave her home for days or perhaps weeks.

The Duchess thought of her late husband and would give anything to have him back as well as her sister. If that happened, all would be well with this world. She planned to move on with her life and she didn't think her late husband, the duke would care if she did that with the McLellan. She hoped David was beginning to feel something for her.

She heard the knock and smiled while she watched her butler walk to the door. "Sir?"

"The Duchess sent for me."

Portia looked up and over the rim of her teacup a startled look on her face. "You sent for my husband? Why ever for?"

The Duchess rose, holding out her hand in greeting when Melbourne strode arrogantly into the room. "Field Marshal Melbourne, how are you doing? I see you got my message."

Melbourne looked from his wife to The Duchess. "You asked my wife here? I thought you wanted to talk business."

"Oh, I plan on it but what business we discuss depends on the status of my query to you about my niece. Brandy?" The Duchess smiled and watched Melbourne run his finger between his collar and neck. "Of course you remember the missive and what I asked of you."

"I'm not sure I understand what your intentions are." Melbourne accepted the drink, his words sketchy, his body shaking.

He was hesitating, trying to mount a battle plan, but there was only one outcome she meant to accept. If he didn't come through for her and the pardon she sought for Larena, she would apprise Portia of all his indiscretions including the embezzlement of funds to feed his gambling habit. News of his dalliances and the mistresses he kept over the years as well as the name of his current mistress would change their relationship but the embezzlement would send him to Newgate.

"Do you want me to explain all the details?" She smiled at him before sipping her tea. "I thought I made them perfectly clear." She was obviously not beyond blackmail.

He cleared his throat several times. The Duchess looked to Portia. "I'm hoping he can grant my niece Larena Graham a pardon. She was in the wrong place and his soldiers tried to arrest her for something she had no part in. Actually, they did arrest her. Larena's husband, the Duke of Millsglen, rescued her from the prison cart as he should have."

"He bribed my soldier." Melbourne shot in his piece.

"Pshaw..." The Duchess waved one hand in the air. "Ah, a minor indiscretion made out of love for another person. I believe he loves my niece as much as the late duke loved me. Can you say the same of Portia? Do you love her unconditionally and are you willing to make a few sacrifices for her?"

"Of course I love my wife. Why..." It seemed he realized where she was going with this. He should have comprehended her intentions when she sent for him. Any man of intelligence and integrity would have. Yet Melbourne had always considered himself above the law.

"I'm not bluffing, Melbourne," The Duchess told him sternly before offering Portia another lemon bar, hoping the sweet would distract her from the conversation. She didn't want to play her cards unless she had to.

"I'm not sure I can grant the pardon. It has to go through several—"

Leaning toward Portia, "You understand of course why Melbourne is not interested in you. Did you know he has property in the country that he regularly visits?"

She watched Portia's jaw drop as her eyes widened. "No. I always wanted a home in the country. Why didn't you tell me?" Her gaze seemed to shoot daggers at the Field Marshal.

The Duchess hesitated for a moment, enjoying the drama, "I suppose he didn't want to share it with you. Perhaps now that you know about the beautiful and isolated home, he will give you a tour in a day or two. If I were you, I'd hold him to that promise. About three years ago, Melbourne purchased a second sailboat too. Did you know he likes to sail on the Thames?"

"The pardon will be granted," Melbourne spoke up quickly. "Portia, come with me, now. You've eaten enough lemon bars to make you sick."

She stood up, brushing powdered sugar from her skirts. "I was..."

"You must give cook time to pack you some of the lemon bars your wife loves. I promised her she could have some."

Chapter Nine

The lean-to Cale and Jonathan built did little to keep the pounding rain from penetrating the structure before soaking into their skin. Cale felt chilled through to the bone.

"It's a fine fix we got ourselves into, but I don't understand why we're stalking a woman who doesn't care about you or even care a fig for you," Jonathan said while he broke twigs to feed the dying fire. "We should keep going northeast and see if we can get a ship out of Scotland for somewhere safe. We could sail to America, we could."

"Larena is our ticket to freedom. We can kidnap her and ask Broon to give us a way out of London in exchange. I don't care where we go but we can't stay here. The United States sounds like a fine destination," Cale reiterated while he kept feeding the tiny flames.

"Well, I don't want our way out to have an endpoint called Australia, thank you. I don't have good health, and I'd just as soon live out what I have left of my life somewhere nicer." Jonathan blew on the smoldering embers. "I'm only here because I don't have anywhere else I'd like to be."

"You want to be freezing your backside off in the rain? No warrant for your arrest exists. I'm not sure but I do believe there is something else going on here."

"Gavin Broon is a lawyer, a damn good one I've heard, but he puts people away instead of defending them. He has enemies, lots of them. The drawings of Larena are the key to all of this," Jonathan said, seeming thoughtful. "I wonder who..."

"The drawings? You mean the articles in the paper where Larena's face was the prominent feature."

"Yes." Jonathan carefully placed a small piece of wood on the fire. "What if we worked with Gavin to find out who is really responsible for the warrant on Larena? If we did that, he might show his gratitude and help us leave England."

Cale thoughtfully stroked his chin and the growing stubble there. "I'm not stupid. I know Larena would never care for me and I don't want Tyna to turn against both of us. If we helped him..."

"This is a much better plan than kidnapping her. Tyna would hate both of us and I can't bear that. I'm glad she's found someone else even though my heart breaks at the thought," Jonathan said.

"What were you able to snatch from the house when they were traipsing around the forest?" Cale's stomach growled. The two of them were not good at foraging for food. All they'd eaten for quite some time were berries and neither one of them had known if what they devoured were poisonous.

"I did well."

"So," Cale waited, thinking of the meals his father had prepared, his mouth watering.

"Not as great as what you're thinking. I've got a loaf of bread and enough cheese to last a few days along with some leftover bacon." Jonathan spread a cloth on the ground and set his treasures on it.

"Our time on the run has not left me picky. I'll eat anything that doesn't move." Cale wished that wasn't true. They made camp about a mile downstream from the couple who made so much noise descending the trail they would have scarred off every animal in the vicinity.

"Me neither. If it fills my belly, I'm happy."

Cale leaned against the boulder, rubbing his face in an attempt to ease his troubles as well as his exhaustion. He never thought his protests against the Corn Laws would come to this. Yes, it was important to him but never worth his life or anyone else's. Somehow he lost control of the situation as well as the protestors.

"First light we are going to talk to those two who have put up a tent by the river. I'm sure they are friends of Gavin's, and if we pitch our case to them, we've a better chance of succeeding than if we go it alone."

"Alright, what are you going to say?"

"The truth, everything, I won't leave anything out," Cale said, wishing the truth was a little more palatable.

"Even your obsession with the Duke's wife?"

"Especially that. They need to understand that I have no delusions about Larena. I understand what a person of my status can have and what they cannot. That's the only way anyone will ever trust us. We have to be straight up from the start."

"Then I need to say only the truth also."

"If we want to find another life in another world, yes."

~ * ~

"You saw the campfire while you were out foraging for fire wood?" Hamilton asked Addie as he sat down beside their fire.

"Of course I did. I even got close enough to hear part of their conversation." Addie was all smiles when she let an armload of firewood and kindling tumble to the ground. Purposely, she struck a pose she knew would entice Hamilton.

"Well," Hamilton looked up from the fish he was skinning and boning with a grin. "Don't leave me in the dark and we need to eat first. Then you can have your wicked way with me."

She plopped down beside him, "Very well then, they don't have nefarious plans. Instead, they want help from Gavin and they're hoping to exchange some knowledge for it," Addie said, stirring the fire with one of the sticks she collected, watching sparks sprinkle the sky.

"So, they are not the ones we are afraid of, not the ones causing all this trouble even though they played a part. Good work, darling, and you really should button your shirt a bit higher or I'm not going to be held accountable for what I do next. The fish could burn for all I might care."

"No, they are not," she said, shaking her head, smiling, her hand playing with the fastenings of her shirt. "They are not. We have solved half of the mystery. When we discover who is behind the drawings and why, we will discover who means to hurt Gavin."

"Well, that is a daunting task." Hamilton kept his gaze on the task at hand, seeming to realize she didn't mean to back down and it seemed she preferred a bout of lovemaking over his fish.

"But that's what we do best." Still grinning, Addie wrapped her arms around Hamilton, hoping for a kiss then something a bit more intimate. She let her hands slide down his arms then back, moistening his neck with her lips and tongue.

"Whatever you say. Dinner can wait. You know how little control I have when you seduce me." Hamilton pulled her close, his hands pulling her shirt from the britches she wore before finding her breasts and loving her.

~ * ~

Larena woke near dawn, spooned tight against Gavin's hard body. She snuggled into him, content then remembered the way their evening ended. Had not expected him to follow her to this room, having thought she'd made her point. She was still angry with his highhandedness.

Not ready to forgive him, she slipped silently from the bed. Striding to the master chamber, she dressed and walked downstairs. The fire still glowed, the embers burning low. The silent peace surrounding her sent a bit of warmth to her soul and a hope she could heal the ever-widening gap between them.

Sleep had been elusive. She had thought over their argument so many times, she wondered if she wasn't being too stubborn as her over-confidant husband had told her. Perhaps Gavin had a point though. She really didn't have experience with danger, especially when that peril involved her. And, she admitted grudgingly, his reasoning might be sound. If the situation had been different, she might have been in jeopardy.

Picking up a piece of paper that had been wadded into a tight ball, she tossed it absentmindedly several times before letting it rest on her lap.

"Oh, excuse me, milady. I didn't realize anyone was up. Just came in to stoke the fire, putting more wood on it. Would you like a cup of hot tea? I've got some brewin' in the kitchen," the cook asked.

"That would be nice, thank you." Curious, Larena stared at the ball of paper before slowly folding it smooth. Seeing the elaborate drawing, her body froze in shock. She looked upstairs, wondering if Gavin had seen this. Of course he had and of course he chose not to tell her about it.

"I was going to throw that drawing in the fire but I forgot last night."

Gavin stepped through the front door, shirtless, his buckskins unbuttoned, drying his hair with a towel.

When she left the bed to dress he must have gone for an early morning swim. "Wish I hadn't but now that I have, can we talk about it?"

From an end table he picked up another piece of paper setting it in front of her. "Another drawing." This one was of her and Gavin when he was sitting on a boulder and holding her yesterday on his lap after she stormed off.

"I'm sorry. There are guards on each door now and still, whoever did this found a way to leave another sketch on the porch. I've a feeling that person or persons could be working for me."

"I feel violated," she whispered, the skin on her arms seeming to crawl. "What could they possibly want from us?"

He sat down beside her, wrapping an arm around her shoulder. "I'm sorry. I'd give anything to keep this from you, but I understand that you must feel you need to know and in this case I agree. As for what they want, I don't know. The only thing that comes to mind is to terrify and unnerve both of us. This person who is drawing these sketches wants us to know he's watching us and can get to us at any time."

"Are you trying to compromise?" she smiled feeling no more at ease after his last words. "Do you think my female sensibilities can comprehend all the intricate components of this danger?" she asked sarcastically, despite her efforts to the contrary.

"No and yes."

His jaw clenched tight and she understood she was reading more into this sudden insight than was there. Well, what did she expect? If he didn't mean to compromise, then she wouldn't either.

"Do you have any plans?" she squared her shoulders, bracing herself for upcoming orders he was sure to issue.

"Right now? No one goes anywhere alone, including me. And I spend a lot of time with Alistair in hopes of discovering who this new employee is."

She wanted to protest, but the addition to his statement kept her silent even though she knew it was calculated to do that very thing. "Do you think Aunt Charlotte has been successful in her attempt to get my pardon? We can all go home if she has, and we won't have to worry about the sketches and who is behind them. This person obviously doesn't mean us physical harm."

"That would be nice. We'll hear from Charlotte when and if it happens, but whoever is doing this," he set the second drawing on the table, "isn't going to stop until we discover who he is and make him cease."

The commotion from the front porch caught her attention. She tried to stand but his arm around her held her in place.

"Stay put," he told her and slanted her a stern look then remained with her waiting for one of the guards to announce the visitor.

Arrogant men.

"It's us, Addie and Hamilton," Addie stepped into the room laughing, "and we brought a surprise. Well maybe not a surprise in a good way, but maybe yes..."

"Cale," she breathed his name as he stepped inside, looking as if he'd been dragged through the bushes. "I think they'd like to sample whatever the cook has on the breakfast table before they talk with us. We found them a mile or so from our tent, starving pretty much."

Hamilton stepped in behind her, volunteering. "We'll keep an eye on them if you two have eaten already."

Hamilton ushered Jonathan and Cale into the kitchen, without a backward glance.

"They are not the ones who are trying for revenge against me." Gavin handed one of the drawings to Hamilton. Addie picked up the intimate drawing before Gavin could show anyone, quickly wadding it back into its tight little ball and handing it to Larena.

"Not meant for my eyes or anyone else's. You must be horribly concerned. Are you any closer to figuring out who could be behind this?" Addie asked before heading for the kitchen.

"What just happened here?" Larena asked. "The two men who got me into all this trouble are here but they are no longer a foe? Have they become friends then?"

"Appears so," Gavin said, rubbing his chin thoughtfully. "I'm going to the kitchen. If you're not, remember to stay in the house."

"I wouldn't think of going anywhere alone," she said sweetly and smiling at him as if she would do his bidding whatever it might be.

"Good."

She watched his back, feeling the loss of the closeness they had shared only two nights ago. This wasn't the way she ever expected a marriage to be. But why not, her mother and father certainly didn't love each other. Sipping the tea the cook had given her, she watched the fire burn.

Addie appeared with two scones and handed one to her. "Trouble in paradise? So soon?"

"I tried to take your advice but it doesn't work. He's not capable of compromise. He's quite willing to look the other way about some things, but when he decides he's right, he expects complete obedience. He acts like he's the king."

"Dear, Larena," she placed a gentle reassuring hand on hers, "He is king of his home. Never forget that if you want a happy life. Is his anger really worth the short time we all have together?"

"We have a lifetime."

"And it will go by before you know it. Don't waste the time you have with him on petty arguments. Do you love him?"

"I haven't figured that out yet." She did love him but she wasn't about to admit the fact to anyone but herself just yet.

"You should tell him," she said biting into the scone, closing her eyes in seeming bliss. "The words will mean the world to him and might well solve half your problems."

"That I haven't figured out that I love him?" she asked, skeptical of Addie's sanity.

"No, that you love him."

"But I don't."

"Of course you do. You're showing all the signs," Addie laughed regarding her with a hint of appreciation.

Tyna walked through the kitchen door and sat down. "Addie's right, you do show all the signs. Sorry but I overheard. Alistair is in the kitchen too."

For the first time since yesterday, Larena felt a tiny bubble of laughter. "And what are those signs? Why does everyone else know when

I don't?"

"Because we can watch you without judging," Tyna said.

"So, what are these signs that let you read me like you can see into my heart?" Larena asked, curious to understand what she gave away to these ladies and hoping she hadn't done the same with Gavin.

"You never stop looking at him if he's in the same room with you. That tells me a great deal. And it's not just that you're gazing at him. It's the look of complete reverence in your eyes. As if you believe he can walk on water," Addie said.

"I do not. Is that true?" Larena squirmed, looking at Addie for an answer. If she meant to be honest with herself, she did regard him in that way. "I'm going to have to be a lot more careful."

"I'm sorry, love, but it is so very true. If it's any consolation, Gavin looks at you in the same light. How do you think about Gavin? That he's special in some way?" Tyna asked. "It's how I feel about Alistair. How I felt from the first second he walked into my life."

"And Hamilton," Addie admitted. "There was some element that he possessed that stole my heart. No one else I've ever met did that to me. I crave him in my life."

"Gavin is unique," Larena confessed outright. "There is no one I've ever met like him. And night or day I can't stop thinking about him. Even when I'm sleeping I dream about him."

"Now, I know you disagree with him about trivial things, but what does he do right?" Addie reached out and touched her hand, a smile on her face. "Think about it. There is sure to be more things he does that you like."

"Just about everything. He's strong and handsome. He knows how to comfort me even when I don't want him to. When I see him, my heart races and I can't slow my breathing. Sometimes my hands tremble just thinking about him. I cried last night when I went to bed in a different bedroom. This, this thing with the warrant on my head, that's what has me questioning everything and is seeming to tear us apart. Ever since he rescued me from the lamppost then the other times, I wanted him to kiss me and yes, make love to me." It seemed to her she was rambling and her thoughts were in chaos.

"You're most definitely in love with your handsome husband,"

Addie said a glint in her eyes. "All you have to do now is admit the fact to yourself and tell him. It's not easy. I know. I had a horrible time admitting it to Hamilton, but I was so relieved when I finally said the words."

"Not until he tells me that he loves me." She suddenly felt just as stubborn as Gavin thought she was. She crossed her arms in front of her, stiffening her back. "I'm not going to make myself even more vulnerable than I already am. It seems he has made me that way." She thought a few seconds longer. "He should tell me first."

"I don't see why but of course it's your relationship," Addie said. "Think about telling him if you see yourself as his equal. Wait for him to say the words if somehow you really don't think of yourself at the same level."

"What if I blurted out the words and..." she didn't want to hear him say love was for fools or that it didn't exist or any number of other horrible things. She didn't want to have him tell her he didn't love her.

"Blurted what words?" Frowning, Gavin stepped through the kitchen door. "Something you want to tell me, Larena. I'd like to hear what those words you might divulge are. My curiosity is high."

"No." she clasped her hands tightly together, gazing at the floor. She didn't want him to see the heat staining her cheeks or the way her hands trembled while she struggled for air. The thought of him overhearing what she and Addie had been talking about terrified her.

"Cale and Jonathan need some help. They want to get out of England. If they shed some insight into the identity of our artist, I told them I'll help with whatever they need," Gavin said.

"They know who drew these?" Larena asked, holding up the drawings and wishing they didn't exist. Thoughts of this man seeing her and Gavin making love horrified her.

"To begin with, it's a woman, one who works for the London Times or used to work for them. When I shed light on what she is doing, I'm sure the job will no longer be hers. Her husband was sent to prison by me, on a charge of stealing. The woman interviewed Cale about the protests."

"Is the man out of prison now?"

Gavin continued speaking. "No. When she saw us together, she concocted a plan, seeking revenge against me. She was content for a while to spread gossip about us throughout the ton, knowing the rumors would hurt both of us. But when she saw you on the platform with Cale, the intent turned deadly. With her drawings along with the articles she wrote, she knew she could create huge problems for us."

"She didn't get me arrested," Larena said. "I did that, well, Cale did when he forced me on the platform with him."

"Yes, she did and it was underhanded. She told the soldier who I bribed where you would be and told the man it would be worth his time in money to make sure you ended up in the prison cart. She guessed I would pay the man to free you and she was right. I would stop at nothing to keep you from harm."

"She wanted you to be arrested for bribing that man and end up in Newgate along with her husband," Addie said.

"That's petty." Larena let all the information soak into her head. "Her actions were subtle and hard to prove."

"True, but she knew my status and didn't expect me to get sent to prison. When she watched us leave, she followed. Her wit brought her to the Broon country estate, and she was able to follow us from there the next day."

"Do you know her name?" Addie asked.

"Isobel McClure," Alistair said from the kitchen door. "I hired her as the cook in the little village down the mountain. She arrived here with the staff you sent ahead. I had no idea who she was. Her credentials were in order."

Larena's nervous laugh caught Gavin's attention, "So," Larena began," I'm in more danger in the house than if I walk outside."

"We had no way of knowing that." Gavin's defensive answer gave her comfort in some strange way. "Yet until the pardon, British soldiers will still be looking for you, intending to take you to jail."

"Sometimes orders are of no use." She smiled prettily, watching his dark features shutter closed. "Perhaps instinct is just as important in dangerous situations as a command." This argument would get her nowhere, and she knew it but some devil inside her head gave her permission to speak before she thought.

"And sometimes it is imperative to err on the side of caution. It's impossible to see every conceivable danger," Hamilton said stepping into this conversation for the first time. "I for one prefer to use both caution and instinct when deciding a possible course. What about you Addie?"

She sent him a heated look before glancing at Larena. "I usually go on instinct first, as you well know, Hamilton."

"I've searched all the outbuildings and the only sign Miss McClure was here is this stack of drawings," Alistair said, placing them on the table near the fire. "When I saw they were of the two of you, I quit looking through them."

Larena felt her gut wrench at his words, "Thank you," she said softly, unable to keep her embarrassment hidden.

"Alistair didn't want to say anything but she left drawings of us too. He has them in our rooms." Tyna said, her voice trembling with emotions. "That woman is no lady."

"I wasn't going to say anything," Alistair spoke up. "It was supposed to be between the two of us."

"I understand, but they need to know everything and I know you now. You would have told Gavin eventually. You're not capable of keeping secrets from him," Tyna said.

"He did tell me, but Addie and Hamilton needed to know also. They are part of all this..."

"And I'm not?" Larena interrupted feeling as if he still treated her as a child and heard nothing she'd said recently. "Oh, I comprehend everything you're telling me now, my sensibilities are not adequate to, to..." she fled upstairs, tears rolling down her eyes. He would never believe she was capable of anything but satisfying his baser needs. All she was to him was a brood mare. He was just like her father.

She had already come to the conclusion Gavin would never treat her, a woman, as an equal, but Addie was obviously on the same level as was Tyna. Face down she fell on the master bed, sobbing for a few minutes before sitting up and forcefully brushing the tears from her cheeks. Crying was what a child would do.

Larena thought for a few moments. Addie might take her down the path to the village below. She couldn't stay here, with Gavin Broon Duke of Millsglen, arrogant man, any longer than she had to. Deciding not to take anything with her she didn't need immediately, she packed a small bag.

The soft knock on the door sent her heart racing and in hopes of Addie sensing her needs, she opened it. "Tyna. What are you doing here?" It wasn't Tyna's fault but at this point in time she resented her as much as she did her husband.

"I thought you might want something to eat. Gavin said you haven't had anything yet. He bade me bring something to you." She held a small tray of food with a steaming pot of tea.

"Thank you, you're very kind but what I need now is to talk to Addie. Can you get her for me?" She bit into a scone, one just like the one she left on the table in the living room. It was dry and tasted like ashes in her mouth.

"You're not planning anything foolish?"

She waved her hands in the air. "Of course not. I've thought about this all of five minutes and with or without Addie..." she thought better of telling Tyna. While she trusted her, it was only so far. If Gavin found out what she planned, he'd most likely hogtie her to his bed. "I don't need the advice of anyone else to make decisions."

"I'll get her but whatever it is you're planning, I hope it's not dangerous."

"Please don't tell Gavin. I have to be able to trust you. You can't be my maid and confident without complete and loyal trust," she paused, her arms wrapped around her. "I must have your silence if I request it and I'm requesting it now."

"How do I not tell him that you've sent for Addie?"

"Promise me you won't let him know anything you think you might have figured out."

"I won't tell him. I promise. But you know he will come after you." She left to find Addie.

"I can find somewhere to live where he can't find me." She doubted it. If Gavin wanted to find her, he would and perhaps then we could get at the root of their problems.

Too late, Larena knew the truth. Tyna would tell Alistair and he would in turn inform Gavin. She closed her eyes tight, fighting the anger and frustration welling inside. She could not live with a man so closed minded as Gavin. She had one hope at her disposal. She prayed there would be enough time in the interim for her to make it down the mountain to the inn before he discovered she was missing.

At the window she watched the early morning sunlight sparkle on the water, remembering the idyllic evening when they made love there. Memories collided in her brain, memories with Gavin and the delightful way he introduced her to pleasure. Bloody hell, there was more to a relationship than lovemaking and gratification. She needed more from him than he was willing to give. Most of all she yearned for respect and to be treated as an equal.

Gavin Broon, duke of whatever, I might be enamored of you, but I don't like the way you treat me.

"What do you want, Larena?" Addie was there, her head tilted sideways in question.

"Will you take me to the inn today, down the mountain to the village?" Larena watched the hint of surprise before Addie quickly guarded her emotions.

"Without Gavin's permission?"

"Yes, and I don't want him to know either. I'm going with or without your help," she said, determined to do this.

~ * ~

Gavin knew the second Larena left the living room, her back stiff. She was angry with him, furiously so. He searched his past words for the reason but came to no definitive conclusion. Meaning to discover what he did wrong later, he set his mind to finding Isobel.

"Where would she go? Wouldn't Isobel need help getting down the mountain?" Gavin asked, trying to recall all he learned about the couple when they were at trial. They were both Scottish and here they were, in Scotland. He understood relatives might be there for her. Clans stood by each other and would give aide in any way possible.

More than one way to the lodge existed. The path he took from the village below was the easiest and shortest. When he was worried about escaping English soldiers, he scoped out other ways to leave, ones that were not as well known to anyone but those who lived in these parts.

From the corner of his eye he watched Addie speak to Hamilton outside. He kissed her quickly on the lips then said something to her before she walked toward the stables. He admired Addie and her ability to be independent and strong, wishing for a moment Larena could be a little more like her. Larena wanted him to compromise in certain ways. He could never do that. She was too fragile and small and needed his protection. Larena would never be able to take care of herself.

Hamilton sat down then held the side of the large map Gavin was staring at. "What are you looking for?"

"See this line, right here?" he pointed at it. "This path is another way down the mountain. Several clans live in this secluded area. He drew circles around the regions. At the bottom in this valley, here," he put an X where his finger rested, "is one of the McClure clans."

"You think she might have gone there?" Hamilton raised one eyebrow in speculation.

"Yes, if she grew up in this area, she might be more familiar with the land and her family could still live here. They could hide her from us for as long as we wanted to search. A pursuit would be a waste of time."

"Do you want to go after her anyway?" Alistair raised the question. "We'll back you in whatever you want, but we might find a good deal of opposition. I'm not liking the thought of taking on the clans."

Gavin's first inclination was to do exactly that but with more thought he decided no, Alistair was right. "It wouldn't be prudent to head that way in search of Isobel. My thought is that she's done as much damage as she could inflict and won't bother us again. We can all move on with our lives. Her husband will remain in prison for the rest of his life."

"She wouldn't dare show her face in London again. No one would accept what she did and that she tried to have you and your lady imprisoned on false pretenses," Hamilton said. "Between our families we have many more resources at our disposal."

"London would be a fiasco for her as well as dangerous," Alistair agreed. "She has no other options that I can tell."

The conversation went on like that for some time. The men exhausted any ideas of capturing Isobel and returning her to stand trial.

Gavin wasn't too sure of what the charges would be, drawings of intimacies she should have never seen. At least one of the drawings could be used to convict him of a crime, but most were only invasions of privacy. Now that he was in possession of them, he liked the one depicting him making love to his beautiful wife in the lake.

"Ah, my wife, what did I say to her?" He sat back, his hands on his stomach, wondering where she was. Hours had passed since she left the room in anger. Once he thought he saw her walk down the stairs to go outside, but he couldn't recall seeing her return.

For a few seconds more he rested, closing his eyes and thinking about making love to his wife. Then he rose and strode up the steps to their bedroom. She wasn't there. Retracing his steps to sneak a look in the other bedrooms, he found nothing.

Downstairs he looked in the kitchen, thankful there were no more drawings on the table and relieved too that Isobel had vanished without creating many more problems. If they were all lucky, Isobel would remain in Scotland.

Hamilton had left several hours earlier with Alistair to take Cale and Jonathan to the Graham home near Berwick on Tweed where he hoped Hayden Johnston, Larena's brother-in-law, would find them a ship headed to parts unknown. Alistair was only going to go half way with Hamilton and Addie then he would return to the lodge.

Stepping outside he stood on the porch, soaking in the dark clouds that were gathering in the sky. Thunderheads grew on the horizon, threatening another storm. Larena would want to watch the storm tonight. He remembered holding her through a tempest such as this. His heart chilled recalling the horrible things that had happened to her as a child. One of his reasons for living was to keep her safe from the fears that tormented her especially at night.

He didn't understand her though. He wanted to love her and keep her safe from anything that might harm her. But, he realized, that wasn't what she wanted. She didn't want him to wrap her up in a cocoon so she couldn't move. In time he might understand all that swirled around her intricate and amazing head. She had ideas he'd never heard before, thoughts that were too new for him to process. She wanted to be his equal and he would try to make that happen, but he knew so far he'd failed miserably.

She wasn't at the lake or anywhere surrounding the lodge. He prayed she didn't stalk off angrily into the forest. That had caused both of them such a fright, he really didn't think she'd do the same again. He wandered to the out-building that Alistair and Tyna shared. The pair were thinking about marriage. Alistair deserved happiness. He'd served him for so long and so well. When he knocked, no one answered.

He shrugged it off believing Tyna might be outside somewhere with Larena or napping. Chuckling, he was sure Alistair would keep her up most of the night.

Walking back to the cabin's porch, he realized he'd been wrong. Tyna was standing by the railing, watching the path from the village. Her eyes wide with what appeared to be concern or even fear.

"Alistair should return soon. He was only traveling halfway down the mountain with them," he told her, striding up the steps to stand next to her.

"Yes, I understand but he needs to return soon." she nodded, alternately wringing her hands then gripping the porch railing until her knuckles turned white.

"What has you so at odds with yourself?"

"I pray that he does return soon. He doesn't know and so you don't know." Tears slipped from her eyes. "I didn't know he was going to leave so soon and I promised milady. Then he vanished before I could tell him. I cannot break a promise."

"What did you promise?" Baffled by the strange outburst, he turned her so he could see into her eyes. "You can tell me."

"I can't. Truly I can't. I promised milady." She seemed truly distraught.

His gut wrenched in two, his heart pounding. "What has she done? You have to let me know so I can protect her."

"Cannot say." Tyna refused to look at him, keeping her gaze riveted on the trail. "Don't think she's in any danger though."

She's not in any danger, repeating Tyna's words silently. If she were outside in this storm, Tyna's statement was false. Lightning slashed across the sky and a few seconds later thunder rumbled echoing across the lake and sending his already frayed nerves to a breaking point. Rain sluiced from the sky along with hailstones, the rattling on the roof so loud he couldn't hear himself think.

"Alistair!" she cried, starting her descent down the steps to meet him with arms open wide.

Gavin held her back. "No, it's too dangerous. He will be all right and you'll be in his arms in a few seconds. He must see to the horse first. Then I'm sure he'll return and you can tell him whatever seems to bother you so much." Then he can tell me what exactly was bothering Tyna, because Alistair would not have made such a promise.

Minutes later when Alistair rushed up the steps, Tyna was in his arms. "Come," she tried to drag him into the house. "Hurry."

He resisted, taking off his rain slicker and shaking it out before laying it over the porch swing to dry. Then he turned to her. "Now, what has you so eager to talk to me? Or is it something else you want?"

"We have to go inside. It's private, very private and I can't say anything where Gavin will hear me. I promised. I made a solemn vow to milady." She pulled him until they were far enough away from Gavin that he wouldn't be able to hear anything she said.

Before she could speak, Alistair pulled her into his arms and kissed her soundly on the lips, running his hands along her back. Gavin was afraid his friend wasn't going to let Tyna talk until he'd bedded her. But Tyna pushed him away, slapping at his roaming hands.

Gavin watched the pair intently, worried about the conversation and beside himself to know what it was she was telling Alistair. Relief washed through him as Alistair strode to the porch.

"What is it that Tyna couldn't tell me?" Gavin asked, realizing Alistair's frown lines were deep, etched with worry.

Alistair paused, looking at the storm before nervously running his hands through his hair. "Lady Larena left this morning with Addie. Together, they took horses and traveled down the mountain. We were all so busy with the map and the discussion about Isobel, we failed to notice the departure."

"Bloody hell, what was Addie thinking taking Larena away?"

Gavin started for the stables.

Alistair put out a hand to stop him. "You can't travel in this storm. You have to wait until it's over. Tyna also told me if Addie had not agreed to go with Lady Larena, she would have gone by herself, she was so determined. She told Addie as much."

"Larena could be in the middle of the storm...and Addie." He searched his lungs for air that wasn't there.

"I doubt that. The storm just hit here in the mountains and if all went well, Lady Larena and Addie will be at the inn in the village, safe and warm, when the tempest finally reaches them. They should have arrived a few hours ago. Where this storm is concerned, you have nothing to worry over."

Gavin's fist connected with the railing. "Where the storm in concerned, but there are predators out there, natural as well as man. She cannot survive on her own. She doesn't have the skills. They are both women." His body shuddered uncontrollably.

"You underestimate your wife. Indeed, I doubt if you truly know her or understand who she is. She's more Scot than English. I've watched her, and she has a solid head and can handle herself well. Addie is with her and I believe Hamilton will catch up with them at the inn or perhaps before. I think Addie might have told him."

"Did Hamilton know they were leaving? I'll have his head on a pike." Gavin started pacing, his heart racing as energy pumped through him. He needed to be on the road now not later. He had to reach the inn before his wife left tomorrow morning.

"I don't believe he did. Neither of us knew. I wouldn't have left here knowing, and I don't think Hamilton would either."

"Will you ride with me at first light? No, never mind, you can't. Take care of Tyna."

"You're right, I can't leave Tyna here alone even with all your men," Alistair was shaking his head, "And if we took her down the mountain with us, she would slow you. She can't ride very well although she can talk to the horses. They seem to understand every word she says. Will you be fine on your own?"

"Have to be, don't I?" He mulled the things in his head Alistair told him, wondering about the talking to horses bit.

"Tyna and I can follow at our pace as soon as the lodge is packed. I'll arrange for your things to be moved down the mountain. Where do you want them to go? Back to London or..."

"Ferguson estate near the crumbling castle. I've a house I'm building and plan to move into with Larena."

"Will you be there?"

Gavin laughed softly, not feeling the humor in it. "I will follow Larena. If I catch up to my elusive wife, that's where we'll head, and we'll all pray the pardon comes through before the soldiers find us."

He would follow her to the ends of the earth if necessary. His emotions turbulent, he searched for a logical reason for her hasty departure but could think of nothing that would cause such drastic measures. She had been angry with him when he refused to give in to all her wishes. But he was more than willing to listen to her and what she wanted. Searching deep inside himself, he didn't believe that argument would be enough to cause her hasty and sudden departure.

"If Tyna is agreeable, we can stay at my parent's home. I'm sure mother will enjoy the company now that she's getting older. If you're going to be up early, you should get some sleep now. The sun will rise soon enough," Alistair said.

Alistair's words had merit but he didn't think he'd be able to sleep. His body was a tight bundle of nerves wrapped up taut. Pent up energy ruled him right now, pulsing within. He needed to take action, not wait until the sun decided to rise.

Hours later, and after pounding his pillow most the night, Gavin mounted and with Alistair wishing him God speed, he started down the path toward the village and his runaway wife. In places water from the rain and hailstones the night before ran in rivulets making the trail more hazardous than ever before. Several times he was forced to dismount and walk the horse, avoiding downed trees and standing water.

When he finally rode into the village, the sun was nearing its zenith and the community was wide-awake and bustling with the day's chores. He had hoped he would reach the inn before Larena and Addie left for parts unknown. Although his best guess was Larena's family home, he still needed to be sure of their destination before he began his search.

Dismounting and giving his horse's reins to the stable boy, Gavin strode quickly inside. He stopped at the desk and inquired about the ladies.

"They left several hours ago, the crack of dawn to be exact," the man behind the desk told them.

"Bloody hell," he swore beneath his breath, cursing the storm and the eroded trail for slowing his pursuit down.

"Seemed they were eager to leave. Shot out of here as soon as the sun rose," the receptionist told him while he scribbled something in a ledger.

"Was there a man with them?" Gavin prayed Hamilton had caught up to the ladies and was now escorting Larena and Addie. Addie would have known Hamilton was following and once again he hoped Addie would make sure they didn't leave before her husband arrived.

"Oh, yeah, that reminded me. The man left you a note." Bending over and searching the papers in a cubbyhole below him and after several seconds he came up with a sealed note. "He told me to give it to a man named Gavin Broon. Are you him?"

Nodding before taking the note, Gavin walked outside, waiting for privacy before he tore it open with trembling fingers.

Gavin,

I had no idea the ladies had left and were in front of me on the trail. I would have pushed the horses harder, but as it was I had no reason to be concerned. I caught up to Addie and Larena later in the evening when they were going to their rooms after eating. I know you'll be here in the morning. The storm rolled through the valley too. Take some time to rest and eat something. I will do my best to slow our progress today. Addie is astute so I'm sure she'll notice my delaying tactics and use counter measures. You should catch up with us sometime after the midday meal, provided everything goes as planned.

By the way, according to Addie the trip was eventless and Larena was more than capable of keeping up. Addie told me to tell you that you should learn to see Larena for the competent and capable woman she is and give her a little credit about making decisions.

I'm sure you would like to know where we are headed. I should leave you guessing because I know you're berating Addie and more so your wife. But I understand the torment. We are headed to Berwick on Tweed, the Graham family home as previously planned with Cale and Jonathan. I'm sure you'll see us before then.

Cheers,

Hamilton

"She set off by herself. That isn't a good decision," Gavin growled under his breath while he crumbled the paper into a pocket.

In the back of his head he could hear Hamilton berate him. *She set off with Addie, not alone and Addie knew I was following. I'm sure she gave this a great deal of consideration before she left. I'm sure it wasn't easy for her or Addie, knowing you're married. You should take some time to consider how you're going to fix the real problems between the two of you.*

In this case Addie didn't make a great decision. She didn't realize she would have to take care of Larena every step of the way. Gavin paused in his thoughts. Did he really believe Larena was that helpless? No matter, she was his wife and he was going to make sure she understood that concept.

After a quick bite to eat and a cup of coffee, he set off, leading his stallion and two others as spares and riding one he purchased. After an hour he wondered if he'd ever catch up and if Hamilton out of some perverse reason didn't do anything to delay the party.

A group of soldiers passed him with a nod and grim expressions. Their presence set a new round of fears beating in his mind and body. He pushed his horse harder. If the soldiers were after Larena, he wouldn't be there to help. Hamilton can handle the situation. He has a title and money. Perhaps they were trying to find her to tell her she has a pardon. Isolated at the lodge, he'd received no messages from The Duchess. Larena's status was unknown.

The sun had begun to set when he saw the horses in the distance. His heart flew to this throat as relief swept inside. His wife, and he didn't know what he was going to do or say to her.

226

Chapter Ten

Addie stood inside the large reception room of the inn, Hamilton beside her. "I understand this decision isn't final but are you sure you want to do this. Gavin is bound to come hunting for Larena and you as well. He won't be happy."

Larena tried to clear her throat of the moisture lying inside. She'd already cried too many tears on the way down the mountain, going over all their conversations and attempting to understand him and wishing she could be what he wanted her to be.

Hamilton mumbled something indefinable beneath his breath then told Larena, "He is a bloody idiot and I don't think he has any idea just how callous he's acted towards you."

"All of this is not his fault. I allowed him to win my heart without really knowing who he is and how he thinks about me or life for that matter. We are far too different on so many levels to be compatible. He needs a submissive wife. One who will say, yes dear, and never question him. I'm not that person, never will be." She'd gone to hell and back trying to figure out a way to ignore his taunting insults but she couldn't. Once she believed she could prove herself to him, but she finally realized that was an impossible task.

"You sure you want to keep going?" Hamilton asked once more as if asking would change her mind.

"I don't have another choice. I can't live with him and I'm not going to try to see everything his way," she stubbornly said and *I'm going to have one hell of a time living without him.*

"He's going to come for you. What then?" Hamilton asked the probing question.

"If he does, which he won't, I'll make him see reason. He can get a divorce or an annulment, whichever is most plausible without a problem, having the money and the means. I think he'll understand. Then I plan on staying at home. Don't want to go back to London ever."

"Don't believe that nonsense for a second," Addie said, joining into the discussion. "Your man is head over heels in love with you, but he's too damn stubborn to admit it even to himself. He's so enamored of you and afraid for you that he can't see who you really are. Give him some time, a chance if you will. Marriage is something men have great difficulty understanding."

She stared at Addie, thinking she was touched in the head then, "You don't have to believe anything or make judgments. You just have to take me as far as you're going, Berwick on Tweed. I know the way home from there."

Hamilton stared at Addie, inhaling a long deep breath. "I hope you're right about this but, like Addie, I don't believe it for one second. If your plans work, you're going to regret them. Leaving Gavin is a foolish idea."

"I don't think so. He won't either. He'll be pleased he can find someone who does not act and make decisions like a child. Perhaps he can find someone he can love as well as respect." Larena said in a clipped voice, wishing that person could have been her. Perhaps if he loved her, she could overlook some his other faults.

"I doubt that," Hamilton retorted. "Seems like a man as possessive as Gavin is just might love his wife."

"Passion and desire aren't love and neither is possessiveness," Larena said in a small tight voice. "Trust me, he doesn't love me and I don't think he's capable of that emotion."

"Larena—" Hamilton began only to be interrupted.

She waved a hand in the air, "We were wed because he could help me escape the law. As a duke he had power he could wield. I needed him. He didn't want the marriage. I'm giving him his freedom from the frail incompetent wife he believes he's married."

"Larena—" Addie began then stopped seeming to sense argument was futile.

"Are the horses ready? With any luck I'll be in my family home before he realizes I've left the hunting lodge. If everything goes as planned, it will only take a couple of days to get to Berwick on Tweed then a few hours ride after that," she said, cutting across Hamilton's attempts to argue her out of her plan.

A taut silence followed but Larena chose to ignore it, finding solace in her thoughts.

"Bloody eyes, but I'm tempted to hogtie you in a room upstairs and wait for Gavin," Hamilton said finally. "This has got to be the most ridiculous decision ever made."

"I can't stop you from doing that," Larena said softly. "But I will fight you."

"And I can't stop you, either, is that it? You'll cut and run off in the wild the first chance you get," Hamilton said.

"That's the only reason Addie agreed to ride with me in the first place and why the two of you are going along with my plan now. The fact you're heading in the same direction just makes my plan simpler."

"Blackmail," Addie agreed with Larena.

"Of course."

Hamilton's expression turned inward. "Have it your way. You will do as you please whether or not we help you. Devil take the man who harms you. All I can do is make sure you stay alive until Gavin comes to get you. You understand he will."

"He won't," she said, feeling a bit too calm. "He doesn't love me and now that I've left, he'll be pleased he can move on with his life." She said the words but tears clogged her throat.

They rode for hours and to Larena it seemed Hamilton took every opportunity plus some to stop and rest the horses. Addie berated him several times, and even Cale and Jonathan questioned his tactics. As the sun drifted even higher in the sky, Hamilton looked over his shoulder more often as if he anticipated Gavin's arrival.

"You're not looking for Gavin, are you? He's not coming." A hot June sun scorched the earth and she was soaked through to the skin with perspiration. "So what are you looking for if not Gavin?"

"An avenging angel of mercy," Hamilton muttered as he turned his attention back to the horses and the stream where they were drinking.

"You need to realize and admit to it, Gavin isn't coming after me," she said softly, trying to clear the moisture in her throat, wishing somehow all this would have turned out differently and that perhaps Gavin did care enough for her to follow.

"For a bright woman you can be pretty damn stupid." Hamilton checked the cinch on the all the horses, taking his time. "Gavin was in love with you from the time he pulled you off the damn lamppost, probably before. That hasn't changed and never will. Neither of you know what's good for you."

"He wants me. That isn't love. It's lust. He'd be the first to tell you love doesn't exist except in fairytales. I think I was a mere challenge to him, one he wanted to conquer and explore. Now that he thinks he has conquered me, he's lost interest."

"You're wrong. Ask Addie. Want and love for a man, well the whole damn thing gets awful confusing."

She turned to Addie, expecting to hear some type of agreement with what she claimed. "Hamilton is right, Larena. A man like Gavin doesn't marry a woman he doesn't love just for convenience sake. It makes no difference whether he says the words or not. True, he felt a need to protect you and he would have done so without marrying you if he didn't love you."

Hamilton swung up on his horse and started everyone moving once more in the direction of the road, leaving Larena staring after the tiny group of travelers before finally following. He kept to a slow steady pace. She wasn't stupid, he was right. She knew he could have traveled faster, and she wasn't at all sure if it was because she was with him as well as three other people or if he hoped he gave Gavin enough time he would catch up to them.

"He's not coming after me," she said again. "You don't have to keep one eye on the road behind you."

The sun was lower in the sky before Hamilton reined in to study the surrounding terrain. The road had been following a stream and so they could camp anywhere. It seemed too early to stop. "I like the look of this place. We can set up camp and still have protection at our backs."

"Why would we do that?" Larena asked. "There is still plenty of daylight. We should keep going."

"We'll camp here for the night," Hamilton said.

"So soon?" Addie asked.

"Why? Don't tell me you still believe Gavin will suddenly appear out of nowhere. The avenging knight, come to rescue the damsel in distress. I can keep going and the sky won't be dark for another hour or more. I'm sure everyone else can too," Larena said, frustration at Gavin growing with each second.

Hamilton slanted Larena a cool know it all glance before speaking. "There might not be another decent place to camp that we could reach in an hour. If we don't camp here, we'll be picking our way through the dark when we could have a decent night of sleep as well as cook some dinner. Are you so eager to sleep sitting up in the saddle?"

"I would like food in my belly," Cale said, having remained silent throughout the day.

"I completely agree," Jonathan said. "We starved for too many days. Don't want to repeat that situation."

Larena met Hamilton's glance, sighed and looked uneasily over her shoulder. She thought she had caught movement behind them, but neither Hamilton nor Addie seemed concerned. When she looked back, Hamilton was regarding her with an odd smile on his face.

"I'll have hours of boredom and sleep once I get back home. I'd just as soon ride now," Larena said her heart suddenly pounding harder than she could imagine.

"Don't worry, Larena," Hamilton said kindly. "I gave you enough lead on that blind fool you call a husband, he'll work off the worst of his temper before he catches you."

"Gavin is not coming." She protested even though she understood Hamilton wasn't listening.

"Of course he is."

Larena gave Hamilton a startled look.

He smiled gently as though she were Addie.

"Even if you're right," Larena said with a catch in her voice that nearly turned to a sob, "Gavin wouldn't get here this quickly without riding a horse to death. I know him and I know he wouldn't do that."

Hamilton let out a long whoosh of air then, "One horse couldn't get the job done," Hamilton agreed as if he spoke to a small child, "but three could." His gaze riveted on the road behind them.

"Bloody hell," Larena whispered, her heart stopping for a moment. "Tell me that isn't him."

Hamilton looked past Larena at the open ground they had just covered. "Can't do that. Looks like Gavin Broon to me. Told you he'd come for you."

"I don't..." she began licking dry lips.

"If I were you, and of course, I'm not, but if I were, I'd spend the next few minutes thinking up a way to ease Gavin's temper. See that dust cloud down the road. He's riding hard and fast, and it's not me or any of the rest of us he's looking for. He's not going to have a great deal of patience when he finally reaches our little group. A man who's tired, hungry and forced to chase after his wife is going to need a damn good explanation before he can forgive the indiscretion. Hope you can come up with one." Hamilton chuckled softly, seemingly unable to relate to her problems. "In any case you're no longer my concern."

The finality in Hamilton's words sent a shiver of ice down her spine. She stood in her stirrups and looked past Hamilton.

"Bloody hell," she breathed, feeling deflated and at Gavin's mercy once more. If she was honest with herself, a part of her was happy he followed her.

"Looks like you're wrong. Your man's come for you," Hamilton said dryly.

"I'm not his possession and I'm not going with him. I can choose where I go."

"Well, now that he's here, I'm not going to stand in his way. He'd kill me and I do believe Addie would miss me just a little bit." Hamilton chuckled, giving his wife a sideways glance.

With watchful eyes, Hamilton waited while Gavin and the horses thundered closer. When he saw Gavin didn't have his pistol in hand, Hamilton let out a silent breath of relief and gave Larena a reassuring smile. Larena turned from him, her breath suddenly coming too rapidly for her to think. She sat rigidly on her horse and waited, knowing if she ran, she'd only regret it and Gavin would catch her. She had nowhere to go except to face him.

Gavin didn't even look at Hamilton or the rest of the travelers when he galloped up and pulled his mount to a rearing dancing stop beside her. His eyes were riveted on her. She stiffened, biting back the undulating terror the expression on his face sent through her. Gavin dismounted, turned the hot horses over to Hamilton then stood silently gazing at her, his hands fisted at his sides.

"We'll just walk on over to those trees—maybe we can make dinner for all of us," Hamilton said, gesturing toward a scattering of trees at least a mile down the road. "We can make camp there."

Hamilton nodded toward Larena and Gavin.

"You might keep in mind she was only doing what she thought was best for both of you," Hamilton said as he handed one of the horses over to Addie and kept the other two. "The same as you were just trying to protect her from herself."

"Good-bye, Hamilton," Gavin said flatly before nodding politely to Addie and ignoring the other two men.

Without looking back, Hamilton, Addie and the other two men reined in their horses toward the setting sun, taking with him all the horses but the one Larena rode.

"Wait," Gavin called out. "Give me the freshest of your horses or the strongest. Don't much care."

Hamilton turned, pushing his hat back. Quickly he dismounted and handed the horse to Gavin.

Without warning, Gavin vaulted on behind Larena, grabbed the reins from her and still holding the ones Hamilton gave him, turned toward the road. Summer flowers and newly leafed out trees caught the fading sunlight. When the small breeze stirred, the leaves quivered as though alive and breathing, taunting her with recriminations.

Larena felt as shaky as one of the leaves. She stared down at the large masculine hand holding the reins and at the arm that half-circled her without touching her. The temptation to draw a finger over the veins in the back of Gavin's hand was so powerful she had to close her eyes against the enticement. A shiver swept through her as she struggled not to show her hunger and craving to touch the life that beat so appealingly beneath

Gavin's measured surface. She might resent his treatment of her, but she admitted she loved him and she recalled all the times he tenderly made love to her.

Gavin didn't stop and neither did he speak. Larena chose to remain silent, terrified of the confrontation she knew was forthcoming and putting it off as long as possible became more appealing with each passing second. They rode for what seemed an eternity before he finally stopped in front of a large farmhouse. He rode around the barn then into the field. A farmer and a young boy walked along a path.

Once again as the sun began to settle beneath the horizon, dark clouds that had been piling up all day let out a roar. Rain fell. Hitting the earth.

"Sir?" Gavin stopped the horse. "Would you mind if we, my wife and I, spent the night in your barn? We wouldn't be a problem and we'll leave at first light. Camping without gear might damage her frail health."

The farmer stared at him for the longest time, and Larena was nearly convinced he would refuse. "Don't mind if you do."

"We'll pay."

"No, who would I be if I kept weary travelers from a night in my barn to stay out of a storm. The weather's not going to get any better tonight than it was the night before. Don't want to be responsible for either one of you taking sick."

"Thank you," Gavin said before heading for the barn.

Once inside, he dismounted then helped her down before motioning for her to sit. He took care of the horses while she watched, her fear now spiraling out of control. Longingly, she eyed the door.

When he finished, he watched Larena for the longest time. She met his narrowed eyes, refusing to show either the pain or the desire that churned beneath her outward calm. In this mood, what could she say to him he'd understand?

"We need privacy." He nodded toward the ladder leading to the loft. "Go on, I'll follow."

She stood her ground, not wanting the intimacy he suggested. She was shaking her head and backing away when he pulled her to him and over his shoulder. "Gavin." She pounded his chest to no avail. "Put me down. I'll walk."

"Too late."

They reached the top and he let her down gently on the hay then took off his rain slicker, spreading it on the straw. He helped her with hers then set it aside, moving deliberately and quickly.

When she sat down again, he regarded her for a few seconds. Tension radiated through his features, his jaw clenched tight.

"Did I notice surprise on your face when I rode up?" Gavin asked, the hardness of his voice belied the cold underlying softness. "Did you really believe I wouldn't come for my wife?"

She slowly scooted away from him. "You weren't coming for me. At least I didn't think you would. You need someone more like Addie, someone who can take care of herself in dangerous situations. I was just doing what I thought you wanted. Leaving."

"I would have followed you if you'd gone to the gates of Hell."

"Why?"

The simple question seemed to enflame Gavin's anger. "Bloody eyes, we're married. You're my wife. Of course I'd follow you."

That was exactly what she thought but didn't want to hear. She needed to hear him tell her he came for her because he loved her or at least cared about her. "A possession. Is that all I am to you? You only married me to protect me from the warrant. It's not real and there is no love. I'm sure The Duchess has my pardon by now. So there is no reason for us to remain wed."

"Like hell there isn't. I had you so deep and so hard it's a bloody wonder either one of us could walk."

At the tone of his words she sucked in a deep breath of air. Heat rose to Larena's cheeks, but she wasn't about to give in to him. "You think so little of me and you gave Addie and Tyna more respect. I don't know what I have to do to convince you I don't need your protection. You can have an annulment or a divorce. It doesn't matter to me. Just do what you want, not what you think you have to do."

"No annulment and no divorce."

"I don't understand," she tried for a calm she didn't possess. Larena shrugged casually despite the tension ripping through her body and the deep shaking encompassing her. "A marriage where there is no respect or compromise or above all love does not make a valid marriage."

"That's just it," Gavin shot back. "I do respect you and will compromise on most everything. I married you because I wanted you not because of the warrant. The marriage is bloody valid and nothing is ever going to change that," he gritted out, his anger seeming to explode from him.

"Are you sure? This trap we made for ourselves will change our lives forever if we don't fix it now."

"You're not making sense."

Her eyes burned even while she tried to focus on him and what she believed they could have had. She felt so weary and saw no hope in this marriage they made with no real thought. Larena was wrong about her feelings for Gavin. It wasn't love she once felt, it was lust.

"I can do everything you ask of me," Larena said. "I can warm your bed and burst into flames with your touch. But it's not enough for me or for you. You despise everything about me except when I'm in bed with you. I can't go back. I don't want to. I don't want to live needing something that is just beyond my reach."

"Nothing you're saying is true."

"What part isn't true?" she asked, determined to discover his thoughts and to stand her ground. "You want a woman who can think for herself and make logical decisions, one who can defend herself when confronted. You will never believe I can be that woman. And so deep down, you despise me."

"Larena, that's not what I—"

"Don't be absurd, it is. I'm not fit to be a duke's wife and the mother of your children. You lust for me but nothing else. In time even that emotion will vanish. Then we'll have nothing but an empty lonely bed and more tears."

"Good God, woman, you're putting words in my mouth. I don't feel that way."

"Yes, it is true!" she said harshly, talking over him. "You have never lied to me no matter how much the truth hurt. Don't start now. I trapped you and now I'm leaving so you can have the life and a woman who is suited to you."

"Damnation. Will you stop talking nonsense and listen?"

"Consummating our marriage was the worst mistake of your life. "

"Wrong." Gavin said furiously. "The worst mistake of my live was promising myself I'd try discussing this with you first."

"What is that supposed to mean?"

With no warning, Gavin pulled Larena into his arms and kissed her hard. She tried to twist away not comprehending his urgency in this situation. He deepened the kiss, and she was helpless to resist him. Unable to deny Gavin, she opened her mouth to his questing forays. And the kiss seemed to go on forever. Yet when he lifted his head seemingly to breathe, it had not been nearly long enough.

"Nothing I've ever said to you makes a bit of difference now. You are mine, Larena Broon, and you are not going to Berwick on Tweed or London or anywhere else without me. If we go, we'll go together or not at all."

"You don't love me," she stubbornly persisted, still longing for the words that would never be forthcoming.

"You are my life and all that matters to me. That's why I've been so damn condescending to you. Don't leave because I will not survive a separation, Larena. I cannot live without you."

She was so touched she could barely speak. All she could do was whisper his name.

"Gavin."

Once again he drew her into his arms and beneath him. Their lovemaking was bittersweet yet filled with a promise Larena needed to believe in.

Afterwards, Larena lay in his arms, listening to the rain as it beat down on the roof and the storm's thunder as it roared above. In his arms she knew no fear from the blackness of the night. But they had yet to resolve any differences.

~ * ~

A few days later, Gavin and Larena rode through the portcullis of the aging castle Gavin's mother had owned then bequeathed to Gavin. Summer was upon them and the air was redolent with the aroma of blossoming flowers. He hoped to make a new life with Larena, not in the castle but in the nearby home he was building.

"We are here. What do you think?" he queried, watching the myriad of expressions crossing her face. After the storm and the confrontation, she seemed to regard him differently. Although she'd been quiet and reserved, the few conversations had been eye opening.

"It's a lot like the McLellan castle but in disrepair. Can we fix the crumbling walls?" she asked, as she seemed to study the space.

"With enough money. I know there are people in London who would pay to spend their holiday in a real Scottish castle." He had been thinking about renting rooms in the castle to help repair it. This had been his home for so many years and his mother's before that. The place would be hard to give up. Restoring it was a dream of his.

She laughed softly, and he enjoyed the sound of it. "You want to rent out rooms in the castle? It's quite the idea. I like it and renting rooms would give me something to do with my time."

"You would help do this? I don't want to live there, much too drafty and cold. At least not when I have a new home under construction which I had built with you in mind."

"You did?" she pivoted to look at him. "When?" she asked in seeming disbelief, yet she was smiling.

"I planned on bringing my new bride to Scotland to live, if you were amenable that is. It's closer to your sisters. Well, all save Ravyn," he told her.

"I do like that. I've missed them and their children. Fayth was away for so long and Ravyn longer. It would be nice to be close again."

Her beautiful smile and willingness to grant him a second chance gave him hope for the future. They climbed the stairs, Gavin, giving Larena a tour of the rooms including the master solar. "We'll stay here until the house is ready. Since it's summer the bedchamber will stay cool and we won't have to worry about drafty chills."

The unspoken question for Gavin was if Larena was with child. Her body had changed over the few weeks they'd been wed, but a lot of things could account for those differences. He hoped she would tell him if she knew.

"I'd like that. Are there any hidden tunnels or passages we can explore? There are in the McLellan castle. Many of the servants believed the noises we made in back passages were ghosts. The tunnels were the reason we could keep the island our own and a secret for so long. No one knew where we went each night, not even the laird of the castle."

"Not that I know of. Alistair and I were more interested in the forest and the trouble we could get into there. We spent most of our days hunting and fishing. Now that you present that possibility, would you like to see if we can find some?"

"I'm sure there are but right now I'd like to walk to the parapets. I'd love to see the view of your lands."

Standing at the top of the castle, the vision was amazing. One could see the lands surrounding the stronghold, the vast forest, and a lake far in the distance.

"There is the village." He wrapped his arms around her, holding her close still unsure of her feelings for him. Their conversation from a few days ago ripped him to the bone. He had no idea he made her feel so small. It had never been his intention. He'd been moments from telling her how much he loved her but something held him back.

"Can you see the home you're building from here?"

He pointed to a lake not far from the town. "It's over there, behind the trees. You can see the loch from the windows of the house." Inside his arms he felt her shiver and wished he knew what she was thinking, but most of all he needed to know if she loved him.

He closed his eyes, his hands on her abdomen. Their peace would end soon. The Duchess had sent news she and the Laird McLellan would arrive tomorrow and Larena's sisters, their husbands and children would arrive sometime in the next few days. They were coming to celebrate their wedding as well as the news that Larena had been pardoned.

Alistair would also arrive within the next hours with his new wife, Tyna. He'd sent a message telling him they stopped at a small parish church and wed. He didn't know who else would appear. Servants rushed through the castle preparing sleeping spaces for those they knew would be arriving soon. The cooks would be busy in the kitchen preparing meals for the oncoming hoards. If he closed his eyes, he imagined the aroma of fresh baked bread, apple tarts, roasting boar and so many more delicacies.

It was growing late and he knew Larena was beyond exhausted. When he turned her, she was gazing at him, no, actually she was staring at his mouth. He smiled, a very male feeling. It was nice to be wanted by one's wife. Very nice indeed. He would finish the tour tomorrow. Right now he had other plans.

He coveted his wife now. Downstairs in their solar he took her with all the intensity that was within him, and she was his in those long moments, but at the same time, he thought on the verge of sleep, she'd captured him, completely, irrevocably. He heard a sound and turned his head slowly on the pillow toward her. Another sound. It was a sob. He stilled. He didn't know what to do. He raised his hand to caress her shoulder then slowly lowered it to his side again.

Why couldn't she be as he wished her to be? Was it so much to ask of her? They had this argument so many times he couldn't count. Yet she still fulfilled so many of his needs and wishes.

The sobs trailed off. Gavin listened to her erratic breathing soften and even as she fell into a restless sleep.

He stared upward into the darkness for a long time. He realized just as he was dozing off that Larena never bored him. She enraged, infuriated and beguiled him, but she never bored him. She'd been a mystery to him at the very beginning and she still was. He couldn't imagine his life without her just the way she was.

He recalled the half explanation as to why she ran off and never quite understood how he'd been cruel enough for her to risk her life to run away.

He was a fool and a coward. He married her because he couldn't live without her. And that was the truth. A truth he'd told her only a few days ago, but he was never quite sure she believed him or accepted his words. Perhaps trust was gained by complete acceptance of the one loved. And respect. She had both from him. It was time he told her that and more importantly showed her. Words were meaningless unless there were actions that supported them.

Late the following morning, Addie and Hamilton arrived with all Larena's sisters except Ravyn accompanied by their husbands and children. Chaos erupted in the main room downstairs as everyone rushed to herd the children in the direction of the kitchen for a snack then their bedrooms for a quick nap so they wouldn't breakdown and terrorize the adults.

Thankfully, they arrived with a nanny so there would be some respite for the mothers. The sisters, Fayth and Storm, huddled with Larena. He would give anything to hear what or who they were talking about. With all the commotion he forgot his intention of telling her he loved her.

"The frown on your face tells me something is wrong." Hadden shook his hand, grinning. "Nothing a good game of golf wouldn't fix." He patted Gavin on the shoulder.

"No golf courses here." Gavin said, his mind still on the important conversation he needed to have with his wife.

"What a shame. It's certainly a good way to escape the crowds and find a bit of solace. You look like you could use some relief."

"I'll have to remedy that." Gavin said dryly, wondering why anyone would want to hit a tiny ball around.

A commotion in the front of the hall caught everyone's attention.

"Aunty!" The girls ran to greet The Duchess who just arrived. The laird McLellan stood back, arms crossed in front of him, seeming to absorb the chaos, even enjoying it.

"We're so glad you're here. This is going to be so much fun." Fayth said, clapping her hands, a huge grin on her face.

Larena left to show them their rooms and give them time to freshen up before dinner. Addie and Hamilton had arrived early in the morning and Gavin expected them downstairs soon. Who was left? Allura, with her family, Eveleen and Logan. Tavia and James were at sea on an adventure, Aidan and Tira were in Baltimore and of course Ravyn and Amorica were also in the states. Ah, Christel and Ryder with their children were yet to make an appearance.

There wouldn't be a moment of privacy for them, at least not until tonight in their solar. He would have to wait and maybe that would give him time to figure out what he would say. Using the right words was imperative if he was going to get the correct point across. From past experience he understood how important the right words were.

"Gavin, everyone is resting for now. Absorb the quiet and the peace. With all the children there might not be too much more for a few days," Larena told him, taking him by the arm and leaning into him.

"How do they stay so in love for all this time?" He was really asking himself but the words were spoken before he gave himself time to think and understand how Larena must feel.

"Perhaps their husbands say they love them, and that's all that's necessary," she spoke so softly he barely heard.

He stared at her, his mouth slightly open, remembering his vow, seeing the surge of hope in her expressive eyes. As he remained silent, he saw the hope drain away to be replaced by pain and weariness. She was waiting for him to speak, and in speaking wound her. That wasn't the way he needed their relationship to transpire. Their relationship was in its fledgling stage and it was failing.

"Damnation," he said very quietly and hauled her into his arms. "Forgive me," he said against her hair. "Forgive me, Larena. I'm a damnable beast and I'm sorry for it. You are so good and trusting. I need to figure out why I deserve you." He needed to figure out how to stop hurting her.

She remained tense, and he felt the depths of the pain he'd given her, heaped upon her so gratuitously. He kissed her temple, her ear before his mouth closed over hers for a long drugging kiss. Then looking up, "Forgive me," he said again.

"My lord...oh! Do excuse me, that is—" One of the servants seemed shocked to see them in a tender embrace.

Gavin slowly released his wife and turned. "It's all right. What is it?"

"I, ah, that is, I wanted to tell your ladyship, but—"

Gavin heard Larena's labored breathing from behind him. He said mildly, "Her ladyship is a bit short of breath at the moment. She will fetch you in fifteen minutes."

"No, no," Larena said, quickly coming around from behind her husband. "I'm fine. What is it?"

"More of your—"

The remaining McLellan clan rushing toward her, hugs and kisses all around, cut her off. "Christel. Ryder."

Gavin frowned. He was so full to bursting with words and feelings and vows and apologies and declarations for Larena. When would all this end so he could have a moment alone with his wife? "Go on, see to your family. I'll find something to occupy myself with. Maybe get a few golf lessons from Hayden."

By the time Larena returned, Hamilton and Addie had turned up in the living room where everyone seemed to congregate.

"I see you patched things up a bit," Hamilton said. "At least now your wife is smiling."

Gavin frowned, unsure where Hamilton was headed with his statement. Gavin wasn't about to tell anyone that he had no idea what was going on with his wife.

"Somewhat," he muttered, wishing everyone would disappear. The only solution as he could see was to vanish and take Larena with him. Since that wasn't possible, he didn't have an answer.

Drake sat down, laughing. "Heard you had a rough time at the lodge. Not your heaven sent getaway. At least where Larena is concerned. You got your act together now?"

If Hamilton and Hadden would leave, he could speak seriously with his friends. A little insight into a woman's mind would be appreciated. When Drake nodded toward his wife, Gavin noticed a few words were exchanged between Ella, Storm and Addie.

Gavin couldn't help but grin as both men stood and strode to their wives, disappearing into another room.

"I've made a mess of things and I imagine the only way they will improve is if I tell her I love her."

"Do you? Don't say the words unless you mean them," Drake warned.

"You and I are too much alike," Logan said. "I had no intention of ever uttering those words to a woman, even a wife, at least not tell I met Eveleen."

"Neither did I but once I realized how deep my feelings for Ella were, I also realized those feelings were love. Everything fell into a pattern after that."

"Nothing like having that revelation when everyone descends on us. I can't get a moment alone with her. When I tell her I love her, I'd like to have the rest of the night to show her." Regarding the great hall and all of the people with frustration, Gavin swept his hands through his hair.

"Patience, my friend, you'll have tonight."

"If I could, I'd kidnap her and take her to our new home. She hasn't seen it yet then I'd ask her forgiveness before I tell her how much I love her." Gavin watched the ladies, noticing Larena was no longer with them.

"My forgiveness? That has intriguing possibilities. I never thought I would hear Lord Gavin Broon ask anyone's forgiveness, let alone a woman's." The tenor of her voice sent a shiver down Gavin's spine.

"Time for me to bow out. Too bad she didn't overhear the first part of our conversation." Drake and Logan sauntered away, their laughter following.

Larena regarded him with a shuttered expression, reminding him of the dark expression she told him he used. "You're not going to believe anything I tell you."

"Try me."

"All right then," he hoped for the best.

She sat down, spreading her skirts around her before looking at him. Her eyes wide open she seemed to wait for him to speak, but he didn't want to make small talk. Yet he did, "What were you and the others talking about?" He wasn't all that sure he wanted to know.

"You deflect from my question." She smiled at him. "That seems to be a habit of yours, but it's something I actually enjoy." She paused, "I'm not sure why."

"I don't remember you asking one." In his mind he backtracked what had been said.

"My forgiveness," she said calmly, too calmly for his state of mind.

He cleared his throat, trying to stall for time. "It's a private conversation I'd hoped to have later tonight."

She gestured with her hands, "We're alone, now."

His laughter didn't make her smile, "Hardly alone, when all of your family and a few of my brothers surround us. If I begin a conversation, they are sure to descend upon us and I'll never make my point."

"Well, baby brother, is this your new wife?"

Larena looked to Gavin for answers.

The man gallantly picked up Larena's hand then kissed the back. "I've heard a few things about you. You're much prettier than the drawings," the man said.

"William, to what do we owe the pleasure of your company?" Gavin asked, displeased by the interruption, yet glad to see one of his brothers.

"I see you've grown up and why would I need a reason to help my baby brother celebrate his nuptials?" William laughed. "It seems all of her relatives were invited."

A few years ago, he would have let Will's words bother him, no longer. "Please, make yourself at home. Am I going to be surprised by any more of my brothers?"

"Probably not, the others are in South Africa. Since they didn't inherit, they're both looking to increase their wealth there. We all knew you were mother's favorite but we could never figure out why." He scanned the room. "But no one else would have wanted this crumbling castle. Repairs will eat away all the money you have."

"I have plans," Gavin told his brother, watching disdain slither across his sibling's face. He wished he had a family and extended family such as Larena's. They all seemed so close and loving.

"Good, good for you. Don't mind if I find some Scottish delicacy to eat or to dance with." Will started to leave.

"Where is your wife?"

Will turned swiftly and before walking away, said, "She is at home and with child, not that it's any of your business."

"Is he always like that?" Larena asked.

"Unfortunately, yes, he is." He hoped Will wouldn't cheat on his wife here in the castle but from what William had said, he didn't hold up much hope for that.

Larena seemed to mull that over for a few minutes. "I think we should talk about finding a place where we can speak of your forgiveness. Am I supposed to forgive you for something?"

From a far corner Hamilton waved to them. "Privacy has to wait. It seems we're needed to cut the cake." He stood and extended a hand to Larena.

"Do we have to? A cake, celebrating a marriage that shouldn't have taken place, dancing. I just..."

He stiffened at her comment. His gut rolling, he pulled her into his arms for a swift kiss. "This marriage is valid and I, for one, know you are my wife in every way. I have no regrets about it taking place and I pray you don't either."

She pushed away from him then ran from the room.

~ * ~

She heard the music stop and the collective gasps as she fled, unable to take one more minute of the pretense of a happy marriage, something she wanted with all her heart. Disappointing all the guests had not been her intent but she needed air, time to think an opportunity to believe in a future she would never have with the man she loved more than life.

Before she reached the parapets, she heard the steady rhythm of his footsteps behind her. She felt his presence, recognized the scent of his cologne, knew he could stop her, haul her back to the reception room if that was what he wanted. For some reason he didn't. She sobbed, her body shaking as she continued the steady climb while he continued to follow keeping his distance.

When she reached the top, she set her hands on the wall and looking over the Broon land, she heaved in long deep breaths of air, her lungs and body aching from the exertion.

How had her marriage come to this? She loved him so much; had loved him the first moment she saw him at her first debutant ball so many months ago, what seemed like years ago. What did that matter anymore? She got what she wanted. Gavin Broon as her husband. But she never thought he was a duke, thought he was a brilliant lawyer, the youngest son of an aristocratic family. He never stood to inherit land yet alone a title, but he did. But that wasn't the problem. He didn't love or respect her and it didn't seem he ever would.

"Larena."

His voice behind her startled her, stopping her brooding. She ignored his presence. Instead she looked on the land that would become her children's heritage, if she had children. When her child was born, she acknowledged because she believed she was pregnant. What would it take to make him love her?

"Larena, what's wrong?" He placed a hand on her back.

The familiar gesture sent warmth through her and the feeling of being protected but not loved. "Nothing." If she had the courage, she would turn around and yell at him how much she loved him. She would. But she'd never been courageous. Impulsive and stubborn yes, but never courageous.

"Of course there's something wrong. It's not like you to run out of a celebration in your honor. I can help if you talk to me. Was it something I said or did? My brother can be callous and unfeeling."

Callous and unfeeling must run in the Broon family.

If he loved her, it would help and perhaps she could communicate her thoughts better. That was the problem though; he didn't love her and never would. She warped her arms around herself, shielding herself from the pain and rejection she felt. "No, really, it's just my emotions getting in the way." She wiped tears from her eyes and smiled at him. "I'm better now. Sorry I embarrassed you by running out of the room. Won't do it again."

"I suppose that could be true and you didn't embarrass me. I was concerned about your well-being," he told her, standing by her side and his forearms resting on the wall gazing over the land, his land, their land.

"I'm sorry. We should return." She should tell him about the baby. He would be a father.

"Not before you tell me what I can do to make the pain go away. Tell me why you are half there when we make love." He stood behind her, massaging her shoulders.

"There is nothing you can do." It would be easy to tell him what would bring her back to him, but she'd never believe him if he spoke the words she yearned to hear. What if she told him all she wanted was his love? Then he said the words she needed him to say.

He pulled her close, her back against his chest, his arms wrapped tightly around her. She loved the feel of him against her, his hardness so opposite from her. His fingertips rested on her neck, sliding her hair away, his lips and moist tongue sending shivers throughout. It would be so easy to give in to this sexual dance and tell herself it was enough for a lifetime. The sex would have to hold her through a life of need, and even sex with him was not as it was before she knew he would never love her.

She could never give him up though, never deny him anything he wanted. Clenching her teeth, she moved slightly, giving him better access to her neck, then turning in his arms gazed into his eyes, searching for a sign he cared more for her than he was willing to admit. All she saw in his steel blue eyes was passion and lust, not love.

Giving in to his tender caresses and the sensual play of his mouth against hers, she let him kiss her, pull her closer until their bodies melded as one. His hand on her derrière drew her against his hard arousal, telling her he wanted her, perhaps even needed her in some primal elemental way. Understandably, she yearned for him too.

He pulled away, the kiss brief and hard, his lashes lowering for a moment as if he searched for the right words then after clearing his throat, "We need to get back to the party and I promise you in our bedroom tonight I will make this evening unforgettable."

She nodded, silently agreeing while understanding unless he told her he loved her, the evening would be much the same as all the others. She watched him for a few more seconds, moistening her lips.

"I'd like that, privacy. We haven't had much since we arrived here. For that matter since we married there have been people all around us." She tried to be amenable while her heart was breaking for what seemed like the millionth time.

Hands linked, they made their way down the steps to the reception. Once inside, he swept her into his arms, dancing with the lively Scottish music. She wanted the enchantment of this moment to last forever. She let him guide her around the room, forgetting what she longed to hear and enjoy the merriment. This was supposed to be their night. It was planned for them, and their friends and family would never understand this was the last thing she wanted.

The music changed as did the steps. She forced laughter she didn't feel. They were stopped.

"May I have this dance," William stood beside them.

Gavin nodded and gave her away to his oldest brother. She held herself away from him. This was just something else she didn't want tonight. William was every bit the gallant gentleman, yet something about him made her skin crawl. She didn't like him and she guessed Gavin didn't care much for his brother either. There was unspoken history between them.

The dance ended and Gavin was beside her to take her into his arms once again. Bending close to her ear to whisper, "Would you like something to drink? And," he continued letting his tongue sweep across the lobe of her ear, "the sooner we cut the cake the sooner we can retire to our room."

She nodded but looked away before she acknowledged his question. "I am thirsty. That would be nice, some Chianti or Bordeaux?" She was so at odds with herself. She didn't want to stay at the festivity, neither did she want to go to the solar with Gavin. Courage within her was nonexistent.

"While you were dancing, I arranged for food and drink to be sent to the solar. I've had the fire built up so it will be warm. Maybe you can wear something sheer." His fingertip traced the line of her neck. "Remember the lingerie I gave you on our second wedding night?"

"You've thought of everything." Her tone was not that of a woman enamored by what her husband thoughtfully did for her, and she regretted hurting him. She wanted this night to be different, but she didn't know how to change her attitude or emotions.

He shrugged, his smile fading, his expression clouding over to the dark brooding man he had become since they wed. "Probably not, but I've tried. I want tonight to be perfect."

"I'm sorry. I know you have tried." She turned from him unable to look into his eyes. When she felt his hands on her waist, she inhaled a quick deep breath. Even that small touch affected her in ways she didn't want to admit.

"Let's cut the cake. I've a need for something sweet," he told her as he squeezed slightly. "Then," he paused, "then I hope to taste the sweetest morsel of all. You."

"You're right, of course. It is getting late and some of our guests arrived just this afternoon. I'm sure they're exhausted. They will not feel right retiring before they give us a proper sendoff." Unsure why she dreaded this evening and wanting to prolong this, she headed to the cake, resigned to the knowledge that no matter what she did, the hour would come when she would be alone in their bedroom with her husband.

"Why do I get the feeling you don't believe what you just said?" he asked as he led the way to the cake.

"Time to cut the cake." Hamilton picked up a wine class and called for everyone's attention.

The music stopped. Gavin and Larena stood in front of the three-tiered wedding cake. She swallowed hard. Her hand trembling, she picked up the knife before looking into his eyes. Gavin's hand closed around hers and they sliced the first piece. She didn't know what to expect, only that once this was done, she had more questions, truly feeling as if tonight was their real wedding night.

As if in a daze she did what was expected of her, smiled at the cheering guests and the ribald jokes. They shared a glass of champagne then he pulled her into his arms and carried her through the crowd to the steps then on to the solar.

"We will be in our room soon, just the two of us," he told her, taking the steps two at a time.

At the door, he bent low enough to unlatch it then kicked it open with his foot then shut it. Carrying her to the fur rug by the fireplace, he sat down with her.

She touched his face, lowering her lashes before she spoke, "We've had two wedding nights, now this is number three. Why does this feel like our first time?"

"This is the real beginning to our life together. Before we were on the run and stalked by a woman seeking vengeance. So perhaps this is our real wedding night." He pushed a lock of hair behind an ear, letting his fingertip hover. "There were no vows exchanged but..."

She laughed, "The first night I had too much to drink and I see you've brought wine."

"The second night though..." he paused, slipping her shoes from her feet then evocatively running his hands along the length of her leg.

Her heartbeat quickened. "I don't need a reminder. I remember your easy seduction of me and the way you discovered every inch of me and how much I enjoy the seduction."

"Larena's schooling," he murmured yet he stopped to set her from his lap and pour each a glass of wine. "What would make you happy?"

She sat cross-legged in front of him, wishing once more she dared tell him the truth. Choosing to ignore his question, she said, "I'd like to discover more of you. Perhaps uncover who you really are. I like the way you make me feel, but I want to understand what's inside your head."

She gazed at him over the rim of her glass for a few seconds before sipping then setting it on the hearth, determined to put her fears in the back of her mind and enjoy the evening. On her knees she steadied herself, her hands on his shoulders. Then she pushed his waistcoat from his shoulders, her fingers brushing against his neck then untying his cravat.

"What are you doing, Larena?" His voice was deeper and rougher than she'd ever heard it.

Gavin was a man of control and she meant to take that from him tonight. She meant to take the offense in this evening's sensual play and see how he handled her.

He brought his hands to her waist, fire shooting through her body. "Don't touch me, Gavin, at least not yet. Will you let me tutor you?"

For a few seconds he didn't say anything, but she heard his labored breathing, "I can try."

"Good."

This night would be different than the other two wedding nights. Slowly, she undid each button of his shirt, recalling that time in The Duchess' house when she barged in on him, his shirt off she touched his chest, felt his hard body for the first time.

"I don't know if I can keep my hands to myself."

"Try harder," she told him, her fingers now on his shoulders slowly divesting him of his shirt. Her kisses followed her fingertips touching every part of his chest and shoulders. "Do you like this?"

His groan of pleasure filled her with delight. "More than you could ever know. But Larena, I should tell you something before you take this any farther."

"I don't want to talk. Just want to feel." Her hands trembling and her nerves in her throat, she stalled the seduction afraid of his displeasure. Yet the desire so strong she prayed it would overcome her trepidation.

"Right now I can barely breathe."

"Neither can I." The sensual play of his muscles as she moved lower sent shivers within. "That day when I barged into your room because something crashed to the floor."

He nodded, holding her hands just above the fastenings to his kilt as he sucked in a deep breath of air. "I remember it all too well."

"What were you doing?" She continued her exploration, tracing the waistband.

His laughter echoed in his chest. "I was trying to get you, and what I wanted to do with you out of my head."

"I don't know what that means." The fastening on his kilt eluded her. She looked down to see how they worked. "It seems you are very adept at getting me out of my clothes, but I can't unfasten your garment."

"Probably a good thing and that's my answer to both of your statements." He groaned.

"Am I hurting you?"

"No, my poppet. Anything but that. It's the waiting for you to figure things out that causes pain."

She shook her head, pursing her lips and trying to figure out what he meant. She wasn't at all sure. "You left that night and another one later on. I watched you ride away. Where did you go and why?"

"I'll show you." Quickly he undid his kilt, letting it fall to the floor and taking her hand in his guided her to his shaft. "See how I'm ready for you. So in need I ache, a good ache nonetheless, but when I couldn't make love to you that night, I needed a way to ease this."

Her fingers wound around him and she heard his deep tortured breathing as if he somehow searched for something. "Did you go to another woman?"

He laughed then, "From the moment I pulled you from the lamppost, no from the moment I saw you at the ball, I've not thought of any woman except you. You've fascinated me. No, I rode to a lake near

Drake's summer home and took a well-needed swim in it. The cold water..."

"I don't understand."

He set her hand aside, "Larena, there is something I need to tell you before this goes any farther."

"I don't like the sound of that." She sat back, worried sick she'd done something wrong. Picking up her wine glass, she stood and walked to the window. She was shocked to feel him behind her, his hands on her shoulders, turning her.

"I hope you will like what I want to tell you." His hands ran through her hair, ridding it of all the pins. Time seemed to stand still as he played with the locks, letting them sift slowly through his fingers. "You have the softest hair, silken fire on my fingers."

His mouth descended on hers and he kissed her. Gently, lightly on her lips then it changed. He was hard, demanding, and she opened her mouth for him, needing him desperately as he unraveled, once again, every part of her.

When he pulled away, his eyes were focused on hers. She moistened her lips and tried to swallow. "What was it you wanted to say to me," she blurted out. She hadn't meant to ask but curiosity propelled the question to the forefront of her mind.

"Come here," He picked up her wine in one hand and took hold of her other one escorting her to a nearby chair. Settling the wine on the table, he placed her on his lap.

"You're scaring me," she told him, her hand resting on his chest, feeling the thunder of his heartbeat. It seemed so strange that she still wore most of her clothing and he was naked.

"I'm terrified," he confessed.

"I'll leave. I didn't mean to take liberties that weren't offered." She tried to push away from him but he held her fast.

"Don't be ridiculous, Larena. I don't want you to go anywhere and my body is yours to play with, seduce, take advantage of or whatever pleases you anytime you want."

"Then why are you terrified?"

"I've never done this before, said the words I always believed didn't exist in reality."

"I think you should tell me now," Larena said, her heart in her throat, her head pounding.

"I love you, my little poppet."

"What?"

"Larena, when I told you I couldn't exist without you, I should have said the words then. I love you and if you don't return that love, I'll understand."

"Do you mean it? Really mean it?" she smiled, relief pouring through her.

"I do. I will shout them from the parapets if you want."

"You love me." She mulled the words over for a long time.

He turned her face so she looked at him again, "I'm waiting."

"Waiting for what?" She truly didn't understand. Her world seemed to spin and tilt wildly. "Oh," then she realized what he asked. "I love you too. I've wanted to tell you for the longest time, but you were always so adamant that love didn't exist. I decided, although I didn't like it, I'd rather live with you than without you despite the fact you would never love me. You've fascinated me too."

"Stop talking, poppet. I need to become even more fascinated with Larena."

"And I want the fascination to never stop. I loved you for what seems an eternity."

His lips found hers for another long, soul unraveling kiss that led to so much more.

Epilogue

1823

Larena and Tyna sat on the veranda of hers and Gavin's new home. The two boys were born within days of each other. She had a difficult time believing Donel turned one just two days ago and Fraser a few days before that.

The women sipped wine from a new Chianti Logan, Larena's brother in law, sent a month ago while watching the toddlers play with their fathers. The ball seemed to elude both little boys as they tried to roll it on the grass.

"Alistair and Gavin are like two little boys. They seemed to be enjoying the game more than our little ones," Larena laughed softly as she watched the antics evolve on the grass in front of her.

"I don't know which one is more adorable," Tyna said as she relaxed on the outdoor chair beside Larena.

"I'm more adorable, of course," Gavin strode to Larena, leaving the boys to play with Alistair then kissing her on the forehead.

"Just as arrogant as usual," Larena murmured. "Good thing I adore you."

"As you well know, I prefer confident." Gavin poured two glasses of wine before holding one out for Alistair who was herding the boys toward the patio where an array of toys were spread.

"Yes, you've always been confident." Larena giggled as Gavin set his wine on a table before pulling her onto his lap.

"Isn't it time for the little one to nap?" Gavin nuzzled her ear, his lips sending shivers of delight through her.

"I think that's our not so subtle invitation to leave," Alistair held out one hand to Tyna while he scooped Fraser into the other arm.

"Before you go, our first visitors to the castle will be here tomorrow sometime," Gavin said. "Do you have everything covered? The food, the servants and god knows what else we are going to need."

"We are as ready as we can be," Alistair said. "The staff has been trained and we've complied some lists of places to visit and nearby scenic areas. I suppose we'll learn as we go."

"I'm excited to see how this turns out." Gavin tossed little Fraser high into the air, listening to his giggles.

"Really, Gavin, if you keep that up, he's going to lose everything he just ate. Don't you think you should put him to bed?" Larena rose, smoothing out her skirts then holding her arms out for the little boy.

"I'll put him to bed then I'll come back for you." He laughed as he cuddled the boy, keeping him in his arms instead of turning him over to his wife.

Larena watched his departing back, pleased he had his heir and now she wouldn't have to worry about that aspect of the marriage even though he'd told her a million and one times he didn't care about an heir.

Tyna reached out and placed a hand over hers. "Thank you so much for trusting me. You changed my life in too many wonderful ways to count."

Larena watched the happy couple and their child leave. Her life had changed too. Gavin had made her happy and she loved him more than anything.

"I'm back," he swept her into his arms. "Not it's time to put the both of us to bed for a second nap."

"I love you and you are my fascination."

"Larena's fascination, I love the way that sounds.

Coming by the Author
September 2019
from
Rogue Phoenix Press

Tira's Education
Twelve Dancing Princesses Book Eleven

Baltimore 1821

Chapter One

On board the ship taking her to Baltimore, Tira Hepburn watched the land grow closer until the boat finally docked. Her trunk was unloaded and she walked down the gangplank with a small valise in hand and her heart in her throat. This was her new life, and it was the first time her twin Tavia was not by her side. She inhaled a long deep breath, breathing in the fresh clean air so unlike that of London and listening to the sea gulls as they flew over head.

"Tira," over here. "Tira."

She smiled seeing her cousin jumping up and down, waiving her hands in the air. Aidan McLellan, strands of wild red hair flying in the breeze off the ocean waited by a wagon, ready to take her to the home their families owned in the city. When Aidan finally finished jumping, she ran to her.

With hugs, "You're here. You finally made it. Auntie wrote to me when you would come. Mr. Lundin sent word to me this morning that several fishing boats had sighted the ship and relayed messages. "I've been waiting impatiently for an hour at least."

"Have you heard from Blade?" Arm and arm, Tira and Aidan

walked to the wagon. A dockworker helped put the trunk on the cart. "He left London almost to the same day that you did."

"No, thank goodness. If I never see that man again, I'll be happy." Aidan looked behind her as if the man she spoke of would turn up. "But I'm truly afraid it's just a matter of time before he finds a way to humiliate me again. If he shows up and does that..." She let the sentence hang and Tira put her own meaning to the words.

Tira was pretty sure Aidan wanted to see Blade again. She loved him but she probably wanted it on her terms and where Blade was concerned, that wasn't going to happen. For years their relationship had revolved around Blade's terms and what he wanted or thought was best for Aidan.

"You must live each day wondering if he'll come after you. I know I would find you if I were him. He's always tried to protect you. You have to figure out how you're going to deal with him when he does show up." Tira hated the thought, yet she knew Aidan loved the man. Where the two of them were concerned, it was most likely a match made in hell.

"He won't. If he hasn't come yet, I doubt if he will. That last incident drove the point home for both of us that we're not suited to each other and never will be. At least what happened made it perfectly clear to me. He's never going to see me as a woman, always as a little girl."

"Lundin Ships," Tira read as they stepped passed the building. "Workers needed." She turned to Aidan, "I'm going to apply first thing in the morning. This is heaven sent for me." She clapped her hands together excited by the prospect. Her dreams were about to come to fruition. She so wanted to learn how to design and build ships, and Jamie Lundin was just the man to teach her.

"You don't really believe Jamie Lundin will give you a job, do you?" Aidan stared at her, a skeptical expression of her face. "No one hires women for ship building jobs."

"I can only hope. I'm going to go dressed as a man. Tavia and I bought pants and men's shirts in London. Tavia sailed on a ship as a cabin boy. She even cut her hair short. Haven't heard from her though I've been thinking about her constantly."

"Tavia Hepburn, your twin, she did what?" Aidan asked, seeming shocked at what Tira said. "She's more impulsive than me and you too.

Look at you, trying to be like a man. I've been trying for years to convince Blade I'm a woman grown and less than a year ago he still thought I was a little girl. I would never masquerade as a man."

"Perhaps you should have tried wearing pants. I heard the ploy worked well for Ella. Remember how Drake had her wear britches when he was trying to figure out if he wanted to marry her." They were alone, of course, at Drake's hunting lodge and no one else saw her.

"Ella Hepburn, now Montgomerie, she's a Duchess. Are they doing well, she and Drake?"

"They were when I left. You know, Blade searched London for you. No one would tell him where you disappeared. We all kept our promise to you even though it was hard," Tira said. "Then he vanished without a trace."

"That's a relief, I'm glad everyone kept silent. I need time to figure out things, and the last person I want showing up on my front door is Blade McPherson. I've had a few outings with some men I've met, but none of them make my heart rush with desire. I don't know how long it will take me to get over him. If I ever do."

"Before I left, I heard Blade was called home. His father was ailing. So you may have a longer reprieve than expected." Tira watched Aidan for a reaction. All who had known these two over the years hoped someday they would find a way to get over their differences. Aidan had been in love with Blade since she was thirteen.

Aidan pulled up in front of the house, stopping the wagon and with a huge sigh. "Did you realize it's been over six years since I first met him. I wish he never showed up at the castle that day with his friend Hunter. If I never met him, I might be happily in love now and pinning away for someone I can't have."

"You've been in love with that man for so long. Have you even been kissed by another man?" Tira was sorry she asked that question. After all, she'd never been kissed by a man.

"Have you?" Placing one finger on her lips as if she remembered how Blade kissed her that first time in the gazebo at the Montgomery estate, Aidan turned the question back on her cousin.

"No." Tira didn't want to talk about it. Since Ella and Drake's wedding Jamie Lundin had caught her eye when he escorted Tavia, her twin. She had dreamt of his kisses. Now she meant to parade herself in front of him in men's clothing. He'd never treat her as a woman if she did that.

Aidan laughed softly. "Here we are virgins who've never been kissed," she choked back her thoughts. "Well, I've been kissed that one time when Blade managed to humiliate me in front of all my family. I liked it when I thought he was sincere."

"Maybe that's why we fled London. There are no opportunities left for us in England," Tira said, looking over her shoulder and trying to see Jamie's building and wondering what would happen tomorrow.

"Hello, welcome. I hope you feel at home here." Lilly, the black woman Amorica rescued from slavery stepped from the door. "Do you need help? I can call Joshua. He can get your trunk."

"Yes, please," Aidan said, smiling. "It's the only way we'll get that trunk up the stairs. If not, we'll have to take each piece of clothing a couple at a time."

Tira followed Aidan into the home and up the steps. "So this is the house." She inhaled a long deep breath, closing her eyes for a moment. Here, she was truly independent. She didn't have to answer to anyone except herself and her conscious. She could come and go as she pleased.

"I'll show you to your room and you can freshen up before dinner." Aidan looked over her shoulder at Tira as she followed behind.

Inside her new bedroom, Tira held her breath, looking over the place where she was going to stay indefinitely. Second thoughts about what she was about to do assailed her. She wanted Jamie to court her properly, but she had serious misdoubts about that ever happening.

She plopped down on the bed, staring at the ceiling and thinking about Tavia. Where in the world was she? They'd never been separated before, and now she hadn't seen her twin for closing on seven months. Was she still alive? Tira was pretty sure if something happened to her, she'd know. They always had a way of communicating without speaking. They shared a bond no one else understood.

A knock on the door brought her from her introspective thoughts to the present. The door creaked open and Lilly peeked inside. "I've hot water. Would you like a bath?"

"Oh, yes. Yes, yes, yes, that would be heaven." Tira sat up smiling, her hands clasped under chin. The trunk was brought in behind the hot water as her bath was filled.

Once the door closed and she was alone again, she slipped out of her clothes and into the bath. Famished, she washed quickly then dressed in clean clothes before skipping down the steps.

"Hello..." she peeked into the parlor.

Aidan met her with a glass of wine. "Come, dinner won't be ready for another hour. Let's go into the parlor and have a few dainty dishes before the meal. Lilly loves to put tiny bits of meat in pastry shells with a cream sauce. They are really very good. I have to be careful not to fill up on them before dinner though."

Tira sat back, her eyes closed, wondering what the morning would bring and if Jamie Lundin would hire her and if she could pull off her disguise. "You know, I'm... I guess I'm a bit afraid for tomorrow. What if he recognizes me? What if he doesn't think I'm a man?"

"Honestly, I don't see how you can change yourself enough so that anyone who has met you would not recognize you," Aidan said, blunt as usual. "And if Tavia tried to pass herself off as a boy, I'm sure her true identity will be or already has been discovered. This is all foolishness, but time will tell. If he doesn't recognize or know that you're a woman at first site, I have serious doubts about his character."

"That's what I'm afraid of too. Tavia cut all her hair off. Do you think I should do that?" Tira didn't want to go to that extreme even when she knew it would grow back.

Aidan choked on her sip of wine. "Absolutely not. Don't you dare. Put lots of pins in your hair to keep it in place and wear a beanie of some sort. Do you have one?"

Tira pursed her lips, staring at Aidan and her look of concern. She had more than second thoughts about this crazy endeavor, wanting Jamie to see her as a woman not a man. "I do. I have material to wrap my breasts too. Tavia and I practiced winding the fabric around our torsos, but it hurts. I'm not sure how long I can put up with the bindings."

Again, Tira's thoughts turned to her sister who could have had the same problem. At least she had a home, a place where she could go and unwrap the fabric confining her, but on board a ship Tavia would have none of that, no privacy what so ever.

"This is all foolhardiness. Never, never lie, you know that. Go to him just the way you are and maybe he will see that you're sincere. Men don't like to be deceived, and they can hold it against you forever," Aiden voiced her opinion. "I should know better than anyone."

"You speak from experience?" Tira questioned, wondering what Aidan lied about with Blade. It certainly wasn't her age.

"Not personally but I've watched my sisters and my cousins. Lies tore them apart from the men they loved. In the end they found their way back to each other, but the truth would have served each of them better. I am never going to tell a lie to the man I love."

"Not always real lies but misunderstandings and lies of omission," Tira corrected, knowing as soon as she showed up at the Lundin ship building company requesting a job, she would be in the middle of a lie of omission. "And I can't risk going to him as a woman and asking for a job. He would never hire me if he knew I was female."

"A man's job."

"A man's job," Tira agreed with a huge sigh. "I don't know what to do. I spent the long voyage here believing I would learn how to design and build ships. This is the only way and I'm determined to make it work. He has to believe I'm a young man and give me a chance." Tira picked at the little pastry in front of her, the huge appetite from minutes ago vanishing with her outstanding worries. She sipped her wine, staring over the rim and out the window toward the building, Jamie's building.

"Alright then, you think he'll believe you're a man. What will you do when he sees through your disguise and he will?" Aidan posed the question.

"If."

"If he doesn't know who you are the minute you stand in front of him, I'd be shocked. You have delicate feminine features that no man would have. Of course you could say you were fourteen, but he wouldn't hire you then either," Aidan pointed out.

"I really don't want to think about it right now. Thinking about tomorrow makes my stomach churn and tie in knots. Have you figured out what you will do when Blade turns up here to protect you from yourself just as he always does?" Tira challenged Aidan, determined to change the subject from her and the very real probability Jamie would recognize her.

"Good ploy, change the topic," Aidan laughed, finishing off her wine and pouring them both another drink. "If he turns up, I will dissuade him in the best way I know how."

It was Tira's turn to chuckle. "Have you ever dissuaded him?"

"No. I chased him until he mortified me. If I ever see him again, I will play hard to get. Not sure if I can do that, but I'm certainly going to try. Actually, after what he said to me, I'm not going to forgive him easily. Besides, I've a few suitors here in Baltimore."

"Any you can be serious about?" Tira asked, pretty sure she knew the answer to her question.

"No, but they escort me places and keep me from getting too bored. Lilly has all the chores done by the time I think about them. I go for long walks by the small lake down the hill. Other than that..." she shrugged. "I miss everyone so much and would almost welcome Blade just so we can have a big fight. He challenges me and keeps everything exciting. I really don't want to say this but I miss him more than I care to admit."

"Don't you wish life was easier?" Tira asked thoughtfully, knowing anything worth having was worth working for. "I certainly do. All I want is to learn how to build ships. I don't care about anything else." But she did, she wanted a family and love.

"You will when you find someone to love. Do you care about Jamie at all?"

"Right now, yes. Jamie did touch my heart a tiny bit when I met him at Ella's wedding, but he held himself aloof. He's not approachable. I doubt if he's looking for a permanent relationship or a relationship of any kind. I had the distinct feeling he was hiding something. Do you know if Drake knew what it was?"

"He was merely an acquaintance Drake knew from his ships and business. He asked him to be part of the wedding party so he could tell his brother he didn't need anyone."

"Are you in love even a little bit?" Aidan asked. It seemed her curiosity had risen.

"Not right now and certainly not with Jamie Lundin. I barely know him. How did this conversation change from asking for a man's job to a possible husband? Have you heard from Amorica recently?" Tira changed the subject to her oldest sister.

"She and Damian were here a couple of months ago. Their children are growing like weeds and the two of them are still so much in love..." Aidan let that thought hang in the air. "I so wish I could have what they have," she paused, "with Blade when I finally forgive him."

"I need to fall in love first," Tira said pensively, wondering what it would take to catch Jamie's attention. Could she work as a man on his ships during the day and meet him at night as a woman?

"I've been in love for over six years, and he's thought of me as a little girl for that long. What can I ever do to change his mind?" Aidan let a heavy sigh emanate from her.

"Blade doesn't deserve you."

"Tell him that."

"Dinner is ready, any one hungry?" Lilly stood in the doorway, hands clasped in front of her, a smile on her face.

"Famished, even though the pastries were wonderful." Tira strode to the dining room relieved to put the conversation behind her and eager for tomorrow morning so she would know her fate.

"Lilly, will you and Joshua join us for dinner? I understand you don't feel comfortable eating in this house, but you and your fiancé are so welcome." Aidan took Lilly's hands in hers obviously hoping she would finally get over the slave versus free person status.

"I will ask him, but he is newly emancipated and I know exactly how it feels to have to bow down to a white master." Lilly spun, "I'll be right back."

Aidan turned to Tira to clarify, "When Damian first came here, he bought Lilly and emancipated her. Now he has done the same for Joshua. Because of intense prejudices, they must be very cautious and don't dare go very far from this property. The townspeople understand they are free, but the farmers and plantation owners in the surrounding lands will not accept it unless they see proof. If they go anywhere, they have to carry their papers and in doing so they risk losing them or having them stolen."

"There is risk in everything they do." Tira was appalled at the revelations.

"Many will strive to keep these two apart and put them in chains again. There are several copies of their papers just in case. Amorica also has copies in her home. There is a copy in the safe here and they both have copies of their own."

"My goodness..." Tira was shocked by Aidan's words. "I would have never believed one would have to go to such lengths to prove they are free. Everyone should be free. This is the eighteen hundreds after all."

"The people here use the slaves to plant and harvest their crops. They are not free and it seems never will be unless some wealthy p erson buys them and gives them their freedom."

"That's awful."

"No, it's inhumane."

Lilly returned. "I'm sorry. He wants to give his apologies, but he doesn't' want to intrude on your privacy. So he declines. I will eat with him and I will see both of you tomorrow morning."

"I understand. Amorica told me it took years for yo u to feel this comfortable even to consider eating with us, but I want you to know that we are not above you in any way. We are all the same, equal in every way. What happened to you and Joshua is a travesty that in a better world would be stopped immediately," a tear slipped down Tira's cheeks, wearing her feeling for everyone to see.

"It won't though," Aidan said thoughtfully, placing a hand on Tira's. "Having been in this part of the world for only a short time I understand what drives the men who keep s laves. They are all greedy men who want free labor. Most believe they couldn't afford to farm their huge crops without the slaves who work for them. They think they would go out of business if they paid anyone to work their land. Your Jamie Lundin is not one of them. His farm is slave free."

"I must go. Joshua is very apprehensive. He has a hard time believing Tira came from across the ocean and she is not his enemy. He is constantly looking over his shoulder, believing his master is hunting for him," Lilly said, also looking over her shoulder at the back door.

"Take enough food for both of you then and enjoy," Aidan said, having assumed the role of the lady of the house. "He had the same reaction to me the first time we met." She turned to Tira.

"Thank you," Lilly curtsied then packed a basket of food before leaving for the kitchen then their little cottage beside the big house.

"So, let's talk about tomorrow." Aidan leaned forward, elbows on the table, her chin resting on her hands.

"Tomorrow?" Tira feigned innocence, anticipating and excited but dreading the moment too.

"Yes, you've got this notion you can wrap yourself up all by yourself. If you're going to wake me up at the crack of dawn, I'm going to be very unhappy with you, Tira Hepburn."

"I promise you I can do it." Tira smiled before taking a bite of food. "But perhaps I should practice. If I can't do it by myself tonight, I'm going to want you to help me. I'll just sleep in them."

"You mean lie awake staring at the ceiling all night long, but, yes I'll help you because I don't want you waking me up before the sunrises."

"I promise I won't wake you up."

Finishing dinner and clearing the dishes the cousins strode upstairs. "Lilly will clean this up in the morning or later tonight. She berates me if I try to take over any of the chores she considers her duty."

In Tira's bedroom, "Here are the bindings." Tira pulled out a long length of fabric cut about five inches wide. "And here are the shirt and pants I plan on wearing." She held them up, grinning.

"Oh bloody eyes, this is scandalous. Jamie Lundin is going to be shocked at your brazenness. There is absolutely no way you can hide your curves in those garments."

"He won't know I'm female. Tavia and I planned everything." Tira was determined to make this work, and if she had to tell herself the same thing over and over she would. Aidan shook her confidence and she wasn't at all sure any more if he would believe she was a man.

"Keep saying that and maybe you'll convince him."

Aidan plopped down on the bed to watch Tira try to wrap herself in the fabric and fasten the bindings. Twenty minutes later, Tira frowned at her and lay down on the bed. "This isn't as easy as I thought it would be."

"Thought you said you practiced."

"We did but we weren't able to do any better than this. I kept going over the process in my head, and I thought I had it figured out, but my hands and my fingers just don't work the way I think they should." Tira felt the weight of her plans begin to implode on her.

"Obviously you don't. What now?"

"You wrap me up now so you won't have to get up in the morning." Tira smiled, one eyebrow lifted in silent speculation.

"I want to see you completely dressed." Aidan stood back to look

Tira over when she was done with the bindings.

Tira pulled the britches and shirt from the trunk and after putting them on, "How do I look?"

"Like a woman. Your hips are too wide, Tira, and even with your hair pulled up and tucked under the cap, your features are all female. There is no way Mr. Lundin will believe this ruse. You wouldn't even believe you were a boy. I'm sure Tavia had the same problem."

"Well, I have to try. You knew who I was, so this test wasn't fair in the least." Tira protested, her hands on her hips. "I've got to keep believing he won't see me as a woman."

"Don't do that if you want to ape a man. The way you're standing makes your hips stand out even more and I have a feeling you better not bend over either. Try to pose like a man would."

"And how is that?" Tira asked thoroughly out of her element.

"How would I know?"

"Well, you brought it up. How does Blade stand when he's acting all male?"

"Chest puffed up and feet braced apart. He usually has his hands on his narrow hips. Don't think you should puff up your chest or bring his eyes to your wide hips."

~*~

"What the devil," Jamie mumbled after the incessant knocking woke him up from a deep sleep. "The town must be on fire...the docks, the ships." His heart racing, he slipped on his buckskins and running his hands through his hair, opened the front door.

Tira Hepburn, what the bloody eyes was she doing at his front door at five in the morning and what was she doing aping a man? For that matter what was she doing in Baltimore? Tira must have been the reason her cousin Aidan was inquiring about the ships coming in from London. "Can I help you?" he asked out of politeness but wishing he still lay in bed sleeping.

"I'm here to apply for the job."

"What job?" Sleepily, he ran his hands through his hair, unable to take his gaze off the woman on his front porch wearing men's clothing. Even dressed in that ridiculous outfit she mesmerized him. The only job he knew of was the one for an experienced ship builder.

"The one building ships." She smiled, puffing up her chest and settling her hands seductively on her hips.

Obviously she had no idea how the simple gestures emphasized her femininity.

If he didn't miss his guess, she sounded indignant, but for some reason he couldn't fathom, he didn't want to end the conversation this instant. He had no choice though. His six-year-old daughter was asleep upstairs and needed breakfast before he could continue with this strange encounter. "Come back at eight o'clock. Not here but at the shipyard. I'll speak with you then and not a moment before."

"I went there to begin with but when no one answered my knock, I came to your house. I need this job." Her voice filled with indignation.

You need this job my ass. "Come back at eight and we can discuss this civilly." He started to close the door.

"Promise me you won't give the job to someone else before the interview." She smiled at him.

"Doubt if anyone in town besides you wants the job. The sign has been up for over a month. Besides, there aren't very many skilled ship builders in town. Are you skilled?" He challenged, hoping she would back down and he wouldn't have to be at the office at eight.

"Pa, Pa, who is it?"

"Go back to bed, honey. It's no one you need to concern yourself with." Yet he suddenly knew what he wanted Tira Hepburn for. She could be Annie's nanny. He reminded himself none of the Hepburns could possibly need a job. He was eager to find out more, and the upcoming interview with Miss Tira could be enlightening. Getting to the bottom of this made the day a bit more interesting than he thought it would be. Suddenly, he was eager to start the day and discover what would come of this chance encounter.

"Papa." She stood beside him, tilting her head slightly and pursing her lips.

"Who is it?" Tira shifted her position as if she was trying to see beyond his shoulders.

"She's no concern of yours," he told Tira a bit too harshly, his protective nature kicking in. Where Annie was concerned he would guard her with his life and make sure nothing bad happened to her, ever.

"I'm sorry," Tira said weakly. "I didn't mean..."

"Of course you didn't. Come back at eight. I'll meet you then." He was surprised at her smile and how that simple gesture affected him, touched his heart. What on earth was she doing to him?

Awkwardly, she backed away and nearly fell off the porch before she turned and headed away from the shipyard her hips swaying provocatively as she walked. He felt a crazy urge to run after her and then what? Drag her into his arms and kiss her?

He remembered her from Drake and Ella's wedding months ago. She'd been the first woman who touched his heart since his mistress died in childbirth and left him to raise Annie on his own. Tira Hepburn was not a candidate for his mistress, a wife maybe...

Lizzy, his mistress, had never wanted marriage and after his first marriage, he sure as hell never wanted to be married again, but he cared for Lizzie and mourned her loss. Before she died, he promised her he would take care of Annie and make sure she would never have to sell her body to make a living.

He was too awake now to go back to bed, so he walked Annie to her bedroom. It seemed she was awake now too.

"Would you like a big breakfast this morning?" He ruffled his daughter's hair and delighted in her smile and laughter.

"Pancakes," she asked, "and bacon too? Anything but oatmeal."

"What ever you want today but don't get used to this royal treatment. Get dressed and by the time you get down for breakfast, I should have most of it cooked. We can talk then about the rest of the day." He loved her more than life itself.

"Who was the lady?" Annie asked.

He chuckled softly. Even his five-year-old daughter knew the person at his door was a woman, not a man. For a quick second the thought of going along with her ruse crossed his mind, but he shrugged it off. Truth was always better than lies and if he let her work for him, he could risk her life. He wasn't about to do that. Damian Andrews, her brother-in-law, would have his hide if he hired her. Truth be told, he was more afraid of her sister Amorica.

Annie stopped at the top of the stairs. "Are you going to get dressed before breakfast? Did you know she was staring at your chest, Papa? Why was she doing that?"

For a moment he choked back an answer. He'd been staring at her chest or lack of breasts too. That wasn't the way he remembered Tira. "After breakfast, maybe we can talk about where she was looking." Given time his Annie might forget her question. He certainly didn't want to answer it.

He remembered Tira's form from that one time he saw her in London and she was not flat chested. She must be horribly uncomfortable. It was another reason to let her know she couldn't fool him.

"That's not an answer," Annie said, standing at the bottom of the steps. "Don't forget I want to know why."

Laughter threatened to bubble up from his gut, "Guess I don't know. Now run along and dress." Jamie couldn't help but chuckle at his daughter. He felt a strange sense of elation that Tira liked his body.

With the bacon cooking on the stove, he mixed the pancake batter. He thought about eggs and potatoes but decided with just the two of them that was too much food. For a moment he thought about inviting Tira but shrugged off the thought. Inviting her to breakfast was too much too soon.

"You're not done." Annie raced into the room laughing. "I knew I could beat you." She ran to him and hugged his legs. "I brought you a shirt." She folded it across the top of a chair.

He bent over, lifting her into the air for a quick toss then a kiss before setting her on a chair. "Be patient, little one, and thank you for your thoughtfulness. This shirt is exactly the one I would have picked."

"Do you think the lady is hungry?" Annie asked.

His heart stopped for a moment. "Why do you ask?"

"She's sitting on the stoop at the shipyard office. Every once in a while she stands and stretches then sits down again. I feel sorry for her. We could invite her to breakfast. If you have your shirt on, she might not stare at your chest."

"Probably not a good idea. She's looking for a job. We don't mix business with pleasure." Tira Hepburn was clearly muddled if she thought he would hire a woman.

"What kind of job?"

"She wants to build ships."

"That's mans work," Annie said, a serious tone edging her voice.

"She can't do that."

Those three words shook him to the core. While he didn't want Tira Hepburn in his shipyard distracting his men, he wanted Annie to be able to pursue any dream she had.

"Annie, I want you to think beyond what men and women should do for work or with their lives. Your mother wanted you to pursue whatever dreams you had." Actually, her mother wanted her to find a man to marry and support her, but Jamie found he wanted more for his little girl. He wanted her to have a voice in her life.

"Why would you want that? I want to be a wife and a mother, well, that's what all my friends say they want. Do you want to know what I really want to be?" she asked, eagerly watching him it seemed for a reaction.

"Tell me." Jamie flipped a pancake on to her plate and pushed the syrup and butter toward her. He gave her a piece of bacon then heaped his plate with food.

For a couple of seconds she pushed her food around on her plate before she looked up. "I'd like to be a doctor."

"Really. That's incredibly special. Why?" He didn't want that for her. Hypocrite.

"Because they help people when they are sick," she told him in such a matter of fact manner. "I want to know how to do that."

He was suddenly frightened her dream would come true. Doctors took risks with their lives to help people. "That's noble of you." He meant to encourage her even though he wanted anything else for her. He knew through the course of a person's life, they changed their dreams. When he was a boy, he wanted to be a lawyer.

"If she can't work in the shipyard, could she be my nanny. I like her. Well, I think I'll like her. You told me you were going to hire someone, but that was months ago."

"You don't even know her, but I met her when I was in England and I liked her too. I'll ask her if she'd like that job."

"When you fire her from man's work."

"Yes, poppet when I refuse to hire her because she's not strong enough to work in the shipyard. I'll ask her if she wants to be your nanny."

"Thank you."

"Eat up. I've got to go to work and you will need to go with me."

Except when Mooney's wife wanted to watch his little girl, Annie went to the shipyard with him. Today would be no different.

He cleared the dishes, leaving them in the scullery for his housekeeper. "Are you ready?" Jamie held out his hand and Annie let him take her hand in his. She was so precious, the best thing that ever happened to him. "Would you like to go swimming after work today?"

"Yes, the little swimming hole behind the Andrews house? I love it there. You can help me learn to float on my back."

"The very one." He stopped in front of Tira who stood when they approached. "I see you waited here. Nothing better to do?"

"I did," she nervously wiped her hands on her pants. "Stay."

Inwardly he groaned, noticing the beautiful curve of her hips and imagining the sway of her breasts if she hadn't bound them, and he sure as hell hoped she didn't cut off her hair. He opened the door and waited for Annie and Tira to walk through the door. "Go up on deck. Your things are still there. Practice tying the knots I showed you last week. Now behave yourself until I'm through with this interview. Call me if you need anything."

Jamie walked into his office, Tira following him. He sauntered around his desk and sat then motioned for her to take a seat. For some reason she fascinated him. "What can I do for you?" The only real question was how long he was going to let her think she was fooling him.

"I'm looking for a job." One more time, she ran her hands along her thighs then back. "I want to design and build ships. Wanted to learn how to do that for as long as I can remember."

He couldn't help himself, that small gesture made him think about doing just that to her. He cleared his throat, pushing those thoughts to the back of his mind, trying to focus on her eyes instead of her lips. "So you're an expert ship builder. Any credentials?"

"No, but..."

"But?"

"I want to learn. It's all I've ever wanted to do and I'll work hard," she repeated. Her voice grew soft, almost wistful.

"The job description calls for an expert. I don't have time to teach someone." He watched her expression change from hopeful to full disappointment. "I need this person who I hire for the job to be there for me, so I can spend more time with my daughter."

He watched her squirm in her chair, her lips tilting downward. "I see. So there's no chance you will hire me."

He leaned forward, hands clasped, "However," he peered heavenward searching for divine strength, "Lady Tira Hepburn..." he paused seeing her sit up straight, her demeanor changing to obvious anger and her lips pursing. Red colored her cheeks. "Yes, I know who you are. I don't know why you want to ape a man or why you need to work, but I could hire you as a nanny."

"Please," Annie stood at the door, jumping up and down, clearly excited about the prospect. "She's pretty and I want her for a nanny. I bet she'll be more fun than my last one. I don't even care if she stares at your chest."

"Stare at your chest? I didn't." She turned even redder, if that were possible.

"Yes you did, but it doesn't matter."

"I didn't know you had a little girl." Tira looked from one to the other. "She has your eyes."

"I don't keep Annie a secret nor do I advertise the fact at a wedding in London," he said, his voice curt, his brows drawing together defensively.

"I'm sorry. I didn't mean to imply... well, I suppose I should go." She rose, hesitating a moment to address Jamie. "What gave me away? How did you know I was Tira?"

He sat back, relaxing in his chair, looking her up then down, understanding the advantage was his. "Anyone who looks at you would know you were aping a man. Even Annie knew you were a woman. As to how I know which twin you are, you have one tiny dimple on your cheek next to the corner of your lips. Tavia has none."

"Oh." She backed toward the door, clearly distraught, moisture forming in her eyes. She turned and in her haste, ran into the wall.

Before she could leave, "You didn't answer my question. Would you like to be Annie's nanny?" That would mean he would spend more time with Tira. He wasn't adverse to that notion. She had intrigued him the first time he saw her and now dressed in men's clothing, she captivated him even more.

"You're right. I don't need to work. I've always wanted to learn how to build ships. I did build a small sailboat about six years ago. The vessel didn't sink." Tira turned to glance at his little girl. "I could be her nanny for a little while. I don't want to go back to London right away, and I will need something to do with my time. Why not?"

"Good, then you can start today. She was supposed to be playing in the captain's cabin aboard the ship. Instead she chose to ease drop on our conversation. The vessel is nearly finished." He slanted Annie a stern look.

"I couldn't wait to find out what she'd say. I promise I won't do it again," Annie said, in her defense.

He led the way to the gangplank, which stopped at the ship's deck. Once on board, he showed her the cabin. "Annie has a few toys she likes to play with inside. When she's hungry, you can take her home and fix her whatever she wants or whatever is in the pantry."

"Anything else?" she tilted her head prettily to one side. "Will you be there for lunch too?"

He vowed he'd never get involved with a woman other than a willing widow or someone who would be a mistress. Tira Hepburn was not that woman. So why was he letting her move him in ways he was hard pressed to resist? "If I can spare the time.

"I think Annie can fill you in if you have questions, and I'll be in my office finishing some paperwork if either of you need me." He turned then and left, shaking his head and thinking about his life in a completely different way than he'd seen it when the pounding on his door woke him up this morning.

In his office he poured himself a cup of coffee, realizing Mooney, his assistant, had come to work early this morning. The man must have seen and heard most of the conversation between Tira and himself. Jamie groaned, unready to answer questions and knowing the man would be relentless when he wanted to know something.

"Who's the little gal and why's she dressed like that?" Mooney stepped through the door, rubbing his bearded chin and holding a cup. "I see she caught your eye. 'Bout time you found someone."

"Lady Tira Hepburn." Jamie turned slowly, unable to stop smiling. "She thought...she wanted a job building ships so she thought she could fool me with that get up. I met her on my last trip to London."

Mooney's jaw dropped. "You'd have to be blind as a bat for that to happen. Never seen a lady in britches but..." It seemed he couldn't say anything more. He poured coffee into his cup.

"She's going to be my...Annie's nanny," Jamie put in, thinking how ridiculous that sounded.

"You're going to employ a real lady, a member of the British aristocracy, to be your nanny. She on hard times or something?" Mooney looked out the door as if he wanted to get another look at the real lady.

"Looks like it. Annie likes her. No hard times as far as I know." Jamie didn't want to explain himself. He sensed a note of disapproval in Mooney's voice. He couldn't help but wonder at his motives, and if that was what Mooney was thinking too. He and his daughter were going swimming after work, and he wondered how he could convince Tira to come with them. Those thoughts went directly to motive.

"Well, it appears to me, you're lookin' at a lot of trouble. Thought you told me once you're not the marryin' kind. You keep lookin' at her the way you were just doin, well..."

"I did say I don't intend to embrace that popular institution. You don't have to remind me. Annie likes her and she usually gets whatever she wants," he said again trying to convince himself he didn't have ulterior motives where Tira was concerned.

After his first marriage and the way it ended, he knew he would never give that institution another chance. Three months after they tied the knot, his wife ran off with another man.

Mooney's roar of laughter echoed in his ears, "Bet you're wed before the end of the year. She's not Lizzy and she's certainly not like your first wife. She's not going to sleep with you and have your child without a ring on her finger."

Jamie stiffened. Mooney's words hit too close to his thoughts, and he couldn't figure out why he was regarding Tira in that same light. Two chance meetings and Mooney had him married. "You know I don't gamble."

"She's a pretty little thing, even in those clothes. Wonder what she'd look like dressed in proper female clothing?" It seemed Mooney tried to goad him.

He was about to say something back when Annie's scream caught him by surprise. He dropped his coffee cup and ran.

Mathew Dutton surveyed the inside of the house. It was opulent, designed in golds and reds a mirror on every wall. The women of the house were all beautiful and scantily clad, yet in ways more discreet than in most brothels. They showed their curves but not their bodies. A man had to pay handsomely to play with one of his girls. His was what he called a high-class operation.

Beside him the madam of the house sipped a fine brandy he'd imported from Scotland. Kendall, he kept for himself. No one else touched her. She'd given herself to him years ago, claiming she never wanted conventional things for herself, not marriage and certainly not a family.

"Kendall, I've a new girl in mind, but I don't think she'll come along as easily as most. I'm not sure. I'll have to look into her situation more extensively. At first look she appears to be British aristocracy."

"Who is it? Do I know her?" Kendall Mackenzie asked.

"No, she's new it town. Just arrived yesterday. Heard she asked for work at Lundin's ship yard."

"What's the problem? If she looked for work there, she must be down on her luck." Kendall sipped the brandy, sliding her hand along Mathew's leg, her meaning clear.

"We could take this upstairs?" Mathew said, catching her exploring hand and kissing the back before she could reach her destination.

She moistened her lips. "Not until I know who your talking about and why there might be a problem. You've always had a way to convince the ladies. Besides this job at the shipyard had to be gossip. No member of the British aristocracy would stoop so low." Kendall sat back, pouting provocatively and letting him take full advantage of the view of her cleavage.

"Don't know her name, working on that little piece of information, but Aidan McLellan picked her up at the docks and took her to the Andrews home. Could be she's connected to that clan in someway."

"You think she's kin. We don't want to mess with any of them. They've got too much influence here and in England. Andrews and Lakeland could have me run out of town if we provoked them. I like it here and I don't want to move."

He trailed a finger along her bodice. "I don't want that either. I'll make sure I understand who it is before I take action. She'd make a beautiful addition to the stable of girls we have here. She's looks aristocratic, long black hair and enticing curves. I couldn't get close enough to see her eyes, but I will."

Kendall swatted his hand away. "We can take this upstairs later. Need I remind you, I've a business to run?"

She rose and flounced away, greeting a customer before calling for one of her girls. The man and the lady disappeared upstairs. Mathew's gut tightened. He downed his brandy, standing. On the front porch he leaned on the railing, looking over the town.

Meeting Kendall had been a godsend. Together they built this brothel as well as two others in neighboring communities. When he met her they were both dirt poor. Now he could buy anything he wanted, and he wanted the girl he saw yesterday.

Kendall wasn't like most women. She had a fire inside that couldn't be tamed. At first, she had been the main attraction, now she only serviced him, unless someone came to the home she was attracted to. He knew she had been intimate with more than just him. Of course he saw other women too. He looked forward to making love to the new girl in town. Mentally, he undressed her, his breath quickening in anticipation.

The evening was clear, barely a cloud in the sky. A few stars shone in the darkening sky. A crescent moon rested on the horizon and a cool breeze blew off the ocean.

Kendall appeared at his side, two glasses of brandy in her hands. She handed him one. "You really smitten?"

"I don't know what it is. I thought I was too old and too experienced to feel this way. She's just another woman."

"You're going to have to find a way to convince her this is the life she's been craving."

"It would help if I understood why you chose me and all this." He gestured with his hands.

She paused, seeming to think. "I've never told you this, but my mother was never happy. She married a bastard and had his children, one after another until he left her. I didn't want a bastard dictating my life. When I met you, I'd slept with several men and I liked it. The thought of having to make love to just one man my entire life wasn't appealing."

"Variety is nice." His hand rested at the small of her back. "No regrets?"

She gasped when his hand slipped beneath her skirt. "None." She turned in his arms.

His lips molded against hers as her tongue swept the inside of his. He groaned low in his belly, letting his other hand find her breast, teasing a nipple. "Can we take this upstairs yet?" He touched the length of her neck with lips and tongue.

"Another hour perhaps. I'll leave Jessica in charge if we get any new customers."

"Go on then." He stood back, watching her leave and anticipating the night with her in his arms.

firestarter, grew to womanhood as she moved through time to keep the demon from finding her. Though stubborn and courageous, she was ill prepared to use powers she had not been taught. Her first sight of the intoxicating Carr McKenna left her breathless, and her second encounter gave her hope for a future she never thought she had.

A playboy, a second son and a shifter, a man who thought his life would be carefree, Carr McKenna was shocked to discover the woman he'd paid as an escort is a firestarter who is running for her life. He is the leader of all the McKennas around the world and that he has multiple powers. His passion for Margo and the need to defend her might cost him his life as well as hers.

Sweet Talkin' Sugar
Book Four in the McKenna Clan Series

Lyonesse McKenna, was dreaming or was she? From the instant Lyn saw Deacon McClain across a black jack table in a crowed Las Vegas casino the unmistakable attraction sent Lyn's senses flying into overdrive. Her family of shapeshifters believed in soul mates. She'd always been skeptical yet she couldn't help but question the way her heart sped when he looked at her.

When Deacon appeared in Las Vegas he knew his first job was to save Lyn from a Sea Demon, but the next order of business was to convince her he would someday mean more to her than she'd ever expected. But her stubborn nature and unbendable spirit consumed Deacon...and he had to chase away all the demons real and imagined in order to win her heart.

Sweet Surrender
Book Five in the McKenna Clan Series

Ripped from her family at the top of Infinity Cliff, Kimi McKenna finds herself thrust somewhere into the future. Dark elements threaten to destroy the earth unless Kimi can work together with the white witch to stop the destruction. Confused by her mate's role in the conspiracy, she refuses to acknowledge the connection. But amidst raging fire and attacks on the people she is coming to hold dear, she allows Maska O'keefe into her heart.

Maska O'keefe has loved the beautiful shapeshifter for years. Unable to save her life years ago, he vows to watch over her as he is given a second chance to convince her that even though he is a witch and not a shifter, they are indeed soul mates. Kimi's divided loyalties between her family and the cause she is now a part of will determine their relationship. Only the part she plays as the messiah can bring this to a conclusion in the final battle.

Dakota's Bride
The first book in the Lakota/Pinkerton Series

When Emma St. John received her brother's letter imploring her to escape her stepfather's vengeful scheme and to trust Dakota Barringer with her life, she was willing to chance it. But the handsome, brooding riverboat owner Emma found in Natchez a danger of another kind. For Emma soon found herself surrendering to an unrelenting desire.
Raised by the Sioux when his parents were killed, Dakota had been betrayed once before by a white woman. He wasn't about to trust another, especially one claiming that her stepfather, a powerful U.S. senator, had framed her as a murderess. But he couldn't let Emma's intoxicating effect on him. Now Dakota would risk his very life to protect the innocent beauty who had seduced him with her tender love.

My Angel
The second book in the Lakota/Pinkerton Series

A BEAUTY IN BUCKSKINS
When her father decided to send her to a finishing school back East, Angela Chamberlain refused to be confined to stuffy drawing rooms. Instead, the daring spitfire who could shoot like a man and ride like the wind longed

for a life of adventure and romance—and she knew exactly who could give it to her. Devil Blackmoor was a hired gun with a dangerous reputation. But Angela was willing to go to the ends of the earth to capture the handsome devil's heart.

A DEVIL IN DISGUISE
He'd come to America looking for excitement, but Devil Blackmoor got more than he bargained for when he encountered a beautiful rebel who answered his kisses with a wild innocence that touched his very soul. Yet standing between them were more obstacles than either ever dreamed. For Devil had strapped on a gun for the wrong man. And that made Angela his enemy. Now he'll have to choose between his duty and the woman he loves more than life.

The Locket
The third book in the Lakota/Pinkerton Series

The year is 1894. Seeking revenge for crimes against his family, Misha Petrovich follows a path that leads straight to Ariel Cameron's boarding house in Mist Harbor, Oregon. A family heirloom in Ariel's possession leads Misha to believe she is guilty. The locket has been handed down to the oldest girl in the Petrovich family for generations. Ariel is innocent of wrong doing, but her father is not. Misha is torn by his feelings for Ariel and his need for restitution against her father. Knowing that the relationship between them is fragile, Misha does everything in his power to protect Ariel's father. His efforts are to no avail when her father is shot. Ariel comes to realize Misha's steadfast courage and determination to protect her and her father despite what has happened to his family. Ariel's love and devotion heals Misha's heart.

The Talisman
The fourth book in the Lakota/Pinkerton Series

Running from a marriage that lasted one night, Dr. Moriah McKeown discovers the land she has settled on is coveted by determined and lawless men. Yet the proud young woman who once vowed never to abandon her home has second thoughts when her adopted children are threatened. Her only recourse is to enlist the aid of a dark, dangerous gun for hire.

Haunted by the past and a betrayal he will never forgive, Ian Civanovich uses his fast gun and his reckless courage to forget the faithlessness of a woman in his past. He will trust no female—nor will he rest until the threat hovering over Moriah McKeown is put to rest.

Forever His
The fifth book in the Lakota/Pinkerton Series

Struggling to come to terms with the part she played in Jacob St. John's death, Etta Barringer resigns from Pinkerton Agency and seeks peace and solace in a Rocky Mountain Cabin.

Jacob has vowed to discover the reason Etta has betrayed him, sold him out to his enemy and left him for dead.

Isolated in their cabin, they discover their love for each other and learn to trust. But the trust is shattered when Jacob learns she is married to his sworn enemy; the man who left him in the desert to die.

Allura's Secret
Twelve Dancing Princesses Book One

Allura McClellan is horrified by her father's decision to take out an ad in the Times awarding her to the man strong enough and smart enough to win her hand and uncover her secrets. She's an intelligent young woman who takes great delight in the freedom allotted to her by her father. She's well aware that marriage would effectively curtail the adventures she's shared with her sisters and cousins.

Hunter Gray is nothing like the other men who've arrived to vie for Allura's hand in marriage and everything that goes along with it. However, he is the first to refuse to concede defeat and pursue her despite her attempts to disguise her true appearance. It's her temperament that is of more concern to him than her looks. Hunter has worked all his life with the hope of someday owning his own land. Now that it looks like there's a very real possibility that everything he's ever wanted is within reach nothing is going to deter him – including Miss Allura's disagreeable disposition.

Amorica's Wager
Twelve Dancing Princesses Book Two

Amorica Hepburn was sent to London to find a husband. Finding a man was the last item on her agenda. With her two cousins, Amorica wagers she can dissuade her suitor before the others. Despite her efforts she discovers a chemistry that cannot be denied. Suddenly she is the arrogant man's wife, pledged to a marriage neither desire. But swept off to his ancestral home above the Dover cliffs and into his strong embrace, Amorica is soon possessed by a raging passion for the husband she had vowed to despise... Damian Andrews couldn't afford to trust the emerald-eyed spitfire who happened upon his secret. Amorica's hatred of all men of his kind only inflames the war that rages between them. Still, he can not control the intense desire his stubborn bride inspires, or make her surrender to his will until he has conquered the headstrong beauty on the battlefield of love...

Ravyn's Marriage of Inconvenience
Twelve Dancing Princesses Book Three

A REGAL BEAUTY
When the duchess decides to wed her to a wastrel and a fop, Ravyn Grahm takes matters into her own hands and declares her engagement to another man. Instead of fessing up and telling her great aunt what she has done, she goes through with the pretense. Aric Lakeland is the bastard son of an earl and has a dangerous reputation. But Ravyn is willing to do most anything to keep the duchess from discovering the lie.

A DEVIL-MAY-CARE SMUGGLER

He'd bought land in America, looking to put down roots and end his life of adventure, but Aric Lakeland got more than he bargained for when he encountered a beautiful heiress who made a promise she didn't want to keep. But the promise could not be undone and standing between them were more obstacles than either ever dreamed. Aric had made plans to spend the rest of his life in America and that was at odds with Ravyn's plan of living in England and running her father's estate. Now, he'll have to choose between his dreams and the woman he loves more than life.

Christel's Sunrise
Twelve Dancing Princesses Book Four

He Made Her An Offer...

Life has thrown Christel McClellan some experiences that could have devastated a less determined woman. Beautiful, self-assured and fiercely independent, she is trying to forget the loss of her stillborn child. But is the child alive?

She Couldn't Deny...

Life is carefree for Ryder MacLaren who loves to see what is on the other side of the sunrise. Laird of Clan MacLaren, he is wealthy, handsome and happily unencumbered...until stunning Christel McClellan enters his life. When he hears her story, he believes the child she thought dead has been sold to a wealthy buyer.

Storm's Passion
Twelve Dancing Princesses Book Five

SHE MADE A PROPOSAL...

Life strikes Storm Graham a shattering blow when she learns her father has bartered her to a man she detests. Storm is beautiful, self–assured and fiercely independent, and refuses to be a pawn in her father's schemes, yet she can find no way out of this bargain made in hell. Going on the offensive she asks the wealthiest man on the eastern coast of England to marry her, never believing she might fall in love.

HE TRIED TO REFUSE...

For Hadden Johnston life has provided everything he ever wanted, including a sanctuary for homeless children. He is wealthy, handsome and happily unencumbered...until stunning Storm Graham marches into his life and proposes a marriage of convenience. Yet this type of marriage to a woman who inflames his senses is far from acceptable. If he's going to be tied down, he will move heaven and earth to have this woman warming his bed.

Gotta Have Fayth
Twelve Dancing Princesses Book Six

A regal beauty with raven hair and piercing blue eyes, Fayth Graham is unwilling to parade herself in front of the wealthy Lords of England during the season. Seeking a means to dissuade any man wishing to wed her, she seeks a way to ruin herself for marriage. When she unexpectedly meets a man with sparkling gray eyes and an infectious grin, she decides this is the man who will keep her from agreeing to obey.

He returned from six months at sea, looking for a few nights of pleasure with a willing lass, but Jarret Kinsley got more than he bargained for when he met a beautiful debutant who responded to his kisses with a wild innocence that touched his heart. Yet the obstacles looming between them might rip them apart. Both had vowed never to marry, so when consequences of their dalliances got in the way, Jarret would have to choose between the life he's always desired and the woman he loves more than life.

Ella's Pleasure
Twelve Dancing Princesses Book Seven

A WHISPER OF PLEASURE

Ella Hepburn was an auburn haired debutant from the harsh Scottish coastline—a wild innocent to be seduced and tamed. A spirited beauty, she captivated Drake Montgomerie's jaded heart—while succumbing to the smoldering desire she felt for her unyielding suitor.

A WHISPER OF DANGER

In Drake Montgomerie's glittering world of money and privilege, young Ella discovered passion and desire could overcome everything she'd been taught to resist—entangling Drake, the heir apparent, in a lethal coil of aristocratic family intrigue. But grave peril would only nurse the sparks of a love that knew no limits and a magnificent ecstasy that would not be denied.

Eveleen's Seduction
Twelve Dancing Princesses Book Eight

A WHISPER OF SEDUCTION

A brutal attack on Eveleen Hepburn's cherished island off the Scottish coastline leaves her shattered and bewildered. Learning a man she once trusted can kill as easily as he can breathe even though the deed saves her life, creates questions that need answers. An innocent beauty, she enchants Logan Maxwell's cynical heart—giving in to the raging passion she feels for her mysterious suitor.

A WHISPER OF INTRIGUE

In Logan's Maxwell's world of espionage and privilege, young Eveleen discovers truths about herself she never expected, and a need for passion and love can overcome all her fears if she learns to accept certain truths. She finds herself entangled in a lethal battle for land that was once owned by French nobility, taken from them during the revolution and sold to Maxwell. But grave peril would unleash the flames of love that simmers, creating a magical union that cannot be refuted.

Tavia's Deception
Twelve Dancing Princesses Book Nine

WHISPERS OF DECEPTION

When her father decides to send her to London for her season, Tavia Hepburn resolves to see the world instead. The raven haired beauty decides to disguise herself as a lad and find employment on a ship bound for Barcelona as a cabin boy. But she never bargains on finding passion and love to a red haired sea captain who rescues her from certain death.

WHISPERS OF MURDER

For James Macmurra, the world is black and white until he meets a young debutante, who turns his world upside down. He's unable to deny Tavia's intoxicating effect on him. In a match tense with obstacles, unwillingness to divulge secrets, and unforeseen peril, irresistible desire and passion grows into undeniable love. James would risk his life to shelter and protect the innocent debutante who seduces him with her sweet love.

Twelve Days to Love

When Archer Steele shows up at Calanthe Durand's failing plantation with an alligator over his shoulder, Cali thinks she's never seen a more handsome man. During the war she had to defend herself and her servants from both union and confederate soldiers. Independent and self-sufficient, she vows to never marry.

But Archer Steele has different ideas. The first time Archer sees Cali in town, he feels an instant attraction. He decides he will do everything and anything to convince the beautiful Miss Durand he is worthy of her love. During the weeks leading up to Christmas, he gives her twelve gifts in hopes she will fall in love with him. Yet they are faced with challenges they must overcome before Cali can commit to a marriage.

Door to Heaven

Jessica Lawrence is the stepdaughter of a woman born in the twentieth century transported back in time to the year 1868. An acclaimed suffragette, she raises Jessica to believe in the equality of women. Jess Law believes everything she was taught, and when the time is right she becomes a private investigator. Courageous and impetuous, Jess finds danger in her quest to save all women from white slavery. Her passionate mission results in a wedding to Roc Newman, a man she knows can steal her heart...

Roc can't trust the sapphire-eyed spitfire who invades his home in search of secret papers and knocks him flat with her karate moves. Jessica's refusal to obey his wishes serves to inflame the war between them. Still, he cannot control the intense desire his reluctant bride inspires, or make her surrender her independence, until he has conquered the headstrong beauty on the battlefield of love...

Rebel Heart

HER REBEL SPIRIT DEFIED HIS OUTSIDERS SOUL... She was velvet and silk, eyes the color of a summer storm and amber hair. Victoria DeMontville, because of a promise and a codicil to her father's will, was forced to marry one man to protect her from another. She hated Cameron Savage with a fierce passion. But to hold on to her genetic research and find a cure for the deadly Signe virus, she must pretend to love the enemy at her door, come with weapons of fire to melt her icy heart...

HIS OUTSIDERS TOUCH IGNITED RAGING PASSIONS... He wore a mask, disguised as the Phantom, a true legend come to life. Even as war and debate over new genetic research engulfed them all, he would find his greatest adversary in the beauty who'd branded him an outsider and barbarian, the woman he was born to possess, his soul mate.

Safari Moon

Solo St. John, a wildlife photographer, is preparing for a trip to Alaska. Suddenly, Solo finds women of all sorts invading his privacy, his home and his office, all cooing nonsense words and blatantly throwing themselves at him. Solo doesn't know why, and he has no idea how to rid himself of the persistent women. He finally decides to beg a favor of his best buddy Nyssa Harrington.

In love with Solo for the past ten years and knowing he doesn't return her feelings Nyssa doesn't want to talk to Solo. She knows if she accepts his phone call, she will not be able to resist the temptation to hope again.

Straight to Heaven

Running from demons, Alexandra McMurdie stumbles into Forbidden Ground where up is down and elements of nature are contested. Though a strong independent woman in the twenty-first century' she is unprepared for life in the 1800s. Her first site of the formidable James Lawrence makes her heart skip a beat, giving her cause to reconsider her desperate need to find a way home.

Born with a silver spoon, James' life was torn apart during the War Between the States. Moving west he vows to put the life he once knew in the past. When he discovers a half-frozen woman near Gold Hill, his heart begins to thaw. His love for Alexandra and his need to keep her from a man who has pursued her through time might cost him his life as well as hers.

A Valentine's Anthology

The Lending Library-a fantasy by Christie L. Kraemer

Faeries try to fit into the human world when the forest where they make their home is destroyed by a mysterious enemy.

Chasing Rainbows-a contemporary romance by Genene Valleau

An eccentric aunt, an inventive uncle, a mother who wears poodle skirts, and a brother who wears pearls provide a hilarious backdrop for the courtship of a young woman who yearns for a "normal" family.

The Gift-an historical romance by Christine Young

A man and a woman on opposite sides of the Civil War get a second chance at love after one final battle returns soldiers to their war-torn homes to rebuild their lives.

A St. Patrick's Day Tale
by
Christine Young, C. L. Kraemer, Genene Valleau

Tumble through time…

…to Ireland in 1817, when tensions are high between Protestants and Catholics and faey people guide the fate of villagers. A lovely Catholic lass stumbles upon the weakly ritual fisticuffing between Irish lads. She falls into the lap of a handsome young Protestant. Family ties, grudges, and two conniving faeries threaten their budding love. But the faeries outsmart themselves when they hijack a time machine that has mysteriously appeared in their forest and are whisked to…

…Eugene, Oregon in the 20th century, amid a property feud between the local faeries and night elves. The conniving faeries from Olde Ireland try to stir up more mischief. However, a warrior gnome convinces the magic folk to control their own destiny, and forces the intruding faeries to take refuge in the time machine again, spinning their way toward...

...A modern day castle in western Oregon. An eccentric inventor is determined to reclaim his wayward time machine and save his beloved wife from her latest misadventure. If only they can travel safely past the black hole...

a May Day Anthology
by
Christine Young, C. L. Kraemer, Rosemary Indra, Genene Valleau

Highland Miracle -- Christine Young

HURTLED THROUGH TIME, Sean Michael Sterling, landed in the midst of a May Day celebration he didn't understand, assuming the role of Laird Sterling.
ILLIGITAMATE CHILD OF NOBILITY, Reagan Douglas searches for a way out of her half brother's house.

Defying the Odds -- C.L. Kraemer

The night elves on the hill aren't happy without their magic. They concoct a plan to punish those who were involved in the act that rendered them almost human. Meanwhile, Uther, the rogue night elf, has returned to woo the Librarian to be his eternal mate.

Love in Bloom -- Rosemary Indra

When childhood friends reunite it takes two fairies and a matchmaking daughter to help them admit their true love for each other.

No More Poodle Skirts -- Genie Gabriel

After drifting for years in the innocent age of the 1950s, a woman struggles to join today's world by finding a career and a new love, with some help from her zany family.

Once Upon a Christmas Moon
by
Christine Young, C. L. Kraemer, Genene Valleau

TWELVE DAYS TO LOVE

When Archer Steele shows up at Calanthe Durand's failing plantation with an alligator over his shoulder, Cali thinks she's never seen a more handsome man. During the war she had to defend herself and her servants from both union and confederate soldiers. Independent and self-sufficient, she vows to never marry. But Archer Steele has different ideas. The first time Archer sees Cali in town, he feels an instant attraction. He decides he will do everything and anything to convince the beautiful Miss Durand he is worthy of her love. During the weeks leading up to Christmas, he gives her twelve gifts in hopes she will fall in love with him.

BOOTS AND BLADES

An ancient evil from the old country has arrived in the high desert of Oregon. Gnome children are vanishing then re-appearing, showing various stages of traumatization. Tiamoon, warrior gnome, will put her skills to use alongside Killian, a handsome warrior, also in need of a cause.

CHRISTMAS PAWSIBILITIES

With their world destroyed and their space ship malfunctioning, the dogizens of Planet Canid have little choice but to crash land on Earth. They face tortuous experiments at the hands of the Geeks in Green...or they can trust an eccentric inventor and his zany family to deliver the Canine Queen's puppies and help them celebrate new lives.

www.ingramcontent.com/pod-product-compliance
Lightning Source LLC
Chambersburg PA
CBHW071449170626
46811CB00007B/2513